Ro

ROYAL WHODUNNITS

Edited by
MIKE ASHLEY

Carroll & Graf Publishers, Inc.
NEW YORK

Carroll & Graf Publishers, Inc.
19 West 21st Street
New York, NY 10010–6805
USA

First published in the UK by Robinson Publishing Ltd 1999

First Carroll & Graf edition 1999
Collection and editorial matter copyright © Mike Ashley 1999

ISBN 0-7867-0634-1

Printed and bound in the EC

10 9 8 7 6 5 4 3 2 1

CONTENTS

CONTENTS

ACKNOWLEDGEMENTS

The stories in this collection are published for the first time anywhere and are printed by permission of the authors and their respective agents.

"The Mysterious Death of the Shadow Man" © 1998 by John T. Aquino; "The Friar's Tale" © 1998 by Cherith Baldry; "Two Dead Men" © 1998 by Paul Barnett; "The Modern Cyrano" © 1998 by Stephen Baxter; "A Stone of Destiny" © 1998 by Jean Davidson (printed by permission of the author and the author's agent, the Dorian Literary Agency); Foreword © 1998 by Paul C. Doherty; "Natural Causes" © 1998 by Martin Edwards; "A Secret Murder" © 1998 by Robert Franks; "Neither Pity, Love nor Fear" © 1998 by Margaret Frazer; "The *White Ship* Murders" © 1998 by Susanna Gregory (printed by permission of the author and the author's agent, A.M. Heath & Co. Ltd); "Borgia by Blood" © 1998 by Claire Griffen; "The Day the Dogs Died" © 1998 by Edward D. Hoch; "Provenance" © 1998 by Liz Holliday; "Accidental Death" © 1998 by Tom Holt; "The Gaze of the Falcon" © 1998 by Andrew Lane; "Woman in a Wheelchair" © 1998 by Morgan Llywelyn; "News from New Providence" © 1998 by Richard A. Lupoff; "Perfect Shadows" © 1998 by Edward Marston; "Happy the Man . . ." © 1998 by Amy Myers (printed by permission of the author and the author's agent, the Dorian Literary Agency); "The Snows of Saint

Stephen" © 1998 by M.G. Owen; "Even Kings Die" © 1998 by Mary Reed & Eric Mayer; "To Whom the Victory?" © 1998 by Mary Monica Pulver; "Who Killed Fair Rosamund?" © 1998 by Tina & Tony Rath; "Night's Black Agents" © 1998 by Peter Tremayne (printed by permission of the author and the author's agent, A.M. Heath & Co. Ltd); "A Frail Young Life" © 1998 by Renée Vink; "The Curse of the Unborn Dead" © 1998 by Derek Wilson.

FOREWORD

Paul C. Doherty

To coin a phrase: "Murder Always Wears a Crown". The dagger, the noose, the phial of poison have always been a necessary addendum to the sword and sceptre of a ruler. Machiavelli, in his classic work *The Prince*, recognized this, whilst Cesare Borgia personified the murderous ambitions of many a ruler.

It would be pleasant to say such things never happen in England but a number of our monarchs have met highly suspicious deaths, or disappeared in mysterious circumstances. Richard II may have died at Pontefract, starved so the chroniclers said. Nevertheless, his usurper, Henry IV, was deeply concerned that Richard, or a look-alike nicknamed "The Mammet", was wandering around the Scottish court. Harold, England's last Saxon king, was supposedly hacked down by Norman cavalry. Nevertheless, the legend persists that he escaped the field of Hastings though, if he lived, he didn't "fight another day". The victor of Hastings, William the Conqueror, powerful as he was, died in suspicious circumstances whilst engaged in one of his favourite hobbies – burning a rebel town to the ground. According to the chroniclers, William's horse shied, driving the saddle-horn deep into the King's protuberant belly. It took him at least a week to die. Was it an accident? Or had some clever assassin realized how a sharp saddle-horn might be useful as a dagger? Two of the Conqueror's sons also died in interesting circumstances: both Richard and Rufus (the later William II) were killed in hunting accidents in the New Forest. Our popular hero king, Richard the Lionheart, had been wounded many times. So why should an injury he received whilst besieging a castle not have healed properly? Or his brother John who, according to contemporaries, was in excellent health until he sat down to a meal at Newark in 1216.

Other royal deaths can certainly be ascribed to murder, though even then, shrouded in mystery. The most famous of them all is the fate of Edward V and his brother Richard of York – the princes in the Tower. Were they murdered and, if so, was it by order of Richard III? Did Henry V really die of a rotting sickness in the marshes of Meaux? Or did the French, who saw him as the vengeance of God, provide a little help so that this most aggressive of English kings could join the choir invisible? Chroniclers tells of the grisly fate of Edward II, but was his death really as told? Possibly that great mountain of flesh, Henry VIII, may have received assistance out of this world. There are rumours that, like Stalin, when Henry fell dangerously ill, some of his councillors decided it would be better if he were never to recover. And just in case you may feel this kind of activity belonged only to the Middle Ages, then just reflect upon the circumstances of Lord Dawson of Penn, the king's doctor, who admitted to hastening the death of King George V in 1936, through massive injections of morphia and cocaine.

Undoubtedly kings and queens did die in the fullness of time. Edward I, at Burgh-on-Sands, his old body racked with fury against Robert the Bruce; or Elizabeth I, sitting on a palace floor complaining about the ring of fire round her finger. Nevertheless, the list of potential murder victims is extraordinary: Mary Tudor and her half-brother Edward VI join Henry VI and Edward IV as those whose deaths were regarded as most untimely. Edward IV is a good case in point. He was only a young man when he went boating along the Thames on that fateful day. Commentators, both foreign and domestic, remarked on his magnificent physique. And why did the city of York receive notification of his death the day before this merry monarch suddenly collapsed amidst his pleasures?

If English kings and queens can be regarded as victims, they can also be depicted as the red-handed sons and daughters of Cain. Some murders were public and given a semblance of legality: Buckingham's execution by Henry VIII; Thomas of Lancaster by Edward II; Lord Hastings by Richard III. Other murders were done quietly in the dead of night. Whatever really happened to Edward II was immaterial to his wife, the she-wolf Isabella and her lover Mortimer. The king was both a nuisance and a burden and so the king had to be removed, just as the hapless Prince Arthur of Brittany had been by his "sweet uncle" John.

I have always found the royal family of England a marvellous source for "who-dunnits". My thesis on Edward II's wife, Queen Isabella, introduced me to this sordid world of royal murder. Every prince had his henchmen, ever ready to recommend the swiftest and most brutal way of removing an opponent. A close scrutiny of the historical record soon teases these people into life: not just the villains of Shakespeare sent in to dispatch poor Clarence or the hapless Princes in the Tower, but historical figures who lived and died by the sword. Creatures like William Ockle, a professional assassin, who was at Berkeley when Edward II died; or Thomas Nelson, guilty of some involvement in the murder of Henry Darnley, Mary Stewart's luckless husband. These are the "hit-men" who would feel very much at home in today's world in carrying out a contract killing for a gangland boss. They never appear on state occasions but the household books and private accounts illuminate their shadows in the secret chamber of the king or queen they served.

Conspiracy theorists have, and always will have, a heyday with any royal who dies before his or her time, as witness the latest speculations over the death of Lady Diana Spencer. Nevertheless, when you finish this volume, you may certainly be forgiven for agreeing with Philip of Macedon (the father of Alexander the Great and himself a murder victim): "The price of the purple is always sudden death."

In a number of my novels – *Death of a King, The Whyte Hart* and *The Dove Amongst the Hawks* – I have offered my explanation for the deaths of Edward II, Richard II and Henry VI. This fascinating collection of stories offers, in chronological order from Good King Wenceslas to Edward VIII, a compelling range of scholarly exploration and astute detection of the brutal or mysterious fate of many who lived in the shadow of the English or European thrones. In doing so it only confirms Shakespeare's most dire warning: "Uneasy lies the head that wears the crown!"

May 1998

THE SNOWS OF SAINT STEPHEN

M. G. Owen

We begin our tour through the chronicles of royal mysteries not with the English or Scottish thrones but with the Bohemian. It's too easy to forget that Wenceslas, whom we know through the Christmas carol Good King Wenceslas *by the Victorian John Mason Neale, was a real king or, to be more precise, duke. His name was originally Waclaw, and he became Duke of Bohemia in 922 when he was only fifteen years old. He worked hard with the Church to improve the education of his people and to convert the land to Christianity. It was through his religious reforms that Wenceslas created enemies and which led to his death in 929. In the following story Mike Owen has recreated an authentic Bohemian world, which with its schisms and superstitions doesn't seem that far removed from today.*

Prague, 929

Only the crunch of frozen snow under the monks' feet broke the dawn silence as they shuffled towards the cathedral. Cold, as much as the Rule, kept their hands folded inside their sleeves and they did not let freezing air into their mouths by speaking. Two tiny clouds of frost-breath hovered before their bent black cowls, four eyes anxiously searching for ice underfoot.

As they turned the corner of the chapterhouse into the cathedral square, Brother Pavel looked east to take in the sight of the new Cathedral of St Vitus, built on the ruins (and ashes) of the old Temple of Radagast and now the first stone building in all Prague. Only the morning star remained above its stub square tower, fire-bright in the eastern sky, a glistening pinpoint sun and a herald of the true Sun that would rise within the half-hour. Nine hundred years ago, at that first Christmas, there had been such a star. The snow on the roofs of the merchants' houses around the square made a dog-tooth white line above the brown timber, rising and falling with the gables, then leaping over the grey stone of the cathedral. Brother Pavel could even forgive the pagan dragons carved at the houses' eaves and over their doorways. He and his companion, Brother Stanislaus, were almost the first ones awake this St Stephen's morning, for the snow lay unbroken but for a single trail towards the shrine of St Agnes in the centre of the cathedral square, where a fur-muffled figure kept vigil, prostrate on the steps. Brother Pavel brought his hands out into the cold in a gesture of prayer and smiled thinly. Prague's Christians were fortunate indeed to have such a king, who could endure the cold so patiently, who would be about his devotions on this frozen St Stephen's morn, when most of the court, Pagan, Christian and Priest, had not yet awoken to their Christmas hangovers.

As soon as Brother Stanislaus had closed the great door of the cathedral behind them, its grey stone pillars and lime-washed walls seemed warm as a wooden hall. The new frescoes broke up its austerity. On the north side of the nave a procession of naked sinners marched over the tops of the round window arches. The fire-red demons with heads of goats, wolves and cats (signifying lust, greed and vanity) pitchforked them westward, away from the altar, to a corner where Hell's gate, in the form of a blood-red dragon's mouth, gaped wide to devour the unrepentant. On the south wall, the Righteous broke out of their coffins on the Day of Judgement, ready to climb the ladder to Paradise. The great blue sky of Heaven, ladder, angels, stars and all, would have to wait until Bishop Anton could find the money for the lapis lazuli pigment. It would not be wise to ask King Wenceslas for money, not yet, he had already paid for the minium for the red parts on the north wall. First things first – paint in Hell's fire; Heaven can wait.

Brother Pavel let his hands linger in the warmth of the Presence lamp as he trimmed it, while Brother Stanislaus gathered up the spent wax under the votive candles, for re-use.

When they returned across the square, young King Wenceslas had not moved. Brother Pavel called out "Christus Natus Est". The king did not respond. Pavel called again. Wenceslas lay in a strange, unprayerful, position. The monks stumbled into a run, snow-clouds flying above their ankles.

The knife in the king's back bore a two-tailed lion engraved on the silver pommel. Only the king and his brother had the right to wear the royal lion of Bohemia, and now the king lay dead at the monks' feet. As Stanislaus drew breath to shout the alarm, Pavel's hand slammed over his mouth.

"Think, lad! This is Prince Boleslav's knife and Boleslav's work – King Boleslav, now. Even as we speak, his heathen dogs may be cutting every Christian throat in Prague!"

Stanislaus quietly calculated the speed of a fast horse, the distance to the nearest city gate and how much cathedral silver would fit into his saddlebags. Pavel tugged at his sleeve.

"We must warn My Lord Bishop. There may still be time."

Stanislaus shuffled after Pavel, cursing the other's bravery, all the way to Bishop Anton's palace, all the time it took them to persuade a half-sober deacon to admit them to the Bishop's chamber. My Lord Bishop's vow of poverty had brought him a well-carved, well-locked (and well-filled) elm chest, a silver wine-flagon and beakers to put on it, and even the luxury of a special linen shirt, just for sleeping in. A great mace, a mail-and-scale shirt and a helmet crowned with a mitre hung on a post in a corner – his vow of humility did not prevent him commanding a small but adequate private army. As for his vow of chastity, the brothers tried to ignore the suspicious double dent in Bishop Anton's pillow as he shook the sleep and wine from his head.

"Stanislaus – wake up my guards. I don't care how you do it, but get them armed and sober and close off the cathedral square. Above all, don't touch the body. Pavel – tell every priest, canon and Christian lord you can find to meet me in front of the chapterhouse – now!"

Fast though Bishop Anton moved, scarcely a dozen of his followers had gathered before the chapterhouse when he heard the muffled stamp of armed guards in the snow, marching down the lane from the royal palace. A lone figure in a grey wolfskin robe, its hood trimmed with miniver, trod silently at the head of the double file.

Anton saw a headband of tiny gold owls under the white miniver and, below them, pale green eyes, unblinking, unweeping. When she spoke her voice was level.

"My son the king is dead."

Bishop Anton made himself look directly into Queen Dragomira's eyes. Somehow it seemed to him that they picked up a tint of the yellow of the headband. He made the sign of the cross, partly in benediction, partly for his own comfort.

"God rest his soul."

"And God save King Boleslav. Say you Amen?"

Bishop Anton counted Queen Dragomira's guards. All had their spears, some had even found time to pull on their mail shirts.

"Amen."

"Then you will crown my son Boleslav king on Twelfth Night."

"A pagan king crowned in the House of God!"

"The king enters any house he pleases. Whether you give the crown or he takes it for himself is your choice. And think on – Pope and Emperor are beginning to speak out against holy concubines. Wenceslas listens – listened. Boleslav may be more tolerant. Now, this snow fell yesterday afternoon and evening and froze overnight. Your priests saw my son's body at dawn, with no footprints in the snow but his . . ."

"Only the Devil's servants leave no footprints. There are Vlachs camped out on the downwind side of the city," Bishop Anton spat out the tribe's name.

Queen Dragomira considered this option. Vlachs came, more or less, from Transylvania. But there had been no reports of a vampire attack, this far west, for seven years, though it was not strange that Bishop Anton should suspect the Vlachs of reverting to their old customs. Vlachs were Eastern Christians, and the Church of Rome hated them for heretics and barbarians. It was fortunate that Bohemia lay astride the line between Eastern and Western Christendom – into that crack a skilful servant of the Old Gods could insert her wedge. She considered the intricate political tapestry of Bohemia, and mentally compiled a list of suspects, as she walked up to her son's body . . .

There was very little blood on the ground, only a small stain on her son's cloak. She unlaced his collar, looking for bites. Nothing, only six garnets she had given him at his coronation, now set in a cross.

Wenceslas had always liked pretty things, bright colours. Only last week he had asked her to lend him the money for the powdered lapis lazuli to paint the church wall. Too late, now.

There was something odd about the footprints. They weren't sharp, they were too big and too deep. Then she saw several with a double print, the pointed mark of a sole on top of another. Dead bodies don't bleed. Someone had killed her son somewhere else, carried the body to the shrine and walked back in his own tracks. Now who was clever enough, and sober enough, to do all that on Christmas night?

Not young Boleslav, apparently. She found him in the palace, stretched out on a pile of skins near what remained of the Christmas fire, and he was still too drunk to curse her when she poured a bucket of cold water over his head and greeted him with "Hail, King Boleslav!"

"What – King who? What's happened to Wenceslas?"

"Ask your silver-handled knife! Why did you do it?"

"Big brother Wenceslas was a pious, girlish idiot!"

"Radagast knows that's true. But he would have done the praying and let us – you – do the ruling. He would never have got sons. You were his heir."

"Anything to avoid a fight, that's Wenceslas. He was ready to hand Bohemia over to Germany. Their harbingers would have been in Prague as soon as the snow melted."

"A dozen German princes under our roof all at once. Think, little Boleslav! I could have done the cooking . . ."

"It's a bit suspicious if they all have your mushroom soup for supper and none live to eat breakfast. You were lucky to get away with killing Grandmother Ludmilla."

Dragomira didn't bother to explain about her subtler delicacies – wild boar, smoked over yew chippings, that keeps for weeks, and when the victim chooses to eat your present, gives him a copious, dire and fatal flux, just like accidentally tainted meat. Ergot of rye, that clouds the reason and leaves the body unharmed, if the dose is nicely judged. The less young Boleslav knew about his mother's kitchen cupboard, the better.

Boleslav belched deeply, his hands pressed to the sides of his head.

"Wait – did you say he was stabbed with my knife? My silver

dagger? I missed that knife some days ago. Find the thief, he's the killer."

"You are talking sense, for once. When did you last have the knife?"

"You know Raika? The little blonde piece? Well, whenever her man is on guard duty, I go to her. Last time, when I got dressed, the knife was missing. I thought she'd just taken it for a souvenir – she's well worth it, so I didn't say anything."

"Does her man know about your night-games?"

"Igor? I hope not. Have you seen the size of him?"

"Who else knew of this?"

"Only Vassilli, my page. Each night the guards draw lots, so they never know, until the last moment, who will be guarding which door."

"Why do you let that sneaky little Christian, Vassilli, follow you around?"

"He plays the lute well. Also, like most musicians, he has good hearing, and he speaks four languages. That makes him a very useful listener at doors."

"My son, you are not as stupid as you look. Now get cleaned up, look regal, look sorrowful. Wear your black wolfskin, no jewellery – second thoughts, wear that black agate I gave you. You have a coronation eleven days from now."

When Dragomira returned to her chamber a large black hairy shape rose up out of the rushes and growled at her.

"Down, Rofi!"

He sniffed and whined from his sheepskin. Strange, she thought – until she remembered the smell of blood and death on her gown. She threw some birch sticks into the brazier's embers and, while the flames curled around them, took four candles, a knife and some cord from the elm chest against the wall.

Let the small candle be Vassilli. Take a hot needle, and draw a boy's face on it, and two arms holding a lute. Now tie a cord around it.

Her sons were big lads. Vassilli was far too small to carry the body through the snow. *Tie a backward knot in the cord.* He had no reason to kill Wenceslas, *tie another backward knot.* But he was a sneaky little thing, he could have stolen the knife for someone else – *tie a forward knot.*

Take a big candle for Boleslav, crown it with a golden ring. He had the best of reasons; the brothers had always quarrelled – a younger son's natural ambition for the crown, and another kind of jealousy – maybe she had shown too much favour to her quiet, biddable elder son. There was respect between her and Boleslav, but mother and son were too alike, too hard, to show much affection even when they felt it. *Tie a forward knot for a younger brother's jealousy.* Boleslav was certainly strong enough for the business, and possibly sober enough, in the early part of the evening. *That's two more forward knots.* But he was too drunk to have disposed of the body so cleverly. Also, he was a vicious killer (where do the children learn such habits?) but he was not a coward, to stab in the back and then hide his guilt. A quarrel is face to face. No, he would have stabbed from the front, then proudly acknowledged his work and claimed the crown by right of strength. *That's two backward knots.*

How could her one belly have bred two boys of such different natures? They had had the same father, so far as she remembered.

Give Igor the biggest candle. He could have forsaken his guard post, stolen the knife and returned unnoticed (*tie a forward knot*). Did he know how his woman consoled herself on lonely nights? Probably. Doors opened in Dragomira's mind, spreading like Radagast's great wings, and she saw the ikon revealed – two brothers so different in natures but alike in build and hair. Igor could have confused them from the back, allowing for drink and darkness. *Tie a second forward knot.* Igor's blunder had been fortunate for Bohemia, caught as it was between Germans to the west and Magyars to the east. As a king, Wenceslas would have made a good monk. Igor could easily carry a body (*that's three forward knots*) but could he carry his drink? She must find out how sober he had been last night.

Shape the last little candle into a woman. Give it breasts and yellow silk for blonde hair. Raika could have stolen the knife and given it to anyone. Where there is a murderer and an accomplice there is a traitor and a betrayer. It is only a matter of chance as to who talks first.

Dragomira sent Axel, her guard, to bring Raika in. While she waited, she threw some charcoal on the fire and left the poker in it.

Raika was a slim little thing of about sixteen summers, baby-pink skin, big blue eyes, long blonde hair tied in purple ribbons, a scarlet woollen dress and a necklace of amber and silver. Amber and scarlet

together! the girl had no sense of colour. But then again, scarlet
wouldn't show the blood.

"Where were you, all yesterday, and where was Igor?"

"We were at the Christmas feast. Everybody saw us."

"All day?"

"Igor and I came together, in the hut, just after sunset. Then we
went back to the hall for the drinking. I left and went back to bed,
after a couple of hours."

"So there you were, a little girl alone in your bed, on Christmas
night. Who came to you? Boleslav?"

"He could hardly stand when I left."

"Then who?"

"No one, My Lady. All the men were drunk."

"Igor just let you leave him on his own?"

"He was well drunk by then. He didn't come home."

"Standing drunk, falling down drunk or fighting drunk?"

"Standing – but swaying a bit. Not fighting drunk – nobody
crosses Igor when he's drunk."

"Nobody crosses Igor when he's sober, if they've got any sense."
Dragomira towered over Raika. "You've been a very silly girl. Is it
sweet to bed a prince? Would you rather bed a king? Would you like
to be a queen?"

With each question Raika backed away and cringed lower, until
the elm chest against the wall caught her behind the knees and she
slumped down, her hands over her face. Dragomira stirred the fire,
moving the poker to the hottest part.

"My girl, you haven't got a prayer – not to any god you can find.
Were you wearing that scarlet dress yesterday?"

"Yes, My Lady. It's my best."

"Your only decent one. Take it off."

While Raika shivered in her shift, Dragomira waved the dress over
Rofi's muzzle. He whined softly, like a dog that hasn't the energy to
snarl and wants to go back to sleep. So there was no smell of blood
or death on the dress. Dragomira threw it into a corner, then
snatched the necklace from the girl's throat and held it up to the
firelight, watching the brown amber turn to a clear orange glow.

"Pretty, pretty. Who gave it you?"

"I got it from that Polish trader who came south in the rutting
season."

"I know he sold it, but who bought it? It cost money."

"Boleslav," she whispered.

"And you wore it all through leaf-fall and pig-killing time. How do you think Igor felt? You didn't think."

"When my grandmother died I said it was hers."

"And you were so stupid you thought Igor would believe the story. He knew. He took Boleslav's own knife to kill him. It was exciting, wasn't it, to have a man who would kill for you. But it went wrong and he killed the wrong brother. Now the two strong men in your bed are both alive. Which will be first, do you think, to break your scheming little neck?"

Dragomira pulled out the poker and spat on it. The spittle hissed and danced, a hot pearl on the redness.

"What really happened? You want to tell me, you know you'll tell me sooner or later."

"I don't know, My Lady, I swear it!"

"Try to remember something in the next couple of days. Axel!"

The door opened, after a sufficient pause. Either Axel had not been listening to her interrogation, which meant that he was obedient, or that he *had* been listening, but had also been clever enough to wait a second before he opened the door. But which?

"My lady?"

The look on his face suggested that he was not surprised to see Raika half-stripped. So he was a clever listener. Well, that was useful to know.

"Take this girl away and lock her up, nobody feeds her but me. Tell everyone that she has a fever, called Queen's Madness, and that it may be catching."

Alone now, but for the dog, Dragomira studied the wax dolls. Raika wasn't clever enough to think of a convincing lie, or brave enough for a conspiracy. *Tie a backward knot in Raika's cord.* But apparently Igor had been had been half-sober last night, and he knew all about Boleslav tupping the little blonde hoggit. *Tie two forward knots for Igor.*

There was one other possibility. She took a fifth candle and, with the hot needle, gave it wings and two sharp teeth. A vampire was unlikely, this far west, but she had to make certain. It was time to pay a call on the Vlachs. The sun was at its noon-peak by now, so she put on her furs.

At the northern city gate a guard courteously moved a rowan wood cross aside, to let her pass. The cross, and the seven crossed nails and bunch of garlic at its centre, had not been there yesterday. Bishop Anton could move fast, when it was a matter of keeping out the Devil's servants. In truth rowan wood had never bothered her, but she was careful to give as wide a berth as possible, for the looks of things. She walked on out of the city, down the river towards Hunter Island, where the Vlachs were camped. A crust of snow merged with the river's grey ice, almost reaching across to hide the swift black channel in the middle. Vampires could cross a bridge over a running stream, but could they walk over ice? She wasn't sure.

Rofi bounded on ahead, then started at something in a ditch. She ran after him. The sheep's guts lay in red coils and loops, just beginning to freeze, not even a branch to cover them. Messy people, the Vlachs. Wenceslas, like many Catholics, would not eat mutton, the Lamb of God, but the Greek Christians ritually killed and ate a lamb, every Easter. Boleslav would eat anything, at any time. She called Rofi back from his find and continued her journey into the Vlach camp. A woman was scraping a sheepskin clean of flesh and fat. A grizzle-bearded Vlach greeted her from the door of the largest tent. The brown and white patches of his goatskin clothes were artistically matched, which among the Vlachs marked him out as a person of quality. He beckoned her inside the tent. When the flap closed behind her, it also trapped the foul air – sheep grease, human grease and imperfectly dried firewood. One of the chief's women brought her a bowl of chopped sheep's liver and kidneys, fried in kidney fat. From her pouch Dragomira took her own spoon – silvered bronze, its tail in the form of a serpent with tiny garnet eyes.

"My son, the king, is dead."

"May his spirit sleep easy, until the Last Day," the chief replied. He crossed himself, but to Dragomira there was something odd, something sinister about the gesture. "I did not need a black mirror to see that you would come. The killer who left no footprints was, the Roman priests say, a vampire. Vampires come from the East, and so do we."

He told his story too quickly, too easily, like a man who had rehearsed it. Dragomira chewed on a piece of meat that was too tough for kidney but too tender to be heart, and so was probably udder.

"Are there vampires in your tribe?"

"Maybe – why should a vampire need to strike with a knife, like a Christian mortal? And a silver knife, at that?"

"My son wore a garnet cross at his throat. He was protected from vampire bites."

"How could a vampire strike near a Christian cross?"

"They hunt among graveyard crosses. Saint Agnes's bones lie under her cross, which makes it a graveyard."

"The moon is but three days old, yet vampires hunt only on the dark side of the moon."

Dragomira acknowledged the truth of that. As she left the camp she noticed that over every tent flap there hung a blue clay eye – to outstare the devil. Everybody trusted Raika, with her baby blue eyes. Dragomira's green eyes had always attracted suspicion. Well, it is better to be feared than loved.

As she walked westward back to the city she saw a speck fly southwards out of the sun, then circle round, left to right. A hawk? no, too big, a kite or an eagle. Either Radagast himself, come to claim the late King's royal spirit, or a common eagle, famished by the snow and attracted by the gralloch of the sheep that the Vlachs had left in the ditch. Now it drew closer, Dragomira saw that it was nothing more than a red kite. Nevertheless, Dragomira took no chances, but put her hand to her brow and made the Sign.

It was unlikely that a vampire could strike at this time of the moon. Neither Raika nor Vassili could have carried the body. The killer had to be Boleslav, in drunken anger, or Igor when his simple revenge plot had gone wrong. Maybe a complex plot had gone right? Wenceslas's bargain with the Germans had made him a raft of enemies. Perhaps someone had hired Igor as assassin, to remove Wenceslas, disgrace Boleslav as a fratricide and stir up a rebellion?

The red kite circled lower, making half a dozen crows break from their feeding and leave the great red bird to scavenge on the gralloch of the sheep. The crow's protests seemed to come from far away. A kite does not fly silently, like an owl, the beat of its wings scares off lesser scavengers, yet to Dragomira this bird sounded strangely quiet. Of course, the snow sucked up all sounds.

Frozen snow cracked under her feet. Rofi walked behind her, out of sight, knowing when he wasn't wanted, or glad of the easier walking made by her footprints. Dragomira could feel the cold, seeping up to her knees. Her hands were white, skin pulled back, their tendons showing high – the cold had driven out the blood.

There had been no blood on the snow; a dead body doesn't bleed – but neither does a frozen, living one. A second time the doors of the ikon opened and she saw a picture – she saw her son's murder happening, but this time she saw the truth. She knew why the footprints were double. She pulled her robe clear of the snow and carefully stepped back in her own footprints, on her own trodden snow. Silence. Then she stepped out across fresh, frozen snow, breaking the crust. Crunch, crunch, crunch.

The guilty fear to make a sound, especially if they themselves have very clear hearing. Now she knew the "how" of her son's murder, and she knew the "who", but she needed to know the "why". She trudged home, towards the sunset over Prague's stockade.

While Rofi snored on the floor of her chamber she took a doll from the chest, studied it, and tied an extra "yes" knot in its cord. Then from the chest she took a stone jar of ale, a silver jug, two silver beakers set with moss agate and some spiced biscuits. She half filled one beaker with water, then ordered Axel to bring Vassili to her.

When they came, she sent Axel away, to go and feed Raika. Rofi could guard the door, she wanted privacy for this interview. Just Vassilli and her.

"How does my son, your master?"

Vassilli smiled nervously.

"He has no wish for music at this moment. Maybe he won't want my simple melodies, now that he's king"

"He isn't king yet. The Christian bishops might try to prove fratricide."

Vassilli did not blink at the Latin word. Boleslav had said that the boy was educated. She poured ale into both beakers, taking the watered ale for herself.

"God rest King Wenceslas's soul"

"Amen!" the boy replied.

There was something odd about the way the boy crossed himself before drinking, something strange but familiar.

"Tell me everything that happened last night," she asked.

"Prince Boleslav – King Boleslav now, forgive me, gave me leave to go to Christmas vespers. Then I went back to the Great Hall, to attend him."

"Did he want your music?"

"A song or two. He himself sung a bit."

"How drunk was he?"

"He remembered all the words."

"When did you leave the party?"

"About midnight – but I think I dozed on a bench."

"When did you last see King Wenceslas alive?"

"He was at Vespers, of course. I didn't see him after that – Yes I did, he was in the Hall for the wassail, at least at the start."

"Was Boleslav on his feet when you left?"

"Swaying a bit and shouting a lot, but walking straight."

"Shouting about what? Act the part, be Boleslav. Here, let me fill your cup."

The boy took a big gulp and dropped his voice to Boleslav's baritone.

"A king should be king! A king should defend his people!"

Light-headed from the ale, living his part, the boy drained his cup. Dragomira only half filled it, there was more in her ale than he knew, and she wanted to aid his tongue without marring his memory. He seemed vague about Wenceslas's movements, yet certain that Boleslav had been only half-drunk at the end of the evening. She put her fingers into the ale.

"My Christian son was a good friend to the Roman church. What now? Is Boleslav able to step into his . . ." she paused, and walked her fingers across the table, leaving a trail of ale-droplets ". . . his footprints?" The boy looked away and giggled.

"You are a Christian. Will you pray for Wenceslas's soul?"

"I have done so already."

"I wish I knew how. Kneel down and show me."

The boy obeyed and started an *Ave Maria*, while Dragomira stood over him.

"Tell me, who needs Christian prayers more – a virgin saint, murdered at his prayers, or he who stabbed him in the back? Pray for *his* soul."

The boy crossed himself, the same strange way, and the third time the doors of the ikon opened for Dragomira. She saw the roads to her son's Calvary, and on every road a Judas. Vassilli had a Greek name. He had crossed himself right to left, Greek style.

Wenceslas was a true friend of Rome, and of peace at any price. He would have let in the Germans, Pope's men every one. Yet Boleslav kept to the old ways, Eastern ways. "The Enemy of my Enemy is my Friend". She handed a spiced Christmas biscuit to Vassilli and took one herself, but dropped it in her lap, where Rofi would not find it.

"Tell me – why do you suppose my son's killer left no footprints?"

"Maybe he was a vampire. Vlachs are vampires. Vampires can fly."

Vassilli giggled again and flapped his arms. The ale, and the far stronger biscuits, were doing their work.

"So a vampire came behind him. Why didn't he hear its wings?"

"The snow swallowed up the sound."

"Are there many vampires, east of the Iron Gates?"

"My grandfather told me about them. They've got big white teeth, like rats, and big red eyes, as big as bowls, they swing towards you like cartwheels."

Vassilli flapped his shirt in and out, like one who was too hot – he was sweating, not just from fear.

"Look, there's one on the doorstep, it's shiny blue, it's got scales!" His eyes were fixed on Rofi. "It's your dragon, you're a witch, your dragon is burning me, my skin's on fire!"

He ran from the room, out into the snow, tearing off his clothes, rubbing snow over his burning bare skin. His shouting drew a crowd who saw a naked page, crying out that there was a great white bat on the Cathedral tower, and dancing in the snow.

Dragomira looked up to the tower and saw an eagle owl, its plumage turned silver by the moonlight reflected off the snow. Vassilli fell over, and none dared approach a bewitched man.

Dragomira left him in the snow and went back to her chamber, her work was done. Whether her son's killer died from frostbite, or the ergot of rye in the ale and the biscuits, was of no concern.

She threw the waxen image of Vassilli into the fire.

Macbeth 🍂

NIGHT'S BLACK AGENTS

Peter Tremayne

We move forward just over a hundred years to the time of one of the best-known kings of Scotland – Macbeth, or MacBeth as Peter Tremayne more accurately spells it. The name is from the Gaelic Mac Bheatha, meaning "son of life".

The historical Macbeth, who became High King of Scotland in 1040 and for seventeen years ruled wisely and well, according to contemporary chronicles, was not the "butcher" of Shakespeare; nor was his wife, Gruoch (Lady Macbeth) a "fiend-like queen". The grandson of Malcolm II, he was a legitimate heir to the kingship. Accepted as the last great Gaelic king, he was buried on Iona, where all legitimate Scottish kings were buried.

Peter Tremayne, who under his real name of Peter Berresford Ellis has published a study of the historical Macbeth, turns his attention to an historical incident which occurred in 1033, seven years before Macbeth became High King but just one year after he became mórmaer (equivalent to earl) of the province of Moray. The murder of Malcolm Mac Bodhe, the brother of Gruoch, is recorded in the annals. Who was responsible? Macbeth investigates.

> Good things of day begin to droop and drowse Whiles night's black
> agents to their preys do rouse
>
> *Macbeth*, III, 2

*　　　*　　　*

"It is plainly murder, my lord," the elderly steward announced unnecessarily.

What else could a stab wound in the back mean but murder? It would hardly be self-inflicted. The fact that Malcolm, the son of Bodhe, prince of the House of Moray, lay stretched on the floor of his bed chamber with the blood still seeping across his white linen nightshirt did not need a fertile imagination to conjure an explanation of what had befallen the young man.

The corpse lay face down on the wooden floor boards, clad in nothing else but the shirt which meant that he had just left his bed to greet his killer. A bloodstained knife had fallen near by, apparently dropped by the assassin in his haste to be gone.

MacBeth, son of Findlay, the *Mòr-mhaor* or petty king of Moray, which was one of the seven great provincial kingdoms of Alba, answering to no man except the High King whose capital was south in Sgàin, stared down with a grim face. Indeed, this was his castle and the dead man was his wife's brother. He stood with a cloak wrapped around his shoulders to protect him from the night chill. It had only been but a few minutes ago when he had been roused from his sleep by his anxious steward and requested to come quickly to the bed chamber of Malcolm.

It certainly needed no servant, nor seer nor prophet to tell MacBeth that someone had entered this chamber and brutally struck down the young prince and then discarded the weapon.

"Is the castle gate still secured?" he demanded, his voice raised as if in irritation and glancing into the corridor where a warrior of his personal bodyguard stood impassively.

"Aye, noble lord," replied his steward, an elderly man named Garban. "As custom decrees the gate was secured at nightfall and will not be opened before dawn. Your warriors still stand sentinel at the gate and walk the ramparts."

"So the culprit may yet be within these walls?"

"Unless he has wings to fly or be a mole that can burrow under the walls," agreed the old servant.

MacBeth nodded in grim satisfaction.

"Let it continue to be so for we may yet snare this evil-doer. Now where is Prince Malcolm's servant? Why is he not here?"

"He was injured, noble lord. He now is being attended to for, in truth, he received a blow to the head which caused it to bleed. He it was who discovered the body of his master."

"Then send for him straightaway, Garban. And send for my Brehon to oversee these matters, according to the law. There is little time to delay in our pursuit of this assassin."

While a king or even a chief could be a judge and arbitrator in the law courts, it was, by law, known that a professional and qualified lawyer, a Brehon, had to sit with the king to ensure the letter of the law was obeyed and a fair judgment delivered.

The old steward was turning towards the door when there was a cry at the portal and MacBeth turned to see his newly wed wife, the Lady Gruoch, standing there, a hand to her mouth. Garban, the steward, jerked his head to her in nervous obeisance before he hurried forward to carry out MacBeth's instructions.

MacBeth turned to his wife. He had thought her still sleeping when he had left the bed chamber to follow Garban.

"Madam, I am afraid your brother is dead," he greeted her quietly, not knowing what else to say but the blunt truth.

Lady Gruoch had seen much violence in her five and twenty years. It had been only one year ago that her first husband, Gillecomgàin, the previous petty king of Moray, had been slaughtered in his castle near Inverness with fifty of his warriors. The castle, with its occupants, had been razed to the ground with fire. No one was caught but whisper had it that the man who ordered the deed was none other than the man whose bed she now shared and who had been acclaimed with the mantle of *Mòr-mhaor* to replace her dead husband. Yet the Lady Gruoch had long been persuaded to discount such a notion and she had come to love the young, red-haired monarch who offered her and her baby, the young prince Lulach, his protection.

Gruoch had not been in the castle of Gillecomgàin at the time of the attack but away visiting with her newly born son. The people of Moray, bereft of their ruler, turned to MacBeth, whose father Findlay had been king before Gillecomgàin. For kingship, like chieftainship, descended by the rule of the ancient laws of the Brehons and not by the inheritance of the first born male. A king, or chief, had to be of the blood but they were elected to their office by their *derbhfine*, four male generations from a common great-grandfather. The law of succession had always been thus so that the most worthy and able should succeed.

No one questioned that MacBeth was worthy nor that he was able. Indeed, he was also of the blood royal for he was grandson of the High King, Malcolm, the second of his name to sit on the throne at Sgàin. Thus the red haired young noble had been duly installed as the petty king of the province.

Within the year MacBeth had convinced the Lady Gruoch that he had not been responsible for her husband's death and had won her love. Scarcely a month had passed since their marriage at which he had even adopted her son, the baby Lulach, as his own. Yet the evil whispers still remained and some said that he was ambitious and was only reinforcing his claims to the High Kingship because Gruoch, too, had been the grandchild of a High King, Kenneth III who had died some thirty years ago. Only in these lands which comprised the former ancient kingdoms of the Cruithne was a succession through the female allowed by Brehon Law but the Pictish custom, as it was called, had not been claimed since Drust Mac Ferat ruled over two hundred years before. So the gossip did not hold water.

More logical tongues pointed out that the Lady Gruoch's brother, Malcolm Mac Bodhe, as grandson to Kenneth III, had a more popular claim to the throne as next High King. Even if he had not, it was well known that Malcolm II, who had sired only daughters, did not favour his grandson MacBeth, nor, indeed, any member of the Moray House. The old king favoured his grandson, Duncan Mac Crinan, the son of the Abbot of Dunkeld, and son of his eldest daughter.

The old king and his grandson, Duncan, were of the House of Atholl, and they maintained they had a superior right to the High Kingship at Sgàin than the House of Moray even though his second daughter, the Lady Doada had married Findlay of Moray and was MacBeth's mother. The death of Gillecomgàin in the previous year, was attributed by many of the House of Moray as being a deed carried out at the whispered order of Malcolm II to ensure that Duncan was placed on the throne. Gillecomgàin alive had been a threat to Atholl's claims. Gillecomgàin had been slaughtered. But Malcolm Mac Bodhe, grandson of Kenneth III, had become the next challenger to the continued Atholl dominance at Sgàin. Some were already acclaiming him as successor to Malcolm II.

But now Malcolm Mac Bodhe, too, was dead; laying on the floor of his bed chamber in MacBeth's castle. Murdered.

The young king appeared troubled as he stood regarding his tearful wife who stood, leaning against the door jamb, her breast heaving, a hand across her trembling mouth.

"There will be many who will blame me for this death, my lady," MacBeth addressed the grief stricken young woman quietly. He held out a hand to comfort her.

She took it and gave a single heartrending sob, trying, at the same time, to gain control over her feelings. The years of threatening danger had taught her to suppress her emotions until she could indulge in them without distraction.

"How so, my lord?" she asked, succeeding in the effort.

"They will say that I have killed, or had killed, your brother, in order to secure my place nearer the throne at Sgàin."

The woman's eyes widened and she shook her head vehemently.

"I will swear that you never left my side since we parted from my brother after the meal last night."

"Can you so swear?"

"Aye, I can, for I have not closed my eyes these last hours. You know well that I am still beset by nightmares and have visions of our being burnt while we slept, as happened to my . . . as happened to Gillecomgàin, your cousin. I heard Garban come into our chamber and ask you to follow him here, that is why I came after you to see what was amiss."

"They will say that your witness for me is what might be expected of a wife or that you had good cause to see your brother dead so that your husband could claim the throne that you might sit by his side as queen at Sgàin. Indeed, some might even say that, while I slept, you did the deed yourself for ambition's sake."

The Lady Gruoch paled as she stared at him.

"What fiend-like creature will people have me be?" she whispered in shock. "To kill my own brother? Even to think such a thought is to pronounce speculations hateful to the ears of any justice."

"It may be said just the same," pointed out MacBeth impassively. "Many things are said and done in the court of my grandfather at Sgàin. I do not doubt that the vaulting ambition of my cousin Duncan, the son of my mother's own sister, will do more than make hateful speculations to secure the throne. His father, the unnatural abbot of Dunkeld, even tries to poison the entire Church against anyone who stands as rival to the resolution of his son to secure the throne."

"I fear that it is so," sighed Gruoch. "I have long laboured, as you know, in the belief that the destruction of Gillecomgàin was brought about by your grandfather who encouraged the rumours which laid the deed at your door."

MacBeth lowered his head. It was true that rumours still circulated accusing him of Gillecomgàin's death.

"There will be more whispers yet," he agreed heavily, "unless we speedily resolve this unnatural death of your brother".

A tall, elderly man stood at the door. It was clear that he had just come from a deep sleep. His hair was a little dishevelled and his clothes had not been put on with care.

"Garban has informed me of these tragic events, noble lord," the man muttered, his eyes moving swiftly from MacBeth, to Gruoch and to the body on the floor. They glinted coldly in the candlelight and seemed to miss nothing.

"I am glad that you have come, Cothromanach. It needs your skilled touch here for I was saying to the Lady Gruoch, there are many who will wish to taint me with this killing. Your word is needed that this matter has been properly conducted and resolved so that none may level any accusation against me."

Cothromanach, the Brehon, set his face stonily.

"The truth is the truth. I am here to serve that truth, my lord."

MacBeth nodded. "Indeed, let us proceed with logic. Garban has told you that we have a witness to this deed in the prince Malcolm's servant?"

Cothromanach nodded.

"I am told that he has been sent for."

"He has. The Lady Gruoch and I were in our bed chamber until Garban summoned me. The Lady Gruoch says that she is prepared to state that I did not rouse from our bed all night. I have told her that her testimony might be dismissed on grounds of her relationship to me."

The Brehon pursed his lips wryly.

"Madam, is there any other witness that will say that you and your husband did not stir until Garban summoned your husband here?"

Gruoch thought a moment and then nodded in affirmation.

"Little more than an hour ago I asked my maid Margreg to bring me mulled wine to help me sleep. She entered our chamber with the wine while my husband slept on obliviously."

MacBeth raised his eyebrows in surprise.

"I did not hear her."

"You were tired, my lord, after yesterday's hunt and last night's feasting."

"This is true. So Margreg brought wine and saw me sound asleep beside you? This, you say, was but an hour ago?"

"It was so."

MacBeth turned to the Brehon.

"And I was roused to come here but a quarter of the hour past, and if the deed were committed not long before it would mean that we have the best witness yet in the maid."

"What makes you think the deed was done but an hour ago?" queried the Brehon.

"Easy to tell. We have a witness to the deed." He turned to his wife to explain. "I have sent for your brother's servant who, it appears, was attacked by the assassin. He has already indicated the time to my steward, Garban."

The Lady Gruoch stared at him in surprise.

"This servant was attacked by the assassin? Then we have no need fear our innocence of the deed."

MacBeth sighed: "Perhaps," he said softly. "Truth does not still malicious tongues."

"You sound defensive, lord," observed the Brehon. "As if you already stand accused and found guilty."

"It is why I want you to examine this matter closely, Cothromanach. I fear it may be so unless I demonstrate that I had no hand in this. Now, here comes Garban and Malcolm's servant. Do you return to our chamber, my lady, and dress yourself for it is near dawn and this may be a long day." He paused and turned to Cothromanach. "That is, unless you wish the lady to stay?"

The elderly Brehon shook his head.

"I have no objections to the Lady Gruoch withdrawing."

As Gruoch left the chamber, with a single glance back to where her brother's body lay, old Garban came forward. Behind him followed a younger man, tall and well built. There was a gash over his eye that still seeped blood. His face was pale and he walked with an unsteady gait. He stood hesitating before MacBeth looking from him to the Brehon.

Old Garban gave him a gentle nudge forward.

"Tell my noble lord your name, boy."

The young man took a pace forward.

"I am called Segan, noble lord," he muttered, his eyes downcast.

"How long have you been in the service of the prince Malcolm?"

"I have served him ever since I can remember and my father before me was a steward in the house of his father, the prince Bodhe."

"Then this will not take long, Segan. Tell us the circumstances in which you received this blow to your head and how you discovered the prince?"

"Little to tell, indeed, noble lord. Prince Malcolm had retired after the feasting last evening and went straightaway to his bed. He told me that he would not want me until the morning. So I, too, went to my bed . . ."

"Which is where?" Cothromanach, the Brehon, suddenly interrupted.

"In that small chamber opposite," the young man indicated through the open door.

Garban, the steward, intervened with a clearing of his throat.

"I placed the servant there so that he might be near his master in case of need," he explained to the Brehon.

"What then?" MacBeth did not wait for the Brehon to acknowledge the explanation.

"I fell asleep. I do not know what time I was awakened nor what had awakened me. Perhaps it was the sound of something falling to the ground. I roused myself and listened. All was quiet. I went to my door and opened it. I thought that I heard a sound from Prince Malcolm's room.

"Wondering if anything was amiss, I went to his door and called softly. There was no answer. I was just about to turn back into my chamber when I heard a distinct sound from this room. I called Prince Malcolm's name and asked if he needed anything.

"There was no response and so I tried the chamber door. It was secured."

"Secured?" interposed Cothromanach quickly.

"It was Prince Malcolm's custom to secure the door to his bed chamber from the inside." The young servant hesitated and dropped his gaze. "These are troubled and dangerous times, lord. There are many who would not weep over Prince Malcolm's death."

"Go on," the Brehon instructed.

"I called again. Then I heard the bolt being withdrawn. I tried the handle and this time the chamber door swung open. I took a step inside and saw the prince even as you see him now, laying on the floor there. The blood on his shirt and the knife at his side."

MacBeth glanced towards the Brehon and saw his puzzled gaze. He preempted the question.

"You saw Malcolm lying there and saw all this clearly? How so?"

"How so?" repeated the young man in a puzzled tone, not understanding what he meant.

"Was the room not in darkness?"

"Ah," Segan shook his head. "No, there was a candle alight by the bedside, even as it is now."

MacBeth turned to examine the candle and saw that scarcely a half inch of tallow was left flickering in its holder. Satisfied, MacBeth turned back in time to see the young man wince and stagger a little.

"Are you hurt?" intervened the Brehon anxiously.

"I am a little dizzy still. Yet I rebuke my own stupidity," lamented the young man. "I cannot believe that I could be such a dim wit. Seeing the body, I took two steps towards it and then something hit me from behind. Now I realize, whoever had drawn the bolt still stood behind the door and who would it be but the assassin? I came in, like a lamb to the slaughter, and thus he could strike me down from behind."

Old Garban pursed his lips wryly and nodded in support.

"It could happen to anyone, seeing their lord dead. It was a natural error. No blame to the young man."

MacBeth nodded absently but Cothromanach was examining the young man with his sharp eyes.

"Yes. It was an action not governed by thought. So you say that you were struck from behind? What then?"

The young man frowned at the elderly man.

"Then?"

"Yes, what happened then?" pressed Cothromanach.

"I must have fallen unconscious to the floor for the next thing I knew I came to with blood on my head and a throbbing which was more agonizing than anything I can remember. I was lying just there." He pointed downwards. "Then I remembered the prince and raised myself. It was obvious that he was dead. I turned, the door was closed and no one else in the room. I left the chamber and went in search of Garban. I roused him and he came here. He then sent me to his wife to clean my wound while he went to tell you of this news."

Garban now intervened once more in support.

"This is true. The young man roused me and I put on my clothes and hurried here while my wife tended to his wound which was bleeding more profusely than it is now. Having ascertained what Segan had said was true, I felt I should come to rouse lord MacBeth. The rest is as he knows."

MacBeth turned to Cothromanach.

"Indeed. I immediately followed Garban here. My wife followed moments later. That was when I sent Garban to you and asked him to bring Segan back here."

The Brehon stood head bowed in thought for a moment.

"How long, Garban, do you estimate the time between you being roused by Segan and you rousing the lord MacBeth?"

The old man held his head to one side and thought.

"Scarce five to ten minutes, Cothromanach."

"And you, Segan, is there any way you can estimate the time you lay unconscious?"

"Not long, I think. It may have been a matter of minutes."

"What makes you say so?"

"The candle. I said it was burning when I entered. It had not burnt down too much when I regained consciousness. And, even now, you can see it still flickering there."

MacBeth went towards the table to examine the candle, noting the spilled grease on the table and the floor. He bent down and picked up a stub of tallow and frowned in annoyance at Garban.

"These chambers should be better cleaned," he snapped, throwing the tallow at his steward, who caught it and began to apologize.

Cothromanach hid his impatience.

"It is not the time to discuss the dilatory habits of the servants, noble lord."

MacBeth looked guilty and turned back to Segan.

"So the chamber was well lit? Did you get any impression of your assailant?"

Segan looked puzzled.

"Impression. I did not see him at all."

"Yet you are certain that it was a male?"

Segan was now entirely bewildered.

"If you did not see who struck the blow," explained MacBeth patiently, "how can you tell it was a man?"

In spite of himself, Segan raised a laugh.

"I cannot imagine a woman delivering the blow that would have laid me low, noble lord."

"Perhaps not," agreed MacBeth. He turned to the Brehon and saw the man still examining Segan's features thoughtfully. MacBeth turned back to Segan and suddenly realised what puzzled the Brehon. "But there is a question that intrigues me. You say that you were struck from behind?"

"Yes, noble lord. Had it been from the front I would have seen my assailant," he added patiently.

"Quite so. Then how is it that your wound is on your forehead and not on the back of the head?"

Segan's eyes widened and he raised his hand automatically to his forehead as if to touch the gash that was there.

"I was struck from behind, noble lord," he insisted. "I feel the hurt there even now. So that I know as a fact. Perhaps, as I fell, I also struck my forehead."

"There is no other explanation," agreed the Brehon quietly. "There is too much of Malcolm's blood on the floor to see where you might have fallen. Well, there is little more we can discover from this young man, I think."

"I have no further questions, Segan. I suggest Garban take you back to his wife to have your wound examined further. It looks a bad gash and a bruise surrounds it."

"I would rather lay down a few moments, lord," said Segan but Garban took his arm with a firm grasp and smiled. "Plenty of time after my wife has made a poultice for that cut and bruise."

Alone in the room, MacBeth turned to the Brehon.

"What do you think?"

Cothromanach shrugged.

"Little to think about, noble lord. There are few facts at our disposal to make any clear deductions."

"The facts seem that the killer gained entrance to this chamber and stabbed Prince Malcolm. The body falling to the floor must have alerted his servant, Segan, who came to the door. The killer had secured the door but, hearing Segan call out, realised that if he remained locked without, he would raise the alarm and the assassin would not be able to escape. So he slid the bolt and waited behind the door."

Cothromanach smiled.

"I cannot fault your logic, noble lord."

MacBeth continued, warming to the theme.

"Standing behind the door, the assassin waited as the young man open the door. The killer relied on the fact that the young man would react at the sight of Malcolm lying in his bloodstained shirt on the floor; he knew that the servant would take an involuntary step forward into the room. That was when the blow was struck. Then the killer left the room."

"Again, the logic is without a fault."

MacBeth smiled thinly.

"If nothing else, I answer to logic," he replied complacently.

"Very well, my lord. Let us turn logic to the following matters. Firstly, let us regard the body of the prince."

MacBeth looked down, his face wrinkled in distaste.

"What can we learn from it except that the killer stabbed the prince in the back?"

"That he did so presents us with an important question that needs a resolution."

"How so?"

"We have heard that the prince was in fear of his life for the reasons well known to you, noble lord. He slept at night with his door bolted from the interior. How, then, when his assassin came to his chamber did he gain entrance?"

MacBeth raised his eyebrows and turned to examine the door. The bolt was in place and there was no sign of any undue violence being used against the lock. He did not have to go to the small window in the chamber for he knew that it was a long drop into a rocky ravine through which a river meandered. There was no way anyone would climb in through that window. He would take an oath on it.

"If . . ." he paused and framed his words slowly, "if the door was bolted then Malcolm himself must have let his killer into the chamber."

Cothromanach made a gesture of approval.

"In order to do that, the prince Malcolm must have known his assassin. He must have known him well enough to have trusted him, to have let him into his bed chamber while not yet dressed and . . ."

MacBeth interrupted, for now he saw what the elderly Brehon was getting at.

"He must have trusted him to be able to have turned his back on him for the two stab wounds are in the back. The killer, as Malcolm turned away from him, stabbed him twice."

"Then dropped the knife and was turning to go . . ."

"When he was interrupted by Segan?"

"Perhaps," the Brehon said. "Yet what would be the motive for such a deed?"

"Surely the motive is obvious? Malcolm was a popular candidate for the High Kingship. The likely motive was to eliminate him."

"So we are saying that whoever did this deed was a servant of Duncan who aspires to the throne?"

MacBeth nodded and then grimaced.

"You are forgetting my claim for, with the prince Malcolm gone, I am now the head of the House of Moray and challenger to the kingship at Sgàin."

Cothromanach smiled briefly.

"I have not forgotten. Nor have I forgotten that you are not the only one who stands to gain."

MacBeth frowned.

"Who?"

"The Lady Gruoch would benefit by your elevation to the kingship."

For a moment MacBeth stood in anger but then he shrugged as if in acceptance.

"You mean more than she would have done had her brother gained the throne?"

"Of course. Much more. However, this is hardly a woman's work."

"With that, I agree," MacBeth was emphatic.

The door opened and Garban the steward re-entered.

"Segan is having his wound redressed. Can I render more assistance?"

"Find the maid Margreg and bring her here," instructed MacBeth.

The Brehon held up a hand to stay him.

"You knew the prince Malcolm well, didn't you?"

Garban blinked in surprise and shrugged.

"That is common knowledge. I was employed in the house of

Bodhe before I took service with my lord MacBeth. I taught young Malcolm to ride his first horse. His death grieves me sorely."

"Indeed," sighed the Brehon, and dismissed him with a wave.

When Garban had gone MacBeth turned to Cothromanach.

"Let us hear from the maid's own lips that we were in our beds at the time the deed was done," he told the Brehon. "Then you may be able to quench any malicious rumours which may be spread about us."

"You are sensitive on this matter," observed the Brehon.

"I know my grandfather, the High King, and my cousin, Duncan Mac Crinan," MacBeth said grimly.

"So be it," Cothromanach sighed.

Margreg was young and youthful, scarcely seventeen. She was dark haired, fair skinned and attractive and, what is more, she knew it. There was a boldness about her that might have been interpreted by some as a speculative lasciviousness.

She entered the chamber, dropped a half curtsey to MacBeth and was about to acknowledge the venerable Brehon when her eyes caught sight of the body on the floor. Her features wrinkled distastefully but she did not avert her gaze.

"The Brehon wishes to ask you a few questions," MacBeth said, stepping to one side and motioning the Brehon to proceed.

"You are maidservant to the Lady Gruoch?"

"You know so," retorted the girl with confidence. "You are as familiar with this castle as I am."

Cothromanach suppressed a sigh of irritation.

"This is an official inquiry, girl. Just answer my questions and leave your impudence for those who appreciate it."

The girl pouted in annoyance.

"Yes. I am maid to the Lady Gruoch."

"How long have you held that position?"

"Full one year since she came to this castle with her baby in search of sanctuary."

"Did you attend your mistress at bedtime."

"I did. Her dressing room is next door to the bed chamber and that is where the baby, Lulach, sleeps and that is where I sleep as well. I helped her undress and prepare for bed. That was just after the feasting."

"So you sleep in the next chamber. Were you disturbed in the night?"

"Yes. I awoke and heard the baby coughing. He is a good little soul but inclined to a night cough. So I arose and tended the child. I had quietened him and was about to go back to bed when I heard a door open and footsteps in the corridor. Curiosity made me go to the door and I looked out."

MacBeth had turned with a frown.

"What time was this?"

The girl shrugged.

"I have no means of knowing, my lord. It was dark and cold and the embers in the fire I had built in the chamber were grey." She turned to Cothromanach. "I try to keep a fire going through the night for the good of the baby. Warm air eases his poor little chest."

"You said that you went to the door and looked out," MacBeth observed heavily. "What did you see?"

"The Lady Gruoch, walking down the corridor. She was carrying something in her hand."

"How could you see that it was her? Did you or she have a candle?" asked the Brehon quickly.

The girl shook her heard.

"No. There are torches kept alight in the corridor there."

"So the Lady Gruoch left the bed chamber during the night?" pressed MacBeth unnecessarily.

"What time did she return?" demanded the Brehon.

"I do not know. Having seen that it was my lady, I simply returned to my bed, for it was chill, as I have said, and I was asleep in no time."

"Were you disturbed again?"

"Yes. I thought me barely asleep when I awoke and found my lady bending over me. She said she could not sleep and asked me to prepare her a goblet of mulled wine. I did so."

"And you had no idea when that was either, I suppose?" sighed MacBeth.

"Of yes. It was not long before Garban came and knocked at your chamber door. I prepared the wine and went in, finding the lady Gruoch sitting up in bed. You were there also, my noble lord, fast asleep by her side. I don't think that you had been disturbed at all during the night for you were deep in sleep and . . . and snoring with a sound fit to wake the dead."

She grinned provocatively at him.

"How long was it before Garban came to our chamber?" he snapped.

"I went back to bed but could not sleep. Perhaps he came within the hour. I cannot be sure, only that it was not very long."

The Brehon looked troubled.

"The Lady Gruoch told you that she could confirm you were by her side all night. Yet now we find that she left the bed and who is to provide her with an alibi? We must send for her again."

Lady Gruoch stood before them shortly afterwards.

She looked guilty but not alarmed.

"Yes. I left the chamber. I have already told you that I do not sleep well. That was the reason why I asked the maid Margreg to fetch me mulled wine."

"But you were seen going down the corridor," pointed out the Brehon. "Where did you go, lady?"

The Lady Gruoch raised her chin defiantly.

"If you must know, I came to see my brother." MacBeth looked unhappy. He glanced at Cothromanach who was gazing thoughtfully at her.

"This is a sensitive matter, lady. You know of what you might be accused? You know why I need to clarify the matter?"

"I know it well enough, my lord. But I came here for a purpose that I would keep between myself and his soul. All you need to know is that my brother was well and alive when I came here. Furthermore, when I left him he was still alive and well."

"That is not all I need to know, madam!" MacBeth almost shouted.

"Softly, noble lord," intervened the Brehon. Then he turned to Lady Gruoch. "But in truth, the noble lord is right, madam. We need to know the reason that you came here like a thief in the night. What intercourse could you have with your brother that needed such secrecy as to be conducted in the blackness of the night, that needed to be kept secret from your own husband?"

The Lady Gruoch was flushed and unhappy. She gazed at MacBeth for several moments and turned back to the Brehon.

"Very well. You will already have the evidence so I will confess to you."

MacBeth groaned helplessly.

"Evidence? What are you saying, lady?"

"It is common knowledge that my brother, Malcolm, was going to claim the High Kingship when my husband's grandfather dies or abdicates the throne at Sgàin. It is well known that MacBeth's cousin, Duncan, is favoured to succeed. Yet he is not the choice of the people, even in Atholl. My brother planned to raise the clans of Moray against Sgàin. For that he needed money. I was given many jewels by my husband as wedding gifts when I married him. Much that I owned perished in Gillecomgàin's castle. So I decided that my brother could make better use of the gifts from MacBeth."

"You say that you brought these jewels to your brother in the middle of the night?" asked MacBeth, doubtfully.

"It was just after midnight, an appointment that I had arranged with my brother last evening so that no one would know of the gift."

"Was his door secured?"

"Yes. It was bolted but he opened when he heard my voice call to him."

"You say that you left him alive?"

"I did so. He secured the door after me."

"And you went straightaway back to your bed chamber?"

"I did. And that was, as I say, just after midnight."

"The trouble is that you have no witness that he was alive when you left here," the Brehon sighed.

"I did not think I needed a witness. I understood from Margreg that the servant Segan disturbed the killer and was knocked unconscious by him some hours after I left my brother. That shows that I am innocent of the deed."

As she had speaking the elderly Brehon had been examining the room very carefully.

"What is it?" demanded MacBeth curiously. "What do you seek?"

Cothromanach looked at him and smiled thinly.

"Why, a bag of jewels, what else?"

Lady Gruoch stared at him in disbelief.

"You found no jewels? But that was the evidence that I thought you had and would trace them to my ownership. Why . . ."

MacBeth, ignoring her, was also searching the room carefully. Finally he stood before her.

"There are no jewels here, madam," he observed heavily.

"I do not understand it. He would not have given them to anyone else for safekeeping unless . . ."

Her eyes widened as she stared at her husband.

MacBeth turned to the Brehon.

"Do we not have another motive before us, Cothromanach? The assassin was not solely a murderer but a thief."

"It would appear so. Yet, let me remind you, noble lord, that the killer, thief or no, was still known to the prince. Why else would the killer be let into the chamber, why else would the prince have turned his back on the hand that then struck him down?"

MacBeth bowed his head in thought. Then he smiled grimly.

"I have an idea. Garban!"

The servant came forward.

"Are the gates still secured and my sentinels in place?"

"Not even a mouse could have left this castle without them being aware of it, noble lord."

"Good. Then we shall search for Lady Gruoch's jewels. I doubt whether our assassin has had time to dispose of them."

"Very well, noble lord. Where shall I start?"

MacBeth looked through the opened door into the corridor.

"We will start with Segan's chamber, it being nearest. Proceed, Garban. You, madam, will return to your chamber until I send for you."

MacBeth and Cothromanach followed the elderly steward into the servant's bed chamber. As Garban entered he seemed to stumble and reached out a hand to steady himself on the wall. He cut short an exclamation and brought his hand away. His finger tips were stained with blood.

MacBeth asked Garban to bring a candle, which he did. There was a small patch of blood on the wall, at shoulder level.

Garban had began to make a diligent search and it was not long before, examining beneath the bed, he emerged with a cry of triumph. He held out a small leather sack. They watched with fascination as he opened it and poured its contents on the bed. The muddle of jewels glittered and sparkled in the candlelight.

"Are they the jewels that you gave to the Lady Gruoch?" demanded the Brehon.

"They are, indeed," replied MacBeth with satisfaction. "Garban, fetch the servant Segan back here but do not mention this discovery to him."

"I understand, noble lord," Garban said with a grim smile.

Cothromanach the Brehon looked thoughtfully at MacBeth.

"Did you expect to find the jewels here?"

"As soon as I heard my wife's explanation – yes. I began to understand how and why this foul deed was done."

"Explain your deduction, my lord."

"Not hard. This is what I believe happened. Maybe the prince Malcolm told his servant that he would be receiving the jewels from his sister. Maybe Segan saw the Lady Gruoch come to his master's chamber and observe her enter with the sack. It was not politics that motivated Segan but greed. He waited until the castle was quiet and then he went to rouse his master by tapping at the door. Malcolm let him into the chamber, half asleep. Seeing only Segan, a servant he trusted, he turned his back on him. That was when Segan struck. Two swift but fatal stabs in the back. He found the sack of jewels and took them back to his own bed chamber and hid them where we have now discovered them."

"How then did Segan receive his own injuries?"

"Easy to tell. He had his story ready, that the murderer had stood behind the door and had given him a blow on the head which rendered him unconscious so that he could not recognise who it was. But this was the difficult part. Have you ever tried to give yourself a blow on the back of the head? Nevertheless, he needed some visual sign to show that he had been attacked. In fact, I might not have spotted the flaw in his story had not you realised it."

"That the injury was in the front?"

"Exactly. He went to the wall and banged his head against it causing the abrasion. Then he pretended that he had just come round and went to rouse Garban with the news of his attack."

MacBeth suddenly smiled and pointed to a small blood stain on the wall. It was shoulder high where a man might have banged his head to make the abrasion.

"I presume we do not have to explain that mark away?"

The Brehon sighed.

"It is a stupid man who leaves such a trail of clues."

Just then Segan entered the chamber with Garban close behind him.

He stared from MacBeth to the Brehon with a slight flicker of puzzlement in his eyes. Then his glance fell on the bed and the pile of jewellery.

"My lord, this . . ." he began, taking a step forward.

Then he froze, his eyes round in surprise. He half twisted and attempted to reach for something at his side. Garban withdrew the six-inch blade from the young man.

He watched dispassionately as the servant fell to the floor. There was no need to examine the body. Segan was dead long before he hit the floor.

"He was reaching for his knife," Garban explained. "He meant to harm you, noble lord."

"A pity," muttered Cothromanach. "Better to have him live awhile and receive his punishment as a warning to all thieves and murderers."

"Indeed," MacBeth acknowledged grimly. "Have the body removed, Garban, and have those jewels gathered up and returned to the Lady Gruoch. I will walk a way with you Cothromanach."

The Brehon glanced at him.

"You are still anxious, noble lord?"

"There are still willing tongues to spread rumours. Many will be quick to lay the blame for this at my door."

"Have no fear. I shall write my account to my fellow Brehons throughout the land. They shall know what has transpired here."

MacBeth smiled in thanks and, hauling his cloak more tightly around his shoulders, turned and made his way back to his bed chamber. Dawn now filled the castle with a grey, cold light.

After the morning meal, while the light was still grey and cold, MacBeth found old Garban on the ramparts of the castle. He was standing in a quiet corner away from the scrutiny of the guards leaning with his back to the ramparts.

"A close call, noble lord," observed the old man as he turned and peered over the ramparts, looking down into the rocky ravine below. "I had to kill him."

"Indeed you did," agreed MacBeth, pleasantly enough. "Yet the plan was nearly ruined by not clearing away the extra candle stub."

"It is easy to make a mistake. But all ended well. After Lady Gruoch left her brother, I knocked on the door and the prince opened it knowing it was I. The problem was that his falling body was heard by Segan who came and knocked on the door. Had I not opened he would have roused the entire castle. So I let him in and gave him a blow on the back of the head. While he lay unconscious, I struck him on the temple, for I knew that this might arouse suspicion. Then I hid the jewels in his bed chamber, in case we needed evidence and also spread his wall with his blood to make it look as though he had faked his wound by dashing his forehead there. Then, to confuse him over the time the deed was committed, I exchanged the burning candle with a new one which would put his timing out by an hour or two."

"That was the mistake you made, in dropping the stub of the first candle on the floor and not taking it with you," observed MacBeth. "It could have made the Brehon suspicious."

"None of us are perfect, noble lord," sniffed the old servant.

"True enough."

"And now you stand one step closer to the throne at Sgàin, noble lord. Prince Malcolm is no longer your rival and the Lady Gruoch is there to support you."

"True again."

"You have much to thank me for, noble lord," smiled Garban. "I trust I will be properly rewarded."

"That I have and that you shall," agreed MacBeth and, turning swiftly, he gave the old man a violent push, sending him flying over the rampart. There was scarcely time for Garban to scream as he plummeted downwards into the rocky chasm below.

MacBeth turned and seeing that he was unobserved allowed a smile of satisfaction to spread over his features.

William the Conqueror 🖤

EVEN KINGS DIE

_____

Mary Reed & Eric Mayer

If there's any date we know in history, it's 1066, the year that William, Duke of Normandy, defeated Harold II, the Saxon king of England at the Battle of Hastings. By sheer force of arms William crushed the English into submission and established a new order with the Norman nobility as the "aristocracy" and the Saxons as the under class of serfs. What William achieved in England he endeavoured to do in northern and central France, expanding his lands throughout Normandy, Brittany and Maine. His whole life was one of conquest and he changed the future of western Europe for ever. He ruled England for twenty-one years before he died, as he lived, besieging the French town of Mantes. At his death many believed his past deeds caught up with him, as the following story explores.

It was in early September that the earthly remains of William, Duke of Normandy, arrived at the abbey at Caen and the task of his interment fell to those of us, humble Benedictines, who had lived in the conqueror's shadow and would not be remembered by history, but who, by the grace of God, still breathed the sweet air of the temporal world.

With the Duke's entourage was an old Saxon cleric named Osbert. I took him to be a person of special standing because, although he was dressed in a plain tunic of undyed wool, his faded belt was embroidered in the ecclesiastical style.

The road from Rouen, where William had died, had almost claimed the last of Osbert's strength. Our abbot, a kind man, recognized in Osbert's shuffling gait and stooped back the ebbing of his life. He instructed me to keep the old man company. This kindness also served to keep out from underfoot a novice monk – myself – whose thoughts too often wandered.

So it was that I heard a story whose meaning has troubled me all my life. How strange that the unraveling of a mystery should have posed questions I had never thought to ask.

We had been sitting silent for some time on a stone bench beside the dispensary, warmed by the last of the late afternoon sun. I could see that the snows of age clung to Osbert's hair. His thin hands trembled as if cold were already creeping through his veins

I remarked upon the beauty of the day.

Osbert nodded, then spoke, his voice as crackling as the parchment his skin resembled.

"But do you not see that the shadows are growing long, and have a blue tint? They remind us that, inevitably, winter must come at last, and frost must kill the fairest flower."

I couldn't see the blue tint discerned by Osbert's pale, watery eyes. I murmured a commonplace concerning man's life, time, God's will. As if there was anything a young man such as I could tell an old man about such things. The other smiled thinly.

"I have lately been thinking about life, time and God's will, Brother Jean," he began. "And since you have mentioned these very things, I shall take it as a sign that you are the person to whom I should relate a story which has been much on my mind. It concerns a great man, a terrible crime and a holy sister who had a secret.

"The great man is he whose body has been delivered into your care. I have followed him for many years."

My expression must have betrayed my puzzlement, because he added, "For William to have a Saxon priest in attendance was not so odd as it might appear. Unlike many of my countrymen, I readily learned the Norman tongue and, unlike many Norman priests – forgive me for saying so – I did not shy from ministering on the battlefields."

I nodded, for it was all too true that William had spent most of his life at war.

"Although you are too young to remember the old duke, William was not unlike his father, Robert," Osbert continued, "who was, it is fair to say, what men expect a duke to be. Hard as iron in the field, ambitious, and, of course, lusty enough to sire a son without benefit of priestly ceremony. To this day, I still hear people refer to William as 'The Bastard'. Although not in his hearing.

"Now whereas William became duke at the age of seven and spent his life commanding armies and fighting for kingdoms, I lived a different life, among the peasants. The children I baptised had often enough been conceived before the wedding ceremony, but they were not heirs to kingdoms. I buried many of them a few weeks later. And of course there were adults to be shrived on their deathbeds. Marriage bed, childbed, deathbed. Such was my labour. And I continued my work even after William arrived, though it seemed strange to do so."

I asked him why this should be so, for such is the labour of the Lord.

He agreed, continuing, "But in those days, though I was not young, I still had a young man's hot blood and it angered me that my people could be so happy with their lot. I wonder now if perhaps it was because although the language of their masters might change, their lives did not. Mark you, there were changes for their lords. William soon enough confiscated their lands. But land was not the first thing he took.

"You Normans are always saying how crude the Saxons are. But, forgive me for saying it, even Normans get involved in, shall we say, extremely regrettable incidents?

"Oh, it all comes down to human nature, but let me tell you that certain Normans of noble blood were married with little ceremony to ladies whose acquaintance was made in a very hasty, not to say forceful, way. Not all of the ladies were originally high born, either, which, I know, amused William immensely. But after all, he had had to endure taunts about his birth from these very men for years.

"I performed more than one such ceremony, the altar illuminated by a single lantern, while owls called in the darkness. That is how I became acquainted with those close to William. But my most painful memory . . ."

Osbert's words trailed off and he pressed a liver-spotted hand to his heart. I could not say whether his obvious pain was physical or spiritual.

"Perhaps we should go inside," I suggested. "It will be dusk before long." In fact, the slanting sunlight had slid away from the bench, leaving us in shadow.

He shook his white-haired head. "There is something inside I want to show you, soon enough. But I must first tell you the rest of my story. It concerns a devout, high-born lady, whose name I will not reveal.

"This woman's husband had died of a fever when she was still young. She was renowned around all our part of the country for her beauty. Her face, at times, was radiant, like the stained glass face of the Virgin, when the evening sun illuminated the windows of the chapel. God forgive me for saying so.

"She was courted by many – rich and powerful suitors who desired the hand of one of the most beautiful women in their land – but she chose none of those men. She withdrew from worldly things and passed her days in prayer or at her needlework, or reading the scriptures.

"One day, when I entered the family chapel – I often attended the private chapels of lords and ladies – I found her kneeling before the altar. At first I did not realize there was anything amiss.

"Lady," I addressed her by name. But still she did not answer.

"Light through the stained glass seemed to fall in a crimson swath across the gilt embroidery at the hem of her linen skirt where it lay across the tiled floor. It was only as I approached that I saw that the red was not reflected light.

"Nor were the purpling marks on her face shadows.

"Her fine garment was torn, her silky hair was tangled. It was obvious that a terrible crime had been committed.

"I fell to my knees beside her and cradled her head in my arms. 'Lady,' I whispered, tell me – who has done this?'

"As I smoothed her hair away from her face I felt her breath against my hand, faint as a breeze on a still summer night. But she said nothing.

"Nor did she ever speak again, for her attacker had taken her voice as well as her honour, as surely as if he had torn out her tongue."

The old man fell silent.

"But you said she was lettered," I exclaimed. "She read scripture. Surely she wrote down the name of her attacker before she died?"

Osbert inclined his head wearily. "She did not die, for many years, Brother Jean. But the – incident – robbed her of all human speech. Perhaps she no longer wished to communicate with any of the race that had done this to her."

I asked what became of this lady.

"She entered a nunnery."

"Why does God allow such things?"

"I asked myself that, though I was older even then than you are now and should have known better." He paused. "I wished to exact revenge on her attacker.

"I could not appeal to the authorities, for I suspected that one of them – one of your countrymen – our foreign masters – was responsible.

"For weeks, until it became apparent the lady would never recover her speech, I came to pray at her bedside, little more than a pretext to questioning the members of her household.

"No one had seen anything. At least nothing they would admit to.

"I walked the streets of the town, inquiring after the health of my flock, but really attempting to gain information on the crime. God forgive me, I even questioned those I was shriving.

"But, in the end, there was nothing I could discover, except it was common knowledge that the invaders, at that time, moved from encampment to encampment in that part of the country, putting down unrest, confiscating estates."

I interrupted the old man. "Even if you had discovered some evidence – something that pointed to a particular soldier –"

"I doubt a mere soldier would have been free to wander into a private estate."

"Well, then, if you had found evidence pointing to an officer – what justice could you have expected, even so?" In mitigation I can only repeat that I was young and still arrogant.

Osbert made no reply beyond a tightening of his lips, but I saw his trembling hand trace out the worn stitchery in the belt of his tunic.

He continued. "I wanted nothing more of my native land. I learned the language of our new masters. I left the south and for years I was with William's son, Rufus, in the barren country of the north. A man, I may say in confidence, I fully expect to come to a bad end. But that is by the way. When he rejoined William's court, I went with him.

"That is how I came to be with William when he died. It was by the sword, as one might have expected, except that he died not by a Saxon sword in a foreign land, but during a dispute over Norman soil.

"He lingered for more than a month. He had been brought to Rouen when the messenger came for me.

" 'The Duke's wounds have proved to be mortal,' I was told.

"I went with all haste to shrive him. His guards argued, but in the end bowed to the authority of the church and withdrew, for a man's final moments are both sacred and secret, and no other ears may hear what the dying heart must speak. And so I heard his confession, and so, as all men must, be they kings or peasants, William died."

For some reason, at these last words, I felt myself shivering. Was it something in Osbert's voice, or just the sinking sun? By now the courtyard was in shadow. The only vestige of sunlight was the gold that touched the top of the ivy where it climbed the arbour against the dispensary wall.

"You have, indeed, told me about a great man, and a terrible crime, and about a nun with a secret," I admitted, "but what is the connection between these things?"

"To know that, one must discover the secret."

"An impossibility, since the lady – the nun – was left mute. I have heard that this may happen in cases of great trauma."

"There is a chill in the air, as well as in my bones. Help me up," he responded. "There is something I must show you."

I rose and took the old man's hand. I could feel the fragile bones beneath the flesh but, contrary to what I had expected, Osbert felt terribly heavy as I helped him to his feet.

"You are aware of the embroidery commissioned by Bishop Odo of Bayeux, honouring of William's military exploits?" he asked. "Of course, he is his half-brother."

"Yes, it arrived from Bayeux yesterday. We are to display it – or unfurl part of it, at least, for the funeral service. It is a most beautiful piece of work, allowing even the untutored to understand William's courage, strategy, the character of the man. A fitting tribute. Or so I'm told."

Osbert smiled, rather grimly, I felt. "No doubt," he began obliquely, "you have noticed the great comet embroidered on it?

The superstitious claim that such a thing foretells the death of kings, do they not?"

I shrugged. I had only glimpsed the rolled embroidery as it was being carried into the church. "Well, even kings die, comets or not."

"True enough. But as a member of William's court I found myself often in Bayeux and the embroidery, quite apart from its beauty, was of special interest to me, having been sewn by Saxon hands in my own country.

"I sensed something was there that I was not seeing. It took me years, but in the end I found it, or rather them. They are small, and overshadowed by the battle raging but once you notice – once you really notice, it is plain enough."

I accompanied Osbert across the courtyard and now we entered the church.

The embroidery had been partly unrolled in a side aisle, preparatory to its hanging for the service. Enough light filtered through the tall windows to illuminate the bright wool in the narrow length of linen.

I walked along, gazing down at the story.

Osbert asked me what I saw.

"The gathering of the fleet, the landing, the march, the battle. Death, glory, the fate of nations, what would you have me see?"

"You are seeing what I saw, at first. What everyone sees. But look, along the borders."

Bending closer, I saw that, in fact, along the top and bottom of the embroidery were smaller figures, dwarfed by the giant pageant of history. And among these smaller figures, a huntsman blowing his horn, a dragon, a cross, a unicorn and a tree entwined by a vine.

Osbert instructed me to look closer, near the unicorn, asking me what I saw there.

I looked, and, seeing, drew back, averting my gaze. Both the man and the woman were naked. The woman was trying to cover herself, while the man advanced towards his victim, his intent graphically obvious despite the simple stitchery. His outstretched hands were already red.

"This is not a proper scene for a funeral," I protested.

"Nor was the original a proper scene for a chapel," Osbert grimly replied. "Some might say the embroidery itself was not proper, even in its conception. Are not men of good will instructed not to gloat over an enemy's downfall? And beyond that, to order the conquered to make this thing, glorifying their own defeat, was this not even worse?

"Yet, the ways of God are passing strange. For one of the Saxon nuns ordered by Bishop Odo to labour at this work was that very lady who had been so terribly violated, and who had lost all power of language, but who, by God's grace, could still speak with her needle."

Horrified, I asked him how he could know such a thing.

Silently he untied the belt that cinched his tunic. When he held it out I could see its faded embroidery – a huntsman, a dragon, a cross, a unicorn and a tree entwined by a vine.

"This belt was made for me by the lady, as a gift when I was ordained," Osbert said simply. "And so, what was intended as a memorial to William's victory, Our Lord turned into a testament to his guilt."

"His guilt? He brought the invading armies, of course, but how could he personally –"

"Her beauty was renowned. Was it not the conqueror's desire to take all the best? And why else depict the crime with William's great triumph! Look at it! The lady is the pure unicorn, he the evil dragon.

"Is this not justice? A woman who is mute, but who, because of a bishop's desire to force Saxon nuns to glorify war and pillage by this work is miraculously given the opportunity to tell of William's wrong. And so exquisitely detailed, so beautifully wrought a thing it is, so that it could hang in the house of God, where truth must be told.

"Since I deciphered this message I have more than once thought how fitting it would have been to have smothered William in his unspeakable embroidery."

The old man's hand tightened in a spasm on the belt and he swayed. I caught him by the shoulder, steadying him, and we made our way out of the church, back into what remained of the light.

At the bottom of the steps leading into the church, Osbert stumbled. I tried to assist him but his surprising weight bore me down with him. A vortex of crows rose out of a twisted oak at the edge of the courtyard, and swirled across the darkening sky.

It was just after vespers that the abbot summoned me to the cell where Osbert lay. There, a solitary candle cast a kindly golden light over the old cleric. The ridges of his nose and brow stood out sharply from his shadowed face. The shadows, I realised, were not merely a product of the candlelight. It was obvious that the old man would soon be learning the solution to the last great mystery.

"Osbert will not be much longer among us," the abbot said softly.

As sparse with words as if they were included in his vow of poverty, the abbot quickly explained that Osbert had regained consciousness, was failing fast, but had specifically requested my presence.

When the abbot had left, imparting a final blessing, I sat on a stool at the head of Osbert's pallet and took hold of his thin hand.

"I am here," I said quietly, thinking how he would die so far from his own country.

His finger's answering squeeze was weak.

"Brother Jean, I wanted to speak to you once more, because I do not wish to die without finishing my tale."

"I thought I had heard the end."

The dying man smiled. His teeth looked huge in his bony face. "You heard only the beginning of the end, my young friend. In fact, it ended on another deathbed, on William's, to be exact."

I had thought his pale eyes were focused on the shadows beneath the ceiling, but he noticed the surprise in my expression.

"Remember," he reminded me, "I was at William's court for many years. I stayed at his side, whether on the grounds of a palace or a tent on a battlefield.

"He grew to be impressed by the Saxon clergyman who spoke his own language so well, who praised – yes, I admit it – who praised his great deeds.

"Year after year, I waited. And so, just as I had planned, when his death drew near the great villain summoned me to his bedside to carry out my priestly function."

It struck me that the old man might be delirious, or, even worse, that he might be about to disclose secrets he should not; hastily I protested that he could not reveal anything said in that situation.

"Of course, of course. But this concerns less what William said than what he left unsaid."

It seemed a dangerously fine point to me. "Even so, the recollections of a dying man, suffering as he had been from wounds and blood loss, might be incomplete. In all conscience we cannot hold that against him."

To my horror, Osbert laughed. The candle's flame trembled at this sudden exhalation.

"Ah, but in this case," he said triumphantly, "I was able to remind William of the incident about which I told you, asked him if he remembered a beautiful lady and a chapel in a foreign land, long ago. Then I asked him if he repented –"

"– You should not be telling me this," I broke in, desperate to stop the flow of words tumbling out. If only the abbot had remained!

"But you see," Osbert went on, oblivious to my protests, "he denied it all. A king, mark you, and yet a man like us, dying with lies on his miserable lips. And so I had to punish him."

"But, surely you didn't –?"

"No, I did not take his life. But what I did was much worse. I refused to shrive him. He went to judgement weighted down with all the black sins of his foul life. Every single one of them."

In a panic, I jumped to my feet. The candle guttered and my suddenly monstrous shadow flew around the walls. "To kill a man is one thing, but to murder a soul –"

"I fear the night is creeping across my eyes." Osbert's voice was weak now. "Have someone sent to shrive me, Brother Jean."

I heard myself calling for the abbot. As I watched, Osbert's eyes took on the sheen of a newly frozen pond. Then I noticed that his free hand tightly clasped his embroidered belt, two fingers resting, as in benediction, on the stitched unicorn there.

Osbert died later that evening. Afterwards, I told myself that his unspeakable revelations were nothing more than the wanderings of an old man.

And I might have remained convinced that it was thus had I not been present at William's funeral in Saint Stephen's Church two days later.

Though I was at the far back of the nave, I could still see clearly what occurred when the bier on which his body lay was lowered into the stone sarcophagus.

William had grown very fat in his later years. The sarcophagus, although of elaborate design, was too small.

Attendants, aghast, pushed at the body but it would not be wedged in. It was as if what remained of this mortal being who had bestrode his world could not resign itself to a cold, dark, resting spot.

Those assembled murmured their alarm. Then, as the attendants began to panic and pushed harder, the corpse burst open and the air was filled with an indescribable stench.

Later, there was talk of sickness, decay, too long an interval between death and burial. But the odor of death is not so unfamiliar. This was not it.

Even as I tried to shield my horror, I knew that Osbert had gained his revenge, for William, dying unshriven, had gone to eternal damnation and what filled the church was the unbearable stench of what awaited him in the burning pits of hell.

William Rufus ❦

ACCIDENTAL DEATH

———

Tom Holt

William Rufus was the third son of William the Conqueror. His eldest brother Robert inherited the Duchy of Normandy. His elder brother, Richard, was killed in a hunting accident in the New Forest in about 1081, so that it was William who inherited England on his father's death in 1087. No one seems to have liked William, least of all the Church, and the records that have come down to us show him as a perverse individual, almost certainly homosexual, who went out of his way to antagonize his counsellors and barons. How ironic that he too should meet his death in a hunting accident in the New Forest. But was it an accident?

In the last year of my lord's life, there were many reports of terrible omens and portents. A party of monks making their way home through the forest near Derby said that they met the devil, who walked with them for half an hour, talking quite freely and pleasantly, and warned them that he had business in the country that would soon become evident. At Finchamstead in Berkshire, a well flowed so freely with blood for fifteen whole days that it fouled the Abbot's fishpond and killed most of the carp. When my lord heard about these things, he laughed; he knew perfectly well what was going on, he said. I remember him pointing out that the Derbyshire monks had based their conversation with the devil on a passage in Notker's *Life of St Anthony*, without even bothering to change most of it because they imagined he was too ignorant to recognize it (but Rufus had heard the passage several times, and he always had a remarkable memory), and that if the Abbot of Finchamstead insisted on using red lead to simulate blood when concocting false portents, he had only himself to blame if he killed off his own fish. I said that I was shocked, and asked him if he wanted these fraudulent priests arrested. He looked at me, smiled, and changed the subject.

On the first day of August, the day before Rufus died, a French monk told Lord Robert Fitzhaimo (who was then the leading man at court) about a terrible dream he'd had, in which the king had swaggered into a church and tried to eat the crucifix, whereupon the crucified Christ leaned forward and kicked him in the head, knocking him to the ground. Robert told the king, who smiled and said, "He's a monk, he dreams for money. Give him a hundred shillings." I'm certain now that Rufus knew he didn't have long to live; there had been quite a few such dreams and visions reported over the previous few weeks, and Rufus himself remarked how things foretold in the dreams of monks about the enemies of the clergy had a strange habit of coming true. Robert took him at his word as far as the hundred shillings were concerned, and nothing more was said about it at the time. Afterwards, of course, much play was made of it, just as everybody was impressed to hear that on that very same evening, at Marcigny, the exiled archbishop Anselm was reported to have told Hugh, the abbot of Cluny, that he had seen a vision of the heavenly tribunal, with Rufus standing in chains before the throne of God and being condemned to death for his crimes against holy religion.

Less well known is the exchange between Robert and my lord later in the evening, when Robert asked him where he planned to keep Christmas, and Rufus grinned at him and said, "Poitou". But I remember that when he said that, there was a long and embarrassed silence, as if the king had said something foolish or insane. In fact, as I and several others knew, he had been considering the situation in Poitou and the dreadful mess his namesake Duke William's ambition to take the cross and go to Jerusalem had made of the duchy's finances. Rufus was a shrewd man, in many ways more like a merchant or a banker than a king, and I have little doubt that if he'd decided to make an attempt on Poitou, he would have succeeded, if only because he would never have considered it unless it was a viable proposition.

The next morning, the king had a great deal of work to get through, and I wasn't needed; so I sat down in the courtyard on the mounting block and plaited myself a spare bowstring. It was a warm day, and several of the leading men were out of doors, keeping themselves occupied with small, congenial tasks of one sort and another. Among them was Walter Tirell, whom I'd known for many years. He walked by and saw what I was doing, or rather trying to do. It was about that time that the Flemish method of laying in the loops of a bowstring was starting to become fashionable, and I was trying it out for the first time.

"Have you allowed the extra thumb's width for the serving?", Tirell asked, sitting beside me on the mounting block. "If you haven't, it'll come up short and ruin your bracing height."

I frowned. "You, of course, know what you're talking about," I said. "I've only ever seen this done once, and I wasn't really paying attention."

"Give it here," Tirell replied with a sigh, and he took the string and the board from me and set about unpicking most of what I'd done. "If you don't know how to do it, you'd be better off sticking to the old method. Otherwise you'll just waste good twine, and risk breaking the bow as well."

"Yes, Walter," I said. "What I should really do is buy a string from someone who makes them for a living."

Tirell grinned. "I'll make you one, for a penny," he said. "Give me the twine."

"Please yourself," I said. "I know you're always banging on about how poor and destitute you are, but I didn't know you'd taken up bowyery to help make ends meet."

"Cash in advance," Tirell said, with mock gravity, so I fished out a penny and handed it over. When he'd finished making the string he did give me my money back; at least, he gave me a penny, but (typically) not the same one. I'd given him an English penny, made of good silver. I got rid of the bad penny a little later on by turning it into cheese and beer in the buttery.

In the event, I didn't join the hunt that afternoon. An hour or so before the hunting party was due to set out, two dusty and exhausted-looking individuals presented themselves at the lodge demanding to see the king and have their action at law settled. Now Rufus was a conscientious man, and when he was told about this he sighed and said, "Well, I suppose I'd better hear them if they've come all this way." (The litigants had walked to Winchester from Stafford, presumably arguing and calling each other names every step of the way). I happened to be standing near him at the time and saw the disappointment in his face; he'd been kept busy for several weeks with a backlog of pleas and appeals, and the strain was beginning to show. Accordingly I suggested that he let me settle the matter. "Are you sure?" he asked. "It looks pretty tedious to me." I made some remark about two human beings tearing each other to pieces being far better sport than a few dogs chasing a deer; Rufus smiled and said I was welcome to the chore.

As it turned out, it wasn't such a dull case after all. As you may remember, for several years Rufus had refused to ratify the appointments of a number of abbots and priors, partly to irritate the Archbishop of York but mostly because he'd taken the trouble to find out about the candidates and felt that they weren't suitable for the job. The defendant in this action was a miller who ground for the small priory of Bromley, near Stafford; as was the custom, he took a share of the finished flour as his payment. In practice, he didn't grind each consignment separately, fifty sacks for the priory, thirty for the manor, two each for the yeomen and so on; he ground everything together and gave each customer the amount of flour he was entitled to, less his share. However, because there was no prior at the priory, there was no-one to authorise payment of the miller's wages; accordingly, the chapter decided that the miller must hand over the full amount of flour from the priory's harvest, and wait until a new prior was installed before getting his share. Unfortunately, by the time they got around to telling the miller about their decision, he had already given out the flour to his other customers on the assumption that he'd be keeping his usual percentage. When the lay brothers from the priory turned up demanding their full allocation (and he had no choice but to do what they told him, since he owed his fealty to the prior), he found that even when he'd handed out his own share he didn't have enough left to satisfy all his customers. The plaintiff in the action was the last customer to collect, and when he arrived at the mill and was told that the miller had no flour to give him, he lost his temper and took the miller to law. The case should have been heard before the prior, as both men's temporal lord, but of course there was no prior . . . In consequence, they had ended up walking halfway across the country to put their case before the king.

·Well, the two men gave their evidence and stood in front of me, waiting to hear what I had to say. Both of them looked at me as if I were King Solomon – as far as I could see they were heartily sick of the matter and would have been happy with any verdict that put an end to it – and I must confess that I hadn't the faintest idea what judgement to give. To buy a little time, I asked whether they had discussed the question with the priory chapter; if the chapter would undertake to pay the plaintiff as soon as a new prior was appointed, surely that ought to satisfy both sides. Of course, I knew perfectly well that that wasn't a fair decision, as Rufus had no intention of giving way over the question of the appointments, and so the poor yeoman would have a long time to wait for his flour. It would be law but not justice – still, if people go to law, law is what they must expect to get; if I'd been in their shoes I'd have made sure the matter was settled at the mill and never allowed to fall into the hands of Justice.

I wasn't surprised, therefore, when the plaintiff greeted this suggestion with a great show of agitation. The situation at the priory, he said, was rather more complicated than that. The prior designate was eighty-one years old and likely to die quite soon; it was generally believed that that was why Rufus refused to ratify his appointment, believing it was fatuous to promote a senile, dying man to a responsible position. But because the bishop had made the question a matter of principle, he had refused to consider an alternative, and so nobody knew who the next or next-but-one prior would be; without knowing that, the chapter refused to enter into any undertakings whatsoever. Matters were complicated further still by the fact that the prior designate fervently believed that he had been chosen by God to be prior of his house, and flew into a terrible rage when any matter was discussed that had any bearing on the question. Since he was in practice running the house and leading the chapter, there was no point in looking to the priory for any co-operation.

My heart went out to them, poor honest men, victims of my lord's determined effort to make the Church conduct its affairs in a responsible manner. Up till then, I had seen the issues only on the grand scale; I had supported my lord against the savage attacks of the exiled Archbishop Anselm, encouraged him to continue holding back the ratification of the three bishoprics and twelve abbacies, and so on. The more the Church raged and thundered against my lord, the more I supported him, as it was my place to do. It's always easier to think about issues than people, particularly when one's loyalties are directly involved.

In the end, I awarded a joint writ to both plaintiff and defendant against the priory, demanding that they pay the miller what they owed him at once so that he could pay out the yeoman. It was, on the face of the document, a fair and equitable decision; and completely unrealistic, of course, since the priory was outside my lord's jurisdiction and the writ couldn't be enforced against the property of the Church. In other words, I sent the two unfortunate men back to Stafford with a useless piece of parchment and nothing decided, because nothing could be decided until there was a prior to decide it. It had been an interesting but depressing afternoon, and on balance I wished I'd gone hunting instead.

It was just after Vespers when the cart arrived at the gate. I had attended the service and was sitting on the step outside the church eating an apple. Two monks and a man-at-arms came up to me and asked me to go with them and look at something. At first I wondered what was going on; then it occurred to me that I was the only senior courtier who hadn't joined the hunting party.

They showed me a small four-wheeled cart, the sort that you see on the roads between the towns; the paint was too new and smart for a farm wagon. Four men were standing beside it; there were men-at-arms behind them, and they looked bewildered and frightened. There was nothing in the cart except a bundle, wrapped in a coarse woollen blanket.

"That looks like a dead body," I said.

The man-at-arms who'd fetched me nodded, and pulled the blanket back. The dead man was my lord, Rufus. His eyes and mouth were still open, and his face was grubby with dirt and leaf-mould. I reached across and touched his forehead. It was cold.

"These men brought him here," said one of the monks. "They say they met the hunting party in the wood, and were told to bring the body here. They told me they've no idea what happened."

I pulled the blanket away. "Then let's see what we can find out for ourselves," I said, in a matter-of-fact voice. None of them recognized the turn of phrase, which was one of Rufus's favourites. I don't know why I said it just then; it seemed to jump into my mind as the right thing to say. Thoughts and words and memories were jumbled up together in my mind at that moment, like tools on the bench of an untidy craftsman; among them the practical matters that would have to be dealt with between *The king is dead* and *Long live the king*. I swept those thoughts back into the clutter of my mind, for there would be plenty of others who would deal with such matters, and perhaps I would be the only one to concern himself with this.

The first thing I noticed was four inches of arrowshaft sticking up on his right side between the third and fourth rib. His shirt was sodden with blood and still wet. There didn't seem to be any other wounds. I looked more closely at the arrowshaft; it had been snapped off, either by hand or by the body falling on it. The point of the arrow stuck out through the skin of his back by no more than the width of a wheat-stalk. I borrowed a penknife from one of the monks and cut away the skin carefully around the arrowhead, which turned out to be an ordinary broadhead, just the sort you'd use for hunting deer. There was dirt in the splintered end of the arrowshaft, suggesting that it was the fall that broke the arrow. That implied that the arrowhead had been forced in deeper than it would otherwise have been, suggesting that my lord had been shot with a light hunting bow, no more than forty pounds' draw weight; the seventy-pound bows that soldiers use would have driven the arrow clean through. A finger's breadth higher or lower, and the arrow would have fouled a rib and been stopped, and my lord would still have been alive, for a while at least; it had been the extra force imparted to the arrowhead when the body fell forward onto the shaft that had killed him, rather than the wound itself, and when I examined the point where the arrow had entered, I found that it had indeed struck the rib and been pushed home thereafter, unlikely if the arrow had had no further assistance after it left the bow. That suggested to me that this might have been an accident rather than a deliberate killing, if only because a wound from a light bow such as this would be as likely to leave a man alive as dead; even if he were to die later, he might well live long enough to name his killer. The fact that the body was cold but the blood was still wet puzzled me, and I looked closely at the bed of the cart. There was a lot of blood there, too.

"Everybody knows," I said, looking up at the four carters, "that a murdered man's wounds flow freely in the presence of the man who killed him. What have you got to say about that? The body's cold, it should have stopped bleeding hours ago."

The four men looked at each other in horror. "We don't know anything," one of them said. "It was just like we told the monk; we were on the road and we met a hunting party. We don't even know whose body it is."

"This is King William," I replied, watching them carefully. The expressions on their faces were a pretty study in horror when they heard that.

"Honestly, we don't know anything," said the man who'd spoken before. "Wait till the hunting party gets here, they'll tell you. We were just passing on the road, we saw a man lying on the ground with a lot of other men standing over him, and we stopped to see if we could help."

I shrugged my shoulders. "What were you doing on the road?" I asked. "Your cart is empty."

"We were taking barley to the mill at Langley," one of the men replied. "We unloaded the grain, then set off for home."

I thought about that for a moment. "Tell me your names and where you live," I said. "We can easily find out if you're telling the truth."

They told me their names, and that they belonged to the manor of Langley, which in turn belongs to the Abbey. I told a man-at-arms to send to the mill and the manor to check what the men had said, and sent a monk to have the body carried to the church. I had the four men taken off to the lodge, where they could be held until the hunting party returned. When there was nothing else left to be done, I went out into the courtyard and sat on the mounting block, although it was quite dark by now. I felt as if I was drunk, too numb and distant to feel anything much. To keep my thoughts from going where I didn't want them to, I went over in my mind what I'd seen and heard so far, and tried to make some sense of it. I told myself the story as if it were a riddle or an adventure, something that isn't real.

The king goes hunting in the forest; he's shot with an ordinary hunting arrow from a lightweight bow, and by wretched and unpredictable chance falls on the arrow, thereby making death more or less immediate. The body is found, and a passing cart is hailed and told to take the body back to the Abbey. When it arrives, it's cold but there's still wet blood on the body and the cart.

There were, of course, several things about the story that didn't want to fit any obvious version of events. If my lord was killed early in the hunt, before the hunters split up and dispersed through the wood, I would have expected the whole party to have come home at once. If he died after the hunt had started, only those who were with the party and able to follow him would have known where he was; an assassin coming to the spot from outside would have had no guarantee of finding him in the heart of the forest, with fifty or so men spread out through the undergrowth, each intent on finding the deer before the deer noticed them. If I was right about the bow, that argued against a deliberate killing, since the weapon was unsuitable and might well have left him alive. But if it was an accident, why hadn't at least some of the party come back yet? There were enough of them gathered together for the carters to talk of a group of men standing over the body; that they entrusted the corpse of the king to a passing cart suggested that they had some particularly urgent business to attend to there in the wood, and the only thing I could think of was the pursuit of a murderer. Finally, the business of the cold body and the wet blood puzzled me greatly. Let me say that I have never believed the story about a murdered man's wounds bleeding when his murderer is nearby; I know it isn't true, because I have seen murdered men not bleeding as their murderers stand over them. I've served two kings for over thirty years. There is no truth in that story.

I was considering a version of events that would reconcile all these difficulties when I heard the sound of horses in the distance. The porter came out with a lantern; I took it from him and sent him away, then leaned in the corner of the gateway arch and waited.

Robert Fitzhaimo wasn't with the party, and neither were Walter Tirell and one or two others. All of them seemed exhausted and thoroughly dejected. I called out to one of them – Bernhart de Peguilhac, whom I'd known for years. He nearly jumped out of his saddle.

"Oh, it's you," he growled, when he saw my face. "What do you want to go hiding in corners and startling people for?"

"The carters brought the body back safely," I replied, walking beside him as he rode into the courtyard. "I thought you'd want to know."

"What carters?" he replied, frowning. His voice suggested that he was too tired to think, and certainly too tired to be bothered with remarks that didn't make sense. "We sent the body on ahead with Walter Tirell and the monk."

It was my turn to be confused. "What monk?" I said.

"The Poitevin," Bernhart said. "The one he gave the hundred shillings to."

"Ah," I replied, "that monk. Can you remember how long ago that was?"

Bernhart slid off his horse and handed the reins to one of the lay brothers who'd come out to look after the hunting party. "No idea," he said, with a shrug. "It's been rather a long day, what with one thing and another. We found the body about an hour before sunset, if that's any help." He turned and looked at me. "What's all this in aid of?" he said. "What's going on?"

"I was about to ask you that," I replied. "Stay there a moment, there's something I've got to do before this lot go off to bed."

I jumped up on the mounting block and cleared my throat loudly until all the hunters had turned to look at me. "I'm sorry to keep you from your beds," I said. "I imagine you're all tired out, so I'll keep this as short as possible. Because of what's happened, there's going to have to be an inquiry, so I'm going to conduct it. The clerk here – hey, you, brother, over here – the clerk here will write down your names and I'll need to speak to all of you tonight, so if you'd care to go over to the chapter house –"

"Just a minute," said an angry voice, which I recognized as Gui de Bornel (we've cordially disliked each other since before the Conquest). "What gives you the right to go around setting up inquiries, particularly," he added with feeling, "at this time of night?"

I smiled. "This does," I replied, and pulled out from my sleeve the Great Seal, which my lord had left with me to seal the writ for the two sorry litigants. "The king entrusted this to me before he left here today, and until I hand it over to his rightful heir, I suppose it means I'm, well, in charge." I was talking absolute nonsense, I knew, but maybe they were all too tired to realize; my official position under my lord Rufus was that of someone who stands about waiting to make himself useful, nothing more or less. In any event, there was some low-key grumbling, but they all trooped dutifully off to the chapter house, with the hapless little clerk scuttling along behind them with his tablets and portable ink-horn, trying to take down names he didn't know how to spell (he was English, poor man, and you try spelling Aimeric de Villehouardin for the first time, in the dark and on the move).

In the event, they were all quite cooperative, if uncharacteristically subdued for a party of Norman noblemen. Their fatigue made my job much easier; they were too tired and fed up to bother lying or embroidering the truth to avert suspicion from themselves or deflect it towards their enemies. As a result, there wasn't too much in the way of conflicting evidence, once I'd weeded out things that were obviously due to perspective and personality.

The story that emerged was that the hunting party had been directed to a part of the forest where the Abbey's foresters reckoned there were a couple of good trophy stags and about ten or twelve hinds. Once they'd reached the spot, they'd split up and set off to comb through the area, which was dense with undergrowth and quite hard to pass through without making a noise. In the event, the whole thing turned out to be a washout; nobody saw anything, and they started trickling back to the place they'd agreed to meet. Eventually, when it was getting dark, everybody was accounted for except my lord, and this left Robert Fitzhaimo in a dreadful state. On the one hand, there was the possibility that Rufus had met with an accident, which meant it was Robert's duty to organize a search. On the other hand, it was rather more likely that the king was simply lost. In due course, he'd find his way back to the meeting-point, almost certainly tired and hungry, and he wouldn't be best pleased to find out that the entire court was crashing about in the pitch dark looking for him, and he wouldn't be able to go home and have his dinner until they'd all given up looking and meandered back to the rendezvous. After a while, though, Robert did give the order for the search, and almost immediately the body was found, though curiously nobody could remember who the finder was. Meanwhile, Robert had the problem of rounding up all the rest of the searchers, which was evidently going to be a much harder job than merely finding the king. That was the point at which he left the body with Walter Tirell and his companions and set off to lead the search for the searchers. When at last he'd tracked down all the members of the party, he went back with them to the meeting point, but of course Tirell wasn't there –

needless to say, since he'd been told several hours before to go straight back to the Abbey with the body.

When I'd finished the last interview and sent the last yawning huntsman off to get some sleep, I went back to the lodge, had the four carters woken up, and went through the whole thing with them once more. Finally, on the offchance that what I wanted might still be there, I kicked Brother Cellarer out of bed and had him go through his cashbox. Then I went back to my own quarters, sent for a clerk with parchment and ink to write out a detailed account of what I'd been told, and fell fast asleep before he arrived. Bless him, whoever he was, he didn't have the heart to wake me, or else he was eager to get back to his own bed; I slept through and, as is often the way, woke up with a much clearer picture in my mind than I'd had when I fell asleep.

On waking, I was told that they'd buried the body already, quickly and quietly and without telling me. I said nothing about that, and when first light came I set off for the forest with one of the huntsmen and inspected the place where the body was supposed to have been found; then I attended Matins; then, when the service was over, I had the abbot announce that I would declare the results of my inquiry after Chapter, and until then nobody was to leave the abbey without my permission. There was plenty of grumbling at that, needless to say, but I wasn't in a good mood by then.

All through the service and the Chapter that followed, I thought long and hard about what I ought to do. I wasn't happy with the decision I reached, but I came to the conclusion that my lord was dead and there wasn't much point making things any worse than they were. If I believe in anything, it's loyalty; but I draw the line at being loyal to the dead. Wherever they go, Heaven or Hell, they have more important matters on their minds than human law, or even human justice.

When the time came I stood up, waited for silence and looked round at the faces of the men around me. Then I coughed once and began.

"I have examined the facts," I said, "and my conclusion is that our lord the king died by accident, at the hand of Sir Walter Tirell, who mistook him for a deer and shot him. It would seem that Sir Walter, appalled by what he did, has gone off into the forest, and I propose that he be left to return to the court in his own time, if he chooses to return at all. Sir Robert Fitzhaimo also has not returned; I believe he may still be looking for Sir Walter, or he may simply be lost." As it turned out, I was right about that; he'd fallen over a tree-root, twisted his ankle, fallen in a briar-patch and got himself hopelessly stuck. Two lay brothers found him that afternoon and brought him home, and it was a full day before he was well enough to get out of bed.

And there matters rested; because there were many far more interesting and important things to think about than a dead king who nobody had ever liked. Three days later, my lord's younger brother Henry, that brutal, savage man who once threw a wealthy and respected merchant of Rouen off the town walls with his own hands because of some minor altercation – Henry, loved by his people and the model of Christian piety, was crowned in London, having ridden like a madman to Winchester as soon as he heard the news of my lord's death and scooped up the royal treasury. Of course he recalled the saintly Archbishop Anselm from his exile in France, and the Church rejoiced to be rid of their enemy Rufus, a man who (so they said) had been sent by God as a foretaste of the Antichrist. Well, so much for all that. I took my oath to King Henry and I have served him well for eight years now. I believe in loyalty, and not much else.

A week or so after his coronation, I asked King Henry for half an hour of his time, which he was pleased to grant me. When we'd shared a cup of very fine wine and spoken for a while of important matters of state, I asked him if he would like to hear the results of my inquiry into the death of his brother.

"I thought Walter Tirell killed him," Henry replied. He seemed genuinely surprised. "You said it was an accident. Look, I know Tirell's your friend and I suppose you're worried for him. But it's all right. I've already said I don't hold him responsible."

"I know," I replied. "But perhaps you'd like to hear what actually happened. Or what I think actually happened, at any rate."

"Go on," King Henry said.

So I told him about the lawsuit I'd heard that afternoon, and mentioned in passing that the road from Southampton to Newbury, which is the way you'd take if you were going from the Abbey to the coast, or to Oxford or the Midlands, ran through the forest not far from where Rufus's body was found. I reminded him of the enmity between my lord and the Church, of how Rufus's policy of not ratifying the appointments of bishops and abbots was bringing the business of administering the Church and its property to a standstill, and, thus endangering the moral and financial health of the realm. I reminded him of Saint Anselm's timely dream, mentioned the visit of the mysterious monk from Poitou, the one who got the hundred shillings. Finally I reminded him of Rufus's stated intention to interfere in the affairs of the County of Poitou.

"I didn't know that," Henry interrupted. "Good God. It makes sense, though. Poitou's ripe for the taking, after all."

"Perhaps you would care to bear it in mind," I replied. "Now then, consider these things. The body was found shortly before dark, and it was left with Walter Tirell and some others, including, I think, the Poitevin monk. But Tirell didn't take it back to the Abbey. Quite some time later, when the body was good and cold – it may have been cold when it was found, I don't know, but it was cold when I examined it – four carters, servants of one of the Abbey's tenants, brought it to me, and when I saw it, the wounds were wet with fresh blood."

"You don't say," Henry remarked, leaning forward with his chin cupped in his hand. "I didn't know that, either."

Then I told him about what I'd deduced about the bow that killed him, and pointed out the difficulty an assassin would have had in tracking him through the forest. "Which I take to mean," I went on, "that if he was murdered, either a companion led him to where the assassin was waiting, or else the murderer was someone close to him and trusted by him, who went with him to the place where he died. Does that sound reasonable?"

Henry nodded. "I suppose so," he said. "Though you mentioned a road that passed close by the place. Could it possibly have been someone who hated him – there were enough of them, God knows – who passed by, recognized him, and made the most of his opportunity?"

I shrugged. "Let's go back to the matter of the cold body and the fresh blood," I said. "We know that when a cold body bleeds, it's because the murderer is close by."

"Which means the carters did it," Henry said. "Or you did."

I smiled. "I don't believe that tradition," I replied. "But I know I'm the exception. Consider; when Tirell and his companions met the carters, the body must have been cold. When it reached the Abbey, there was fresh blood on the King's wounds and in the cart."

Henry frowned. "You think Tirell and his friends put fresh blood – deer's blood, or whatever they'd been hunting – on the wounds to make it look as if the wounds were bleeding –" He paused, closed his eyes, opened them again. "To make it look as if the wounds were bleeding, which would make it seem as if the carters were the murderers." He blinked again. "And the carters wouldn't have bothered to see if the body was cold or not, so they wouldn't have suspected the trick. But what on God's name would be the point of that?"

"I have no idea," I replied. "Unless, as you say, it was to make people think that the carters killed him. They were the abbot's men, and the king was actively oppressing the entire monastic movement; indeed, the Church as a whole."

Henry thought for a moment. "I can see that the abbot, or indeed the bishop or the whole damned synod of bishops, not to mention the sainted Anselm and not forgetting God Almighty, might want him dead. There were all those portents," he remembered. "Maybe the lords spiritual were helping God to make good on his promises."

"Anselm's dream," I said. "But the carters didn't kill him, or at least I can see no evidence whatever to suggest that they did. If I'm right, this foolery with the blood was all a forgery of Tirell's."

"Designed to make us think the Church murdered him," Henry said. "This gets more complicated the more I think about it. All right then, if Tirell wanted to put the blame on the abbot and the Church in general, it must be because he murdered my brother himself."

"Well now," I said. "Walter Tirell was a soldier of fortune, always protesting his poverty. Remember the business with Poitou. A Poitevin monk comes to court and prophesies the king's death, and he dies. And, for what it's worth, that same day Walter gave me this." I reached in my purse and produced Walter's bad penny, which I'd taken back from Brother Cellarer. "Can you read what it says on the coin?"

"No," Henry admitted.

"It says 'Carlus Rex' and on the back, 'Metullo', it's a coin minted by the Count of Poitou, from bad silver, so you rarely see them outside the County. As I told you, I had it from Tirell that morning."

"So Tirell killed him on the Count's orders," Henry said, "after getting his wages from the monk. I suppose that must be it."

I shrugged. "It's possible," I said. "That did occur to me when I was about to make my speech in the chapter house; and Walter Tirell is my friend, as you know, and he's still missing, which is suggestive in itself. But I don't think he killed the king. I believe it's possible that he intended to; that once the king was dead and his body had been found, he may have been afraid that others would reach the same conclusion we've just reached, and that he devised the pantomime with the blood to point the blame at the king's other great enemy; possibly that after he'd done that he still reckoned he'd be suspected and ran away, just to be on the safe side. But there's no evidence."

"True," Henry said. "All right, what do you think happened?"

"I don't know," I said. "But it's possible that my two wretched litigants, the miller and his creditor, walking home to Stafford after their wasted journey, may have come to the conclusion that since their dispute couldn't be settled until a prior was appointed, and since a prior couldn't be appointed while William Rufus was king of England, then only the king's death would solve their insufferable problem; at which point, the king himself steps out from the bushes holding a bow and arrow, and asks them if they've seen the deer."

"*They* killed him?" Henry muttered, shaking his head. "I really don't see . . ."

"As I said," I went on, "I don't know. But what killed the king? An arrow, an arrow with a broken-off shaft, with mud in the splinters. As I said just now, if you were planning to kill a king, you wouldn't choose to use a forty-pound bow, and you'd probably wouldn't aim the arrow at his ribcage, where it could easily be deflected. But if two men were walking along a road unarmed, and met their enemy carrying a bow and an arrow, it's possible that they might try to take the weapons from him. There may have been a rough-and-tumble struggle; my lord might have fallen on the arrow by accident in the course of that struggle, or one of his attackers may have grabbed hold of it and stabbed him with it, like a dagger. But I stake my reputation as a soldier that the arrow wasn't driven home by any bow."

Henry looked at me for a long time. "And then," he said, "they took his body and dumped it in the forest, and carried on back home to Stafford."

"And my lord's bow and arrows weren't by his body when it was found." I nodded. "You might care to look into the matter of the priory of Bromley," I said. "It strikes me as a great injustice."

"Shocking," Henry said. "There are a great many things wrong with this country that I intend to put right." He looked away, then back at me. "But it's also possible," he went on, "that it was just an accident, and that the arrow was driven in when William fell on it, and, come to that, that his death was a judgement on him for his wicked oppression of Holy Church."

"Very possible," I said.

Henry smiled. "In any case," he said, "he's dead now, and I haven't heard anyone complaining. I'm quite happy to stand by the decision you announced at Chapter. Are you?"

"I serve the king," I said.

THE *WHITE SHIP* MURDERS

Susanna Gregory

We have already met Henry I, the brother of William Rufus, who succeeded to the kingship in 1100 and usurped the Duchy of Normandy in 1106, capturing and imprisoning his brother Robert. Henry married Edith, daughter of Malcolm Canmore, king of the Scots, and great-granddaughter of Edmund Ironside, one of the last Saxon kings. She changed her name to Matilda upon their marriage but kept her Saxon way of life. Their son, William, was known as the "atheling", the old Saxon title for the heir to the throne. Disaster struck in 1120 when William was drowned when his vessel, known as the White Ship, *foundered off Barfleur in Normandy. Susanna Gregory investigates what happened.*

November 1120, Winchester

Robert, Earl of Gloucester, sat at the king's side and looked at the silent courtiers who formed a circle around the bed, some of them fighting their own grief at the terrible news that had caused King Henry of England to faint from shock. Eventually, he felt Henry stir, and took one of the strong, capable hands in his, chafing it in awkward sympathy.

"Are you sure, Rob?" the king whispered, fixing tear-filled eyes on Robert. "Everyone on the *White Ship* was drowned? My only legitimate son and heir to the English throne? The children of half the nobles in the country? All dead?"

Robert looked away and nodded. "I'm sorry, my lord. A butcher was the sole survivor."

"But there were more than 200 people on board," said the king hoarsely. "How could this have happened?"

Stephen of Blois, the king's nephew, stepped forward, his usually cheerful face sombre. "The *White Ship* was due to sail for England shortly after your own boat left, but it was delayed by bad weather. This butcher said that by the time the wind was favourable again, everyone on board was drunk, even the captain, and the ship hit a rock outside the harbour. It was dark and cold, and no one stood a chance."

The king closed his eyes tightly. Young Prince William had represented all his hopes for the kingdom and for a lasting peace between England and France. Now that William was dead, there was no male heir to the throne, and all Henry's efforts to pass a stable and prosperous realm to his son had been in vain. It was ironic that Henry, who had more than twenty illegitimate children – Robert among them – had only produced one son and one daughter from his marriage to the queen.

"The *White Ship* was supposed to ferry me to England, not William," said Henry in a low voice. "At the last minute, he begged me to allow him to take her instead, because she was such a splendid vessel. When I agreed, all the other youngsters decided to go with him. I wish to God that I'd refused!"

"The butcher said William died bravely," said Robert, trying to be gentle. "The captain put him in a boat and instructed that he was to be rowed ashore, but William insisted on returning to the sinking ship to try to rescue the others."

Henry's eyes brimmed with tears, but then he took a deep breath and sat up in his bed. "I wish to speak to Robert alone," he said, waving away the assembled courtiers. He touched Stephen's arm affectionately. "You go, too. Don't look so anxious – I won't faint again."

When they had shuffled out of the chamber, the king turned to Robert. "This tale has the stench of treachery about it, Rob. This was no accident!"

"You think someone deliberately sank the ship?" asked Robert, aghast.

The king met his eyes. "That's what you must find out. I can't accept that 200 people were so drunk they couldn't even swim to shore when the ship went down. You must speak to this butcher you say survived, and to Fitzstephen, the merchant who presented me with the *White Ship* – the finest vessel ever built, so he claimed!" The king almost spat the last words.

"I know Fitzstephen. Do you really think he gave you a ship he knew would sink?"

The king gripped Robert's hand fiercely. "There are several people who might benefit from William's death. For example, there's my daughter Matilda, who thinks she would make a better king than any man in my domains."

"But Matilda's in Germany. How could she be sinking ships in France?"

Henry sighed. "She's not in Germany, Rob. She was supposed to return there last month, but who can blame an eighteen-year-old girl for not being keen to surrender to the embraces of an ugly husband twice her age? She's still in France."

"I can't believe she'd harm her own brother," said Robert, although a derisive snort suggested Henry did not concur.

"Then there's young Stephen," the king continued. "He owns nothing of his own, and looks to me to further his ambitions."

"Not Stephen," said Robert immediately. "He's devoted to you, and is too gentle – and lacks the intelligence – to have a hand in anything like this. Anyway, he's too far down the line of succession to make killing William worthwhile – he has older brothers for a start."

The king rubbed his temples tiredly. "I suppose so. The shock of this tragedy has made me suspicious of everyone, even people I thought I trusted. Such as you, Rob."

Robert stared at him in horror. "Me?"

"You're my oldest son, and my barons respect you. Why shouldn't you aspire to the throne? Bastards have worn crowns before – look at the Conqueror – and with Prince William out of the way, it could be yours."

"You think I'm the kind of man to murder my half-brother for personal gain?" asked Robert, shocked. He stood abruptly, wanting to leave before hurt and anger led him to say something he might later regret. Henry caught him by his sleeve.

"Well, someone killed William for his inheritance," he hissed. "Who, other than you, Matilda, or Stephen would stand to gain from his death?"

"Your other nephew, Clito," said Robert shortly. "You *have* been at war with him these last few years, after all, and he hates you for ruling what he considers to be his kingdom. He might have paid someone to sink the ship."

Clito was the son of the older brother Henry had incarcerated in Cardiff Castle. Many people believed Clito had a strong case, and even Robert, wholly loyal to Henry, felt uncomfortable when he pondered Clito's claim.

Henry made a face of disgust. "That pathetic boy couldn't hatch a plot like this."

"He's still bitter because you defeated him at the battle of Brémule earlier this year," Robert pointed out. "He'd stop at nothing to strike at you."

Henry sighed. "Perhaps you're right. But you must solve this vile crime, and bring the murderer of my beloved son to justice."

"But what do you want me to do?" asked Robert uncertainly. "You trained me as a knight, not an inquisitor."

"I want you to go to France and find out what really happened on the *White Ship*."

Robert saw he had no choice. "Then I'll leave tonight."

"Good," said Henry softly. "But take care: murderers are often desperate men."

January 1121, Barfleur, France

As soon as the ship was secured to the slimy green pier, Robert disembarked and strode towards the town centre, his cloak billowing about him in the wind. It was dusk, and warm yellow lights seeped from sturdy stone-built houses. Robert wished he were in one: the journey across the Channel had been the roughest he had ever known, and several times he thought he would die like William, with his lungs full of frothing water as he sank below the waves.

Robert had been surprised to discover that Stephen was also on board. Between bouts of seasickness, the king's young nephew had made clumsy attempts to discover Robert's whereabouts when the

White Ship had sunk. It did not take a genius to discern that Robert was not the only one who had been charged with the task of catching William's murderer: the cautious Henry had dispatched Stephen in case Robert proved to be less than innocent, and Robert lest Stephen should be implicated.

Robert was furious that Henry should still consider him a suspect, and was resentful of Stephen's crude attempts to question him. But Stephen's affable nature and easy charm made it impossible to be angry with him for long, and by the time the ship reached Barfleur they had made their peace and had agreed to work together to uncover William's killer.

While Stephen went to discover what he could from the constable of Barfleur, Robert started to track down the butcher who had survived the wreck of the *White Ship*. It was not as difficult as he had anticipated: the butcher was regarded as something of a celebrity in Barfleur, and everyone knew where he lived. It was not long before Robert was sitting in a smelly quayside tavern, ordering a jug of wine to pay for the privilege of hearing the butcher's story.

The butcher, a florid, sweaty man called Berthold of Rouen, made a show of tasting the claret to assess its quality before accepting it, apparently aiming to impress the prostitute with black teeth and knowing eyes who lounged next to him. Sensing Robert's reason for wanting to know Berthold's story was more than ghoulish curiosity, the prostitute stretched a hand towards him.

"I saw it all," she declared, revealing her rotten teeth in a calculating smile. "I was with a customer on the quay, and I saw the ship go down. Pay me to tell you what happened, too."

"Not a man or a woman was sober when that doomed ship left port," began Berthold quickly, unwilling to lose Robert's custom to the woman. "Even the captain was drunk. He hit that rock." Berthold pointed through the window at a black mass just outside the entrance to the harbour. "The ship went down like a stone. The captain had put Prince William in a boat to be rowed ashore, but that brave boy returned to the ship when he heard the piteous cries of his drowning half-sister. The little boat was swamped when too many people tried to climb in it."

"If the captain was so drunk that he hit a rock, how did he suddenly become sufficiently clear-thinking to put William in the boat?" asked Robert.

Berthold was immediately wary, while the prostitute cackled with laughter that her friend had apparently been caught out in an inconsistency. "The cold seawater that flooded the ship must have sobered him," he said shortly.

"Why would a big boat like the *White Ship* sink so fast?" asked Robert, puzzled by the tale, but speaking more to himself than to Berthold.

"It did, though," said the prostitute. "Give me a few sous and I'll tell you all about it."

The butcher did not appreciate his story being questioned by the soberly-dressed knight who sat across the table, or his companion's attempts to upstage him. He shot her an unpleasant look, and then turned an indignant glower on Robert. "It went down so quick that not even the king's treasure could be saved. And that's God's honest truth!"

"His treasure?" asked Robert, confused. "You mean his son?"

"I mean his jewels," said Berthold impatiently. "The gold coins and precious stones he always takes to France, because he daren't leave them with the thieving English."

"Why was everyone on the ship drunk?" asked Robert, uninterested in treasure when there might be treason afoot. "My brother Richard was on board, and he never drank excessively."

"Because the captain provided free wine," said Berthold with a shrug. "By the time we left, everyone – passengers and crew – had been drinking for several hours."

"And how did you escape?"

"I float well," said Berthold, patting his ample stomach and winking at his companion. "While the skinny sank like rocks, the fat bobbed like corks on the surface and were washed ashore."

"It must have sounded terrible," said Robert, imagining the rocks tearing through the ship's hull and the screams of the drowning as the waves surged around them.

"Not really," said the prostitute, ever-hopeful hand extended yet again. More to silence her than to buy information, Robert tossed her a coin. Black teeth bit the metal in delight, and she leaned forward confidentially, making Robert recoil from the stench of old garlic. "In fact, there was scarcely a sound. I might have missed it altogether, had I not been on the quay. There were a few wails, but that was when the ship was almost gone."

Robert rubbed his chin thoughtfully as he watched her drink from Berthold's jug. A ship hitting the rock Berthold had indicated would surely have been heard from the shore, and it would have taken longer than a few moments to sink. Robert felt sick as he realized the ship had probably not hit the rock at all, but that it had been deliberately scuppered. King Henry had been right to be suspicious. And, furthermore, it was very convenient that everyone on board had been blind drunk – something his abstemious brother Richard would never have allowed to happen to himself – suggesting further still that foul play was afoot.

Icy fingers of unease clutched at Robert's stomach as he clarified his suspicions in his mind: not only had the *White Ship* been deliberately sunk, but her passengers had been given more than simple wine to speed them to their watery deaths.

"Here we are," said Stephen, as Berthold pointed to a shabby building with peeling plaster and rotting timbers. "The Dolphin Inn, where we will find Thomas Fitzstephen, the unfortunate owner of the *White Ship*."

Robert entered the tavern cautiously. It was as unsavoury inside as it was from the outside, a dark, crowded room with dirty rushes on the floor, and stained tables with sullen customers huddled around them. Berthold pointed out Fitzstephen, who sat near a smoking fire, deep in conversation with two people swathed in thick cloaks against the winter chill. When he saw Robert, Fitzstephen stood.

"A man of your means should be able to afford better lodgings than this," said Robert, looking around him in distaste.

The merchant grimaced. "I spent my last sou on that damned ship. When it sank, it took my fortune with it."

Stephen gave him a sympathetic smile. "It was tragic for you that the ship floundered. The king would have rewarded you handsomely for making him such a fine gift."

Fitzstephen nodded gloomily. "But now I'm ruined, and will never be able to set foot in England again."

"Take this," said Stephen, thrusting his full purse at Fitzstephen in a spontaneous gesture of compassion that was typical of him. "And at least remove yourself from this hovel."

"Such generosity from a relative of our miserly monarch?" came a low, husky voice from behind them. Robert and Stephen spun round in surprise, recognising the purring tones of the king's only legitimate daughter instantly.

"Cousin Matilda!" cried Stephen in delight, throwing his arms around the haughty figure in an affectionate hug that made even her rigid features crack into a smile. "But what are you doing here? I thought you were with your husband in Germany."

"The old goat won't miss me for a few more days," said Matilda carelessly. "And I was keen to discover what really happened to my brother on the *White Ship*."

Robert looked from her to her cloaked companion. "And why are you here, Clito?" he asked softly, as the king's most bitter enemy pushed back his hood to reveal his face. "To plot against the King of England with his only surviving child?"

Robert sat apart from the little group that clustered around the fire, and reflected that all his suspects were now together. At his suggestion, they had left the seedy tavern and were lodged in a nearby abbey. Logs blazed cheerfully in the hearth, and the remains of a fine meal lay on the table.

Stephen and Matilda sat next to each other, his fair head contrasting sharply with her dark one, while Clito slouched opposite, straggly brown hair bundled under a dirty cap. All three were grandchildren of the Conqueror, and had a claim to the throne when Henry died. All, therefore, had reason for wanting Henry's only son dead. There was also Fitzstephen, who had owned the ship and who would have known exactly how to make her sinking look like an accident, and there was Berthold, the sole survivor of the wreck, who claimed his fat body saved him. Had Berthold acted on the orders of one of the four, chopping a hole in the bottom of the ship while the other passengers drank themselves insensible?

Robert watched them carefully, concentrating on their conversation about the tragedy to see if he could detect any note of triumph or guilt that would indicate a role in the plot. But he could identify nothing tangible. Each of the four claimed innocence, while accusing the others, with varying degrees of subtlety, of having the motive and opportunity to kill William. All had good alibis for the actual sinking of the ship, but, as Clito pointed out, that was irrelevant: any of them could have hired a saboteur and then withdrawn to a safe distance until the deed was done.

It was not long before the discussion grew acrimonious, and Robert rubbed his eyes wearily as loud, angry voices echoed around the chamber. The room was hot, and he wanted some fresh air.

"I wager King Henry sent you – his lapdog – to spy on us to see if the *White Ship* was deliberately sunk," sneered Clito as Robert headed for the door. "So, do your duty, man. Ask Matilda about it. She knows more than she's telling."

Matilda gave a harsh bark of laughter. "You'd do better talking to Stephen, Rob. He's a man, and men, not women, inherit English thrones. Killing William would do *me* no good."

Even the easy-tempered Stephen's patience was wearing thin. "I've brothers who would inherit the crown before me. But look at Clito: he's the son of Henry's older brother and has a greater claim and therefore a stronger motive."

"Are you going to fetch the castle guard to arrest us all?" asked Matilda, as Robert, disgusted by the whole affair, opened the door to leave. "Do you think I seduced Fitzstephen, so that he would order his captain to steer the ship onto the rocks? It's no secret that I hate Germany, and would relish the opportunity to return to England. I suppose I'm your main suspect?"

"He thinks *I* killed William because I hated him almost as much as I hate his usurping father," said Clito, eyeing Robert defiantly.

"But William behaved honourably towards you, Clito," objected Stephen. "After the battle of Brémule last year, he returned your horse after he had captured it."

"You think that was done for honour, do you?" demanded Clito bitterly. "That, my naïve little Stephen, was to humiliate me – it served to make him look chivalrous to my detriment."

"You're wrong!" protested Stephen hotly. "William would never have done anything like that!"

Clito gave Stephen a pitying look. "I only wish Henry had been on the *White Ship*, too."

"Keep your traitorous thoughts to yourself," snapped Robert, finally goaded to anger.

"Ever loyal, Rob," teased Matilda, amused. "And such loyalty will not go unrewarded – you will 'prove' to Henry that William was murdered by one of us, and Henry will make you his heir to express his gratitude."

"Yes," said Clito, eyes glittering. "Being a bastard did not prevent the Conqueror from ruling England, so why should it stop you?"

Fitzstephen regarded Robert in horror. "Surely *you* didn't kill William. How could you betray the king so vilely?"

"Of course I didn't kill William!" shouted Robert, uncomfortably aware that Clito and Stephen were gazing at him as though he had. "I've no wish to spend the rest of my life fighting for a crown that could never be mine. But someone killed William, and I assure you that I'll not rest until I discover who."

As he stalked out of the chamber and down the stairs, he heard the raised voices of his suspects. Stephen's was defensive and confused, unwilling to believe ill of his cousins, yet equally determined that no one should think the worst of him; Clito's embittered whine was incredulous, still grappling with the possibility that Robert might have had a hand in the end of the *White Ship*; Fitzstephen's was wreathed in self-pity, claiming he was the one to have lost most when the ship had gone down; while dominating them all was Matilda's arrogant, mocking laugh.

It was cold on the quay, but Robert scarcely felt the biting wind as confused thoughts tumbled around in his mind. He sat for a long time, gazing out across the black waters, not wanting to fail Henry, but not knowing how to proceed. After a while, he sensed he was not alone. Sword in hand, he spun round, peering into the shadows cast by piles of crates and discarded rope.

"Easy, sir. It's only me."

It was Berthold's prostitute, reluctantly abandoned when Robert had demanded that the butcher take him to Fitzstephen. He sheathed his sword as she swayed towards him. Realising that the loss of Berthold had condemned her to a night without pay, he gave her a coin and told her to find herself a bed somewhere.

"I'd like to introduce a friend," she said. "Someone who wants to meet you."

"I'm very tired," said Robert, not feeling inclined to romp around in some dismal hovel with the likes of the black-toothed whore and her cronies.

"This is Anton," she said, gesturing to a slight figure who stood behind her. "That fat butcher wasn't the only one who survived the *White Ship*. Anton was its helmsman."

"Then why isn't Anton profiting from his miraculous delivery from a watery grave like Berthold?" asked Robert, suspecting that the pair of them had dreamed up a story in the hope of earning easy money.

"Because I daren't," said Anton in a whisper. "Everyone believes the crew was so drunk they drove the ship onto the rock. I was the helmsman – they'd hang me!"

"And did you steer the ship onto the rock?" asked Robert, still sceptical. He sat again, and was startled when Anton suddenly snatched up one of his hands, holding it like a supplicant kneeling at the feet of a venerable bishop.

"No! It was no rock that caused her to founder. Please! I don't want to spend the rest of my life waiting for an arrow in the chest – you must find these villains and bring them to justice."

"I'm trying," said Robert, freeing his hand firmly, "but people keep telling me all manner of lies."

"You must believe me!" begged Anton. "I'm not asking you for anything – except that you catch these men. But think about it – if the *White Ship* had hit a rock, the crash would have been heard by half the town. No one heard a thing."

"I see," said Robert non-committally. The prostitute had said that the ship had made no sound as it sank, but that could have been something she and Anton had fabricated together to secure his interest.

"I complained to the captain that she felt sluggish when we left the harbour, but Prince William didn't want to turn back to see what was wrong. I think someone had hacked a hole in her hull to flood the holds, and then opened the hatches when we were underway to let water into the lower decks. She went down like a stone – far too fast for the rock alone to have been responsible."

"She did go down fast," affirmed the whore. "I saw her myself."

"And you and the butcher were the only survivors," finished Robert, not believing a word of it.

"No," said Anton unsteadily. "Five crew made it ashore. Three were found drowned a day later, although they were alive when they reached the beach, while the other is in an alley with an arrow through his neck even as we speak. I'm the last one."

"Other than the butcher."

"I never saw Berthold on the ship," said Anton miserably. "And anyway, do you think that great fat lump could swim to safety when fit and agile sailors could not?"

"He says everyone was drunk," said Robert, standing and moving away as he grew bored with the man's litany of untruths.

"No one was drunk!" shouted Anton in exasperation, running after him. He relented at Robert's raised eyebrows. "Well, maybe we were a little tipsy, because the wine that was provided was unusually strong. But you've been on ships; you must know that it would be impossible to manage a ship on a lively sea if we were drunk. The passengers were a different matter: they were senseless. But not the crew. The captain sacrificed his own life to try to save the prince, but the prince wouldn't row to safety. He insisted on returning to the ship."

"Rallying to the piteous cries of his half-sister," said Robert dryly. "Yes, Berthold told me."

"Berthold is a liar!" cried Anton desperately, as Robert began to walk more quickly. "And there were no piteous cries! It happened too fast, and most of them went to the bottom without ever waking from their drunken stupors. The prince didn't go back for his half-sister – she was already drowned – but for someone else."

"Who?" asked Robert, stopping to look at the sailor, intrigued despite himself.

"I don't know," said Anton. Robert made an impatient sound and turned away. Anton followed, grabbing at the hem of his cloak. "Berthold made up his story to turn William into a hero. The crew were *not* all drunk, and I did *not* steer the ship to its death. The captain was the hero, not that selfish, arrogant prince, and certainly not those courtiers and their debauched ways!"

Robert did not reply and Anton relinquished his hold on the cloak as the knight strode away. Moments later, thuds and a peculiar gurgle made Robert glance around: Anton and the prostitute were lying on the ground. Puzzled, he walked back to them.

Both had arrows in their chests. The prostitute had died instantly, but Anton was still alive.

"See?" he managed to whisper before his eyes closed. "I told you they'd hunt me down."

As Robert crouched, the sharp hiss of an arrow winging through the air told him that whoever had silenced Anton was now trying to silence him. Heart pounding, he darted into the shadows and began to make his way to where he thought the bowman was standing, painfully aware that his chainmail would not save him from the determined efforts of a good archer.

But by the time he reached the spot, the bowman had gone. Running footsteps made him turn, just in time to see someone disappear around a corner. Abandoning the safety of the shadows, he set off in pursuit, yelling at the top of his voice for the archer to stop in the name of the king. The archer stumbled, and Robert began to catch up, blood roaring in his ears and his breath coming in ragged gasps.

Suddenly, the archer swung round. There was an arrow already nocked in his bow and he brought it up to point directly at Robert's chest. Desperately, Robert tried to duck out of the way, but his leather-soled shoes skidded on the damp cobbles, and he fell heavily. With horror, he saw the archer could not possibly miss him, but just as he fancied he could already feel the steel tip of the quarrel lancing through him, the archer faltered as someone hurtled out of a nearby alley. A weapon flashed briefly, and the archer dropped to the ground.

"That was close," said Stephen shakily, looking with distaste at the stained sword in his hand. "He almost had you, Rob."

Another figure emerged from the shadows. Clito, seeing the archer was now harmless, slunk towards them.

"He still lives!" he yelled suddenly, and, before Robert or Stephen could stop him, he had seized the archer by the hair and had slit his throat with a dagger.

"We needed him alive!" shouted Robert, furious that a possible avenue of investigation had been so mindlessly blocked.

"I suppose he might still have been dangerous," said Stephen, loyally trying to defend Clito's action, although his voice lacked conviction. "You probably saved our lives."

Or did Clito have his own reasons for killing the wounded archer? wondered Robert as he looked from Stephen's open, honest face to Clito's closed, secretive features.

"You were lucky Stephen and Clito thought to go looking for you," said Matilda, as she watched Robert poke dubiously at the lumpy oatmeal the monks provided the following morning. "Another moment, and you wouldn't be here to complain about the quality of breakfast."

"I know," said Robert. He looked to where Stephen sat in the window, strumming on a rebec and humming to himself. "How did you know where I would be?"

"You always head for the sea when you want to think," said Stephen, smiling. "And then I heard running footsteps and I sensed you were in danger. Just when I thought we'd never find you, I saw that archer about to shoot."

"It was rash of you to fight an archer with a sword, Stephen," observed Clito, unimpressed by his kinsman's impulsive act of courage. "He might have released his arrow at you."

"That's why my cousin is more chivalrous than you will ever be," said Matilda, regarding Clito with cool disdain. "He's bold and brave and thought only of saving Rob. You, meanwhile, skulked in the shadows until it was safe, and then dispatched a dying man with a dagger."

"Then Stephen is a fool," said Clito scathingly. He gave Robert a smug smile. "You can take him off your list of suspects, Rob. He is far too stupid to make England a good king."

Robert tensed, anticipating a fight, but Stephen merely smiled away the insult. "I have no wish to quarrel with you, Clito – or anyone for that matter. Quarrelling achieves nothing, while good manners and patience always win the day."

Clito was right, thought Robert disapprovingly: Stephen would make a dreadful king with peculiar notions like those.

While the others attended church, Robert went to look at the body of the archer in the abbey stables. He wanted to see it in daylight, although a close inspection told him nothing about the man other than that he was probably a hired mercenary. But hired by whom? Anton had died telling his story, which proved he had been speaking the truth and Robert's suspicions had been right: someone had deliberately sunk the ship, while the passengers had been fed unusually strong wine to ensure that they would drown.

Robert was about to leave when he saw the archer's belt was one that had pockets sewn into it, so coins could be hidden. There was nothing unusual about it, but he unbuckled it anyway and began to make a pile of the coins. He was surprised at the amount of gold the archer possessed, and he could only conclude that whoever wanted no survivors from the *White Ship* was prepared to pay handsomely for it.

He took the coins to the door to inspect them in better light and then gaped in astonishment. They were not any old coins, but were bright new ones from the king's own mint in Winchester. They were, without a shadow of doubt, part of the king's treasure that everyone had assumed had gone down with the *White Ship*.

Robert gazed at the gold in his hands and cursed himself for a fool. All along, he had assumed that the wreck of the *White Ship* had been to assassinate the future king of England. But the ship's saboteur and not been interested in the august personages on board at all: he had wanted nothing more than the king's treasure!

Everything was suddenly crystal clear to Robert. What better place to rob a ship than just off the coast on a dark night? It was safer than attacking far out to sea, and it would allow the thieves to row out to the floundering ship, grab the treasure chests, and make off with them while the crew struggled to keep the ship from sinking. Powerful wine had been provided in copious quantities to ensure there were no witnesses – and any survivors had been eliminated by well-paid mercenaries like the dead archer.

Robert hurled the gold away from him into the dusty depths of the stable, disgusted that its bright colour could induce men to sacrifice a shipload of promising young people and malign the dead crew. As he watched the coins fall, he saw fingers emerge from under a pile of straw to claim one. Startled, he watched as the hand snaked towards another before he gathered his wits and strode towards it to seize its owner by the scruff of his neck.

"Berthold," he said flatly, giving the fat butcher a shake. "What are you doing here?"

"It wasn't my idea," squeaked Berthold in alarm. "I was just carrying out orders."

"What orders?" demanded Robert, shaking him harder. When he had first recognized the greedy butcher, he had simply assumed the man had been doing some opportunistic snooping, perhaps to garner more information to sell for a drink in a tavern. But Berthold, it seemed, had more to confess than spying, and Robert's rough treatment was prompting him into revealing it.

"It was Fitzstephen!" Berthold cried. "My business was doing badly and I needed the money. Fitzstephen paid me to row out to the *White Ship* as she foundered, to pick up his accomplice and the king's treasure chests."

"Fitzstephen organized the sinking of the *White Ship*?" asked Robert, releasing the man abruptly. "For treasure?"

Berthold nodded miserably. Robert stormed out of the stables, yelling to his men to take the quaking butcher into custody, and headed for the church. Matilda and Clito were just leaving, their voices low hisses as they engaged in one of their interminable arguments. He let them pass and then entered, his metal spurs clanking on the tiles as he made his way to the chancel where the merchant and Stephen still knelt at the altar. When Fitzstephen saw Robert's grim expression, the blood drained from his face and he had to grasp a pillar for support.

"I know what you did, Fitzstephen," said Robert softly, his voice dripping contempt. "And I know you did it for treasure!"

"Did what for treasure?" asked Stephen, looking from one to the other in confusion. He went to help Fitzstephen stand. "What's the matter?"

"Leave him!" snapped Robert, his voice ringing in the empty church. "He has committed the most dreadful of crimes – for money!"

"What's he done?" asked Stephen, still bewildered. He took Robert's arm. "Don't yell in a church, Rob. Come outside. I'm sure we can talk about whatever it is that's distressing you and come to a perfectly acceptable arrangement without all this shouting."

"Always the peacemaker, Stephen," said Robert, sorry that he had maligned his affable cousin by including him in his suspicions. "But we'll talk here, in God's hearing. Fitzstephen sank the *White Ship* and murdered everyone on board, just so that he could steal the king's treasure."

"No!" gasped Fitzstephen, horrified. "I admit to stealing the treasure, but not to killing!"

"But the ship belonged to Fitzstephen, Rob," Stephen pointed out. "It was so costly that it broke him to build. Why would he sink it?"

"But it wasn't his – he gave it to the king, remember?" said Robert. "He probably promised it in a moment of rash patriotism, and Henry would never have allowed him to renege on giving such a gift. It was more expensive to build than Fitzstephen anticipated, and it left him with nothing. He decided to let Henry pay for it by stealing the treasure chests he always carries with him when he travels – the treasure chests that were with poor William on the *White Ship*."

"No!" cried Fitzstephen desperately. "It wasn't like that!"

"Once the ship had started to founder, Berthold rowed you out to the ship to collect the treasure your accomplice had already stolen and had waiting," Robert went on relentlessly. "And you paid an archer to kill any survivors lest suspicion fall on you."

"But I hired the archer later, when it had all gone wrong," said Fitzstephen in a whisper. "No one was supposed to die. The ship was meant to sink and I was supposed to take the treasure, but no one was supposed to drown – especially not William."

"Really?" asked Robert coldly. "And did you have boats ready to pick survivors from the icy waves? They were insensible, man! How could you expect no one to die if you intoxicated 200 people and left them on a sinking ship?"

"The ship had to be sunk, or the king would have known his treasure was missing," protested Fitzstephen. "And anyway, I only got part of it. Most is at the bottom of the sea because the ship sank so quickly. It all went horribly wrong!"

"That was Prince William's fault, not yours," said Stephen soothingly.

Robert gazed at him. "What do you mean?" he asked sharply.

Stephen, who had been leaning solicitously over the now-weeping Fitzstephen, looked up slowly to meet Robert's eyes. "Damn!" he said softly.

"It was your plan!" whispered Robert in horror as realization dawned. "Fitzstephen doesn't have the guts to organize something like this, and he said it wasn't his idea. It was yours! You wanted William killed to improve your own chances of succeeding to the throne."

"It most certainly was not my idea," said Stephen indignantly. "And anyway, I have older brothers. How could I inherit over them?"

"Perhaps they're not safe either," said Robert coldly. "But what did you mean when you said it was William's fault. No, don't tell me." He leaned back against a pillar and thought about what Anton had told him. "The captain put William in a boat, but William refused to row to shore. Anton said he insisted on going back for someone. Anton was wrong: it was not some*one*, but some*thing* – the treasure."

He closed his eyes when he saw the brief flash of gloating on

Stephen's usually affable face. It was an expression Robert had never seen there before, and it was one he did not like. He cursed himself for allowing Stephen's honest countenance and pleasant manners to have fooled him so completely: Stephen was a cunning manipulator who used bumbling amiability to disguise his true intelligence.

"And William was your accomplice," he said unsteadily. "Is that why the captain was able to put him in a boat, because he alone hadn't touched the strong wine that left everyone else senseless?"

"Actually, if you must know, the whole plan was William's," said Stephen. "My only role was arranging some very minor details. William recruited Fitzstephen and me; Fitzstephen recruited Berthold on William's orders. Why do you think William asked if *he* could sail in the *White Ship* rather than Henry? Did you think it was fate?"

"But why?" asked Robert. "In a few years everything would have been his anyway."

"Henry is a terrible miser, and William had needed money to pay his debts now. But, as Fitzstephen said, not all the treasure could be rescued before the ship went down, and William insisted on going back for it. His greed killed him. The ship sank and William went with it."

"And that, of course, was very convenient for you," said Robert in disgust. "You might have tried to stop him."

"Me?" asked Stephen with wide eyes. "I was nowhere near the wreck – I was in Winchester with the king. You can't blame me for William's selfish greed."

Robert eyed him with loathing.

"Stephen suggested hiring the archer to kill any survivors," said Fitzstephen in a small voice. "Some of them may have seen William struggling to get the treasure off the ship before it sank. He said we must protect William's reputation, and attempt to save the king from further grief. He even paid Berthold extra to tell everyone the prince had died valiantly trying to save his sister."

"Most noble," said Robert, not trying to hide the contempt in his voice.

"What will you do?" asked Stephen, sounding more interested than concerned. "Will you expose my small role in this, and break Henry's heart when he learns that his beloved son died with his hand in the royal treasury? Or will you keep silent, and allow the stories to circulate about William's courage?"

"More to the point, what will you do?" demanded Robert. "Kill Clito, Matilda, and your brothers to secure the throne for yourself? And what if Henry has sons from his next marriage? Will you murder them, too?"

Stephen gave his open, beguiling smile. "That, my dear cousin, you will have to wait and see."

On 25 November 1120, the White Ship *sailed out of Barfleur where it hit a rock and sank. On board were Henry I's heir William, many young lords and ladies, and the royal treasure. The only survivor was Berthold, a butcher from Rouen.*

The disaster of the White Ship *was a devastating blow to Henry. William's death meant that Henry's closest heir was his detested enemy, Clito, the son of his older brother. Henry remarried within two months, but the liaison produced no children, an ironic twist of fate given that Henry had at least twenty illegitimate offspring, one of which was Robert of Gloucester.*

Clito died in 1128, and Henry in 1135. Stephen immediately seized the crown, and Matilda, Henry's only surviving child, invaded England, thus beginning the period of British history known as the anarchy. Robert of Gloucester remained loyal to his unpopular half-sister for the rest of his life, acting as her chief adviser and leading her military campaigns. His death in 1147 heralded the end of her cause, and she left England never to return.

WHO KILLED FAIR ROSAMUND?

Tina & Tony Rath

Henry II was the grandson of Henry I by his daughter, Matilda, known as the Empress, whom we met in the last story. He was one of England's most powerful kings, lord of the Angevin Empire, which also covered over half of France. He was the father of two of England's best known kings, Richard the Lionheart and John. Henry married only once, the indomitable Eleanor of Aquitaine, but he had many mistresses, amongst them Rosamund Clifford. She died sometime around 1176 and the rumours soon spread that she had been murdered. But how, and by whom?

"There's nothing like following a royal progress for giving a man a true picture of his place in the scheme of things," said Olivier.

He was sitting on a heap of musty straw in a barn in the middle of a muddy field. His companion, Brand, was lying on a pile of sacking, his eyes closed. A dour man, currently travelling with a team of dogs who performed a Morris dance, was picking his teeth, and a girl acrobat was mending some hose. No one paid any attention to Olivier, not even the two old men huddled in the doorway, no doubt waiting for the rain to stop so that they could go and do something rural involving dung, and no doubt hopeful that their exotic guests might do something interesting before they went. They had probably heard that the girl, Alyson, danced on her hands, and wondered, in their simple country way, what happened to her skirt during her performance.

"There's the king," said Olivier, "in the castle. All the food and wine, and hot water and sweet oil, and beautiful women that he wants. And his lords spiritual and temporal getting their share of course. And there's the upper servants all dry and warm. To say nothing of the hunting dogs, and the horses in their comfortable stables. And then there's us. They make history. We just have to take history."

"We'll have our chance tonight. I've arranged it with the cook," said the dog-man. "We're to perform in the kitchens if wet, in the stable-yard if dry, for all the leavings of the king's banquet that we can eat."

"What'll we give them?" said Olivier.

"What do you want to give them?" Brand asked without opening his eyes. "Bit of juggling. Some fire-eating, only you'd better leave the fire-eating to me after what happened at York. A few songs. The Devil's Nine Questions. The Friar in the Well."

"We should try something new," said Olivier. "We're near Godstow here aren't we? Isn't Rosamund Clifford buried there? Why not the Ballad of Fair Rosamunda?"

He unshipped his lute and dashed a dramatic hand across the strings. "It's got everything. A beautiful girl, adultery, jealousy, murder, royal scandal and local connections."

"Take care as the king doesn't hear it," said the dog-man.

"Oh, the king isn't coming to the kitchens tonight," said Olivier. "He sent word to say he was sorry, but he had some ruling to do. Joke," he added flatly when no one laughed.

"Anyway the king wouldn't care. He didn't have much time for his father, as I hear tell," said Brand.

"None of them did," said the dog-man, "and this here John was his favourite, they do say."

"This ballad," said Olivier, seeing his brilliant inspiration in danger of being lost in a lot of gossip about ungrateful children. "It's got possibilities: didn't the king keep Rosamund in the middle of a maze somewhere, so the Queen Eleanore wouldn't find her? I could make it a maze of briar roses in the song, keep the rose theme,

Rosamunda, Rose of the World, and all that. But then somehow the queen managed to track her down, she made her way through the maze with a silken thread, didn't she, and then she killed her and the king nearly died of grief."

"And the queen was haunted for ever after by the scent of crushed rose petals," Alyson contributed. "I wish someone would make a song about me."

"Get yourself murdered by royalty and they will," said the dog-man.

Olivier picked at his lute strings and sang, experimentally. He had a surprisingly sweet, true voice, not the usual ballad singer's roar. Some might have detected a faint echo of the cloister in those clear notes:

> Queen Eleanore lay in her bower
> And sorely did she weep
> For envy of Fair Rosamond
> She could neither eat nor sleep
>
> Her eyes are blue as summer skies
> And mine are black as sloes
> My cheeks are pale as ivory
> And hers are like the rose.
>
> Her hair is like the yellow gold –

He stopped. "Was she a blonde?"

"Ar," said one of the rustics at the door. "Goldy head she was."

"Did you see her!" Olivier exclaimed. He heard his voice rising to a shameful squeak of childish excitement but he didn't care. "Did you really see her! It's like meeting someone who once saw the great Cleopatra."

"No, I never saw no Cleopattera," said the man, slightly taken aback by Olivier's estimate of his age, "but I did see Rosamund. And she was a goldy head. Pretty little thing when she was young but those fairish girls go off early."

Olivier strummed his lute impatiently. Ballad heroines don't lose their looks.

> Her hair is like the yellow gold
> Hangs down below her knee

Small wonder Henry doats on her
And turns away from me.
Oh then –

The flow of inspiration stopped abruptly. "What did happen then? I mean, how did Eleanore find her? Did you ever hear tell you anything about that – the maze of thorns and the poison cup?"

"Twasn't a poison cup," said Alyson. "Queen Eleanore stabbed her right through the heart. Or so they say."

"Wasn't no maze, neither," said the rustic. "She had a nice little manor at Woodstock. Stands to reason, the king wouldn't be finding his way through no maze every time he wanted to visit his lady-friend, would he?"

"Wouldn't take the trouble," Alyson agreed. In her experience men took very little trouble indeed when it came to women.

"So Eleanore came to Woodstock –" said Olivier.

"Why did she take the trouble?" said Brand abruptly.

"What d'you mean?" Olivier demanded. "She was jealous, wasn't she?"

"Yes, but why?" Brand pursued, sitting up. "I mean, Rosamund wasn't the first, nor the last of Henry's light o' loves, and Eleanore didn't murder them all."

"She'd never have had the time," said the dog-man, a cynic by trade after all.

"There was no chance of Henry getting rid of Eleanore to put Rosamund Clifford in her place, now was there? Not even after all that trouble, when Eleanore was disgraced."

"Was she now, and her a queen!" said Alyson, who only knew one way of being disgraced for a woman and assumed it worked that way for royalty as well. She wondered what had happened to the Queen's particular disgrace. Perhaps, she thought vaguely, they had made him a bishop.

Brand went, pursuing his own thoughts: "Eleanore had land in her own right – she brought Henry half of France as a dowry, didn't she, she had allies, and a whole parcel of sons. Everything was in her favour. All she had to do was wait. Henry wasn't exactly known for his fidelity. He'd had a couple of sons by an English woman, hadn't he? And there was Belle-belle . . ."

"Who?" said Alyson.

"She came after Rosamund," said Brand. "A French piece, I suppose. There was a story that Henry gave her and the queen both a cape of samite, each as fine as the other, not a pin to choose between them."

"What did the queen say to that?" the dog-man asked.

"I never heard. But they say she wore the cape. And so did Belle-belle. And I never heard that Eleanore mishandled her."

"Yes," said Olivier, "but women aren't reasonable creatures. Say Henry went on about how beautiful Rosamund was –"

"I thought he was trying to keep her a secret. You don't hide your lady-friend away in the middle of a maze and then make a point of telling your wife what a beauty she is," Brand objected.

"Queen Nell, she was a looker herself," said the rustic who had, so far, remained silent. "Saw her once."

"Ah!" Olivier pounced. "When she came to Woodstock to kill Rosamund!"

"No. 'Twas in London. Free-holder I am, not tied to no estate, so I went for a soldier when I were young and I seen all sorts. Queen Nell never came next or nigh here as I know of."

There was a curious silence, broken only by a faint ching-ring as the dogs, dressed already for their evening's performance, shifted in their sleep on the barn floor. Then Olivier ran his fingers over the strings of his lute, plucking out the tune of that popular crusading classic "L'homme armé".

"She must have come here when you were away at the wars," he said.

"May a done, may a done," the man agreed. "Course, Rosamund was dead and buried long before I went off."

"Why don't you both come and sit down here and tell the story properly," said Brand. "Tell us everything you know about it. Never mind thorny mazes and silken threads, poison cups or daggers. Just tell us what you remember."

"Well. It was a powerful long time ago," said the first man. "The year she died I wasn't no older than this chap here," he pointed to Olivier. "And it was only talk. All I can tell you is what folk said."

"Old bishop turned her out of the church. I do remember that," said his companion.

"What, he turned her away from the altar?" Olivier squeaked. "I never heard that story." He could see the scene: the tall ascetic figure of the bishop at the church door, arm outstretched to reject the king's beautiful mistress as she bent her golden head and wept for guilt and shame. It would make a good verse for the ballad.

"No, no. He never dare do nothing like that, long as old Henry was alive. No, when she died, Henry he built her a great tomb in the nuns' church at Godstow. Paid a lot of money for it he did. But he hadn't been dead long hisself when the bishop of Lincoln made them take it away. Put her out into the churchyard, on account of her being a harlot."

"Oh, poor thing!" said Alyson.

"She was past caring by that time, you daft piece!" said the dog-man.

"Fair play to the bishop," one of the countrymen said heavily. "There were a lot of daft pieces coming to the church to put roses round the tomb. Kind of thought she might put in a good word for them. Get them a rich lover too."

The men laughed but Alyson nodded to herself. She could see the point of that. It wasn't the kind of thing you could ask Our Lady about. She was lovely, of course, and, in Alyson's opinion, a lot more sensible about women's affairs than the priests gave her credit for, but there were some things you really couldn't raise with her. St Rosamund the Harlot would be a useful saint to petition if you wanted to be lucky in love. But she said: "It shows Henry must have loved her. Spending all that money after she was dead. No wonder Eleanore was jealous," she added with a side glance at Brand.

He said, patiently: "She'd only have been jealous if she'd loved Henry too. And she didn't. You don't plot with your sons to get rid of your husband if you love him. As far as she was concerned I dare say Rosamund could have him."

"Did she plot with her boys then?" said Alyson incredulously.

"Yes, she did. That's why she was disgraced, like I said."

"Oh. I thought you meant she'd had a baby who wasn't Henry's."

"Proper rebellion there was," said one of the countrymen, with relish. "Real set-to. Queen Nell she tried to escape from the King's palace in France dressed up like a man –"

"Dressed up like a man," Olivier pounced. "That's how she did it. She disguised herself as a man and came here to kill Rosamund. That's why no one remembers seeing her."

"She was under house arrest in France a year and more before

Rosamund died," said Brand patiently. "Here, let's do this properly. Now, were either of you living at Woodstock at the time?"

"No, but my old dad was a carter and I used to go over to there twothree times in a week with a load. And there was a girl in the kitchens . . ."

"Eadgyth!" roared his friend digging him in the ribs. "She was a goer!"

"Banged like a barn-door, God rest her soul," his friend agreed piously.

"Was she a talker as well?" said Brand hopefully.

"Yes. Chattered like a jay, she did."

"So, what did she tell you about the household? You said the Rosamund 'went off early' – so she was losing her looks?"

One of the men nodded vigorously. "Thin in the face, thick in the waist. Some women go like that."

" 'Specially the goldy heads," his friend, who seemed to have something against blondes, agreed. "Don't last. Lost her complexion too. Yellow as piece of parchment she was before the end. And her teeth were loosening as well."

"Cheeks fallen, body bloated, colour gone . . ." said Brand.

"Poison," said Olivier starkly.

"It does sound like it, doesn't it?" said brand. "But where did it come from? Did Eadgyth ever talk about people who visited Woodstock?"

"Didn't get that many visitors. King didn't like it. Well, stands to reason he wouldn't want no one coming round when he was away, and while he was there, well, there wasn't no need."

"Not many visitors," said Brand. "So there were some. Who were they?"

There was a silence while the man consulted that formidable instrument, the memory of the illiterate which must carry a whole lifetime of events. "Her brother. Rosamund's brother, he came to see her. Specially when she started to ail. And the priest of course. And nuns from Godstow Convent."

Olivier opened his mouth to ask if one of the nuns could have been a disguised Queen Eleanore, but Brand waved him down. "Did the nuns bring her medicine? Or food?"

"May a done," said the man vaguely. "But why should a holy nun want to murder the King's mistress?"

"Unless one of Henry's old mistresses went into a convent," said the dog-man.

"One of Henry's old mistresses —" said Brand thoughtfully. And then: "Did anyone else bring her food — little treats to tempt her appetite when she started to get ill?"

"Yes, Henry. He sent game and such."

"Sent or brought?" said Brand.

"Same thing," the man protested.

"Not really. If he brought food with him he'd have to eat it as well, or give a bloody good reason why not. But if food was sent . . ."

"Well, he'd bring food with him, of course, and he'd send birds and such by that English by-blow of his, the — the one with the tongue-tie, him that wasn't quite a priest —"

"Geoffrey Fitzroy," said Brand. "Not quite a priest, and tongue-tied. Geoffrey Fitzroy, or I'm a black pudding."

"Henry's bastard," said Olivier. "He was probably just trying to curry favour with the new mistress. With his own mother getting old, stands to reason the king wouldn't have much time for her . . ." his voice trailed off.

"One of Henry's old mistresses. Now there's someone who would have been jealous of Rosamund," said Brand. "Henry's cast mistress, Ykenai, the English woman. After all, Rosamund really had taken her place in a way she never could have taken Eleanore's. And you say her son was here when Rosamund was dying." He paused and added: "With game pies, and such."

"He could have been an emissary from Eleanore," said Olivier, still fighting his corner.

"Eleanore wasn't just in disgrace she was under house arrest," Brand repeated. "In France. But he could have been a messenger for someone else. Geoffrey was in favour with Henry. He'd stuck by him when his legitimate sons rebelled. 'This alone is my true son,' that's what Henry said."

"What else did he do for him?" said the dog man.

There was another uneasy silence.

"Rosamund nagged him, they did say," said one of the countrymen, "kept on she did — so Eadgyth say — didn't see why he shouldn't put her wholly in Queen Nell's place, seeing as how Queen Nell was in prison, or as good as."

There was another silence.

A mistress who was losing her looks. Nagging. Demanding. And a king with a terrible temper. Known for his rages, Henry had been, awful seizures when he would rip his clothes, roll on the floor, chewing the rushes . . . when he would do things, say things that he would never have done or said in his right mind, things he would regret for ever. When it was too late. And a young man with a good reason for wanting to get rid of the king's mistress. Henry in one ear, and Ykenai in the other, perhaps . . .

"But he loved her," Alyson repeated softly. "He spent all that money on her tomb . . ."

"He was fond enough of Becket," said Brand. "Had himself flogged at Becket's tomb, didn't he? But he ordered his murder. And all it took was a few words."

"Will no man rid me of this turbulent priest?" the dog-man quoted, hoarsely.

"Yes," said Brand. "And suppose, I mean just suppose for the sake of argument, he'd said: 'Won't someone get this wretched woman off my back'? Something like that. Not really meaning it. But our Geoffrey took him up on it. Maybe he and Ykenai had been waiting for the chance And then Henry was sorry. So he built her a grand tomb, set up a shrine for her, but she wasn't Becket, wasn't an archbishop, he didn't have to do any public penance . . ."

"Maybe the old bishop of Lincoln knew," said one of the countrymen. "Maybe that's why he wouldn't have her in the church. Bit too close to Becket for his liking."

"So," said Olivier. "No rosy maze, no silken clue, no dark jealous queen coming to murder the golden rose of the world. Just a fading mistress, a malicious woman and a man with a nasty temper. And a chancer like Geoffrey. He never came to much, did he, for all his father's favour? Didn't Henry make him a bishop?"

"There is another possibility," said Brand.

"Suicide, I suppose?" said Olivier impatiently.

"No. Rosamund was peevish, losing her looks, how did our friend put it, 'thin in the face and thick in the waist,' so what does that suggest?"

"She was expecting," said Alyson promptly.

"And things went wrong. And she died. As women do. He would have felt guilty then all right."

There was another, different sort of silence. Everyone could

remember a time when things went wrong and a woman had died. It
was the curse of Eve.

"So there's your ballad," said Brand. "You've got quite a choice
there."

Olivier plucked a few discontented notes: "Who killed Fair
Rosamund?" he sang. "Who saw her die . . ."

The rain had eased off by the evening. A little straw spread on the
stable-yard had enabled Alyson to perform her acrobatic dance (with
her skirt ingeniously tied round her ankles with her girdle, to general
disappointment) and allowed the dogs to hop solemnly through their
Morris dance. Brand had eaten fire, and juggled. And to an admiring
silence Olivier was singing a new ballad. It told how the dark thorny
queen Eleanore had found her way through a rosy maze, following a
scarlet thread, and how she so misused the golden rose of the world,
the King's only true love, that she died soon after (he had not been
able to make up his mind between the poison cup and the dagger, so
he left that bit vague) and how the king had almost died of grief
himself. And as for the queen she got her come-uppance for she was
haunted ever after:

> And whyfore no man knows
> She smelt a savour all in her bower
> Most like a bruised rose . . .

Alyson, now on her feet again, took a moment from tying her girdle
back around her waist to dab at her eyes. It was ever so sad. And
coins showered into Olivier's hat, but he hardly noticed them. He
was too absorbed in making, or at least meddling, with history after
all.

Richard the Lionheart ❦

PROVENANCE

———

Liz Holliday

Our picture of Richard the Lionheart, who has long been a national hero, is of a chivalrous warrior king, the saviour of Christendom, who fought the infidel in the Holy Land. In truth Richard cared little for England, other than as a source of revenue, and spent but a few months in the kingdom. He lived only to fight, rather like his great-great-grandfather, William the Conqueror, and spent most of his reign either in the Holy Land, in prison in Austria, or fighting in France. There is no doubt that he was a brilliant soldier, an athletic fighter and a brave man, and in days when men still looked on in awe at a warrior king, he no doubt fitted his role admirably. However, he was good at creating enemies. At one time most of western Europe disliked him. When he set off on the Crusades the fleet was delayed and Richard spent some time in Sicily. Unhappy over the treatment of his sister Joanna, who had married William, the former king of Sicily, Richard allowed his men to run riot in Messina and eventually captured the town. As part of the reparations, Richard presented the new king, Tancred with a very special present. Just what that was and the mystery surrounding it is the subject of the following story.

The silence in the great hall of the Castle of Palermo was broken only by the slow pacing of the English king's servant up the central aisle.

Guillaime cursed the luck that had placed him in one of the pools of sunlight that shafted through the high windows, and restrained himself from fidgeting. His master, Sir Leonarto, stood next to him, tall and still. Guillaime tried to emulate him, for there was nothing he wanted so much but to be worthy of him – of being a knight.

The slow pacing stopped. The servant reached his king. He bowed to Tancred, King of Sicily, before going down on one knee and holding out the velvet cushion and its precious cargo. The English king – Richard, they called him, Richard with the heart of the lion – took up the sword in its battered sheath. Reversing it, he presented it to King Tancred.

"In the name of the people of England, and in the cause of peace, we offer you this sword – once wielded by our greatest king. We pray you take it, that together we may smite the Infidel!" King Richard said, for all the world as if he had never laid siege to Messina or demanded money of Tancred, which he called a dowry for his sister. King Tancred took the weapon. For a moment, all was stillness. Then metal hissed on leather as he unsheathed the blade. He swept it high above his head. Light fractured on its surface and shattered into a thousand points of brilliance. For a moment, it seemed that he held a flaming brand aloft. Then he moved his arm, and the sword became a shaft of glittering silver, with only the rubies glittering bloodily in its hilt to break its clean simplicity.

A great sigh went up all through the hall. Even Sir Leonarto seemed entranced by it.

He glanced at Guillaime. "It's nothing, boy," he muttered.

Guillaime looked away, glad enough to watch the shaft of brilliance that was the English sword. The Sicilian sword, now.

"In the name of the people of England," King Richard said, "We give you – Excalibur!"

There were celebrations that evening – a feast for Sicilians and English alike, with roasted meats, and much wine, and dancing and singing. Late in the evening, Guillaime noticed Sir Leonarto talking to a wiry, copper-haired man. A stranger, to Guillaime at least. There might have been nothing in it, but for the odd intensity in their manner. A short while later, Sir Leonarto came over to Guillaime, who was playing at dice with some of the other squires, Sicilian and English alike. There are no language barriers when there are pennies to be won.

Sir Leonarto scowled. "Outside," he said. Guillaime eyed him warily. He could think of nothing he'd done wrong, but his master was known for his hot temper and quick – and heavy – hands.

He got up and went outside. Behind him, he heard the others whispering. No doubt they thought he'd been caught out in some misdemeanour with the serving girls, or possibly a minor theft from the pantry. The moon rode cold above the palace courtyard.

"Over here," Sir Leonarto said, and pulled him into a shadowy corner.

"Sire, if I've done –"

"Shut up and listen," Sir Leonarto said. "I am given a task which will make my reputation here at the court, if done well. And if I rise, you rise." Guillaime could only nod. Sir Leonarto's fingers bit into his shoulder. "There are doubts about the sword that the English king so very kindly gave to us. We – you and I – are to prove the right of these doubts." He glared at Guillaime. "Do you understand?"

"I think I do, my Lord," Guillaime said. He could barely bring himself to speak. "But what if it is Excalibur?" He stumbled over the unfamiliar name.

"Must you always be so stupid, boy? Sometimes I wonder why I took you for my squire." He pushed Guillaime hard against the wall. "We are told there are doubts. What our king wishes, we will find. We will search out the truth." He glared at Guillaime. "Now do you understand?"

Some people thought Guillaime was not very clever. He knew that, but thought it unfair. He just wondered a lot, and sometimes that got in the way . . . As Leonarto paused, Guillaime thought that he had been going to say something else, and that played on his mind.

But what he could not imagine.

"Yes, my Lord." Guillaime nodded. From inside, the strains of a lute floated out, and the sound of a song being sung in English.

"To that end, you will get to know the English better – not just any of them, but the ones closest to their king. That black crow of a monk – what do they call him? Brother Francis? – that travels with him. He would be a good place to start. After all, he's supposed to be here to vouch that the sword is what they claim." Leonarto smiled: that wolfish smile that had the girls doing whatever he asked, and the other knights – some of them, anyway – envying him for it. "Better yet, try the girl."

"Yes, my Lord," Guillaime said. He knew the one his Lord meant. He had heard that she was the monk's niece – she was clearly not a serving maid, yet she did not have the bearing of a lady. "My lord," he ventured. "Could not you do it? You would be so much better than I."

"The king wants it done in secret – and who would ever suspect you? Besides, I've no stomach for monks and priests, as well you know." He grinned suddenly. "Young lad like you – I'm sure you'll know how to please that wench into giving up her secrets."

Guillaime flushed and muttered something he hoped would be taken for agreement. To his immense relief, Leonarto let him slip away.

He could still feel his face burning when he got back inside. He looked around, but his friends were gone. On the far side of the hall, the English knights were laughing and shouting. Brother Francis was nowhere to be seen. But the girl was sitting quietly to one side, clearly ill at ease.

How to begin? Guillaime wondered. Not from here, obviously. He started across the hall, but even as he did so, she stood up. She murmured something to one of the men, who paid her little attention, then went towards the door. Guillaime changed course, and stopping on the way to pick up a goblet of wine from one of the tables, managed to get there at the same time she did. Faking clumsiness – not hard, he thought ruefully, given what Sir Leonarto was always saying about him – he managed to bump into her.

"My pardon, my Lady," he said in his best French, the language of the English court.

The young woman stared at him, clearly bemused. He hadn't thought his accent was so very bad.

"It was my fault, Sir," she said, with an accent worse, if anything, than Guillaime's. She glanced back the way she had come, clearly worried.

How very odd, he thought. Still, he knew a little English, and if it would make her feel more comfortable – "This is a great day for both our peoples," he said.

"What?" She seemed startled. "Oh. Yes."

"We should celebrate." Guillaime desperately wanted to finish the conversation. Get her to reveal her secrets, Sir Leonarto had said. If only he could. "But you're not. You're –"

"A headache, my Lord," she said.

My lord? he thought. Hardly. He was big for his age, but even to his own eyes he hardly looked like a grown man, much less one of any substance.

"Perhaps you should get some air," he said. It sounded better – more like something someone capable of prising secrets from young girls would say. "I could accompany you, if you are afraid of being alone outside."

"I must not," she said. "I said I was retiring. A headache –"

"Oh come," Guillaime said. "Surely a few minutes in the cool of the night will help your headache more than hours in a stuffy chamber?"

She smiled. *She smiled*. Guillaime felt his heart slamming in his chest.

"Well, perhaps, then. A few minutes."

He never could remember quite how they got to the courtyard, or what they had spoken about. All he could think of was the moonlight on her pale hair, the wonders of her laugh. Out here, she seemed so much more relaxed.

"It is wonderful to be here," she said. "It is so much warmer than England . . . if it weren't for the sword, and my Lord Geoffrey's kindness to my father –"

"Your father," Guillaime said, coming sharply to attention. "I thought you were travelling with your uncle – that Brother Francis was your uncle?"

"Yes," she said. She was flushed, though whether from the chill of the night, or delight in his company, or for some other reason, Guillaime could not say. "Yes, of course. But it was my father who introduced them –"

"But –"

"It's been nice talking to you, Guillaime. But my uncle will be worried about me. I really must go now."

And it was over . . . she was gone.

Guillaime sat alone in the courtyard, trying to think about her and not her smile. Clearly, he thought, there's something untoward here. Could she be the monk's illicit child? Such was hardly unknown. But it was hardly relevant to the problem with the sword.

Alice, he thought. Her name is Alice. That seemed much more important, just then.

"Alice!"

The name, spoken aloud, cut through Guillaime's reverie. He looked round. She was hurrying across the yard, towards a robed figure hardly visible against the shadows. Brother Francis, Guillaime thought. He heard her say something, though he couldn't make out the words. The monk's hand flashed out and grabbed her arm. Guillaime walked closer, quietly but not so stealthily that he could have been accused of sneaking if he were caught. After all, why shouldn't he be getting some of the evening air?

"I swear, girl –" Brother Francis shook her hard.

"It was nothing – he's just a boy. A squire –"

"I told you to keep yourself to yourself." The monk's tone was harsh, and his English accent so coarse that Guillaime could hardly make out his words. Not an educated man, our Brother Francis, he thought. He was getting closer to them, now. Moonlight revealed the monk's face. The man was clearly furious.

"Please, father –" Alice begged.

Father, Guillaime thought, without letting surprise break his stride. He was between them and the hall entrance now. Either he had to go inside, or intervene, and make it clear he'd overheard. And he didn't dare do that.

"One more word out of you, lass, and I'll –"

Guillaime bit his lip and went inside. The heavy door shut behind him, and he heard no more of the conversation.

"I won't be needing you today," Sir Leonarto said. It was nearly noon, and the morning sun was already hot.

"Thank you, my Lord," Guillaime said. The courtyard was half-full of servants going about their chores, and townsfolk with business at the castle. "But I thought you wanted to practise at sword today –" For all his drinking and crude ways, Sir Leonarto was a fine fighter and usually practised at arms for several hours a day.

"Yes, boy, but I've changed my mind." Leonarto pulled his cloak closer round him, and fiddled with the feather in his cloche hat. "I've realised I've business in the town. Business of a certain sort, understand me?"

Guillaime did. By the look on the face of a passing courtier, so did half the residents of the castle. But then, Leonarto had something of a reputation as a ladies' man.

"And," he went on, "I would hope that you could find plenty to do to keep yourself occupied. You can tell me what you've been up to when I get back this evening."

"Yes, my Lord," Guillaime said. He had hoped the subject of the sword might have been forgotten overnight, but it seemed it had not. Still, he thought, it would give him an excuse to talk to Alice again. The thought was almost unbearable to him. He meant to seek her out immediately, but instead he went back to the chamber he shared with Sir Leonarto. He found himself pacing the floor, and then staring out of the window at the sea – pacing and staring, staring and pacing. It was never going to get any easier, he thought at last; and Sir Leonarto was hardly likely to be sympathetic if Guillaime claimed he'd done nothing because he was too shy.

With that thought in mind, he set off to find the apartments the English had been given. A serving girl directed him, with a knowing smile, to the rooms Alice shared with her "uncle". He tapped on the door; there was no reply, so he rapped again, harder, though in truth the hammering of his heart sounded louder. Still no reply. What was he to say to Sir Leonarto – *well, they were nowhere to be found, so I spent the day playing at dice, if it please you, my Lord?* Before he had time to think better of it, he eased the door open and slipped inside.

There was little enough to see – the place was as spartan as any monkish cell. Doors led off at either end to bedchambers. One of these was clearly Alice's, by the garments left on the clothes-stand. Feeling hot and miserable with shame, he backed out. But the other – the other was her uncle's. Her father's, rather, Guillaime corrected himself. A nightstand revealed an earthenware flagon of strong drink; and a trunk, clothes. Clothes such as no monk would wear, surely? Breeches, brightly coloured tunics, a cape of coarse linen. And at the bottom, a dagger and shortsword such as a common soldier might carry. There were dice, too, and a bag of gold coins of a kind unknown to Guillaime. And then, when he'd thought to find nothing useful among so much that perplexed him, he found a sheaf of letters. They were old, browned at the edges, with the ink fading; and they were written in English. Even so, he managed to read a word or two. And then a phrase leapt out at him: it seemed the writer – he signed himself Edmund, an English name – was coming to Sicily, that he had plans to take up residence in Palermo. An address was given – a place in the market quarter.

It was something, Guillaime thought. He wasn't sure what, but certainly something. He put everything back the way he had found it, then carefully closed the lid of the trunk. He regarded it for a moment; if anyone looked at it with a suspicious eye, they might realise it had been disturbed. But otherwise it would pass, he hoped. He went out into the sitting room. Before he could get to the outer door, it opened. Alice came in.

"What are you doing here?" she demanded.

"Waiting for you," Guillaime said, hoping he didn't look too guilty. She arched an eyebrow at him. He'd been hoping for a smile. "I wanted to ask you about the sword –" Subtle, he thought. "The one they say is Excalibur, you know –"

"There's nothing I can tell you," she said; now her tone was cold. "Please leave."

"Look, I'm sorry if I offended you, but –"

"I said leave." She turned to face him. A bruise purpled her left cheek. "My uncle wishes me to stay apart from you foreigners," she added.

"He did this?" He knew he must not reveal that he'd heard her call the monk father.

"It's nothing," she said; she was trembling. "Please go."

"All right," Guillaime said. "I will – before this 'nothing' happens to you again."

Furiously, he went down to the hall to get himself something to eat. So, Brother Francis had heavy hands, did he? Well, he might not be able to do much about that. But the man also had more money than any monk ought, and dice and drink as well. And if Guillaime could do something about that, then he would.

The thoughts were still revolving in his head while he ate. He had hardly made a start on his bread and cheese when a page arrived with a note. Guillaime thanked the boy, and read it quickly. It was from Leonarto, telling him to bring a basket of food and drink to an address in the town. Guillaime sighed. It wasn't the first time this had happened. Leonarto had a taste for low women, but too much regard for his stomach and health to trust himself to the kind of food they could provide. Well, he thought, all to the good – now he had an excuse for a trip into town.

Guillaime set the hamper down on the sideboard.

"There's a good lad," Marie-Angelique said. "He's a good lad," she repeated, turning to Leonarto. The two of them were sprawled across a pallet in the corner of the room, covered only by a thin blanket.

"I hope it's to your liking," Guillaime said. His face was burning; he could feel it. They would think it was embarrassment, but it was shame. Leonarto was a knight; such adventures as this should be below him. Yet here he was, naked as the Lord made him, with this woman who was no better than a common whore. And quite a time she'd given him, Guillaime thought. There was a chain of lovebites on his neck, and bruises darkening on his upper arm.

Marie-Angelique – the latest in a long line of Leonarto's mistresses – got up, clutching the blanket around her. Somehow, to Guillaime's eye, it did more to emphasise her endowments than to conceal them. She turned round and kissed Leonarto sloppily on his cheek, where, Guillaime now realised, he had a wide graze.

"Be a good boy, this time, won't you?" she said. Leonarto slapped her smartly on her behind. She squealed and backed away towards the basket, watched all the time by Leonarto. Guillaime did his best not to look at either of them. Their clothes were spread all over the floor, Leonarto's expensive cape and tunic and her grubby petticoats, all piled on his boots and belt.

"Ooh," Marie-Angelique said. "Bread! Cheese! And look at this – ham. And some pickles and apples." She stuffed a chunk of meat into her mouth. "You say thank you to your cook, mind," she said. "Tell him I said it's just what a body needs after a full morning's rumpty-tump."

She laughed coarsely.

"Come back to bed," Leonarto said lazily. "We can eat later."

"In a minute," she snapped. "I'm hungry now." She eyed Guillaime up and down. "Unless you'd like to join us, sweetheart?"

"No!" Guillaime said. The place stank of unwashed bodies and patchouli oil. It made him want to gag. "No," he repeated. "I have – other chores to do."

He backed out of the door. As it closed, he got just a glimpse of Marie-Angelique's naked body as she dropped the blanket and threw herself down on to Leonarto. Sweet Virgin Mary, Guillaime prayed as he stood on the narrow stairs, if I am ever a knight, I pray I am not like that. A giggle came from inside the room. Guillaime launched himself down the stairs before the sounds turned to anything more.

He hurried down into the street, and though it took him some time – time in which he found his way into increasingly unsalubrious areas of the town – eventually he came to the address mentioned in the letters he had found.

A rickety set of stairs led up to a garret. If this person had come to Palermo to find his fortune, most assuredly he had not done so. For the second time that day, Guillaime knocked upon a door and waited for a reply which did not come. He looked around. There was no one in sight. He pushed the door, expecting to find it locked, and a quick end to his adventure. But the door opened. Late afternoon sunlight shafting in through a high window revealed a workroom. So Guillaime took it for at first – there was a workbench and a set of tools under the window. Only when he glanced around did he notice the box-bed in the corner, the stool by the little hearth and the cooking pot on the open fire. A couple of jugs of drink stood nearby, and next to them a chipped cup, with another standing further off. Most promising, he thought.

"Is anyone here?"

There was no answer. He stepped inside. The workbench was a clutter of equipment – wax for casting, files, planishing and other hammers. There was a pile of boxes under the workbench, covered by a piece of sacking. Somewhere here, he was sure, he would find his answer.

The door slammed.

He spun round. At first he saw no-one. The weight of the door must have caused it to shut, he decided. It was only as he turned back to the bench that he saw what was hanging from the beam in the corner.

A body. An old man's body, hanging by a rope. It swung silently towards him. Away. Back again.

Warily, he approached it.

Edmund, the Englishman, Guillaime supposed. He had been big once, but poverty had wasted his flesh; and up close, he was not so old. A stool lay overturned nearby. His last act, Guillaime thought – to kick away his support. May Christ have mercy on his soul, if it please Mary and the saints to intercede for him; but it was a pointless prayer, he knew. Suicides were damned by their own hand, in the next world as in this.

I should call for help, Guillaime thought. But he would have to account for his presence there, and he did not know what he would say. How could he claim to be on the king's business, when the king wanted it done in secrecy? Still, he couldn't just leave the poor man hanging there; it didn't seem right. Besides, a voice nagged at a corner of his mind telling him that there might be something about the man's person that would help him in his task.

He set the stool upright and climbed on it; the rope was easy enough to cut with his dagger. The body was heavy, and stiff in death. He almost fell off the stool under the weight of it, but eventually he managed to get down and lay the corpse on the floor. It reeked of alcohol and vomit. The man's eyes bulged from his face, which was contorted in agony. Guillaime reached for the noose, with some odd thought of relieving his pain uppermost in his mind. The rope loosened easily enough. An oddity of the markings on the man's neck drew Guillaime's attention. He removed the rope entirely; there was not one set of contusions, but several.

For a moment, he did not know what to make of it. Then he realised what he was seeing. Finger marks, he thought. The man had been strangled. He held out his hands, still puzzled. A moment's more thought, and he had it: the man had been strangled from behind. He glanced around the room. There was no sign of a fight, or that the room had been searched.

So perhaps he knew his attacker, Guillaime thought. If they took anything, they knew where it was kept – and in fact, they must have hanged him after they strangled him . . . to make it look like suicide. It was a terrible thing to do. A suicide could not receive the last rites, or have Mass said for him in Church, or be buried in holy ground.

I must leave, he thought. If they think I did this . . . He stared at the man, noting what he saw even while he panicked. Old wine and vomit stains on the tunic, so the man was a heavy drinker. But newer ones, too. Perhaps his attacker had got him drunk? Nervously, he touched one of the purple stains. It was still very slightly damp, so the murder had happened in the morning. The man's hands were calloused, and index, middle and little fingers of his left hand were malformed, as if they'd been broken and badly set.

"Who killed you, you poor man?" Guillaime whispered. "Who killed you and condemned your soul to hell?" He closed the man's eyes gently, wondering if it were true what they said – that a murdered man's eyes retained the image of his killer.

It must have something do with the sword, Guillaime pondered. This Edmund had known Brother Francis, and it had been no ordinary killing for money or over a gambling dispute. He stood up. There was nothing he could do for Edmund now, except to find out who had done this to him. He felt like a grave robber – and one likely to be interrupted at any moment – but still he forced himself to search the place. The answer's here somewhere, he thought.

He went over to the hearth. The fire was still slightly warm, reinforcing his earlier conclusion that the man was only recently dead. One of the flasks of wine was still stoppered, but the other was open, and half empty. There were dregs in the bottom of the cup. He lifted it to his nose. The wine had an odd aroma – sour, and with a faintly medicinal tang to it. Poison? he wondered. Or a sedative, perhaps; but he didn't know enough about medicine to be sure. The other cup had been washed clean, and told Guillaime nothing more. Perhaps, he thought, the murderer had drunk with Edmund and then killed him, washing his cup to make it look as if the old man had drank alone. Certainly, there hadn't been a struggle – even as he thought it, he noticed that the bottom edge of the stool was splintered. It was very pale, and the wood was jagged. Recent, he thought, rubbing his thumb over the area. It would have taken quite a lot of force to do that. Had Edmund used the stool to hit his attacker? If so, the murderer had done a good job of cleaning up, because there would surely have been some blood. So, he thought, maybe it fell over and hit the hearth?

He tried to picture what had happened in his mind: Edmund had welcomed a visitor. Someone he knew and trusted – a client, perhaps? Or a friend? They had drunk wine together, but the visitor had drugged it, then tried to strangle Edmund. But he had enough of his wits about him to fight back. The stool went over. Edmund died, and the murderer strung him up like a suicide, clearing up the signs of his visit.

"Poor Edmund," Guillaime muttered. He went over to the workbench. There were various bits of jewellery in different stages of manufacture, yet the dust overlaying them showed they had lain where they were for a long while – far longer than the man had been dead, at any rate. Gingerly, Guillaime picked up one of the rings, more because it looked oddly familiar than for any other reason. He held it up to the light, revealing an odd design carved into the metal –

some kind of distorted animal, he thought. A bull, perhaps, or a boar. Heathenish designs; but what else would you expect of the English? Sunshine caught the ring, and he realised that it was made of pewter and glass, not the silver and amethyst he had first taken it for. In a casket to one side, he found a sheaf of receipts. The increasing spaces between their dates spoke eloquently of the decline in Edmund's business.

So, Guillaime thought. He's ripe to be involved in something shady. But what? And why was it so important he had to die for it?

He pulled out the boxes from beneath the bench. Heavy hammers. Bellows. A brazier. Something he could barely move, that proved to be an anvil.

A swordsmith! Guillaime thought. There was something he was missing, something that would make the pattern whole. But he couldn't see it. Edmund had come from England, to be a swordsmith in Sicily – otherwise why would he have dragged his gear with him? He'd damaged his hand. Perhaps lost the strength in it; and so, perhaps, he'd turned to silversmithing and jewellery making. But his work – Guillaime looked again at the pewter trinket, and was again struck by its familiarity – was of no great craftsmanship, and so his business had fallen away, and he'd got involved in something too deep for him, and ended his life at the hands of . . . who?

He searched further, and found a second casket. This one was locked. With a twinge of guilt, he levered it open with the point of his dagger, leaving a splintered mess of wood around the lock. Inside, he found a sheaf of papers. They were covered in drawings of jewellery – rings, armbands, cloak-pins. The designs were skilfully drawn, and extremely detailed – almost, Guillaime mused, like a set of working plans. But who would want to work from them? Like the ring he had found, they were ugly heathen things. Yet Edmund had found a market for such things, at least for a while.

He flipped over a few more pages, and found himself staring at a sketch of a sword's hilt – Excalibur's hilt.

Suddenly he was back in the great hall, and King Tancred was brandishing the sword over his head.

"This gem is a ruby," he whispered, placing his finger on the drawing. "And this. But this one is a sapphire . . ."

So Edmund was involved somehow; but it proved nothing, except perhaps that the sword had once been in his possession, along with

other jewels from olden times. Had he copied them? Perhaps he had
the skill to make such things, but could not invent originals. Then,
perhaps, he had sold the originals – maybe just for the value of their
metal and gems. It was a possibility he had no way of checking. He
flipped over another page. For a moment he thought he was looking
at the same drawing again. Then he realised that there were small
differences in the engraving that surrounded the gems, and in the way
the stones were set.

Guillaime frowned. Nowhere else had Edmund made more than
one drawing of a piece. So, could there be two swords? And if so,
why hadn't they been sold off?

It's not important, he thought. Whatever the circumstances of
Edmund's life that led to him selling off one bauble and keeping
another, they don't matter now. All that mattered was that if there
were two swords, neither one was Excalibur.

Guillaime stood in the middle of the room he shared with Sir Leonarto.
The drawings, which he'd stuffed down the front of his tunic, pressed
against his chest. He'd meant to find his master immediately, but that
would have to wait. Someone had ransacked the room while he had
been out. Every item of clothing had been dumped on the floor. The
bedding, too. His little pallet in the corner had been ripped open, and
so had the mattress on Sir Leonarto's bed. The nightstand had been
turned over, and the water jug and bowl lay smashed beside it. The
water made a dark stain on the stone floor. Even some of the wall
hangings had been ripped down, and the rest had been yanked aside.

How am I ever going to explain this? Guillaime wondered, though
it was not his fault. That had never stopped Sir Leonarto blaming
him before. There was no hope he could get it straight before his
master came back – it looked like a week's work. Suddenly weary, he
started picking up clothes. He supposed he could call a page or maid
to help him, but as Sir Leonarto's squire he was supposed to see to all
his needs.

He righted the wash-stand, and started gathering the bits of broken
crockery. That was when he saw it, cast aside in the corner – Sir
Leonarto's sword, still in its scabbard.

But he was wearing it, he thought. Under his cloak. He
remembered how it had spoiled the line of it. And again, he'd seen
the belt at Marie-Angelique's. A heavy cloak on a hot day, he

thought. Two swords, not one. Yet he'd been at Marie-Angelique's all morning . . . so she said.

And he knew. With bitter, cold certainty, he knew.

The king smelled of patchouli oil, just like Marie-Angelique, and there was a smear of grease on his tunic. Guillaime had never been so close to him before, and he could not believe he was so close now.

It had taken all his nerve to send the message. He had expected to tell Sir Leonarto what he had found. To repeat it, perhaps, to this courtier and that. To have his words written down.

But not to send a note to the king. Still less to have the king take it seriously, or summon Guillaime to his presence, or to make him stand and explain it to him and several other grave looking men.

He had explained what he had found out. What he had noticed, and the conclusions he had drawn. King Tancred had sent him outside, leaving the drawings behind, to pace and sit and pace again, and ponder on what punishments might be meted out to an insolent squire who dared indict his master, while the king consulted with his advisors.

When they called him back in, King Tancred grabbed him by the jaw and wrenched him round. Guillaime stared up at him like a rabbit caught by a weasel's eyes.

"We will summon these men you have accused," the king said. His grip grew ever tighter. "But until I say otherwise, you will say only that you found proof at the peasant's hovel that he had the sword before the monk did. Understand me?" He thrust Guillaime away.

"Yes, Sire." Guillaime could barely get the words out. "But – forgive me, Sire – why?"

For a moment he thought he had gone too far.

King Tancred's face distorted in rage. "Because the cunning fox catches more prey than the ravening wolf, boy! Now be silent and do as you are told."

And then all he could do was wait while the king stood staring out at the rolling sea, and the courtiers stood silently in the corner; and the king's pages went to fetch Brother Francis and Sir Leonarto, and King Richard of the English.

After a long, agonising time, they arrived. Sir Leonarto was alone; his face was flushed and sweaty, and it was obvious to Guillaime that he had been drinking. Brother Francis was accompanied by King

Richard himself; and worse, from Guillaime's point of view, by Alice.

"Now," King Tancred said. "I have summoned you –" he looked around at all of them, "– and requested your presence –" he nodded to King Richard, "– because of some information that has come into my hands. Information that may have the direst consequences."

Sir Leonarto relaxed visibly as King Tancred's translator put the words into French.

"Boy!" King Tancred said, "Tell them what you told me."

"Your Majesty," Guillaime said. His tongue felt swollen in his mouth, and he was desperately dry. Nevertheless, he managed to explain what he'd found. The drawings were produced and placed on a low table.

The courtiers watched King Richard and Brother Francis; but Guillaime's gaze never left Sir Leonarto. He went pale. His hand crept up to his face, and then away again, when he realised that Guillaime was watching him.

"So," Guillaime finished. "It seems to me that someone must have purchased the sword from the artisan Edmund."

"This is preposterous," Brother Francis said in heavily accented Spanish.

King Richard slammed his fist down on the table so hard the wine goblets jumped. He shouted something incoherent in English. His translator looked embarrassed, and then muttered, "By Our Lady, monk, you will give an accounting of yourself or I'll have your balls for breakfast."

Brother Francis said something in English. The translator started to repeat it in Spanish, but King Tancred snapped at the monk, "In Spanish, monk, since you speak it so well."

King Richard looked affronted, but nodded agreement with bad grace.

Brother Francis started again. "The sword . . . it is true, the sword came from the swordmaker Edmund. But that is not to say he made it." He pushed back the cowl of his robe, revealing a bony face much worn by time and hard living. "On my life, I swear it, Sire." He bowed to King Richard, who stared grimly back. "I said that I was a monk from Glastonbury, but that is not entirely true –"

"Is any of it?" King Richard demanded. "On your life, as you have said –"

"Father!" Alice said.

Brother Francis jerked round. "Shut up," he snapped. He turned back. King Tancred glared at him. "She was an error I made before I entered Holy Orders, Sire," he said to King Richard, who regarded him stonily.

An error, Guillaime thought. He wanted to hit the man.

"I was a soldier then. A mercenary, and rough in my ways. I did not wish to dishon –"

"The sword," King Richard said.

"It was found at Glastonbury –" He looked from one king to the other. "But not – not the way I said before, when the brothers there unearthed the body of King Arthur and the noble Guinevere." Again, he paused. Fear? Guillaime wondered. Or working out a new lie? "I found it myself, when I was new to the order. My old comrade Edmund had come to visit me – to try and persuade me to leave before I took final vows. We walked by the marshes at Glastonbury, one early morning, with the crimson sun low in the sky and the mist coming off the water –"

"Get on with it," King Tancred snarled.

"I swear," Brother Francis said. "We found the sword that morning – all wrapped in oilskins, in the shallows of the marsh. We unwrapped it, him and me. A thing of such unearthly beauty that we thought sure some fey had made it –"

"And that was all there was – the sword?" King Tancred asked. Brother Francis looked from one man to the other, wary as a beast at bay. And Guillaime saw – and thought he was the only one to see – that Sir Leonarto looked just as hunted.

"It had a scabbard," Brother Francis said. "But water had warped the wood and rotted the leather." His hands twisted in front of him.

There was silence. At last King Tancred said, "And nothing else – no jewels, no regalia?"

Brother Francis stared at him for a long moment. "There were jewels, my Lord. Rare jewels. But they were of no importance next to the sword."

"It's not your place to decide what's important, dog," King Richard roared.

King Tancred waved him to silence. "Ah," he said. "The sword. Yes. Do tell us what became of it."

"I would have given it to his holiness the Abbot," Brother Francis said. "I would. But Edmund said it wasn't mine to give. He wanted to sell it off – the jewels, the sword." He almost stumbled then. Guillaime wondered if he would have noticed, had he not known the man was lying. "I would not agree. But I gave it to him rather than argue. I had had enough of the quarrels of the world –"

He stared around at them, as if daring them to disagree with him.

"You let some gutterscum take King Arthur's sword out of England?" King Richard was puce with rage. He crossed the room in two strides and backhanded Brother Francis so hard that he fell to the floor. A thin trickle of blood dripped from his lip.

"I did not know, Sire. Not till he wrote to me –"

"These jewels," King Tancred went on, as calmly as if nothing had happened. "Did they look, perhaps, something like this?" He pulled out one of the drawings and held it up.

"Perhaps, Your Majesty," Brother Francis muttered.

"But the sword's hilt, you would agree, looked like this?" The king produced one of the hilt drawings.

"Yes." There was terror in the monk's eyes now. He scrambled to his feet. He stared around, as if looking for somewhere to run.

"My advisors – scholarly men, have no doubt – say that these drawings are in the style of the northern barbarians of centuries long past."

King Tancred smiled. "Are you really saying that your marvellous King Arthur would have used a sword made by such as those?"

"It came from water and went to water," King Richard rumbled.

"Yes," Brother Francis said. "And think – even such a sword must have been made somewhere, by someone. Why not the northern-men –"

"And not some fey?" King Tancred's tone was mild, but his eyes were hard and dangerous. Before Brother Francis could reply, he went on. "Well, perhaps it matters less than I thought. After all, you do say that the sword is unique?"

For a moment, Guillaime thought the monk would crumble. But somehow he held his courage together. "It is my Lord – as far as I know."

"Did you know that Edmund had been selling off the jewellery – after first copying it, in order to bolster his own inferior artistry?" King Tancred asked. He sounded very sure of himself, though Guillaime knew there was no way to be certain that was what had happened.

"He might, my Lord," Brother Francis said. He shot an anguished look at the door, but there were guards either side of it. "He saw everything we found as a way to get money, nothing more."

"Well he did. But he could not sell the sword – it was too distinctive. So when you came and offered him money for it, he was glad of it, yes?"

"Yes," Brother Francis said. "But I swear it is Excalibur. On my honour –"

"What honour?" King Richard demanded. But no-one looked at him.

"So – it is Excalibur, and it is unique," King Tancred said. Brother Francis nodded. The colour had gone from his face, and his hands worked at his sides. 'Then you can offer no explanation for this?" King Tancred held the second drawing up beside the first.

For a moment Guillaime thought the monk would break. But he said nothing, merely shook his head.

"If there are two drawings," King Tancred said, "is it not likely there are two swords? And if there are two swords, neither is unique – and neither one is Excalibur. Is that not so?" He advanced on Brother Francis, who held his ground for one pace. Two. And then backed away.

"And that is why you murdered this friend of yours – this Edmund. Because with him dead, there would be no-one to tell the tale of how you really came by this heathen sword, and its mate. A pity for you that you did not find the drawings."

"Murdered?" Brother Francis whispered. "He was my friend. We fought together. I would not – you cannot think that I would –"

"Oh but I do," King Tancred said. "And I demand satisfaction – he may have started his life an Englishman, but he died a townsman of Palermo, and under my protection."

"This is nothing," King Richard said. "A matter of a slum-dwelling drunkard, Tancred. Nothing at all –"

"Then say I will have satisfaction for the shame and embarrassment your man has brought me – coming here, swearing he has this sword of legends. Has he not shamed you? Are you not foresworn because of him?"

King Richard, already flushed, drew in a deep breath. "Aye, there's that. What would you do with him?"

"Why," said King Tancred, "I'll do nothing at all – we'll let God and his angels sort the sinners from the righteous. Trial by combat.

Since he would live by that sword, let him see if he *can* live by it."

King Richard scowled for half a heartbeat. Then the humour of it seemed to catch him, and he laughed uproariously. King Tancred waited for him to finish, then drew the sword he had been given. Light blazed around it, as it had before. He handed it hilt first to Brother Francis.

"Come on you – monk or soldier or whatever you are. Let's see what you're made of."

Brother Francis took the sword. He wielded it easily, and even through the bulk of his habit it was clear that he had a good stance – a soldier's stance.

"So, Tancred – who's your champion?" Richard asked.

King Tancred glanced round at the assembly. His gaze rested on Sir Leonarto. "You'll do," he said. "Come, draw your sword and prepare to fight for your king."

"Sire, I am honoured," Sir Leonarto said. He licked his lips. "But I am ill prepared. Another would suit you better –"

"But I don't want another, good Leonarto – I want you." King Tancred sounded completely reasonable, but Guillaime knew how fast that could change.

"But Sire, I fear I will not serve you well – I'm afraid I'm indisposed. It shames me to admit it, but I've been drinking this morning, and –"

"But this is Trial by Combat," King Tancred said. "With right on your side, you cannot fail, for God in his mercy and all his angels fight on your side."

"Yes, Sire." Sir Leonarto was shaking. "But I would not disgrace you in front of your guests, my Liege –"

"Come now, my good knight – only your reticence disgraces me. Draw your sword and have at my enemy!"

Sir Leonarto drew a long, hard breath. For a moment, Guillaime thought he would faint. But he raised his gaze to the ceiling, as if in prayer, and then he threw back his cloak and drew his sword. Light ran down it like liquid fire, shattering into a thousand points of scintillating brilliance.

"By our Lady, what is this?" King Richard shouted. "If you're trying some trickery, Tancred, I swear all of Sicily will pay –"

"Explain, boy!" King Tancred said. He pushed Guillaime roughly into the middle of the room.

"I looked through his –" he turned to Brother Francis. "Forgive me. I looked through your things and found a letter with Edmund's name on it. When I went there, I found him hanging. I thought at first he had committed suicide –" And he went on to explain how he had changed his mind about that, and how, when he had returned home, he had found Sir Leonarto's room ransacked and his sword cast aside. "And," he finished, "it was then that I remembered seeing him this morning, wearing a heavy cloak. What for, if not to disguise the sword he was wearing – a sword not his own? And he had called me out on an errand, so that I could see he had been with his mistress all morning." He licked his lips. "Hard at it, they had been. Or so I supposed, from the marks on his body. But they might have been marks from a fight –"

"The boy is touched by spirits," Sir Leonarto snarled. "The devil speaks through his mouth."

King Tancred motioned to Guillaime to continue. "And when I thought of that, I realised where I had seen the likes of the jewellery Edmund made before – round the neck of Marie Josepha, my master's mistress before this one."

"This is ludicrous!" Sir Leonarto snarled. "What would I have to gain from killing a peasant like this Edmund? I beg you, my Liege, do not listen to this young –"

"Silence," King Tancred said. "Well, boy?"

"I believe he knew of the swords – perhaps he saw them when he went to buy jewellery before. And I believe he was blackmailing Brother Francis, with his knowledge – and that it was Brother Francis who searched his room, hoping to find the second sword, and thus save himself."

"No!" The word seemed to be torn out of Sir Leonarto. King Tancred advanced upon him, and Leonardo shrank with every step.

"Will you lie to me? You are sworn to loyalty, remember. And so I ask you: did you kill the peasant?"

For one long moment Sir Leonarto held the king's gaze. Then he looked away.

"Yes," he said. "But not for any base reason. I had discovered their plan some days ago, and I knew it would be an affront to your Majesty. I knew that Edmund had a second blade, and so I commissioned him to make a second hilt. Just a hilt. I thought if I produced it at the right moment, it would discredit them . . . the

English. But then I saw them watching me. Always watching, and so I thought they knew what I had done. I killed him – but only so no-one would know how I had tried to save –"

"You killed him. And not for any good reason – there's no good in you," Brother Francis said. "I attest you were blackmailing me, as your boy said –"

"So you lied to me?" King Richard shouted. "You let me make oaths based on a lie –"

"No!" Sir Leonarto said. "The sword may very well be Excalibur. Whatever he says, there was only the one like it. The other's a forgery –"

"Enough!" King Tancred said. "There's no telling where the truth is, or who lies. So we'll let God decide – and if the pair of you won't fight, I'll have you both executed." He turned to King Richard, who nodded his assent.

And so the assembly moved from the chamber to the inner courtyard. The courtyard was surrounded by high walls in one of which was an ornate window. Guillaime looked through to the sea boiling for frothing at the bottom of the steep cliffs. The sun was starting to set, casting a ruddy glow over the company.

Guillaime found a place against the wall. It was only as King Tancred's marshall dropped his kerchief that he realised how close Alice was. Even as he watched, her hand crept up to cover her mouth. He slipped a little closer. "Courage," he whispered, as Sir Leonarto and Brother Francis circled each other.

Slowly they moved. Slowly. Weighing each other up, weak points and strong.

"Get it over with," Alice muttered.

For the first time, Guillaime wondered how long it had been since Brother Francis had been a soldier – or even if he'd ever taken vows at all. He broke first. He feinted forward, then lunged in low and hard. He had the reach, but Sir Leonarto was too fast for him. Metal clashed on metal. Guillaime could hardly bear to watch. Afterwards, what he remembered were those two perfect blades, dancing in the heavy air like wands of burning silver – slash and parry and feint and chop, neither man gaining an inch of advantage.

Come on, Guillaime thought. Come on! But he didn't know whether he wanted Sir Leonarto to win or not, any more. If he died, Guillaime would be free to seek another –

Brother Francis pressed the attack, using his longer reach to push through Sir Leonarto's defence. There was a flurry of blows too fast for Guillaime to follow. Sir Leonarto backed off, defending all the while. Then he rallied. He pressed forward, and now Brother Francis seemed to be tiring. Feinted high, and came in low, under the monk's guard. Metal hissed on cloth. Brother Francis grunted. Blood spurted out, turning Sir Leonarto's blade to ruby. Brother Francis staggered forward, sword held high and awkward. Guillaime realised that Alice was weeping. He turned to her. Movement caught at his eye. He turned back – Sir Leonarto, walking toward King Richard, stumbled on a patch of blood. He went down. Brother Francis, holding his arm across his body as if to hold himself together, fell on him.

There was a scream.

And then silence.

For a moment, no-one moved. Then two of King Tancred's soldiers rushed forward. They pulled Brother Francis' body off Sir Leonarto. There was a great bloody gash across his back. The two swords, indistinguishable one from the other, lay crossed on the floor.

"Will he live?" Guillaime asked, knowing already that it was a futile question.

"Don't be a fool, boy," King Tancred said. "But you've done well. We will see you find a better master."

"Thank you, Sire," Guillaime answered, barely able to get the words out.

But already King Tancred had turned and was walking away. "Get this trash out of here," he commanded.

"What of the swords, Sire?" a voice asked. Guillaime was appalled to realise it was his own.

"What of them?" King Tancred said. But he paused, then went to them. He held them up. The setting sun turned the bloody steel to ruby.

"Your great gift, Richard," he said at last. "We will show you what we think of your poisoned English generosity." And he went to the great window. "Here's one," he said, and before anyone could stop him he cast the sword into the sea. "And here's the other."

King Richard darted towards Tancred as the king readied to throw the second sword over the cliff.

"You're crazy, man," King Richard shouted. "What if one of them was Excalibur? A king's ransom –"

"Who's to say?" King Tancred looked old, suddenly. He stared at the sword still in his grasp. "Is this the real Excalibur, or was the other?"

For a moment the world stood still as all eyes fixed on the remaining blade. Was this the blade that the Lady of the Lake had given to King Arthur all those centuries ago – the blade with which Arthur defeated the invaders of Britain?

As they stared and wondered, so King Tancred let go his grasp and the sword spiralled out of sight. There was an audible intake of breath from those in the courtyard. Tancred looked steadily around at them.

"Who's to say?" he repeated. "If it was, it's gone back to the water whence it came. But if wasn't, then what difference does it make?"

And they left then, both the kings and their courtiers. Guillaime remained, with Alice weeping beside him. He crossed to the archway, and looked down at the sea, crashing endlessly against the rocks below.

What difference does it make, he thought, if Sir Leonarto killed for greed or to preserve his king's honour? Edmund still died, and Alice still weeps. And I am still here to comfort her. And with that he had to be content.

John 🍂

TO WHOM THE VICTORY?

Mary Monica Pulver

It is perhaps a little unfair that John is remembered as one of England's worst kings whilst his brother, Richard the Lionheart, is held as a national hero. Unlike Richard, John liked England and many of the people liked him, since he had a keen mind for legal administration and often dealt fairly with the cases brought before him. However, he had little time for the Church or his barons, and often annoyed them with his impropriety and disdain for protocol. It was his constant disregard for his barons' counsel and authority that caused them to rise up against him and force him to sign the Magna Carta in 1215 recognizing their rights. Even then John ignored the charter and suddenly found himself in the midst of a Civil War with the French Dauphin invited to England to take over the kingship. In the midst of this crisis John died suddenly, apparently of over-indulgence in an extensive repast. Was that the case, or might there be another story?

I am to have a visitor! I have not been allowed visitors since my husband ordered me confined. I do not even have time to put on a better kirtle or cover my hair, since he is upon the stair even now.

The visitor is a stranger to me. He is tall and thin, with dark hair and an ugly parrot's beak for a nose. His clothing is fine but covered with the dust and dirt of travel. He has not taken the time to wash his hands and face, how discourteous! Unless the news is so important – He is weary, almost staggering with weariness. He goes to one knee, most humbly, a wonder to me, for no one has treated me as my rank deserves for a long time.

"Majesty, I bring important news."

Majesty! Better and better. "What is the news? Has my husband relented? Am I to be set free?"

His head comes up and his dark eyes search my face. "Majesty, your husband is dead."

Something long confined in my heart breaks loose and I burst into tears. My chamberlain makes a sympathetic noise, which nearly stops my weeping – he is become a cruel jailer, not a servant – but I allow the tears to flow a bit longer, then wipe my face with my hands.

"Did – did he die bravely in battle?"

That was a mistake, I know it as soon as I say the word "bravely". John Softsword they call him, and most aptly.

"Nay, Majesty, he died in his bed after a sudden illness." By his reaction he knows that I have misspoken. This will not do, I need time to gather my wits.

I renew my tears, but manage through them to say to my chamberlain, "Take this man away and find him some warm water and a change of clothing. Then bring him –" I am free now, my heart says, and I divert my words in mid-course. "Bring him to the hall, where you will meanwhile build up the fire. And have the kitchen supply us with the best of our poor wine, and wafers if they are fresh, and whatever fruit there is. I will talk further with him when he is rested, and when I can control the reaction of my heart to this news."

My chamberlain bows and says, "As you wish, Madam," as if he has always met my wishes with these words and gesture, as if I frequent the hall of this castle, as if visitors are an everyday occurrence. Better and better!

John is dead, my husband is dead, the King of England is dead. He was a cruel and evil man and is doubtless discovering that his disbelief in the afterlife was a serious mistake. May he roast on a gridiron for eternity, his fat dripping into the flames and making a smoke to stink up all of hell!

Everyone departs but the half-wit they allow me as a personal servant. "Open my chest," I say and she obeys. My son Henry is now to be king, and as the king's mother, I shall once again have a say in the ruling of this country – and Aquitaine and Anjou and Normandy and my beloved native Poitou, which I may visit soon – Oh, la Rochelle and your delicious oysters! But careful, only if I am careful. Doubtless this messenger will report to those who sent him all I say and do. If I appear silly and dissolve constantly in tears, they will dismiss me as a mere female and set me aside. I must appear wise and capable.

At the bottom of the chest I find my finest garment, a deep blue kirtle that covers my feet even when I sit. Gold embroidered roundels set in bands of green mark the breast, hips, thighs, knees, and ankles of the gown, and again around the wrists of the close-fitting sleeves. A white silk wimple and veil cover my throat and hair. Two years of captivity have not put a gray hair on my head, though I am again of slender build. But the messenger has already seen that, so what does it matter if the kirtle was made when I was well-fed? Still, I cinch the waist firmly, and I put rings on all my fingers and put a broad golden collar set with five sapphires around my neck. A very full and flowing woolen cloak in a deep wine color, with five bands of fur, will help keep the October chill away; it would not do for him to see me shiver and think I am fearful. I hold my head very high and turn to look at my maid, by whose awe-struck face I am satisfied I look every inch a queen. Too bad John took the royal crowns with him; nothing like the Crown of England on one's head to complete the image and give one confidence.

John is dead, and I am free. I hide my face in the cloak and laugh aloud, then wipe my face as if to dry tears. My husband's death shakes the Kingdom; for that reason alone, we must not be merry too soon.

Within an hour I am sitting on what was once my husband's chair – how a different chair refreshes one's flesh! – and there is an extravagantly large fire leaping on the center hearth, its smoke rising as if on swift wings toward the louvers in the ceiling. I am glad I thought to order a brazier of charcoal in addition, for the lofty stone hall is cold. But what can one expect? It is nearly All Hallows and this is England.

I have not seen the hall for a long while, and it is equally refreshing

to the eyes to have a different interior to look at. The room in which I
gave birth to Joan was not a dungeon, but it was nearly as confining
to one used to constant travel. I remember when my husband's
mother was let out of her captivity and how she went about the
Kingdom releasing prisoners, saying she knew how marvelous it was
to be released from confinement. I didn't understand that story when
I first heard it, but now I think I shall do the same.

Half of my servants were in my husband's pay to spy on me and
treat me rudely, and the other half were in the pay of his enemies. But
now he is dead, and both kinds hasten to show me they are once
again all mine. Yet I will not smile on them, not until some things are
settled. For example the bowl of fruit on the table. It is very fine fruit,
apples and pears of the best quality. I was not served such fruit while
up in that little room, yet here it is, produced immediately for a
visitor. That means it has been here all the while. Whose money paid
for it? Mine. And who got the joy of it? The man who brought it saw
his error the instant my eyes lit on the bowl; he scuttled out and is
doubtless gathering his belongings in preparation for leaving by the
postern gate. I wonder how many servants I shall have in the
morning? Shall I seek out those who abandon me?

But this is not the time to consider that problem; for the messenger
is coming in. And again he kneels most humbly.

"Rise, sir," I say. "What is your name?" He looks nearly
presentable now, in a grey mid-calf tunic deeply dagged. By its
excellent fit, it is probably his own. But I still find his nose ugly.

"I am Saveric de Mauleon. I am a poet late in the court of His
Majesty, and a sometime adviser as well."

"Adviser?" I look at him askance. John was known to take advice
mostly from the wickedest knaves he could find, and was not a man
to think makers of music or poetry had anything of real value to say
to him.

He reads all this in my face and voice and gives a very charming
chuckle. "On occasion, he would listen to me. I recall last year, on St
Andrew's Day, at the siege of Rochester Castle. The castle had
surrendered and John, in his glee, proposed to hang everyone he
found inside. But I pointed out that one day his fortunes might be
reversed, and how would he like to be treated if he were taken from a
captured castle? Rather to my surprise he listened to me –" He stops,
remembering to whom he is telling this little tale.

I smile to show I am not offended. "He was not a good man," I murmur.

"And who might know that better than you?" he says with what seems real understanding.

But my confinement has taught me to be wary. "Yet he had his good qualities," I say.

De Mauleon nods. "He was fond of sitting as judge in his court, and often his judgment was clever or even wise. Better the law than the sword to settle disputes."

"Yes." But John would rather anything than the sword. He was quick enough to murder women, children, and priests, but he would sooner make an ill-considered treaty with an armed enemy than fight him. I lift my chin and wait, giving de Mauleon a chance to say these things, and when he does not, neither do I.

"Please," I say, "take and eat, pour the wine."

He bows and goes to the table. "May I fill a goblet for you?" he asks.

"Yes, thank you." The wine, not now to my surprise, is excellent. John loved good wine and good food, and would sometimes steal it when he could not buy it honestly. I once thought that very amusing, to see how a host would honor us with a particularly fine wine or delicacy – and John would empty our host's cellar or pantry and leave nothing but a promise of payment that was never kept. I was an honest child; I think it amused John to corrupt me. But I learned many things from others as well; John would be surprised at me now. Perhaps he is; I don't know what interest the dead take in the living.

A little silence falls, during which de Mauleon cuts an apple into quarters and eats the pieces with a swift, neat efficiency, taking occasional sips of his wine. I choose not to eat anything, though the wafers look delicious. John was very greedy, I do not want this man to think I picked up that trait from my husband, for then he might wonder what even uglier ones I have learned from him.

"About your husband, Madam," he says when the last bite of apple was devoured and the seeds tossed into the fire.

"Yes?"

"There are those who think his death . . . unnatural."

My eyebrows lift high. "In what way, unnatural?"

"He was taken ill very suddenly, after a long period of robust health."

I can't hide a smile. "Most people are."

"I mean to say, he was not an old man, going slowly down the road to the grave."

"That is a road we are all travelling, sir. Besides, none in his family make old bones. His father died of a sudden fever, and so did two of his brothers. Why, Geoffrey and Henry were not yet thirty when they died. John was forty-eight. His brother Richard died when a simple neck wound festered, but you see by that example that it is in their blood to succumb easily once they fall ill."

"Then perhaps what is in his blood is contagious, as a good and holy monk who shared King John's last meal also fell ill of a fever and died in much the same manner as he did."

Much startled, I cross myself. "A monk? The same way, you say?"

"Very much the same. But your husband lingered for six days, while the monk was gone in three."

"God rest his soul." De Mauleon seems to expect more of me, so think, think! I say, "But how odd that a monk should come to share a meal with my husband. He was not overfond of the company of clergy."

"Indeed, Madam, this is very true. Yet he was much in the company of monks in his last days. May I tell you how that came about?"

I nod permission.

"As possibly you know, he had been meeting with wonderful military success of late. This was, of course, mostly because the rebellious barons regret their invitation to Prince Louis of France to take the throne of England. Louis is a thorough Frenchman, so naturally he is replacing English officials with Frenchmen. This was not taken in good part by his English hosts, some of whom began recalling their oaths of fealty to the true king. His Majesty broke the siege of Lincoln castle by the very news of his approach. From there he went to Grimsby and Boston, then through Spalding to King's Lynn, where bells were rung and a large procession gave him a most joyous welcome. But it was October 12 that his sorrow began. He left Wisbech in the morning to cross the River Welland. Impatient to continue his victorious path, he did not wait for the tidal ebb to complete itself, but insisted we should cross at once. There are quicksands there, and of a sudden a horse vanished as if the earth opened and swallowed it. An entire wagon followed and before we realized it, all the wagons began to sink. Three men dived after a horse carrying armor and all of them were caught in a swirl of water and mud. A man riding to help them was taken before our eyes. I cannot tell you what a struggle it was for all of us, including His Majesty. All his sumpter horses and the wagons carrying the royal treasure, his arms and armor, the equipment for an encampment, and the royal crowns and scepters were lost. Most of the men escaped, but it was a near thing for many. His Majesty was sick with rage and regret."

"Lost?" I find I am standing with no memory of rising. "All, lost?"

"But few men were caught, it was mostly the wagons and horses."

"The crown jewels? The royal treasure?"

"All gone, I am afraid."

"Surely there are men who are good swimmers, who for a price –"

"No, Majesty; any attempt to recover the treasure would only result in more men dying."

I force myself to sit. "This is most dreadful news! When our enemies hear of this, that we are helpless to defend against an attack –."

He raises a hand, and says, "Not at all, madam."

"Not? Please explain."

"The rebellion was against your husband, who is dead. Even as he died, forty rebel lords were waiting to renew their oaths of fealty to him. With him gone, they are left with Louis, who is in his way worse than John. Yet there is another choice . . ." He looks at me to guess who that might be.

I feel like a very apt pupil. "Why my son Henry, of course!"

De Mauleon smiles. "His highness is a sturdy, lively boy, intelligent and handsome, well grown for his age, with every prospect of growing to adulthood and restoring the good name of his family." I smile as any mother would to hear such praise of my oldest, my firstborn, the pride of my life.

"We will have a crown made for him –" begins de Mauleon.

"No, no," I interrupt. "I believe you are right, the rebellion will collapse once they have a better prospect than a cold French toad. But we must give them that king at once, while they are still confused. Here." I unfasten the collar and stand it upright on my head. "See? It is nearly big enough for me, and so will do nicely as a crown for a boy. Use this and we may have him crowned immediately. You must tell . . . Who?"

I am trying to think which loyal bishop might be nearest to do the coronation, but de Mauleon says, "William Marshall or Peter des Roches, they are the two to whom your husband left the care of your son. You are correct, and such a good idea has probably already occurred to them."

"But I am his mother! And the queen! Surely I –"

"You are dowager queen, Majesty," he amends, in a respectful voice that nevertheless diminishes me just a little. "But may I continue with the story I was telling?"

I must not rage, that would be as bad as tears. "Of course." I resume my seat and even take a little drink of the wine.

"We traveled with His Majesty to Swineshead, to the Cistercian abbey there, arriving near nightfall. He was in such a state that he had not eaten anything at all that day. We were shown to the guesthouse and were preparing for sleep when a monk brought in a large bowl of peaches, each one more beautiful than its brother, and a pitcher of new cider. There were not enough for all of us, so of course they were offered to His Majesty. And the King was so struck by them that his appetite returned. He picked up the largest, made as if to bite it, then stopped and turned to the monk, a young fellow with a good face.

" 'Here,' said the king with a sly smile, for he was ever a suspicious man, 'I would share these with the bringer of such a gift.' The monk took the peach gratefully – these Cistercians eat like paupers; it must have been a rare treat to have a peach all to himself – and took a bite. The fragrant juice fairly flowed across his fingers and dripped on the floor. His Majesty watched him closely, until the monk was halfway through his peach, before His Majesty selected another. After one bite he picked up the bowl and took it to a corner of the room to indicate he was not sharing this treasure any further. And indeed, he ate every one of the remaining peaches, even sucking the stones to get every delicious morsel. He had the monk drink half a goblet of cider before he drank the rest himself, and then went to bed, his good humor restored.

"He woke in the night with a pain in his head and bowels and said he should not have indulged in so much fruit on an empty stomach. By morning he was worse, with flux and vomiting and even greater pain. But he was determined to leave, and we rode to Sleaford, where he was in such a state that a surgeon was summoned to bleed him.

Still ill and now very weak, he nevertheless insisted on continuing his journey, and we rode to Newark on the 16th, where at last even he could see that not only was this journey at an end, so was the journey of his life.

"We carried him to the abbey of Croxton, where he confessed his sins to the abbot, received the last sacraments, and made everyone with him swear fealty to his son. He commended his soul to God and his body to St. Wulfstan. They dressed him in a red cloak, put silver spurs on his feet and a naked sword in his hand, and then a monk's cowl over his head. When I left, they were making arrangements to take him to Worcester, where he will be buried next to the shrine of St Wulfstan."

There is a silence in the room. Sauric de Mauleon is a talented story-teller, his beautiful voice adding to the spell he winds with his words.

"That was well told," I say. "But it does not convince me that there was something unnatural about his death. Getting wet and angry on a cold October day, then riding all day without food, then indulging one's greed for ripe peaches and new cider just before sleeping is a combination to make the most robust man ill indeed."

"But the monk is dead, too, and he was warm, dry, and rested. His symptoms were identical."

I put my hand to my forehead; perhaps I will need to have a headache of my own. "If it is a coincidence, it is a very peculiar one."

"And if it is not, do you not wonder who the murderer is?"

"Why, is someone charged with his murder?" I ask sharply.

"No, not yet. The first question in such a matter is, who might have wished him dead?"

I laugh, I cannot help it. I have often been told it is unseemly for a woman to laugh aloud, but de Mauleon's question must be a jest, and John once told me it was my bold laughter that first made him love me.

But now I see by this man's face that he is not jesting. I wonder if he is not quick-witted after all.

I explain, "It might be simpler to name those who did not wish my husband dead than to try to list all those who did. Begin with Robert FitzWalter, Lord of Dunmow, who is the leader of the rebellion, and go on to the other barons who follow and encourage it. Do not forget the Bishop of London and the other clergy who defied even the Pope to continue in support of those working for my husband's fall. And what of the king of France and his son, who contrived daily to harm my husband?"

"And what of the remaining relatives of Maud de Braose and her son William, whom John walled up in their own home and starved to death?" De Mauleon says as if agreeing heartily with me; but there is a sardonic glint in his eye. "And other women of both noble and mean blood subjected to treatment that left them shamed?"

The silence now is like the wait between lightning and thunder. What can I say? My throat is closed.

De Mauleon says, very gently, "And what of Hugh le Brun, Count of Marche in Poitou? He had an agreement with your father, that you were to marry him. You were formally betrothed, weren't you? And sent to live with his family in Lusignan until you were old enough for the marriage to take place. Though you were just a child, I think Hugh was in love with you – you were a very beautiful child, as you are now a beautiful woman. Hugh has never forgiven John for stealing you from him, and has never ceased to do all he can to bring trouble to your husband, whether by his own deeds or by inciting others."

"I know not what is in Hugh le Brun's mind. I have had no direct contact with him since I left Poitou to marry King John."

"Common talk is that he hated your husband because you were taken from him by a ruse."

"That may be. I know my father told me my brother was ill and we were to go see him. But we never did; instead I was given into the custody of the king." I remember that day, how strangely my father behaved! Full of nervous smiles and constant little pats meant to reassure. And how John kept staring at me, as if I were a delicious meal and he was famished. Hugh never looked at me like that. But Hugh was kind and noble. For all he was a king, there was often little of the noble in John.

I hear a sound as of a throat clearing and am recalled to the present. De Mauleon speaks gently. "While it is a great and honorable thing to be a queen of the most powerful kingdom in Europe, do you not sometimes think you might have been happier to be merely the Countess of Marche?"

I lift my head proudly. "My husband made me Countess of Angoulême in my own right." My father was Count of Angoulême, and so was my brother until he died; it is an old, proud title. My words come with an effort I hope does not show on my face, for de Mauleon must not know that I agree with him. I add, with a little less effort, "I believe God gave me to John for the good of his soul, and the greatness of our son as King Henry the Third will prove it."

De Mauleon bows – to hide the doubt on his face? When he straightens, there is nothing in its expression to read. "I pray daily that that might be true, Majesty." He rises and goes to refill his goblet. He raises an eyebrow in query but I shake my head. He is a very strange man, in turn humble and forward, and until I understand him better I must not fuddle my wits with drink.

A thought strikes me. "If you are looking for someone to accuse of poisoning my husband, look among those men who had come to renew their fealty to the king! The barons of England play turn and turn about with their loyalties, for they are true only to themselves. An oath here, a pledge there, broken as quickly as it was made, that is the way of the world. My husband was known to be a glutton; a quick way to regain his favor was to bring him something delicious to eat or drink. And if the friend were false, how easy it might be to introduce a subtle poison to the gift."

"That is indeed deserving of consideration," he says, sipping his wine. "Your husband had two kinds of enemy. One took action with sword and lance, trying to remove what they consider a menace and disgrace to the kingdom. It might be thought that a man of this sort would strike a blow with the weapons he knew best. The second kind has no ability with weapons, and is thought helpless to exact revenge. I speak of women and children."

"Women and children are at the mercy of men," I say with a nod. "That is why the majority of the souls in hell belong to men, for they often fail in their responsibilities toward the weak. And, of course, why the holiest saints are likewise male, for they have to struggle harder to overcome their nature, and grow even stronger in winning that struggle. Woman is the weaker vessel, their salvation is the responsibility of man." This is, of course, merely conventional wisdom. I myself do not believe it. I think women must make their own salvation, for in heaven there is neither male nor female.

"So it seems even more a shame, what your husband did to those helpless to defend themselves."

"Do you expect me to defend my husband in this regard? He was as cruel to me, a woman, as to any of the others. Would you speak kindly of him yourself?"

"I loyally served my lord, your late husband, and now serve Lords William Marshall and Peter des Roches, protectors of your son, Prince Henry, who will be King Henry the Third."

He speaks with such authority! "In what capacity do you serve these protectors?"

"Madam, to be of any value as a poet, I must be one who sees things as they really are. I am here to tell you what really happened to your husband, and also to look about me, and see if perhaps there is more to his death than first appears. I have often performed this service for His Majesty, though he did not always believe what I told him."

"I don't understand. You are acting as a sort of justiciar?"

"If you like. Except, of course, I cannot enforce any judgements I might make. I can only report on them. In this case, I am trying to discern the truth about the death of the King."

"What do you think the truth is?"

"I think, Madam, you are, at least in part, responsible for his death."

I cannot breathe, I feel my cheeks grow hot. "How dare you say such a thing to me! You forget who you are – and who I am!" I look around for the biggest knave in the room. I will have this man flogged –!

"Majesty, Majesty, please!" He is on both knees, hands upraised. "I but answered your question. I was sent to ask questions, and am ordered to come back with answers. William Marshall is the most honorable man in the kingdom; he wants your son to be King; he would not dishonor your son's mother."

I catch hold of my temper. The silence in the room is very deep, one would think the very stones are listening. I must be very careful. "Then rise, sir, and tell how you think it possible that I am responsible for my husband's death. He has not come here, nor have I written to him for nearly a year. If someone administered poison to him, it was one of his knights or soldiers, someone near him on the day he fell ill, surely."

"Madam, remember what I said about the first kind of enemy, the man who normally fights with sword or lance. The one who poisoned your husband is one who cannot wield a weapon, one who is not a knight or a soldier. In other words, the monk who died."

"Fool, no one who put poison in food would eat it himself."

"If the monk had not first tasted the peaches, the King would not have eaten them. And this monk was determined to kill the King, so determined, he was willing to die himself to accomplish that end. I have discovered this monk had a private audience with the abbot, and went from that to the kitchen, where he prepared the dish and brought it to His Majesty. The peaches were taken from a large basket of them gathered that day, and others were eaten the next day with no harm. The cider was drawn from a barrel that others drank from, with no harm. The poison was in the cider or on the peaches brought to His Majesty. No one else handled the food or drink. The abbot will not say what the monk told him, invoking the privacy of the confessional. Yet the monk was shrived again before he died. What did he do between those two shrivings that necessitated the second one?"

My opinion of de Mauleon's cleverness rises again. "Do you know anything else about this monk? Who is he?"

"He was a de Vere, whose uncle is the third Earl of Oxford and one of the rebel barons. His great-aunt was Juliana, mother of Roger Bigod's wife. And Roger Bigod is another of the rebel barons, whose holdings are in Norfolk. Neither baron was among the forty rueful ones waiting to see your husband."

"That is very interesting, and possibly a true explanation. But I still fail to see how you think I am connected with any of this. Today is the first time I have been out of that room you found me in since the Feastday of St Nicholas two years gone!"

"You have always maintained a voluminous correspondence, even before your confinement."

"But I never wrote to a monk at Swineshead." I smile – then frown at him. "And how do you know about the Queen's correspondence?"

"When men go to war, there is a great deal of marching and even more waiting between battles. They talk, they write their own letters, and read and share information, rumor, and gossip. Your husband was, naturally, the subject of much speculation. Men whose wives have written you hear from those wives of your reply."

"I see. Very well, I have been closely confined, so I sought however I could to maintain contact with friends. What of it?"

"Indeed, what? Madam, in your correspondence, have you written to Amicia, the wife of Richard, Earl of Clare?"

"Yes – and I am aware her husband is of the enemy's camp, but she and I were friends before the rebellion, and anyway, he is in London while she stays at home. As is the case with most wives, of course. Not all of us could be Queen Eleanor."

"Of course. She is, I believe, in her manor house not far from here."

"Yes. It is a shame I have been forbidden visitors, because for her it would be a very short ride."

"But I believe that Amicia had reason to hate your husband."

"Why, pray, would Amicia hate my husband?"

"Your husband raped her."

I can only stare coldly at him. "My husband cut a wide swath among the noble and gentle women of England, sir. But 'rape' is too ugly a word to describe what he called seductions."

"Amicia called it rape when I spoke with her earlier today."

"Amicia must be a depraved woman to speak with other than her husband or a priest of such a thing."

"Then you believe her accusation to be false?"

"I would not contradict the word of a duchess without more knowledge of the facts."

"Amicia says that most of your husband's so-called seductions were in fact rapes; that your husband enjoyed hurting those weaker than himself. It is a fact that he starved prisoners in his keeping, and hanged children." De Mauleon's voice has grown steadily louder as he makes these dreadful accusations; he speaks the last sentence while standing, one arm lifted, a finger pointing to heaven as if to call God's attention to what he is saying.

The silence that falls now goes on and on, until I feel I have to break it. "You have still offered nothing to prove I had anything to do with my husband's death. Or do you now mean to accuse Amicia?"

"I would accuse a number of women, beginning with you, and then Amicia, and continuing across England until we came to Gunnor, wife of Robert FitzWalter, whose holdings border on the River Welland. Like Amicia, like Hadwisa, like all women, she remains at home while her husband is away to war. I would accuse the ordinary peddlars and tinkers of this land, who are used every day to carry letters and small packets from city to castle, from castle to abbey. But what I am really here to do is to save your life."

"Is my life in danger?" I say this very coolly and with great control, for a wonder, while my mind scrabbles in circles like a trapped rat. He knows, he knows!

"There was a tinker who happened upon us as we stood, wet and shivering on the banks of the River Welland, watching our wagons sink out of sight. He followed us to Swineshead, and was fed at the abbey after repairing a cauldron in the abbey kitchen. He even stayed the night, though he left very early the next morning. He left behind a package."

"Was it for my husband?"

De Mauleon shakes his head. "For the monk. Who went to the abbot and said he could rid the country of a heavy burden by adding just a little to it."

My breath catches in my throat, and I must cough to clear it.

"Yes," says de Mauleon, "that is what you wrote on that note you sent along with a parcel addressed to Amicia, isn't it? That to rid herself of a terrible burden, she must only add this trifle to it."

"N-no," I say, and put my hand on my throat.

"Yes, you did, Madam. And Amicia sent the package on its way with the same message. It has been chasing your husband across England, from woman to woman, all of whom he has wronged. Even Hadwisa, your husband's first wife, whom he cruelly set aside, had the package in her hands for awhile. Her second husband rescued her, and paid an enormous fine to the king in order to marry her. De Mandeville is dead now, and I think Hadwisa blames your husband for that, too. The package has passed through Norfolk, where Earl Bigod's holdings are; his wife was also shamed by your husband. But it was Gunnor, Robert FitzWalter's wife, who found out John was near The Wash, and who put it into the tinker's hands. But the package passed through your hands first."

I lift my head and say in my most arrogant voice, "How do you know that?"

He reaches into the heavy sleeve of his robe and pulls out a small pottery costrel. It is a lovely clear yellow with darker stripes, shaped like a barrel. There are handles of a sort on it, through which a thong can be strung so it may be carried around one's neck or over a shoulder. It is small, not larger than my fist, closed with a cork. He turns it so I may see one of the flat ends. A roundel of brown clay, cut to resemble a man's face has been stuck on one end.

I had thought it a pleasant surprise when it was unpacked, a new year's gift from an old friend in Poitou. But it did not gurgle when shaken, and when opened, there was only a fine white powder inside, and not much of that. With it came a note: "When your burden is too much to bear, you must yet add this to it, and it will be relieved." I puzzled over that for several days, and then stirred just a very small amount, as much as two grains of wheat into a goblet of wine and let my monkey drink it. And my monkey died in agony a few hours later.

"I should not have sent it in its original container, should I?" I ask.

"No, madam. But you did not know the final recipient would not have time to dispose of it."

"So you know. Yet you say you are here to save my life?"

"Yes. You are going to see your son safely crowned, and after a short interval, you are going to take a ship to Normandy, and from there you will go home."

"Home? This is my home. My parents are dead, and so is my brother. I have no home in Angoulême."

"In Lusignan you do." My heart leaps, I put both hands to my throat to contain it. Then de Maulean continues, "But not with Hugh the Brown, of course."

"Why 'of course'?"

De Mauleon says gently, "Brown Hugh is also dead."

My tears this time are from real pain and sorrow. "What happened to him?"

"I am not sure. In fact, I am not sure he is dead, yet. But he was the one who sent the casket to you, and set this ugly thing in motion, and such a deed cannot go unpunished. We cannot have it rewarded in any way, especially by you. Why, you might have thought one day to go back to see if that old agreement could be resurrected."

"I would not do that!" I say very loudly, to contradict him, to conceal the truth he must have seen when he said I still had a home in Lusignan.

"But Hugh has a son, also named Hugh, and now to inherit the title Count of Marche. He is not as much younger than you as his father was older. And he is as yet unmarried."

I stare at de Mauleon. The entire world holds its breath while I try to decide what to do. He knows, this poet. I sent the little casket on its way, not knowing if it would eventually reach my husband, but I did not send all the white powder it contained. Perhaps I should prepare a special drink for him in the morning before he departs. Or perhaps I should drink it myself. Or perhaps I should retire to my homeland, and seek out this young Hugh. I wonder if he resembles his father.

A FRAIL YOUNG LIFE

Renée Vink

The dynasty established in Scotland by Malcolm Canmore in 1058 died out after five generations in 1286 with the tragic death (another accident?) of Alexander III. His two sons had predeceased him and the nearest heir to the throne was his daughter's daughter, Margaret, an infant still not three. Her father was Erik II, king of Norway, and her mother had died in childbirth. The infant was raised in Norway and it was not until 1290 that the child left her home to travel to Scotland. She did not survive the journey – or did she? Another mystery rears its head.

Mikael Skotte, chaplain at the Royal College of Bergen, had just said early Mass when the messenger met him outside the Apostles' church. He was summoned to the castle by the king himself. Suppressing his desire for breakfast he followed the man; empty or not, even a stomach had to defer to royalty.

King Håkon Magnusson seldom stayed in this westernmost town of Norway these days, as it was no longer the residence of the Norse kings. When his brother Eirik had died two years ago, *anno Domini* 1299, he had turned his former ducal court in Oslo into a royal one. Some people claimed the new king hated Bergen because of the rain.

They seemed to have a point, for even now while Mikael scurried after the messenger a soft drizzle moistened his cloak and hood.

Upon his arrival at the castle, further to the west on Holmen, Mikael was led into a room opposite the great hall built by Håkon Håkonsson. Inside, the builder's grandson occupied a carved chair serving as a high seat, sitting very erect and looking lofty and stern – the very image of *Kongespeilet*, that mirror of monarchs written for his mighty grandsire. Mikael involuntarily thought of the book's central statement: "The King is so elevated that every man must bend to him as if to God, and die or live according to his judgement." And so, though he wasn't sure he agreed with such an approach to temporal sovereignty, he knelt before the royal presence.

Looking up, however, he realized the image was less than perfect. The king's brow was clouded as a Bergen sky and he was dressed in simple travelling attire instead of stately silks and velvets. He must have arrived recently, using the first light of this late spring morning to reach this town with the day ahead of him.

Apart from the guards at the door there were only three men with the king, and Mikael knew all of them. The warlike figure behind the chair was a member of the *hird*, the personal retinue and bodyguard of the Norse kings. In the tall, middle aged fellow with the balding head standing at a window-slit he recognized the royal councillor Weland of Stiklaw, an old acquaintance. The third man was the aging bishop Narve of Bergen, seated on a folding chair at Håkon's right. Obviously Narve had only just arrived from his own residence, for the hem of his robe was still dark with moisture.

"*Sira*," King Håkon said without preamble, gesturing him to rise, "we gather you know about the woman in the Prisoners' Tower?"

Rising to his feet the chaplain nodded, slightly apprehensive. "Yes. my lord king." Though he had no bent for gossip it was impossible to be ignorant about her. Bergen was talking of nothing else these days.

"What do you think of her?"

"That – that she cannot possibly be your late brother's daughter, God rest their souls."

"And yet?" The king bent forward.

Mikael blinked; Håkon had unerringly caught his hesitation. Weland of Stiklaw pursed his lips as if to hide a smile. The bishop rubbed his dry, wrinkled hands, an unnerving sound.

"Yet some of the rumours are very disturbing," the chaplain murmured at last.

King Håkon said nothing.

Narve stopped rubbing his hands. "You see, my lord king?" he croaked. He turned to Mikael. "Of course you know better, yet no doubt you have noticed how the voices saying this godforsaken witch" – and he crossed himself – "truly is Margareta, are increasing in number and strength. This was never a trifling matter to begin with but now it has become nothing less than dangerous. Saint Olaf protect us! Some fools demand we make war to win back Margareta's kingdom for her, others even say the laws of succession ought to be changed so she can be queen of Norway! And that, of course, is treason."

The king's jaw set. The bishop went on: "As if we do not have enough troubles already with the rebellious barons, the Danish pirates, and the English robbing our merchants since we allied ourselves with the French. Under such circumstances the king must display his power when and wherever it is necessary. That is why I requested his presence."

"And I suggested yours." Master Weland's accent was still much more pronounced than Mikael's own.

Mikael opened his mouth to profess his unworthyness for what he feared would come yet hoped to avoid. But before he could speak Håkon raised a hand.

"I trust you will be able to talk sense into her, *sira*. As the woman is not our niece, she must be someone else. Find out why she claims to be Margareta and what she hopes to gain by it. Try to discover if she is part of a conspiracy against our throne. Make her reveal her true name, and we will let her swear to it in Christ Church itself, on the bones of the blessed Saint Synnøve and on little Margareta's tomb, in the presence of a host of witnesses, that all rumours finally be laid to rest!" King Håkon Magnusson straightened. For one fleeting moment he *was* the image of the King's Mirror.

"Why me?" Mikael almost whispered. He didn't want to be involved.

"You're clever," murmured Weland.

Nobody else seemed to notice. "Why not?" The bishop began rubbing his hands again. "You also accompanied the Maid on her last voyages – the one she made alive and the one she made in her coffin. The prisoner refuses to speak to me anymore but she may trust a simple chaplain. You make her confess. Once she's done that . . ." His voice trailed off.

What about the seal of the confessional? the simple chaplain thought. But all he said was: "And if she doesn't?" Narve's eyes gleamed fanatically when he said: "Let us pray that even though she is female, she will see reason. For if she does not, she'll burn."

Little Margareta Eiriksdottir, also called the Maid of Norway. Born of the Norse king Eirik Magnusson, and of Margaret, daughter of Alexander III, King of Scotland. Motherless from birth. Proclaimed Alexander's sole heir when his last surviving son died. Reluctantly acknowledged as Queen of Scots when Alexander himself was killed in a mysterious fall from his horse after an ill-boding ghost had appeared at his second wedding. Destined to become the wife of Edward of Caernarfon, heir to the power-hungry king of England – who had been remarkably eager the two should become a pair. Departed from Norway at the age of seven, never to return alive. Margareta. Margaret. The child of many hopes and some grudges that all expired when she breathed her last before having set one foot on Scottish soil.

The child had died in Kirkwall, in the Norse fief of Orkney. Mikael, who had been among those who were to take the little queen to her new home, had seen her slip away quietly, the last in a disquieting series of royal deaths that had plunged Scotland into strife and political disorder, occupation by the English, and bloody war.

And now, more than ten years later, a woman from the town of Lübeck in Germany had come to Bergen claiming she was Margaret, Queen of Scots. The real Maid had been dead and buried for more than ten years. So the Lübeck woman had to be an imposter, whatever the people believed. If the rumours were correct she was too old to be Eirik Magnusson's child anyhow.

Yet rumour also had it that she remembered a clergyman intoning the ancient hymn Veni, Creator Spiritus *when she was brought from Bergen castle to her ship.*

And that was the plain truth.

The Prisoner's Tower was across the yard on the castle grounds, but Mikael wished it was miles away. He hadn't come far yet when someone came marching up behind him and a voice remarked: "You don't seem to be in a hurry, Michael Scot. Why am I under the impression the task you've been set is not to your liking?"

Slowly the chaplain turned. He knew the man before he saw him, as the voice was familiar and the language had been Scots. Evasively he said in the same tongue: "It is hard to be put to work on an empty stomach. I had not yet broken my fast when the summons came." He refrained from saying he had been fasting yesterday as well.

Weland of Stiklaw, once a member of the Scottish clergy, looked every inch the Norse baron he was since King Håkon had made him councillor and entrusted him with a fief. Eight years ago Weland had accompanied lady Isobel Bruce to Bergen, where she was to marry the widowed king Eirik. As a Bruce adherent, he had decided to stay in Norway rather than submit to the new Scottish king, John Balliol, on whom he thought the crown was wasted. When that toom tabard was deposed and Edward of England invaded Scotland, Weland also refused to do him homage as King of Scots and was promptly declared an outlaw.

Now he stood towering above the chaplain and said with a condescending smile: "I'd have thought you would be used to fasting. But this won't take long, as the woman will never recant. Narve doesn't believe there is a conspiracy; he thinks she's just mad, or even possessed, and it's no use talking to her. If this king wasn't the kind of perfectionist that always has to get to the bottom of everything her fate would be sealed already." He glanced up at the dripping clouds as if expecting to read the final verdict in the grey scrolls of heaven. "So let's get on."

Inwardly, Mikael groaned. He did not like Weland to be present when he questioned this imposter. But he could hardly send him away.

The false Maid had been thrown in the underground dungeon destined for traitors, rebels and heretics. She lay on the cold floor like a ragged sack of bones, and by the light of the torch the guards had given him Mikael could see she was in bad condition: thin and dirty, her shift – the only garment she wore – torn and bloody, and her skin covered with bruises and crusts. It was obvious she had been maltreated and perhaps tortured, and he failed to see why such a weak and pitiable creature should be chained to the wall.

Then his eyes came to rest on her head. The matted hair that obscured her face was filthy, and the red torchlight unsteady and treacherous, but even in this shadowy dungeon it was visibly white. The hair of a crone. He glanced at Weland, but the other Scot merely wrinkled his nose at the rank and offensive smell that pervaded the dungeon.

Since he couldn't call her Margareta or my lady, Mikael loudly cleared his throat to draw the woman's attention.

After a few moments she turned her head. The lank, unkempt hair fell to one side, revealing a face that gave him a shock. The woman's face was as dirty as the rest of her but looked much younger than the hair. In fact, it could hardly be older than twenty-five –

He took a deep breath to steady himself. *Don't start imagining things!* It had to be the eyes: large like a child's, very blue, and remarkably unclouded for a woman who had been treated as harshly as she.

Again he looked at Weland – had he lost a little of his composure now?

To Mikael's surprise, the woman took the initiative. Raising herself to a sitting position she asked: "What do you want?"

Though she did speak Norse a shade of a foreign accent coloured her speech. Low German? The chaplain, who frequently heard that language in the streets of Bergen, wasn't sure.

"Your true name," he said. "In your own best interest." He rubbed his softly rumbling stomach.

"My true name is Margareta Eiriksdottir. I am the rightful queen of Scotland."

"Nonsense!" Weland said. "You're a common woman from Lübeck!"

"Who are you to doubt me? I am who I say I am." Weland gave his exasperation free rein. "Margareta is dead and has been so for more than ten years!" Mikael wished the man would leave, as he was not precisely creating an atmosphere of confidence.

As if he sensed it Weland promptly swung round, raising a fist to bang on the door. "I've heard and seen enough," he said. "When you're done here, Michael, join me in the room where the king received you."

When the dungeon had been locked again Mikael put the torch in a low ring on the wall and squatted on the cold, mucky floor of the dungeon to avoid looking down upon the woman. Hopefully she'd appreciate the gesture.

"Why do you claim to be Margareta Eiriksdottir?" he began, trying to sound friendly and at the same time wondering if Weland was standing outside with his ear to the door. "The child is truly dead. I saw her die. For your own good let me warn you that you'll burn at the stake if you persist in your errors. Confide in me. Tell me who you are. I am a priest; confess, and you may live. Think of your immortal soul!"

She looked at him unblinkingly with those very blue eyes but remained silent. In the end he had to avert his.

"Don't tell me it wasn't Margareta," he added. "When the ship returned to Bergen, her father ordered the coffin to be opened. He inspected the body inside and confirmed it was his daughter's." And wept, Mikael remembered, for the child he had begotten as a child.

Poor Eirik. The most ill-starred monarch Norway had seen in a century. Limping, suffering from severe headaches after two bad falls from his horse in childhood, a widower at the age of fifteen, burying his only child at twenty-two, and dead at thirty-one. And a weak king as well, *Kongespeilet*'s contorted reflection.

"It's true. I saw him inspect the body," he said pleadingly when she still didn't respond. "I returned to Bergen with the coffin."

"How can you be sure she was dead?"

Mikael frowned. "Are you suggesting she was merely unconscious? That she was somehow smuggled out of Christ Church before we could bury her? Impossible. We had a sea voyage ahead of us. It was October, and we had every reason to expect rough weather and delay. So Bishop Narve decided to have the body embalmed. Among other things that means the intestines are removed. Not even queens can survive without bowels."

She was not taken aback. "Did you witness the embalming, too?"

"No," he had to admit.

"It never happened."

"Of course it did!"

"I know I have bowels, if only because they feel empty."

He refrained from pointing out that she had them because she was not Margareta.

"But I may indeed have been dead," she went on, her voice dreamy now. "Somebody woke me up when I lay in that coffin, an angel of

God, or perhaps Saint Sunniva. I never saw who; it felt more like a presence than a person. And being raised, I found my hair had turned snow-white to remind me of God's power to forgive sins and renew our lives. And there in Christ Church I met a friendly skipper from Lübeck who had come to pray for his safe return home. He took me –"

"Did you tell this to the bishop?" Mikael interrupted her when he had more or less regained his composure. If so, he could imagine why Narve thought her mad or possessed.

"Yes. I told him I was taken from my coffin by an angel or a saint. He cursed me and said I was speaking heresy."

Agitatedly, Mikael jumped up. "He may well be right!" He grabbed his pectoral cross. "And if it doesn't defy the teachings of the Church it does defy logic. If the coffin had been empty the men who lifted it to bury her would have noticed. And if Margareta had risen from the dead she'd have run to her father instead of disappearing."

Why am I unable to end this appalling conversation? Has she bewitched me, this strange creature with her oddly white hair and her haunting eyes?

"And so I would have," the woman said, "if it had been safe. But they were after me."

"Who were?" Mikael asked in spite of himself.

"Everyone." For the first time a hint of pain crept into her face. "I could trust no one. They gave me poison."

A wave of dizziness washed over him. He was on the ship again, that last week of September more than ten years ago. Not long after they had set out from Bergen the wind had freshened up, and the vessel was heaving more than some stomachs could bear.

Lady Ingeborg Erlingsdottir, who was in charge of the Maid's personal household, was bending over the child with a wooden cup. Margareta had repeatedly been sick over the railing and refused all food but now Ingeborg seemed to succeed in making her drink a little. That would be a good thing, as the girl's health was frail enough already.

The ship should have sailed earlier but the Maid's departure had been delayed because King Eirik had been fighting the Danes all summer. In May, Edward of England had sent a vessel with colourful banners and exotic foods and spices to take his son's future wife to England. But Eirik had refused to let his daughter go.

He wasn't satisfied with the marriage agreement the English and Scots had reached between them, and even less satisfied when they turned it into a treaty without him. Eirik felt he had not been taken seriously. Until this would be amended his darling was not going to leave Norse territory. She certainly wasn't going to a king of England who in fact considered himself overlord of Scotland and seemed to foresee at least the same role for his son and heir – in spite of the safeguards for Scotland's independence included in the marriage treaty.

Now at last Eirik was sending her to Orkney, a Norse fief held by the Scottish earl John of Angus, whose Norse allegiance usually prevailed over his Bruce sympathies. There, the Norse ambassadors were to confer with the Scots and with Edward of England's envoys, who would travel north by land. When a final agreement had been reached the Maid would sail on to Scotland, to be inaugurated on the Stone of Scone.

Among the Norsemen accompanying her on her ship were Bishop Narve of Bergen and baron Thore Håkonsson, Ingeborg's husband. Among the Scots was a lord Weymiss, sent by John Balliol; there was Michael, a young, Orkney-born Scot designated to become one of the queen's chaplains; and finally there was Weland of Stiklaw, a canon of Dunkeld and former chamberlain of King Alexander III sent to Bergen by the Guardians of Scotland to ask Eirik Magnusson if he was ever going to give them their queen.

But perhaps Eirik had been right to be reluctant. His daughter was not bearing this sea voyage well. Children were so vulnerable. Many died at birth, others just faded away before they could grow up, and only the fittest survived. There was little one could do to repel that great harvester, the Angel of Death. Sometimes he even received the support of adults who sincerely believed they were doing the right thing.

Everybody but the sailors concerned themselves with the young queen's condition. Singing, telling stories, making her promise to eat if she lost one of the games they played with her – though that didn't work. They all brought her drinks, rejoicing when she took a sip, which she did all too seldom.

As Margareta's doctor sighed in exasperation: "Why is this slip of a girl too stubborn for her own good?"

"I shall do as I'm told when you let me go home," Margareta said

again and again, in a voice growing increasingly weak and listless.

"That is impossible," they all told her.

"Why do you say I am queen if you don't do as I wish?" she complained.

They tried to explain to her why they couldn't turn back just yet, and made all kinds of vague promises, the way adults do. She merely turned her back to them.

Two days before Michaelmas the ship anchored in the bay of Kirkwall, and Margareta was brought ashore. Earl John was waiting to welcome the Queen of Scots to his isles, though of course he had not expected her to be laid in his arms as a pathetic bundle of clothes. He personally carried her to the jarlsborg, where she was put in bed.

When asked if she would recover, the physician – as doctors would – refused to say either yes or no.

Chaplain Mikael had to steady himself against the dungeon wall before he was able to turn to the door and knock.

"Want to leave?" asked the guard who finally opened it. No sign of an eavesdropping master Weland.

Mikael shook his head. "No, but I need something to eat. If you would be so kind . . . ?"

"I'll see if there's anything left."

When the guard had gone Mikael turned back to the woman, who had been waiting motionlessly all the time. He squatted again. "Do you mean to say the Maid was – murdered?" He felt really faint, and not only for lack of food.

Now she shifted position, and the chain rattled. "I remember being so miserable I wanted to die. Then I just drifted off. It must have been because of the poison."

"Margareta was seasick. She refused to eat, and she drank very little. By the time we reached Orkney she was simply too weakened to recover."

"I was made to drink a poisonous concoction," she insisted. "To kill me. Or to render me unconscious, so they could more easily smuggle me away and sell me."

"Who would want to do such a thing?"

"The lady Ingeborg, for one. I overheard her talking about 'selling the child'. To her husband, I think, though I'm not sure."

"On the ship?"

"No, not on the ship. I was lying in a proper bed."

A Norse baron and his wife, talking about selling their king's child? Most likely Ingeborg Erlingsdottir had meant Margareta was being sold in a figurative sense. A subtle difference that would have been lost on a seven year old.

On the other hand, he *could* think of one particular buyer. An agent of King Edward could have approached lady Ingeborg in May, when the ship with spices – At that point Mikael checked himself. The woman was not the Maid, so this was merely one of her senseless ramblings. Ingeborg Erlingsdottir had said nothing of the kind.

The door creaked open, and the guard returned with a lump of bread and an earthen mug containing a liquid probably meant to be ale. He thrust them into the chaplain's hands and left without a word.

Prodding in the bread Mikael felt it was stale. But he was hungry, and she had to be ravenous as a troll, so he blessed it, broke it and gave one piece to the woman.

She accepted it as if it was the body of Christ, and waited a moment before she began to eat, with surprisingly dainty bites.

He took heart; maybe she would trust him now. But at that instant the door opened again and the guard put his head inside the dungeon.

"Time to leave, *sira*. You're wanted elsewhere."

That was much too soon! "Will I be allowed to return? She has not – I have not –" The chaplain faltered.

The guard shrugged and shooed him out.

"Is it the king who summons me?" Mikael asked when the man put the bar back in place.

"The king has just left for Christ Church with the bishop and half of his *hird*. To pray at the shrine of Saint Synnøve, and at – the little maid's tomb, it is said." The guard cast a glance at the door as if he wondered if there was anything in that tomb. He had also forgotten to remove the half drained mug and the torch. Perhaps Håkon ought to be warned the loyalty of his jailers needed testing?

The same messenger who had dragged him out of his complacency earlier in the morning waited at the entrance to the tower to wave him to his destination in the castle's main building.

"Who has sent for me?" the chaplain tried again.

"Lord Weland," the messenger answered cheerfully. "Or perhaps the late king's widow and her guests. They were with him when he sent me here."

The late king's widow – Isobel Bruce?

While the company that had sailed from Bergen anxiously hovered around the ailing little queen, several rumours about Scottish affairs came oozing into Kirkwall. Old Robert Bruce, lord of Annandale, had seized the royal castles of Dumfries and Wigtown, and one castle of Balliol's in Kircudbrightshire. He had gathered most of his vassals and was now said to march on Perth and the Stone of Scone with his army. Balliol had been less provocative, merely styling himself heir of Scotland until the queen would bear a child, or be dead.

That last possibility was by no means remote. Though Margareta managed to keep down a few spoons of gruel her condition hardly improved. On the vigil of Michaelmas, both Earl John and Lady Ingeborg quarreled with the doctor, accusing him of incompetence and lack of dedication. The man left in anger. Several leeches and herbalists who heard about the girl's illness, came to the jarlsborg to offer their services.

Most of them were sent away but the situation being desperate, a local healer and a wisewoman were admitted into the Maid's presence. The healer soon gave up hope; the woman thought something could be done yet. And on Michaelmas the little patient did indeed seem a little better, though the healer called it the final flickerings of life and left before she could die, and he be accused of having failed. The wisewoman continued her ministrations, confident her treatment would restore the child to health.

Mikael visited the sick-room twice that day, in the morning and after Vespers. Both times he entered upon the same scene, with the wisewoman mixing or stirring a potion and Lady Ingeborg softly humming a tune at Margareta's bedside. The first time the chaplain was invited to sing for the sick child, and he chanted the hymn she loved most. The second time Bishop Narve and the Balliol liegeman – Weymiss was his name – entered shortly after him. Mikael seemed to remember Weymiss asking the wisewoman some questions about herbs.

On the last day of September, disaster struck. Margareta was found unconscious in her bed. It was obvious she was dying. The wisewoman had gone – fled, it was thought, before she could be forced to swallow her own harmful concoctions, or worse. All those

who had sailed with the little queen gathered around her to aid her
passing into eternal rest. Bishop Narve administered the last rites to
her, and she died between his hands.

Balliol's man immediately departed south with the dire news.
Weland of Stiklaw waited until after the Requiem Mass in St.
Magnus Cathedral before he, too, left Kirkwall. Mikael chose to
follow the body home. When offered a position as a royal chaplain in
Norway, he accepted at once. If Margareta had lived he would have
served her as a priest. Why not fulfill that role by saying
commemoration masses for her in the town where she was buried?

The search the Earl of Orkney ordered for the wisewoman turned
out to be fruitless. She had vanished as if swallowed alive by the
mouth of Hell.

In the lesser hall where the king had received him earlier in the day a
tall young nobleman in red and green was pacing to and fro. "If that
brother-in-law of yours does not support our cause we'll have to
make peace with Edward, curse his long shanks and his even longer
fingers!" he cried in Scots to an equally young lady lounging in the
chair vacated by King Håkon.

Mikael saw the lady was indeed King Eirik's widow. But far from
being garbed in black Isobel Bruce was dressed flamboyantly in a
crimson bliaut embroidered with bramble motives, as if she had
something to celebrate. Her face was dark, though.

"You shouldn't have made all those promises to Wallace," said a
deep-voiced man with rather puffy cheeks from the the folding chair;
him, Mikael recognized as well.

"His success was rather short-lived," Earl John of Orkney went on,
"as I –" He broke off, and the chaplain knew he had been noticed,
though that was not the reason for the pang of remorse he felt.

"There he is!" Weland said from the window, apparently his
favourite spot. He turned to the young man. "This is the chaplain I
referred to, my lord Robert. Any news from our false Queen of Scots,
Michael?"

Belatedly it dawned on the chaplain who the nobleman had to be:
Robert Bruce, grandson to the late lord of Annandale, come *ta*
Norowa o'er the faem to seek aid for the Scots in their struggle
against the English, but discovering Håkon Magnusson to be deaf on
that particular ear.

Young Bruce stopped acting the restless lion and looked the chaplain critically up and down.

"Not yet, my lord. I hadn't finished interrogating her yet," Mikael answered Weland's question, not quite at ease.

"And I thought I had provided you with an excuse to escape from that dungeon! You were making progress, then?" Weland's face suggested the reverse.

Loath to admit defeat to that sort of face Mikael said: "I suppose the woman told the bishop that Margareta was to be abducted or killed?"

She hadn't, it appeared; Narve must have stopped listening after the resurrection story. It was gratifying to hear Weland's sharp intake of breath, but the effect the words had on John of Angus was disturbing. The Earl of Orkney grimaced as if in pain, and one hand flew to his chest.

Nobody else had noticed. Mikael just wanted to ask what ailed him when Robert Bruce suddenly said: "This is about the Maid of Norway, isn't it?" He turned to his sister. "Remember how our grandsire used to say she ought to marry me instead of Edward of Caernarfon? How different things might have turned out if –"

"It's just as well she didn't!" Isobel interrupted him tartly. "When the ghost appeared at Alexander's wedding it was clear that his house was doomed. The Maid was Alexander's grandchild, and she died as well. You might have become ensnared in their doom!" She crossed herself.

Her brother scowled. "I might have been king; crowns want to be worn by men!"

While they were talking Mikael felt a shiver run down his spine – as if that same auld ghost could reappear any moment, foreboding a new doom. He gathered all his courage. "My lord Weland, do you remember who hired that wisewoman to treat the Maid when she lay sick in the *jarlsborg* in Kirkwall?"

Weland shook his head as at a particularly dim-witted pupil of the Bergen cathedral school. "Do me a favour, Michael. Don't tell me you believe this imposter's fancies!"

But Earl John cleared his throat, apparently recovered from whatever had caused his distress. "I see no reason for secrecy. I engaged the woman. She was recommended to me, and she seemed to be more than the average old crone mumbling pagan spells over some unsavoury brew. She even claimed she used to try out her medicines on herself and her own children from the time they were as young as the Maid. I thought we could take the risk. So did Ingeborg Erlingsdottir."

Did his words really convey more than he seemed to say? "But you were wrong," Mikael stated flatly.

The flames on the Earl's cheeks screamed against Isobel's bliaut; he looked positively unhealthy. "How could we have known? I'm no leech! Ingeborg Erlingsdottir knew a little about herbs. She was supposed to keep an eye on the woman and watch over the child. But she obviously failed to do so."

"The lady is dead. *De mortuis nil nisi bene*," Weland said sternly.

Earl John shot him a withering glance. "So I alone am to blame? Pray tell me – who thought it a good idea to hire that wisewoman?"

What were they fighting about? As Weland didn't reply Mikael ventured to ask: "Where did she come from, my lord?"

The Earl shrugged. "I believe she was an Irishwoman, come to Orkney as a young girl. But what difference does it make?"

Heavily he rose from the folding chair. "This is meaningless. Margareta died because she was mortally ill and we were desperate enough to trust an incompetent peasant. That's all there is to it." He turned to Isobel Bruce. "I believe we have an appointment, my lady. Shall we go?"

Isobel looked expectantly from Weland to John of Angus. When neither face showed any inclination to prolong the exchange she nodded with all the grace her disappointment allowed her to muster. "As you wish. Are you with us, Robert?"

He was, with only a little less reluctance. When the three of them had left Mikael asked: "Can I return to the prisoner now, my lord?"

"That would be a waste of time."

"King Håkon commanded me to discover the imposter's true identity," the chaplain pointed out. He took a deep breath "I believe I know now, but I need confirmation from the woman herself. It may save her life."

For a while, Weland stared at the point of his shoes. "Forget it!" he said at last. "Let me repeat it once again: that woman is out of her mind. She won't confirm anything. Nor will the king want to listen to another concoction of lies and nonsense."

"Being the man he is, the king will want to know the truth."

"What truth, *sira*?" Almost casually Weland interposed his tall frame between Mikael and the door.

The chaplain braced himself. "About the death of the Maid."

"Go on," the other man said after a short silence.

"There was an attempt to abduct her – but not by Edward of England, as I thought first. It was old lord Bruce of Annandale who was behind it. Until Alexander III was born Bruce was heir to Scotland but since then the situation had changed. If Margareta should die he was merely one of several candidates for the throne. As his main rival Balliol stood a fair chance of reaping the profits, killing the girl was no option. Securing the crown for his descendants was. Bruce was old, and ready to pass on the torch of his ambitions. Young Edward and the Maid were not yet formally betrothed; if Bruce's grandson were to wed the Queen of Scots . . . we have just heard young Robert say it: Crowns want to be worn by men. I guess he was quoting his grandsire."

"And how was lord Bruce going to attain that goal?"

"The plans were to be carried out by some trusted friends whom I don't need to name."

Weland's hand had been scratching his chin; now it went to the hilt of his dagger.

"Give the poor girl something to make her seem dead," Mikael went on, trying to keep his voice steady. "Then carry her off while the right man is keeping vigil with her. If the doctor seems a liability, engage someone else to do the job. A wisewoman, for instance. Sadly enough, you were too impatient to wait until the patient had recovered. The dose the wisewoman administered to her must have been too high for a body as frail and weakened as Margareta's. She truly died, God rest her soul – and damn those who were responsible for it!"

"John Balliol had an unmarried son, too." Weland mused with feigned detachment: his fist was clenching his dagger. "Don't you think it could just as well have been his man – Weymiss I think his name was – who tampered with the girl's medicine, or bribed the wisewoman? Or he poisoned her on the ship, and she just never recovered."

Mikael gestured in the direction of the Prisoner's Tower. "You know it wasn't Weymiss, or you would allow me to go back. As it is now, you're afraid the truth does lie in that dungeon, locked behind bars and chained to the wall."

"I don't even know who it is that lies in there! Why should I fear a riddle? I only want to prevent you from returning there before I know what you think you've discovered."

"I think she is the wisewoman's daughter."

The other man laughed rather loudly. "Much too old!"

"No doubt you, too, noticed that she's younger than the hair suggests. Not yet thirty, I think. She had a rough life – or some dark sorrow or terror made her hair turn white. As Earl John told us, the wisewoman used to try out her medicines on her children. What, if she made one daughter swallow so many dangerous potions during childhood that it bleached the colour from the girl's hair? I've heard of such things before.

"And what, if this daughter had come close to death after her mother made her try out an untested medicine when she was about the Maid's age? Later, when the wisewoman told her the whole story, the daughter felt an intense compassion with the hapless child. A compassion that with the years grew into identification, and made her raise the dead girl in her own, private way. How and when she ended up in Lübeck is hard to say – fled from Orkney with her mother before the earl's men came. Though I bet the wisewoman was never seriously searched for."

"Conjecture!" Weland said curtly. "Where's your proof?"

"The prisoner knows about the hymn. I sang the *Veni, Creator Spiritus* in the sick room at the request of the girl herself." A great sadness crept upon Mikael. "It was her favourite hymn. I recall lady Ingeborg telling the wisewoman the same hymn had sounded when we departed from Bergen. The woman in her turn may have told her daughter."

Staring intently at Weland's face Mikael suddenly realized the other man believed him – had probably done so all along. Had Weland seen the wisewoman's likeness in the false Maid's face?

"There is one other reason," Mikael went on. "How would you call the saint who rests in the shrine in Christ Church?"

"Synnøve. Like the Norsemen do. Though I know she was given another name at birth," Weland added after a short pause.

"Yes. She came from Ireland, where they know her as Sunniva. The false Margareta called her by precisely that name. Like almost everyone on Orkney she speaks Norse, but with a foreign accent that is not German. And the wisewoman was Irish."

During the silence following his words Mikael could hear voices in the yard, the familiar sound of rain, the rustling of the rushes under his own nervous feet.

"Very clever," Weland said at last, finally taking his hand from the dagger's hilt. "You have missed only one point – and that is just as well."

Weland was right but he had been wrong to mention it. Mikael needed no more clues to realize he had overlooked Ingeborg Erlingsdottir. Wasn't this lady the one who was supposed "to keep an eye on the woman and watch the child"? Ingeborg had been on remarkably good terms with the common wisewoman, chatting with her over the patient's head. About selling a child, for instance. Not to King Edward, but to lord Bruce of Annandale.

Ingeborg had been in the conspiracy. Why? That was a harder question. She might have acted entirely of her own accord, because she didn't like the way others were using the child. But of all possible answers one leapt at him with such force that he was unable to ward it off. He thought of the man who had been most unhappy with the marriage treaty, and who had refused to let the girl depart to England with Edward's glorious ship.

Eirik Magnusson. A tool in the hands of his powerful barons, and above all of Bishop Narve, not only as a minor, but also after he had come of age. Had King Eirik desired an alliance with the Bruces, to find himself thwarted by everyone around him? Had he then decided for once to sail a course of his own, rejecting the English alliance, throwing in his daughter's lot with some dissatisfied Scots who seemed to have better plans with their little queen – plans that would not lose him Orkney and Shetland to a united British kingdom? It would also explain why Bruce had thought he would get away with an abduction.

Had lady Ingeborg really been instructed by her king? If so, Eirik had unwittingly brought about the death of his only child. Improbable, but not impossible. Ever after that fall from his horse King Eirik had had his strange moments. And he was Håkon's brother.

If you are the King's trusted servant and councillor you will hold his brother's memory sacrosanct. No one will be allowed to besmirch it. The past must rest in his tomb, and his daughter's.

*   *   *

"You are not going to tell me," the chaplain said.

"Most certainly not." Weland kept blocking the way to the door. "And you will return to your duties now and never speak to the false Maid again."

"So she will burn."

"She will. There was never any other option. Though the king may think otherwise, he cannot let her live under any circumstances. If you see what I mean."

He did. Even if she truly were Margareta, she would still have to die. The chaplain gave Weland a hard stare. "Of course. The king is but a man. Only He who is above all kings can give life to the condemned. All the same, I will not stand by and watch when they tie the poor wretch to the stake" – *and see the Maid of Norway die a second death.*

"Not even if you're commanded to?"

"By that time, I hope to be on my way to Scotland. Perhaps Lord Bruce will accept my company. I guess you won't join us."

"I'm exiled, remember?" Weland said. "But I do wish you well, Michael Scot." He stepped aside.

The chaplain made for the door but then halted. "One last question, my lord." As Weland nodded he went on: "I was wondering why the Earl of Orkney is here. Did he come along with Lord Bruce to support the Scots' request for help? Or did the earl consider the rumours about the Maid alarming enough to hurry to Bergen in full sail?"

"That, too." The councillor smiled thinly. "Though the main reason is that lady Isobel has promised him her daughter. The betrothal is to take place tomorrow."

A little maid of four and a man old enough to be her grandfather? *Lord have mercy . . . especially upon high-born girls, tossed on the waves of other people's ambitions.*

Without looking back Michael Scot left the room.

Robert the Bruce ❧

A STONE OF DESTINY

Jean Davidson

The death of Margaret of Norway left Scotland without an immediate heir and this gave Edward I his opportunity to control Scotland. He removed the Stone of Destiny, upon which all Celtic rulers of the Scots had been inaugurated for centuries. Edward also nominated Scotland's next king, John Balliol, but Balliol proved not to be the puppet ruler Edward had anticipated. Balliol was soon dethroned, but before Edward could integrate Scotland into a United Kingdom, other rebels fought for freedom. First there was William Wallace, and then Robert the Bruce. Bruce, like England's Richard the Lionheart, is depicted as a national hero, but he was not always as valiant and heroic as history likes to portray, as the following story reveals.

"Tell me again about your pilgrimage to Glastonbury," William begged. He touched one of the badges I wore, each showing a completed pilgrimage. "Did you really see the Thorn Tree that grew from Joseph of Arimathea's staff? And to be where the Chalice once rested – did you feel an atmosphere of awe, of wonderment?"

We were in the church of Dumfries Greyfriars Abbey replacing used candles. A menial task at the best of times. But this was exactly where I wanted to be, and when. Besides, it was warmer in here than out in an icy February day, even with the sun shining.

"The Thorn was in full flower. But I didn't take to the Somerset levels. Too much water and flooding for my taste."

"I'm longing to make my first pilgrimage." He eyed the array of cockleshells, brooches and miniature flasks of holy water that bedecked my Franciscan friar's habit with admiration, his sense of adventure clearly stirred. What would he say if he knew I'd never made a pilgrimage in my life, though I had travelled a great deal. "Tell me again about the pirates who attacked your ship on the way to Santiago de Compostela."

I smiled. "You're encouraging me in at least three sins I'm sure, of which hubris or pride is the biggest, young William. But if you really want to hear it again, then what does my sin count against pleasing another?" I was playing my role to perfection. The trouble was that William's innocent gaze made me feel something a little like shame. If I were capable of such a thing any more. "Only first, let's make sure these candles are set straight, or they'll smoke and drip on people's heads."

"Friar Gregory," William said solemnly, "These past two weeks since you arrived at our monastery have been the best weeks of – well, since I can remember."

I snorted. "Admit it, lad, it's the badges that caught your eye. You've followed me around like a puppy with its tongue hanging out. You just want to squeeze me dry of my experience and then you'll be off."

He grinned. "You see right through me. But what I can't understand, Friar Gregory, is why you've come to Dumfries? What could interest a man of the world such as yourself in our Scottish backwater?"

"There are plenty of heathens up in the Highlands, so I'm told, who could do with some fiery preaching." We both chuckled, then I added casually. "And I've a mind to visit Iona, the Holy Isle, where St Columba first landed and tamed the Picts. Didn't he bring the Stone with him too, where the old Scottish kings were enthroned?"

William's face turned stony. I was, after all, English, and I'd found mentioning this touchy subject soon showed who believed in a Scottish kingdom. Then his expression cleared. "Oh, that old bit of sandstone. There's another tale, that Joseph of Arimathea brought it from the Lost Tribe. Did you learn anything about that at Glastonbury?"

So he'd decided not to trust me and dissemble. He wasn't as naive an eighteen-year-old as I'd taken him for. Sensible lad.

"No. And we'd better get on with the job. Here, I'll use my dagger to prise that stubborn bit of used candle out, then we can talk." I was now adept at manoeuvring within the folds of my Franciscan friar's habit, and was soon gouging at the used tallow. All these pieces were collected and saved to be melted and reused. Abbot John of Greyfriars was not one to spend two farthings when one would do.

"Such fine work on the hilt," William sighed. "I'm not surprised you didn't want to give up such a possession. You must prize it highly."

"I prize my own life even more. I would feign give that up on some lonely track. In order that I might continue to do God's work, of course," I added, hoping that my voice didn't sound too hollow. But it's always like that, when you're a spy. Constantly pretending and unable to share your innermost thoughts with anyone, except your master, who in my case was King Edward of England.

William nodded eagerly and spoke with the idealism of youth. "That's it. Doing God's work. I feel that I'm wasting what good I could do, living here comfortably at the abbey. I would far rather be spreading God's word where it's needed."

He held out the sack into which we were putting the used candles and I tossed the last piece in. Then we pushed the big fat new candles in place and lit them. Soft candlelight now illuminated the entire church, winking from the cross at the altar, casting light into the darkest corners. I felt inner satisfaction. I would miss nothing of the meeting to come. I prided myself on precision planning, and I wanted to make sure it went as I intended. Or as I was being paid to make happen.

I glanced at William's bent head, where he was fastening the sack, with its fiery red-gold Celtic hair. I surprised a far-distant memory. I too had been an idealistic young man once. But I'd left that pointless aspect of myself behind a long time ago.

He looked again at my badges. "Glastonbury, Waltham, Westminster, Santiago de Compostela," he recited under his breath, then burst out, scowling, "I am determined to go. I don't know why Father Abbot keeps refusing his permission, though he grants it to others. There's some secret he's keeping from me. But what? Or is he teaching me some lesson?"

"Patience?" I suggested. "Obedience?" But I had my own thoughts on that subject, having observed Abbot John. It always paid to watch those around you carefully. You never knew from what quarter the next attack or betrayal might come. That, of course, was one reason why I did this job – the fear, the risk, gave me a huge thrill. That, and pretending to be other people. They filled the empty space that had once been me.

"Scrubbing floors, polishing, weeding the gardens and cleaning out the fishponds – jobs for old men who are past it. No, what I really want is to be . . ."

As he poured out his young man's dreams, his fair skin flushed and his blue eyes fixed on some distant horizon, I spared a thought for the man who had really done the things young William so admired. I had not killed him to obtain this disguise, for once. Nature or God was doing that for me. I had huddled by his side as cold winds blew snow through the cracks in our withy hut as he coughed and retched from an inflammation of the lungs through his last hours on this earth. He had rambled in his final fever, unravelling his entire life, as if to leave something of himself behind before passing towards the great unknown. He even made confession to me, perhaps mistaking me for the silent hermit who had built this traveller's shelter by his own solitary cell near Carlisle. The dying man never knew how paltry his misdeeds were beside the sins of his imagined confessor.

I told the hermit I would write to the dead man's family, then asked if I might take his robe, staff and other meagre and well-used belongings. He had been a friar of the old school, having renounced most worldly possessions. Not many of them left these days. The hermit inclined his head towards me, considering; then as if his blind eyes saw something I could not, something of the future, he nodded. So I became a Franciscan friar with a dead man's memories.

I always kept my own name when I could: Gregory Deschamps. I'd been caught out once early in my career as spy when I didn't recognize my assumed name. I'd wriggled out of that one, but I never ran that risk again.

"Friar Gregory, will you teach me how to use the staff and knife? I must learn to defend myself. If I promise not to use these skills to hurt or attack unprovoked, will you teach me? Father Abbot has refused me permission on this too."

"Then perhaps I should not disobey his rule?"

"It's not a Rule!" he protested, then cooled down when he saw I was joking. "Promise me this?" He grabbed my arm. I looked him up and down.

"You've got a slight build, but a wiry one, which usually means plenty of staying power. You're tall, like me, which has reach advantages."

It must have been a trick of the light. It was as if I wasn't with William, but my own son. He too would have been eighteen in this year of 1306 and I would have been teaching him. But a fire had ended his life, and that of his mother. I closed my eyes against the unwanted memory. When I looked again it was William. "Maybe I will," I said shortly. "Now, have we finished our job here? The candles are all lit for prayers later."

The bells rang. My heart quickened. It was mid-afternoon. It was time, now, and I'd let William make me dawdle. "Come along," I said brusquely. "We must go."

But William stood his ground. "That's not the first time," he said. "One minute you are Friar Gregory – the next you become a stranger. Possessed."

"Do not fear me, William," I said gently as I could, then tried to lighten the atmosphere. "It is Father Abbot we must fear."

He was not to be budged. His face was pale, his jaw set with pride. "If I have said something wrong, then I apologize. But no insult was intended –"

"None taken. It isn't you – only shadows from the past, and banished now. Come along," I urged again, "You must be gone."

He moved forward, but so slowly, towards the vestry door behind the altar. Through the vestry we could reach the monastery. "Why? Why must I be gone?" he asked stubbornly.

I ground my teeth in frustration. but I was obscurely glad to see this toughness in him resisting me. "Because we must."

We were in the vestry, and I was just pulling the curtain part closed and pushing William ahead of me, when the outer church door opened, and I knew it was too late.

"Please go, William," I urged. I did not wait to see if he obeyed me but turned to watch through the curtain, and learn the outcome of my mission.

It was John Droxford, who commanded the King's Wardrobe, who usually gave me my orders, though the king's voice was apparent in everything. Edward kept a tight control everywhere with a stable but vengeful and sometimes strangling grip. He held England steady, and who was I to question his motives or his methods? My reasons to live had been lost long ago, and I neither judged nor cared. But I should be grateful. More than the first half of my forty years were happy, only the lesser part oblivion.

After the loss of my family, my elder brother had managed to ruin our small estate, and then conveniently died of the pox. What else was there to do but follow the army and fight? My ability to stay alive, yet not caring if I did so, and to find the best food and quarters must have been brought to Droxford's attention. I was recruited as a spy. Fifteen years in the service of the king. Moments of great excitement and forgetting, with the dreary bleak down periods in between kicking my heels. I was in one of those bouts when I was sent for a couple of months ago.

I was surprised all the same when I was ordered to attend the king in person, especially since he was in such poor health. Grey in face, in the hair, his eyes were as grey and cold as the North Sea. Despite the fire burning in the King's Solar, a shiver ran down my spine when he fixed me with that stare.

"It is simple," he said. "Who can I trust, and who is against me? I must and will have Scotland join us. She will be mine. But even though nine years ago I took their ridiculous relic, that red lump of stone that was not even dressed, carved or polished, that they can call by no better name than the Stone – the Stone of Scone. A so-called Stone of Destiny, needed for their enthronements. Hah. Even though I have it tucked under my own throne at Westminster, still the Scots defied me. King Balliol," he sneered, "after I so carefully chose his claim above the others, even he turned against me. And when I beat him in battle he ran away to Normandy." He glared at me. "As for that great betrayer William Wallace I've spiked his head to be jeered and spat at and had his entrails scattered across the realm. But still they obstruct our will. But our – my – will *will* prevail." His wintry voice took the heat from the fire.

I waited. No doubt he'd get around to my instructions soon enough. It paid not to interrupt kings.

"And now, now I'm ill, what are they saying?"

He looked at me. Wisely, I shook my head. "What are they saying, Sire?"

"Merlin's prophecy, yet more horse manure. Have you not heard it? After the death of the covetous king, the Scots and Welsh will unite and have everything as they want it. Or something like that. And guess who is the covetous king? Me. So I must do what I can and nip any last thoughts of rebellion in the bud. The new council for Scotland will be inaugurated next April, in 1306. I want there to be no hitches, understand me? Especially as there is this other rumour, that our Stone is a copy and the real one still up there."

I nodded. "What do you want me to do?"

His face softened slightly. "Carry a message to Robert Bruce at his home in Annandale near Dumfries. He at least I feel I can rely on. He has too much land and too many houses in England to lose, for one thing. Besides, we get on well. Such a merry fellow, and a good fighter. A man could be proud of a son like that." I kept a tactful silence. Edward did not get on with his own son.

"Robert has a lot of friends up there. Tell him to make a deal with John Comyn, Red John they call him. He's clan leader."

"And has the strongest claim to sit on that lump of red sandstone you have hidden under your own chair, now Balliol's disgraced."

"Exactly. And he's a miserable man. Always flying into a rage. Overfond of money, too. Well, I don't want those two to make an alliance against me. My spies are hinting at secret meetings between them, no doubt Comyn's doing. Divide and rule, don't you agree?"

"Yes," I said. "You think it would be better for me to deal with Bruce, not Comyn? Could Comyn be bribed?"

The king smiled nastily. "Not as easily as you, Gregory. Believe me, there will be your biggest reward yet for pulling this one off. I hear you have quite a golden egg somewhere."

I declined my head in false modesty. He had my measure.

"No, Comyn is too stiff-necked to take a bribe. And I don't want you to bribe Bruce – he requires more subtle treatment than that. Make a deal. Suggest that he negotiates with Comyn but does nothing until the council's inauguration, and I will ensure that he receives more power than anyone else, bit by bit. Which I may or may not do. But promise it anyway. Can you do it?"

"I can try," I replied. "You know these men well, I've only seen them at a distance."

"It's a hazardous trip."

"Especially in the winter months," I agreed, but already my pulse was quickening, my spirits rising.

"And while you're at it," he added carelessly, "look into those rumours about that wretched Stone. Have I been duped with a replica?"

"Perhaps the rumours are just that – sent abroad to unsettle you?"

He smiled. "A nice thought. But it's the power of the thought that's holding them together. I must find the real Stone if it is there – and this time destroy it. Break it into pebbles and scatter them to the four winds. It may have been created for the Pictish people, but that was a long time ago, and time marches forward." His tone was passionless, his purpose was iron.

"How much time do I have?" I asked.

"Perhaps six months, Gregory. And then, no more Scottish kings. There is only one king in these isles. I want nothing left to chance."

I had few farewells to make, and travelled north as inconspicuously as possible. Some of my enemies still lived. I was fortunate in that my features were not outstanding either way, neither malformed nor beautiful, and my hair is mid brown. But I am taller than many, with broad shoulders.

Then I encountered the dying Friar, also a well built man, and on a whim adopted his guise I guessed it would be easier to penetrate his household and approach Robert Bruce as a friar and I was right. We had our talks, and this meeting now, this very moment, was the result.

Through the gap in the thick curtain I saw Robert Bruce strolling down the aisle with his kinsman, Christopher Seton. Robert, a thickset thirty years old or so, with an open expression was looking around with those lively eyes of his. He said something, and both men laughed. I wondered if he guessed that I was watching.

Then the outer door opened and two more men came in, striding towards the first two at the altar.

"The Red Comyn," whispered a voice behind me, "and his uncle."

"I told you to leave," I whispered back to William, but I had no time to deal with him.

Robert Bruce and John Comyn greeted each other with a kiss on the cheek and then moved a little apart to stand by the altar, talking animatedly but in low voices together. Their kinsmen companions stood nearby, quite relaxed, exchanging a few words. The candles settled down after being disturbed by the open door. The bells were silent now. I felt that heady sense of elation and release I always experienced when I had engineered a master stroke. A rush of power perhaps.

I could feel William pressing close behind me. Comyn listened carefully to Bruce, then replied – and suddenly they were staring each other down face to face, the one white and tight lipped, the other red and stormy. Two furious men. Then John Comyn spoke again, very slowly and deliberately. It all happened in an instant, yet time seemed to slow down. Bruce's hand was at his waist. The dagger gleamed silver as it plunged forward – then seemed to enter Comyn's body so slowly, inch by inch – then it was out. Blood seeped and Comyn gasped long and loud before collapsing to his knees, then the floor.

Behind me William too gasped. I glanced round. He was waxy pale with shock, murmuring, "No. Not you. No." I hesitated, my heart thundering . . . What to do? Now time speeded up. Christopher Seton struck Comyn's uncle a massive blow on the head, felling him, in order to save Bruce as the man lunged at him. Then the two men stared down at Comyn, wounded on the ground. Bruce did not try to help his rival. His face was a mask.

"There's no time for this, Robert. I've slain his uncle there, and now I'll do for the nephew too." Christopher raised his sword.

"Wait, Christopher. In cold blood –"

He was too late. Christopher plunged his sword into Comyn. His act seemed to unfreeze Bruce. Wildly he grabbed Christopher's arm and dragged him from the church, shouting incoherently.

The shackles fell from my legs too. Released, I ran into the church. "Quickly," I called, "I think he's still alive."

I bent over the wounded man. He groaned.

"Can you hear me?" I asked.

His eyes flickered open. "I'll live," he said faintly.

William was beside me. "We'll carry him into the vestry," I commanded – a quick glance at Comyn's uncle confirmed he was dead. "Make him comfortable on the bench there. But no further or we'll make him spill more blood. We must keep him warm."

He was a heavy, brawny man, but we got him there. I was right about William's wiry strength. William was uncharacteristically silent, avoiding my eyes. I assumed it was shock until we had laid Comyn on the bench and I said, "Look after him while I fetch help and try not to be sick, there's enough to clear up." Then William spoke.

"You," he said. "You made this happen. That's why you're here. You knew they were coming – you volunteered to help me – you planned this – this –"

"No! Listen to me, William." I seized his shoulders. "Yes, I suggested the meeting, yes I suggested the time and place. But bloodshed? No, that was not my idea. Not my idea at all."

I was in my visitor's cell packing when they came for me. Abbot John of Greyfriars Abbey, Dumfries sent his two strongest monks to fetch me. They were polite, but to be obeyed. They kept a respectful distance in case I lunged with my dagger, and made sure I left my staff behind.

This abbey had been endowed by Margaret, the second, and English wife of the great Alexander III of Scotland. A devout woman she had spent most of her later years praying in the chapel she had built on Edinburgh's heights. The weight of history pressed down on me as I was led to the abbot. What had William told him? Was the boy so disillusioned he'd blurt out everything? And Devorgilla, who'd married a Balliol and therefore into the Comyn clan, had built Sweetheart abbey and bridge here in Dumfries. I was on very dangerous ground.

Had my luck deserted me?

Did I care?

Before the monks came for me I'd completed my dispatch to the king, telling him what had happened, promising to do my best to discover what Robert Bruce's deuced plan was.

Obviously the man would have to flee if Comyn died, a fugitive from justice and ripe for excommunication. Both their lives hung on a thread. Which meant the king had lost two powerful men – who would swim into that gap? I saw my reward slipping away.

Or had that been Edward's scheme all along? No, surely even his strategizing mind could not have foreseen such results from my meddling?

I had also told him my life was in danger. Then I had paid a boy passing in the Friar's Vennel to take the letter, hidden in a small pouch inside a rough sack of dried apples, not worth stealing, to a reliable messenger waiting nearby.

"What's all the commotion in town?" I asked the lad, pointing to flickering flames and smoke clearly visible even in the darkness.

"That's the Bruce. He threatened to set the castle on fire if the justices in the pay of the English king meeting there didn't let him in to take possession. They ran out like mice. He got the fires stoked to show he meant business. Everyone's running round demented, there's such a hullabaloo through town. Is Red Comyn truly dead?"

I pretended to cuff the lad round the head and showed him another coin. "That's for you if you bring me a sign you delivered the package." We had agreed a signal, the messenger and I.

I stood in front of the abbot thinking: so Robert Bruce thinks he can hide from Edward's wrath in the castle. No doubt he's waiting to see if Comyn lives or dies. Maybe he'll claim it was a personal quarrel. But only I know he deliberately flouted Edward's will. My life is worth less than nothing.

I was surprised to see the abbot looked as if he was in the grips of some terrible emotion. His face sagged and he could barely speak. He motioned to the monks to leave then beckoned me forward. He spoke in a low voice.

"You killed him."

"Comyn died despite your best doctors? But I promise you, I did not kill him."

"Not Comyn. Yes he is dead," he waved a hand. "We were still caring for him in the vestry an hour or two later when Bruce sent his men back and they overcame our monks, dragged Comyn back to the altar and made sure he was dead. Lindsay was the leader, I've heard. So. These men live and die by the sword. But the evil sacrilege committed in such a holy place has led to greater darkness."

Something in his tone stopped my mind racing through all the probable outcomes from Comyn's death. I stared at him. He stood and gestured to a curtained alcove. Inside, on a plain wooden trestle, lay a dead body. It was William who lay there, as composed as if sleeping. I stretched out to touch him, utterly confused. I had seen enough of death to know that William was dead. But how could he be? Only hours before he'd been alive and well.

"This is a sudden sickness, to work so fast," I said.

"No sickness. He was found in the Scriptorium, slumped over his desk, his manuscript smeared. A bodkin had been thrust into the base of his skull."

My stomach lurched. "Instant, then. And by an experienced hand."

"Exactly. Yours. You had an air about you that said you were more than a friar. When I saw William after Comyn was really dead, he said, 'Gregory – I can't believe he had a hand in this.' And then he tried to take it back. He idolised you, so even then he was loyal."

I could not take my eyes from that dead body. It should not have happened. What little shred that was left of my heart was torn from my body. Could it be my fault that he was dead?

I sensed that the abbot was a desperate man in his grief. I had to talk fast. It was becoming plain that he may well try to kill me himself. He had loved the boy.

Brusquely I turned away. "Have you questioned the monks here? Did he say anything to anyone else about this afternoon? Was anyone here jealous of your – preference for him?"

Shock made the abbot go white. "You are accusing me? And of what –?"

"Though I'm a stranger here, even I could see."

He covered his face then straightened up. "I thought I would kill you; a life for a life, as it says in the Old Testament, but perhaps I have been too hasty. And supposing you were to overcome me then falsely accuse. It would harm William more. I will therefore tell you something which you must swear on his dead body will go no further – I believe you were fond of him."

"I make no promises, but will do what I can to uncover his killer."

He nodded, sat down heavily again. "William was my son. I fell in love only once. She was already married, to a man she hated. When the child was only two years old, her husband was killed in battle against the English, and Constance was taken away to England a prisoner, where she eventually died. But before she left Scotland she managed to smuggle our child to me for safekeeping. I had already joined the Order then, but I arranged his upbringing and guided him here. He was my only son."

This second possibility had crossed my mind too. "I did not kill him," I reassured him again. "Now, are you sure it was no one here at the Abbey? No personal rivalry or grudge?"

He shook his head. All his energy seemed to have drained away. He went to sit in his carved chair again, slumped there, trembling with grief but still in command of himself. "No. I would have heard whispers and complaints in a small community like this. My fierce questioning only revealed that he was well liked and will be sorely missed."

"I can believe that." My own emotions, suddenly painfully released, made me pace up and down. "Then it's most likely connected with Comyn's murder. Bruce's or Comyn's men – was anyone seen in the abbey before William died?"

"William was alone, and the Scriptorium is easily reached from the outside without passing places where we habitually walk. An assassin could have entered, killed him, and left unseen. A dark winter's night, the monks either at prayer, or probably talking about what has just happened."

"But why didn't he protect himself?" I asked, then answered, "He was probably trying to settle his confusion by working alone on the manuscript. Concentrating hard, he didn't hear the assassin come up behind him." I nodded, and bunched my fists. "Bruce," I murmured softly to myself and thought, "He's betrayed his king, and now this. Did he find out that William witnessed everything? Or was it because William was alone with Comyn while I fetched help. Bruce perhaps fears what Comyn might have said."

"I think William was silenced," I concluded aloud. "But not by me –"

The abbot lifted his head. "Whoever pays you, I will pay you more, and not just in intercessions with Our Lord. Find his murderer."

We stared at one another. We could each betray the other. We stood on equal ground. I felt anger, such anger. William's murder had betrayed me, had allowed thoughts and feelings to emerge I never wanted to have again.

"I'll do it," I said stiffly. "I don't want your silver or gold, though you may talk to Our Lord about me if you wish. When or if I find the truth I will let you know – but I must be free to govern my own actions then. I must have an independent hand."

He was still for a moment, then relaxed and nodded. "I don't have any other choice – but then, I am free also to do as I will. Go then, with my blessing." He wanted me gone so that he could be alone with his misery. I lifted a hand in farewell – to both of them.

Sheeting rain blown by a freezing north-westerly gale cut mercilessly against any exposed skin. The night was pitch black, all stars and moon hidden by thick storm clouds. I slipped and slithered along the muddy path, cursing under my breath. Ahead of me were men, and behind, as well as pack animals. But I could not hear them above the the roar of the wind. Each of us plodded on, lost in his own world of discomfort.

It was nearly six weeks since I had left Dumfries. Time had dulled my grief, but only increased my dogged determination to unravel the mystery and honed my desire for vengeance. I had spent that time following Robert Bruce's trail. He seemed to sense I was behind him, and kept one step ahead of me all the time.

I would never have predicted what he did. He did not hide from shame or guilt. Instead, after seizing Dumfries Castle that very first night, he had blazed a trail – seizing castles, rallying support – across the lowlands, but always heading north and east, his eventual goal the town I hoped to reach tonight. Scone.

Extraordinary events had unfolded in those scant six weeks. English men had fled south of the border. Bishop Wishart had brought out of hiding the Scottish Royal Vestments, Robes and Banner that he'd saved years before when Edward took the Stone of Scone, and gave Bruce his blessing in Glasgow. Men from all walks of life, rich and poor alike, flocked to the cause of Scotland, and to Robert Bruce. It seemed that he had built up an enormous store of not only goodwill, but also faith in his abilities as a leader. There were powerful men who were afraid to shake off the traditional yokes of England and Balliol, and there would be battles ahead against them. But for now, Bruce carried all before him.

I realized, as events moved with bewildering speed, just how much manoeuvring must have been going on for years. How enraged King Edward would be to learn that the man who had been his favourite had perhaps only been biding his time to seize power. Had the death of John Comyn been planned, so that once removed Bruce had a free hand? Or was it an accident that acted as spark for the conflagration that now roared across Scotland?

I had not forgotten my other purpose. Was there another Stone of Destiny at Scone? And if not, was it still possible that a king could be enthroned there? Was there enough power in the place to endow him with kingship to lead the ragbag of Scottish people and make them one? Because that was what Robert the Bruce intended. Tomorrow, he would become King Robert. King Edward's vengeance would know no bounds. No doubt he was already embarked with his army on the march northwards to again batter the Scots into submission.

Ahead lay the small town of Scone, with Moot Hill on its outskirts. Kings of old since the days of the Picts had been crowned there, had chosen this place to declare themselves and to govern from, and so had Robert the Bruce. But who would crown him? The young Earl of Atholl, the only one with that power, lay languishing in imprisonment in England. And the Stone of Destiny – surely that too was captive at Westminster? Robert Bruce of Annandale, Earl of Carrick, could never pull it off. Surely it was all a great bluff?

I felt I was closing in on my destiny too. Soon I would meet him again. I was close to him now. Nothing would stop me finding him out, and then I would find the truth.

I had sent no further dispatches to King Edward after that first one (the boy had returned safely with the signal, and got paid). My own motives, for once, had precedence. I had heard that, on February 24th, he'd sent two clerics north to investigate, perhaps a response to my report. But they were blundering about like blind men in the heather.

I'd had plenty of rain-sodden, frost-blighted hours to mull things over. I'd replayed my first interview with Robert Bruce over and over, searching for some clue as to why he had murdered Comyn so unexpectedly. So contrary to our discussion. Or so I thought.

It had been surprisingly easy to get near him. I'd come across his hunting party one day, joined in, and found myself sharing venison roast on a fire outdoors along with a potent spirit that caught the back of my throat. He'd teased me on being a friar with lustful appetites. Later, I'd caught him alone, while his men sang, and played music nearby.

When I revealed carefully I was from Edward he was watchful but not fearful. He sighed and said, "How disappointing. I thought you a jolly Friar, but find you to be playing the game I like to escape from when I can."

"A game you intend to win?" I suggested.

"A game I *hope* to win. It's a risk, a gamble."

"Then here's how to increase your odds for achieving your goal." Delicately I unwound King Edward's proposal, making it as enticing as I could.

Looking back I realized now that he never vowed, nor agreed. He merely appeared to go along with it by avoiding either saying no or putting up objections. He had played me at my own game and I had lost. I thought he was in agreement – but he was simply leaving things open and avoiding conflict.

Oh yes, I would catch up with him. This time he would have reason to look fearful. This time he would not be able to evade me.

I met him at dawn the next day. After sleeping fitfully on a pile of damp straw I went out on the hill overlooking the small grey town. The storm had blown out, the sky was just lightening in the east. There was only the whisper of a breeze in the air. I had sent a message to Bruce the previous night, asking him to meet me here at dawn, "to talk over old times," I'd said, signed Friar Gregory.

I stood looking down, conspicuous in my bedraggled clothes – I'd adopted their more comfortable garb of plaid over the shoulder over a saffron yellow shirt. I could make out the low hump of Moot Hill, the church, and in the distance the mysterious circles of standing stones left by ancient peoples.

Would he come?

As I stood, looking down, what I thought was a rock on the hillside, moved. It was a man, a rough blanket around his shoulders.

"You came, then. I'll sit with you. *Sir*."

"What, sit in the wet grass?" his voice was light, quick, amused. "Well, why not. And less of the sir. I'll be Sire soon enough. For now I'm content to be a man, this one last morning."

"Aren't you afraid?"

He gave a snort of surprised laughter and leaned back on his elbows. "Perhaps I'm learning about taking risks still. Perhaps I want to tempt fate. If I survive until the crown is placed upon my head – why then it was meant to be after all."

"You have a strong claim. Your lineage stretches as far back to royalty as do the others."

"Yes yes," he was impatient. "Always the past. Now I want to look ahead to the future, when we govern ourselves, as one nation. Scotland. For too long I've weighed the pros and cons, tried to make the ends justify the means. No more now. Now my father is dead. It's a straight line I walk."

"Stepping over one dead body on the way, if not two? Why did you do it?"

Immediately his expression changed, and he sat up. "You mean John of course. And the other?"

He was clever. Still he gave nothing away unless he absolutely had to. My voice shook a little when I told him about William.

"I'm sorry," he said when I'd finished. Yet still he wouldn't yield any of his secrets. Suddenly I lunged at him. At this point I only intended to shake him, to get him to talk, but he was more ready than he looked. We wrestled on the wet hillside, panting and cursing, until his youth and no doubt stamina from enjoying dry beds and better food than I, gave him the upper hand.

Once more I stared death in the face, but still it did not come. He grunted and released me. "No more deaths," he said.

We sat side by side in silence for a moment, then he began to talk. "Why did I kill John? Because we had always fought and been rivals, he the Claimant and I the Competitor, and because we had never been in sympathy – chalk and cheese? Some would find that reason enough. But not me.

"Gregory, I did tell him about your message from Edward. 'The man is ill,' I told him. 'We should act now. If you back me as king, you can have all my lands. Our families have dealt this way before.' He said, 'Why should I trust you to act decisively for once? You switch allegiances when it suits you. You were ever faint-hearted in a cause.' He was right of course. In the past it was so.

"But I told him I had changed. Grown up. My father not long dead. Wallace crushed and dead. Suddenly I discovered I was next in line. At last I was ready. He made fun of that, which I expected. I was angry at him for his insults and taunts. But we've exchanged worse before.

"What had changed? I don't know. I felt that this was it. A sense of being outside myself. Very aware. I put it to him again. Yes or No? And all he said was: 'Never. I will never call you king.'

"I was enraged. I felt there was no alternative. He'd never budge. That is no excuse to take a life. I had forgotten where we were – the church, the altar. I only saw that face – him – before me. In the way. I lashed out to remove it. A selfish act, to be sure."

He paused, looked at me. "But afterwards, that was when I murdered him. When reason returned, we could have tried to save him. Instead, I left, and I did not try to stop my kinsmen going back later to finish him off, to be sure he was dead. I did not order it, but I did not stop them. They were determined anyway that there would be no going back this time. This time I would be forced to go forward. I had to take the chance. Seize the moment."

"And William?"

He looked down, plucking at the grass. "Lindsay told me there was one young monk who seemed attached to Comyn. He was sure Comyn said meaningfully to him, 'Don't forget what I told you.' Lindsay asked me what Comyn could have meant? I could not take the chance that Comyn told your friend of my meeting with you and Edward's message. My enemies would claim a double bluff – Comyn's death was Edward's order. One risk I would not take." He looked directly at me. "I told Lindsay to arrange the young monk's silence."

It was as if an arrow pierced my gut. Indirectly, then, I had been responsible. For putting in train events that caused William's death. An accident. Wrong place, wrong time.

"I tell you now, nothing can deviate me this time from the course I have set myself. I had to choose. I could've fled – but spend my life doing nothing in exile? That's not for me. I have these two sins to put right. I will try to make the ends justify the means. And you?"

"I don't know. I must think –"

"Well, I have a coronation to attend, quickly before I'm excommunicated. No doubt the Pope's messenger is en route somewhere. So I'll be away. You can say your piece if you want, but I don't think many will want to hear it."

"Maybe not. I'll be the lone voice. But how can you become king? The Stone of Destiny is in Westminster. Isn't it?"

He gave a brief smile. "Aha. We shall see. Perhaps it's enough to imagine the real one is still here. Just as no one knows if it came from the Lost Tribe of Israel, or St Columba brought it. Maybe every

Scottish hearth is, in a sense, part of that Stone? Now I must go. Will you be trying to stop me?"

I shook my head. "I haven't decided yet."

Later that day, Lady Day March 25th 1306, I watched Isabel, the Earl of Atholl's sister and devoted follower, some say mistress, of Robert the Bruce, lift a golden coronet and hold it high above his dark head. There was a moment of stillness. The packed crowds seemed to catch their breath. Into that silence I could have cried out, "Do not crown this man, accept him as your king. He is a murderer." Even though the cynic in me knew that many kings and councillors had killed and worse to gain their power.

The coronet descended, the church erupted in cheers. My moment was over.

I'd made my decision not to speak. This was what these people wanted. Their choice. Bruce had acted out of heat and passion. Edward's cruelties were cold and calculating. He enjoyed the infliction of pain. In his careless way, the Bruce did not. And as we approached Easter, Gregory too would be reborn.

Somewhere along the way in my journey from King Edward's Solar to this moment I too had changed. My soul – what tatters that were left of it – had been unfrozen. I too had been infected with this talk of new beginnings.

I recalled I had told King Edward I feared I would be killed, and had not communicated since. I could start a new life here – and there were bonny lasses aplenty. Suddenly I no longer wanted to be associated with my old way of life and its creeping in the dark shadows. It brought too many innocent casualties. In a way, this rejection of my old life might give meaning to William's death. As Robert Bruce – or as I should now call him, King Robert – had indicated.

At least I had resolved the murders. As for the Stone? I was sure now the real one must still be here, radiating its power.

And after all, King Robert would need someone nearby to make sure he did not stray from his new path, make sure he continued to atone for these murders.

But in my new country and in this new dawn, I had no doubt it would be done.

Edward II ❦

PERFECT SHADOWS

Edward Marston

It was Edward II whom Robert the Bruce defeated at Bannockburn in 1314 to re-establish Scottish independence. History has not treated Edward well. He was a weak and rather foolish king between two giants: Edward I and Edward III. He fell victim to his scheming wife, Isabella, known as the she-wolf of France, and her lover, Roger Mortimer. Edward was deposed and imprisoned where, history tells us, he met a gruesome fate – a red-hot poker was thrust up through his anus into his bowels. But is this what really happened?

> "But what are kings, when regiment is gone,
> But perfect shadows in a sunshine day?"
>
> Christopher Marlowe *Edward the Second*

"You are to be moved to Berkeley Castle," said Henry of Lancaster gently.

"Why?" asked Edward with alarm.

"Orders have been given to that effect."

"By whom?"

"The king."

"My son would not be so unkind to his father. This is the work of that she-wolf, Isabella, my hateful wife. She and evil Mortimer conspire against me here. I do not like it, Henry."

"No more do I, my lord. But I must comply."

"What lies behind this change of prison?"

"You have been no prisoner here," Henry reminded him.

"I know, my friend, and I am deeply grateful."

Edward the Second had suffered indignities enough by the time he was consigned to Kenilworth Castle and his custodian, Henry of Leicester, who had newly assumed his dead brother's title of Earl of Lancaster, saw no reason to add pain to ignominy. Courteous and considerate, Henry treated the deposed king more like a guest than a prisoner. Edward was allowed the freedom of the castle and lived, if not in state, then at least in relative comfort. He was about to exchange his kindly host for a much more heartless gaoler. It put a note of anguish into his voice.

"Mortimer has stolen my wife, my son and my kingdom. Now he robs me of my peace of mind. There is only one thing left to take!"

"Do not even entertain such a thought."

"I must, Henry. My life is at risk."

"Thomas de Berkeley is an honourable man."

"He *does* know what honour means," said Edward bitterly. "And he has cause for revenge. After my victory at Boroughbridge, I kept both Thomas and his father, Maurice, languishing in a dungeon. The old man died in captivity but his son was liberated by my erstwhile queen, who restored his estates to Thomas de Berkeley. Now that I am his prisoner, Thomas will not forget that he was once mine."

"I, too, suffered at Boroughbridge," sighed Henry. "You defeated us in battle and condemned my brother, Thomas of Lancaster, to a traitor's death. In your mercy, you commuted the sentence to one of beheading. I am eternally grateful for that act of kindness. Though I have grievances of my own to nurse, I have endeavoured to treat you with the respect due to your position."

"Is any respect due to a king who was forced to abdicate?"

"I believe so, my lord."

"My time has come and gone."

"You may still live out your life in dignity."

"Here in Kenilworth, perhaps," said Edward, reaching out to squeeze his companion's arm. "Thanks to you, my misery has been greatly eased. Warwickshire is a beautiful county even though it holds cruel memories of the death of my beloved Gaveston. I have enjoyed gazing out across its green fields as I walk around your battlements." His face darkened. "Will I be given the same licence at Berkeley Castle?"

The question was answered by the arrival of his new custodian. With an eagerness bordering on glee, Thomas de Berkeley came striding into the Great Hall where the two men had been conversing. One look at the newcomer's face was enough to confirm Edward's worst fears. There was a ruthless glint in Berkeley's eye. No compassion could be expected from him nor from the man who accompanied him. Sir John Maltravers, his brother-in-law, was a fugitive from the army which Edward had so soundly beaten at Boroughbridge some five years earlier. Maltravers had joined Isabella's party in France and was one more beneficiary of her husband's fall from power. He and Thomas de Berkeley had a score to settle with the deposed king.

After an exchange of greetings, Berkeley's disapproval was curt.

"Why is the prisoner not chained?" he snapped.

"He presents no danger," explained Henry.

"What is he doing out of his cell? Does he have a degree of liberty here in Kenilworth?"

"At my discretion."

"He will not enjoy such favours in my custody."

"Nor will I expect any," said Edward defiantly.

Berkeley ignored him and gave a peremptory command.

"Have the prisoner taken back to the dungeons!"

Henry of Lancaster bristled. "Only I give orders in this castle," he said with vehemence. "Bear that in mind. While he is in my keeping, I will treat Edward as I think fit. Tomorrow, I hand him over to you, Thomas. Until then, I warn you not to interfere."

Edward was grateful for his host's intercession but he knew that it would gain him only a temporary relief. Thomas de Berkeley was clearly smarting at the rebuff. When the prisoner came into his charge, he would make Edward pay for the stern words of the Earl of Lancaster.

They left Kenilworth at the crack of dawn on Palm Sunday. Manacled on the orders of his new master and surrounded by four burly men-at-arms, Edward rode in discomfort and saw little of the county whose beauties he had savoured from the vantage point of the castle. Out in the fresh air, he yet felt more confined than he had done when in the care of Henry of Lancaster. There were no solicitous inquiries about his health and preferences at table. Berkeley and Maltravers had none of the gracious behaviour which had lessened the ordeal of imprisonment at Kenilworth. When they were not mocking or sneering at Edward, his captors fell into a grim silence.

At the end of a long day, they reached Monmouthshire and spent the night at Llanthony Priory. The monks showed a dutiful kindness towards Edward but he was allowed no privileges. On the following day, they completed their journey. The prisoner's first glimpse of his new abode struck quiet terror in his heart. Berkeley Castle was smaller, neater and more compact than Kenilworth and had none of the latter's craggy magnificence. Set in a wooded plain which swept on to Severn Estuary, the castle was an imposing fortress which somehow combined elegance with solidity. Edward saw none of its handsome features. What filled his mind was the fear that he was riding towards his tomb.

When they entered the courtyard, Thomas de Berkeley was crisp.

"Lock the prisoner up!" he ordered.

"Am I to be allowed books to study?" asked Edward.

"No!"

"Not even the Bible?"

"You will inhabit a dungeon and not a monastery."

"Have care for my soul," pleaded the other.

"We will remember you in our prayers."

Berkeley gave a derisive laugh and gestured to his men. Edward was lifted bodily from the saddle and hustled off to his quarters. The cell was small, fetid and without natural light. A single candle illumined the bleak scene. Dank straw partially covered the floor. A crude mattress stood against one wall. The only other furniture was a rough-hewn stool and a rickety table. A rat scuttled out through a drain-hole. Before Edward could complain, he was thrust unceremoniously into the dungeon and the heavy door clanged shut behind him. When he tried to shout, the stench hit his nostrils so hard that he started to retch.

The comforts of Kenilworth seemed a thousand miles away.

Weeks stretched into months and the privations began to tell on his health and appearance. He was permitted some brief daily exercise in the courtyard but the shuffing figure was unrecognizable as the proud warrior who had put his foes to flight at Boroughbridge. Edward suffered a dramatic loss of weight. His hair was unkempt, his overgrown beard salted with grey. His shoulders sagged and his head was bowed. Sharing most of his time with the flickering flame of a candle, he squinted badly in the daylight. It was a life of sustained humiliation.

Some time in July, he was allowed a visitor. When the Dominican friar was admitted to his cell, Edward was at first disturbed, fearful that the man had come to administer last rites before summary execution. Seeing his distress, the newcomer was quick to offer reassurance.

"Have no fear, my lord," he said. "I come to bring succour."

"I am sorely in need of it. What is your name?"

"Brother Thomas."

"I am much abused here, Thomas."

"So I see," said the other sadly, "and it does not become your rank. They do you wrong to treat you so. Is this some whim of your custodian or does he act under orders from above?"

"Both," explained Edward. "He inclines towards cruelty and is ratified in that inclination by the commands of his father-in-law, Roger Mortimer. The same villain who sleeps in my bed with my wife and rules the kingdom through the person of my young son."

"England has learned to rue the name of Mortimer."

"So have I, Brother Thomas."

"He is a harsh ruler."

"Matched with a harsh woman."

"Both have made the kingdom bleed. God will punish them for it." He glanced around to make sure that the guard was not listening outside the door. "I come as a friend, my lord."

"I hear it in your voice, Thomas."

"A *special* friend. I have done you service in the past."

"Have you?" Edward peered at the gnarled face in the gloom. "At Oxford, perhaps? Were you one of the kind Dominicans who took in the headless body of my dear Gaveston and embalmed it because sentence of excommunication still attached to it and it had to lay unburied?"

"No, my lord. I was not at Oxford."

"Where, then, did you show this special friendship?"

"In Avignon."

"Ah!"

"I was sent hither at the express command of Sir Hugh Despenser to negotiate with the Pope the annulment of your marriage."

"Would that I had never wed Isabella in the first place!"

"I acted as your emissary, my lord."

"Then you are doubly welcome, Brother Thomas. Yours are the first soft words I have heard since I came into Gloucestershire. I am in a dire condition yet you still reverence me like a king."

"I am not the only one, my lord."

"Your meaning?"

"England is in turmoil," said the friar. "Those who supported the alliance between the Queen Isabella and Mortimer are having second thoughts. Our new rulers take arrogance to the point of tyranny. Instead of rewarding their followers, they bully and tax them. Rebellion is in the air. People are starting to remember how well you treated them, my lord. They are angered by reports that you are kept here under restraint."

"Those reports are not false, as you can see."

"I see much more than that."

"In what way?"

"That will soon become clear. Tell me about the castle."

"The castle?"

"Its design, its defences, its garrison, its routines. You have been here long enough to see how Berkeley Castle is run. Tell me all, my lord. The intelligence will be put to good use."

"By whom?"

"Myself and my brother."

"Another friar of the Order?"

"Hardly!" said the other with a chuckle. "My brother, Stephen, is too wild and wilful a man to submit to the Rule of St Dominic. You may understand why when I tell you his full name. It is Stephen Dunheved."

Edward's eyes widened. "Lord of the manor of Dunchurch."

"Banished lord. His estates were seized."

"Does he live abroad in exile?"

"So it is believed."

"And what is the truth of the matter?"

"You will see."

The talked earnestly together for a long time in lowered voices.

Thomas Dunheved was a resourceful man who provided much more than spiritual sustenance. By the time that his visitor was about to leave, he had revived a long-dead hope in Edward.

"Will you do me one more service, Brother Thomas?" he asked.

"Do but name it, my lord."

Edward thrust his hand under his tattered tunic to bring out a roll of parchment. He gave it to the friar with a conspiratorial whisper.

"See this delivered to Henry of Lancaster."

"A letter?"

"A poem," said Edward. "I wrote it during my stay at Kenilworth. It is not safe to hold on to it any longer. I am denied writing materials here and they would take this from me if they knew I had it. Have it put into the hands of Henry of Lancaster. He deserves this record of my time with him at Kenilworth Castle. Can I trust you to see this done?"

The friar nodded then slipped the parchment into the sleeve of his cowl when he heard the door being unlocked. Edward was sorry to see Brother Thomas go but he was heartened by what he heard. It would give him food for thought during the lonely hours of the night. He still had friends. There were those to whom he remained Edward the Second.

Escorted to the main gate, Thomas Dunheved left the castle and picked his way across the meadow and through the trees. Only when he was out of sight of the sentries did he stop to take out the parchment from his sleeve. Unrolling it with care, he read the first verse of the poem.

> In winter woe befell me
> By cruel Fortune thwarted,
> My life now lies a ruin
> Full oft have I experienced,
> There's none so fair, so wise,
> So courteous nor so highly famed,
> But, if Fortune cease to favour,
> Will be a fool proclaimed.

The friar was moved. Edward's plight was far worse than he had imagined. He had now seen with his own eyes the way that the deposed king was treated, kept like a wild animal in a dungeon below ground. Slipping the poem back into his sleeve, he turned northward and moved off through the undergrowth with long and purposeful strides.

The attack was cleverly-timed and well-executed. Primed by his brother, Stephen Dunheved knew exactly when and where to strike. Under the dark blanket of night and taking advantage of a depleted garrison, the banished lord and his men stormed over the walls and dealt viciously with any resistance. Dunheved was a big, brawny man with a love of valiant action and an edge of desperation about him. Having killed, robbed and cheated in order to survive as an outlaw, he now felt that he had a worthy cause and committed himself wholeheartedly to it. Once inside Berkeley Castle, he opened the main gate to admit his brother, Thomas, with the rest of the armed band.

When the guards were overpowered, Stephen Dunheved battered his way into the keep then raced down to the dungeons. Roused from his sleep, Edward was confused by the yells and the sound of fighting. A blood-covered Dunheved soon unlocked the door and beckoned the prisoner out. Thomas arrived with a cloak, hat and sword for him.

"What is happening, Thomas?" said the bemused Edward.

"We have come to rescue you, my lord."

"Where are you taking me?"

"Away from here."

"I am truly free?"

"Only if you move your royal arse away from this cesspit," said Stephen Dunheved, averting his nose from the stink of the cell. "Come, my lord. We have a long ride ahead of us this night."

But the leader of the attackers had other business to discharge first. While Thomas ushered the prisoner into the courtyard where horses awaited them, his brother gave the order for his men to loot and destroy indiscriminately. Only when they had filled their satchels with spoils and set fire to parts of the castle were they ready to retreat. Thomas Dunheved had planned the assault but it was his brother who provided the efficient brutality needed for its success.

Edward was thrilled to have a horse beneath him again. A brilliant horseman, he sorely missed the opportunity to ride. Now he was free once more, galloping through the night on a black stallion, putting distance between himself and the castle which had entombed him. At the first gesture of daylight, they reined in their mounts and waited for the others to catch them up. Stephen Dunheved and his men were a clamorous assembly. Drunk on stolen wine and inebriated with their success, they came hurtling along with loud whoops. They behaved less like loyal subjects than wild marauders but Edward did not mind. These men had risked their lives to rescue their king. It was exhilarating. Edward laughed as loud as any of them as they continued on their way.

Pursuit was swift and decisive. The reckless flight of the attackers was their own undoing. A large posse was formed and it had no difficulty following the vivid trail south to Dorset. Before they could embark and sail to the safety of the French coast, Edward and his supporters were caught and outnumbered at Corfe Castle. Many of the the band died in the skirmish or fled ignominiously. Stephen Dunheved was among them. It was ironic. The man who wreaked most havoc at Berkeley Castle escaped but his hapless brother, Thomas, the Dominican friar, who had organized the violence in which he did not participate, was dragged savagely back to Gloucestershire to face the full wrath of Berkeley himself.

A monastic cowl was no protection. Stripped naked and flung headlong into a dungeon, Thomas Dunheved was cruelly tortured until his body could take no more. Locked in another cell, Edward could do nothing but lie there and listen to the agonised cries of his erstwhile saviour as he went to his Maker by the most excruciating route. The friar had served his king well but paid a frightful penalty for his loyalty.

Having vented their fury on the man who planned the escape, Berkeley and Maltravers took steps to ensure that such a bold rescue could not happen again. Edward was moved to another cell, even darker and more malodorous than the first, serving the castle as a sewer and leaving its occupant ankle-deep in accumulated filth and excrement. Even the robust constitution of the deposed king began to suffer. Sir Thomas Gurney now shared responsibility for the safety of the prisoner and he was as merciless as his colleagues. Gurney was as Berkeley Castle in September when the fateful message came from Mortimer.

It was delivered by William Ogle, who arrived in haste from Wales.

They received him in the Great Hall and read the letter with interest. It was written by William of Shalford, one of Mortimer's lieutenants, and it disclosed details of a second plot to rescue Edward which was being hatched by Sir Rhys ap Grufydd. The intelligence had first been sent to Mortimer himself who was Justice of Wales and in Abergavenny at the time. Mortimer moved swiftly to crush the threatened rebellion, after first dispatching Ogle to Berkeley Castle. The message was clear. As long as Edward lived, he was a source of potential danger. A letter in Mortimer's own hand gave the point more emphasis.

Thomas de Berkeley read out the crucial sentence.

"*Edwardum occidere nolite timere bonum est.*"

"Fear not to kill the king," said Maltravers. " 'Tis good he die."

"There is another translation," noted Gurney, poring over the words. "*Edwardum occidere nolite timere bonum est.* Put a comma in the right place and it becomes the opposite. Kill not the king,'tis good to fear the worst."

"There is no punctuation here," observed Berkeley. "We must provide our own by which I mean a full stop at the end of life. Our orders are plain. Fear not to kill the king, 'tis good he die."

"The sooner, the better," agreed Maltravers.

"Edward is a Latin scholar," said Berkeley with a smirk. "Should we show this message to him and ask him to oblige us by translating his own death sentence?"

"He must himself be translated," said Maltravers, stroking his beard. "From earth to heaven. Or to hell, rather. For the angels will not allow that unholy stink in heaven."

Berkeley nodded. "We know what we must do. All that remains is to decide exactly how we do it."

"Drown him in that sea of ordure down there," suggested Maltravers with a hollow laugh. "Or cut his throat. Or toss him from the battlements and say that he fell while attempting to escape. Any of these ways or all three together will be enough to snuff out a royal life."

"Yes," said Gurney, succumbing to a rare moment of guilt. "A *royal* life. That is what concerns me. Have we really been given licence to kill a king? This is no ordinary crime, sirs. It is regicide."

"A year ago, it may have been," argued Berkeley. "But not any more. What was regicide then is now a service to the nation.

Edwardum occidere nolite timere bonum est. Let us be more precise translators. Fear not to kill Edward, 'tis good he die."

"Edward is not a king," added Maltravers. "He is merely the father of the king. His son has now been crowned."

"And will that son condone this murder?" asked Gurney, still troubled by scruples. "How will he view us if we are seen to be his father's assassins?"

"That is not how we will be seen," said Maltravers airily. "By those who rule the kingdom – Mortimer and Isabella – we will be hailed as heroes because they will know the truth of the matter. Everyone else will be led to believe that Edward died of natural causes."

"But he is as strong as an ox," said Gurney.

"Even an ox must die at the end of its useful life," asserted Berkeley with a dismissive wave of his hand. "Enough of this hesitation. Our instructions are clear and the manner of their delivery reinforces their urgency. This good fellow here has ridden hell-for-leather to deliver the message. While Edward is alive, his name will continue to act as a rallying-point of rebellion. It has fallen to us to rid England of that threat. And to earn the undying gratitude of Mortimer."

"You are right," said Gurney, sweeping aside his reservations. "Let us about it this very night. Whom should we employ to do the deed?"

"There are enough of us here to do it ourselves," said Berkeley, looking around their faces in turn. "Four strong men against one weak prisoner. Whatever method we choose, he will be unable to resist us."

"Beat his brains out," urged Maltravers. "A quick and violent death."

"With the marks of violence left upon him for all to see. No," said Berkeley, pursing his lips reflectively, "we must devise a means to take his life while leaving no trace of how it was done. And let us remember that Edward was once king over us and made us all suffer under his yoke. He deserves a special kind of death. An appropriate end."

Maltravers gave a sudden laugh and slapped his thigh.

"I have it, friends!" he boasted. "I know the perfect way."

*   *   *

The atmosphere of Berkeley Castle underwent a subtle change. There was a sense of imminent violence in the air. Everyone was aware of it except the man at whom it would be directed. Small and unexpected acts of kindness lightened the burden of Edward's last day. He was given a candle and a Bible. One of the gaolers brought him extra food and drink. One of the porters gave him a small crucifix and talked kindly to him. Two of the men-at-arms who had recaptured him at Corfe Castle came to take their leave of him. They found him hunched in a corner, reading the Bible with intense satisfaction.

When night fell, mercy was replaced by vindictiveness. The four assassins had everything in readiness. Down in the dungeons, a poker was laid in the roaring fire. A stout wooden table was placed beside the forge. Ropes were procured. When the poker was white hot, it was time to act. They grinned in the half-dark with anticipatory pleasure.

The prisoner was fast asleep when they struck. Berkeley led the way with Maltravers, Gurney and William Ogle as his confederates. When the door of the cell was unlocked, Berkeley rushed in to rouse his guest and to slip a black bag over his head. Resistance was useless. The prisoner was dragged from his cell by determined hands and carried across to the table. They held him face down on the timber and used the ropes to tie his flailing arms and twitching body. His rags were torn away to expose his bare buttocks. Maltravers and Gurney held down a leg apiece while Ogle pressed down hard on the prisoner's shoulders.

It was Thomas de Berkeley who wound thick leather around his hand before picking up the poker. It glowed murderously in the gloom.

"You have a visitor, my lord," he taunted. "Your dear Gaveston has returned to pleasure you once more. Bid your lover welcome."

And he thrust the poker deep into the prisoner's anus.

They drank in celebration until dawn and congratulated each other on their night's work, convinced that it would bring them rich rewards. Maltravers took the credit for devising a means of death which had a certain poetic justice about it. He had no regrets.

"Those that live by the arse, die by it!" he said with a guffaw. "We gave him a new delight. Even Gaveston's beloved prick was never as hot as that poker. Mortimer will appreciate this jest, I think."

"Yes," said Berkeley, sipping another cup of wine. "And the beauty of it is that it will not show. When the body has been bathed and the wound tended, we may lay Edward on his back and display him to the witnesses we must call. There will be no visible marks of violence upon him. To the naked eye, it will seem that he died a natural death."

"While savouring an unnatural vice."

They shared a crude laugh then decided to gloat over their handiwork. When they got down to the dungeons, however, a surprise awaited them. The prisoner had been untied and the bag had been removed from his head. Bathed and bandaged, he was turned over on his back. Berkeley held a flaming torch beside the face of the corpse and bent over to whisper another taunt into Edward's ear.

But Edward was not there. The sightless eyes which stared up at him belonged to an older and somewhat shorter man. His beard and colouring resembled that of the prisoner and there was the same fine nose but the likeness ended there. The four assassins gaped in horror. They had killed the wrong victim. The vile death had left the man's face contorted with pain but Berkeley was still able to recognize him.

"It is Dickon!" he said in astonishment.

"Dickon the Porter?" asked Maltravers.

"The same. He sought my permission to visit the prisoner so that he could give him a crucifix. I saw no harm in the request and granted his wish." Berkeley looked around in dismay. "But he tricked us all. Dickon must have taken the prisoner's place so that Edward could escape. This is a calamity!"

"Only if it is known," said Maltravers firmly.

"Yes," said Gurney, searching for a means of redemption for them. "Our orders were to kill Edward and we duly dispatched the prisoner. Let it be thought that we murdered the right man. Cut out his heart and send it to Mortimer, encased in a silver casket." He shrugged his shoulders. "Who will know the difference?"

"We will," said Ogle nervously.

"And so will others when the body is displayed," said Berkeley.

"Not if we prepare it properly," argued Gurney. "Faces change during long captivity. Nobody but we have seen Edward for several months. We can swear that this is he. Let us have the body embalmed and dressed in raiment which conceals it. Close this porter's eyes and he may yet have the faint appearance of a king about him."

"It will be done!" affirmed Maltravers.

"It must be done!" insisted Berkeley. "Or we stand accused of folly. Nobody must ever know the truth of this. It is a secret which we four must take to our graves. The body will be shown to witnesses and we will give out that Edward died of a fever contracted in the dungeon. Are we all agreed on that?"

"We are," said Gurney. "And there is nobody to gainsay us."

"Yes, there is," remarked Ogle.

"Who?" said Gurney.

William Ogle ran his tongue over his dry lips before speaking. "Edward himself."

Edward rode hard and thanked God repeatedly for what he believed was divine intercession. Dickon the Porter had been sent from above to save him from the hideous fate which beckoned. The man had not only taken his place in the cell and slipped him a dagger, he had saddled a horse and left it hidden among the trees nearby. Having sneaked out of the castle under the cover of darkness, Edward followed the directions and soon found the animal. His flight was swift but more considered this time. Instead of leaving an easy trail to follow, Edward altered his course time and again, zigzagging his way south.

When dawn came, he felt safe enough to rest the horse, cleanse himself in a stream, change into the apparel which the considerate porter had put in the saddlebags and shave off his beard. Staring at himself in the rippling water, he saw a very different face smiling up at him. He was free once more and he would not surrender that freedom again. Before he set off, he got down on his knees to offer up a heartfelt prayer of thanks. Then he rode on at a steady canter.

Pope John XXII, ruling the Catholic Church from Avignon, was both surprised and curious when he was told who came in search of him. He granted the visitor an audience at once and heard the strange story with rapt attention. Edward the Second was evidently still alive.

"Word reached us that you had died of a fever," said John.

Edward gave a wry smile. "It seems that I did, your Holiness. My body was seen by several eminent witnesses who vouched for the fact that it was me. But nobody wished to claim my body, fearful that they would incur the disfavour of Mortimer if they did so.

Malmesbury and Bristol both refused to accept the corpse of a deposed king."

"Or a deposed porter."

"I was in Ireland when I heard the news," continued Edward. "The goodly abbot of St Peter's at Gloucester took pity on me, I learned. He defied the threats from Mortimer and gave me the most honourable burial. I am almost sorry that I was not there to enjoy it."

The Pope did not share his amusement "This is a wondrous tale, Edward," he said seriously, "and proof positive of God's benevolence. But while you escaped, another died in your place. I will name him in my prayers. What was he called?"

"Dickon, your Holiness. Dickon the Porter."

"A brave and noble man. Buried in Gloucester, you say?"

"At the abbey church of St Peter."

"Then he will find true fellowship in Heaven," said John soulfully. "St Peter is the porter at the gates and he will have a special welcome for this blessed porter. Your rescue is a small miracle, Edward. Few men are capable of such an act of self-sacrifice. Dickon was your salvation."

"Yes," said Edward sadly. "The perfect shadow of a king."

This story was suggested by the contents of an undated letter which was sent to Edward III by Manuel Fieschi, a Genoese priest who held an English benefice. Fieschi recounted the facts which he claimed to have heard from Edward II himself in the confessional box. The details of the events leading up to his imprisonment at Berkeley are remarkably accurate and it is difficult to see how else the priest could have learned them. England, however, was firmly convinced that their former king had died and he was mourned with unexpected fervour.

Edward III soon tired of being manipulated by Mortimer and his mother. He overthrew Mortimer in a coup and had him executed in 1330. His father's assassins – if that is what they really were – never paid the price for their crime. Thomas de Berkeley was prosecuted but his plea of ignorance was accepted and he was acquitted. William Ogle was arrested but escaped to die a free man. Sir John Maltravers found it safer to live abroad but rendered good service to Edward III in Flanders and secured a full pardon before his death in 1364. Sir Thomas Gurney was arrested twice. The first time he escaped but the second time he died in the hands of his captors.

THE FRIAR'S TALE

Cherith Baldry

To many Richard II, the son of Edward, the Black Prince, was a re-run of his great-grandfather, Edward II. Both were weak kings, dominated by court favourites, though Richard II was more outwardly homosexual. Yet Richard II had been heroic in his youth, daring to face Wat Tyler, the leader of the Peasant's Revolt. Despite his homosexuality he was devoted to his wife, Anne of Bohemia. There was always much scandal attached to the king's court, especially after Robert de Vere became the court favourite after 1388. Richard II was a great patron of the arts and under him literature flourished. This is the time of Geoffrey Chaucer, who was in the king's employ. In the following story, when scandal strikes again, it is Chaucer who turns detective to help the king.

"Go, lytel bok, go litel myn tragedye . . ."

Anne of Bohemia sat in the rose arbour, in the garden of Salisbury castle, a scrap of bright embroidery disregarded in her hands, as she listened to Geoffrey Chaucer drawing his great poem to a close.

She could never stop wondering that this small man, his sandy hair and beard already turning to grey, this quietly efficient court servant, should carry within himself the gift of poetry. The jewelled language, the deep understanding of human minds and hearts, sat oddly with Master Chaucer's prosaic outside and almost pedantic manner.

He stood now reading from a lectern placed in the castle garden. It was early for roses, but daisies studded the grass, bright in the May sunshine. Anne's lord and husband, Richard the king, lay prone among them, half-supported on his elbows, his chin resting on cupped hands. Beside him, Robert De Vere, the Earl of Oxford, sat cross-legged, making a daisy-chain. Anne suppressed amusement; they both seemed very young.

The poem drew to an end, and Master Chaucer listened with a faint smile to Richard's extravagant praises.

"Excellent, Master Chaucer," Anne said, when the king had done, "but must you write of wanton women? Are there no good women worthy of your pen?"

The poet's smile deepened, became almost mischievous.

"Indeed, my lady Anne," he said, "if they had goodness and beauty to match yours."

"You flatter me, Master Chaucer." Anne could feel herself flushing. "I am not beautiful."

The poet stooped, plucked a daisy and presented it to her.

"There are many flowers more lovely," he said. "But only this we call the day's eye, the sun, that draws all others to it."

Anne bent her head, hiding embarrassment, and tucked the flower into the lacing of her gown.

"A sweet tongue, Master Chaucer," said De Vere. "And a true one." He had finished making his wreath of daisies, and laid it ceremoniously on Richard's head. "I crown you May King, my lord."

Richard let out a snort of laughter, and launched himself at De Vere. The two young men wrestled amiably, rolling around on the grass. Anne watched, smiling, and did not realize until Master Chaucer cleared his throat, that they were no longer alone.

One of Richard's waiting gentlemen, Sir John Clanvowe, was pacing across the grass from the rose alley that led to the garden gate, followed by a man in friar's habit.

"Richard!" said Anne.

The king and his friend fell apart and sat up. Muttering something, Richard sprang to his feet, brushing grass from the front of his tunic: the king of England, flushed and dishevelled, with flowers still clinging in his hair.

"My lord," Clanvowe said blandly, "this worthy friar would have audience with you."

Now that the friar stood before her, Anne recognized him. He had celebrated Mass earlier that morning, in Robert de Vere's apartments. A tall, gawky figure, with a hatchet face and dark eyes that gleamed fanaticism in their depths.

"Master Latimer," the king said, catching his breath. "What may I do for you? Speak."

The friar stepped forward. His voice vibrated with suppressed emotion.

"My lord king, I bring you word of a plot against your life."

Terror stabbed through Anne. A familiar terror, one she lived with every day, and usually she could persuade herself it slept. It was awake now; she found it hard to believe the icy calm in Richard's voice as he asked,

"And who has made this plot?"

The friar had drawn closer still, and grasped Richard's arm to speak into his ear, though everyone could hear what he said.

"It is your uncle, the Duke of Lancaster."

Richard stepped back, and shook off the friar's clutching hand.

"My uncle . . ." The words were breathed out; he looked completely astonished.

"Have him executed," de Vere said edgily. "Now, before he can act."

Whitefaced, Richard stared at him. "Yes . . ." he murmured, and added more firmly, "Yes. Clanvowe, see it done."

"My lord, I cannot!" Clanvowe sounded scandalized. "Not before my lord of Lancaster has the chance to defend himself."

"Do you question me?"

Richard's temper flared up. Anne could see that he was ready to go flying to disaster. She went to him and caught his hands.

"Richard, listen to me. The Duke of Lancaster has powerful friends. They will be your enemies if you do this. If he is guilty, then a fair trial will do you more honour."

After the first few seconds she realized with relief that he was listening to her. When she had finished, he swallowed and took a breath.

"Very well," he said. "I shall search this further. Clanvowe, have the Duke sent to me here."

Clanvowe half turned towards the garden alley and stopped.

"No need," he said.

John of Gaunt, the Duke of Lancaster himself, was striding across the grass. Anne watched him come. He was richly dressed, in blue velvet and a cloak lined with vair, but somehow she could never picture to herself the tall, rangy figure and iron grey head in anything but armour.

"Yes, he comes, the traitor," said Latimer vindictively. "Take his life now, my lord, or the time will come when he will take yours."

Richard paid no attention to him; his eyes were fixed on Gaunt.

"Richard, your court awaits you for –" Gaunt began to speak impatiently as soon as he was in earshot, and then broke off, as if aware that everyone was staring at him. "In God's name, what's this?" he asked. "Have I sprouted horns?"

De Vere let out a little crack of laughter, and turned aside. Richard said,

"My lord of Lancaster, an accusation has been spoken against you here. Master Latimer, repeat what you have just told me."

Anne thought the friar looked disconcerted at the thought of accusing the duke to his face. He sawed the air uncertainly with one arm; he looked almost like a scarecrow, as if one good wind could have blown him into tatters. At last he said,

"I heard, my lord, that you plotted against the king's life."

Gaunt reacted with no more than raised eyebrows, but his eyes sparked like steel when swords clash.

"And where did you hear this?" His voice was dangerously quiet.

"It was told to me by an esquire of my lord de Vere."

Anne caught her breath. The king spun round and faced his friend. "Robert?"

De Vere, astonished in his turn, spread his hands.

"Richard, no! If this is true, it was none of my doing. You, fellow –" He paced forward and shook the friar roughly by the shoulder. "What man was this? What was his name?"

Latimer pulled himself away, a defensive look on his face.

"I do not know. He told me he was an esquire of yours, my lord, and bade me take news to the king of a plot against him by my lord of Lancaster."

De Vere snorted with disgust.

"A pack of lies!"

"Richard," said Gaunt, cutting through the friar's protests, "I swear to you I have no thoughts of your death. But if the lie has been spoken it must be answered."

The king did not respond for a moment, but let out his breath in a long sigh. He rested one hand on Gaunt's arm.

"I trust your good faith. Master Latimer" – now he spoke commanding, compelling the friar's attention – "go now and write down all that you know of this affair. Sir John, go with him and when the account is finished, bring it to me."

Sir John Clanvowe bowed; the little group around the king remained silent as he led the friar away. When they were out of sight, Gaunt said,

"Is this some trick of yours, de Vere, to rid yourself of me?"

De Vere's hand went to his belt knife; his face flamed with fury. Gaunt was unimpressed.

"De Vere, I could break you in two," he said. "But I'd as soon not be put to the trouble of it."

De Vere breathed heavily, and then relaxed, with a mocking twist to his mouth.

"Even if you suspect me of treason," he said, "acquit me of stupidity. If I plotted against you, my lord of Lancaster, I should do it more efficiently. I certainly should not bid my man to identify himself."

Chaucer had listened to all this in silence, withdrawn a little beside his lectern. He had gathered together the pages of his poem. Now he bowed and said,

"My lords, my lady Anne, I will take leave of you. I swear I will say nothing of what I have heard."

"No!" Anne caught at the poet's sleeve. In all this fear and confusion, he seemed the only source of calm. "Master Chaucer, stay with us and advise us. We have sore need of your wisdom."

Chaucer glanced at the king, brows raised. For a moment, Richard looked uncertain, and then he managed a shaken smile.

"What help you can give," he said, "I will most gratefully receive."

Rumours of the friar's accusation were already flying. John of Gaunt went with Richard to meet his nobles in the hall of council. Anne led Chaucer to a gallery where they could overlook the hall. Seated side by side on a wooden bench, hidden by the gallery rail, they tried to make sense of the clamour of voices rising from below.

Richard was seated on the dais, tense and frowning, with John of Gaunt at his side. Standing before him at the foot of the steps was an elderly nobleman, with a pouchy, discontented face.

"The Earl of Arundel," Anne murmured.

The earl was managing to make himself heard.

"My lord Richard, perhaps now you will see the need to reform your household. This plot against my lord of Lancaster must come from there."

Richard said something in reply inaudible to the watchers in the gallery. Anne was relieved to see that he was holding on to his temper.

"I name no names, my lord," Arundel went on. "But I can –"

"I will name one name." Another voice interrupted him, and the speaker sprang up on to the dais to stand before the king. He was a smaller man, thick-set, with reddish hair: the Earl of Buckingham, Richard's youngest uncle. "The whole of England knows that Robert de Vere hates my brother of Lancaster."

This time Richard's response was snapped out quickly. Buckingham stood with legs apart, hands on hips and head thrust forward pugnaciously.

"I call for de Vere's banishment."

Anne saw Robert de Vere pushing his way through the crowd until he could mount the dais and stand beside the king. He said something to Buckingham, with a mocking look that must have infuriated the Earl still further.

"Save your insults, de Vere," he snarled. "You're a parasite on this court, on the whole of England, and damned into the bargain. Or do you deny that you use the king for your foul lusts?"

The clamour in the hall rose even higher. De Vere flung himself at the earl, only intercepted at the last moment by Richard, who gripped his shoulders and spoke to him urgently. Suddenly furious, John of Gaunt stepped to the front of the dais, thrust his brother back into the crowd, and said something which gradually quietened the noise. When the shouts had died to an uneasy muttering, he spoke the formal words which brought the council to an end.

Waiting for the noblemen to disperse, Anne tried to make sense of what she had heard. Was there, after all, a plot against Richard's life? Or was it an attempt to discredit the Duke of Lancaster? Or, more complex still, an attempt to work the execution or banishment of Robert de Vere?

Anne did not entirely trust de Vere. His devastating looks and charm, his flippant approach to life, made her uneasy. But she doubted he was capable of real evil. And what he had said in the garden was true; if he had plotted, he would have been too clever to expose himself.

Once the hall was empty, she and Chaucer slipped down the stairs. On the dais Richard was seated again with his face buried in his hands, and de Vere beside him. He looked up as Anne approached.

"I will feed my hawks on Buckingham's liver," he promised.

"Unfortunate birds," de Vere said, the attempt at wit falling flat.

"Could we blame Buckingham, do you think, for lying to this wretched friar?"

The king shook his head.

"He is brother to my uncle of Lancaster. He would not slander him."

"Then do you prefer Arundel?"

Richard began to smile faintly, responding to de Vere's gentle teasing.

"Arundel is a prosy old bore. But why would he injure me like this?"

De Vere grinned.

"The other day, in open Parliament," he said, "you told the Earl of Arundel that he lied in his teeth, and sent him to the devil. I doubt he loves you, Richard. Or my lord of Lancaster, who made peace between you."

As he spoke, Richard had coloured. His hands clenched.

"What right have these old men to lesson me? I am the king."

"And unless you learn to govern these old men wisely, my lord," Chaucer said drily, "you may be king no longer."

The king stared at him.

"Do not presume, Master Chaucer," he said. "A word would bring you down."

"Richard –" Anne began to protest, but the poet was smiling.

"My lord, I own you care little for Master Chaucer the wool clerk. But I believe that Geoffrey Chaucer the poet will always have your good will."

For a few seconds Anne thought that Richard would give way to a towering fit of temper, but then he relaxed, laughing, and reached out to clasp Chaucer's hand.

"And in return, my lord," Chaucer added, "I will do my best to bring the truth of this affair to light."

Anne herself saw that Chaucer was comfortably lodged that night and the next morning brought him into Richard's presence in his private apartments.

Gaunt and de Vere were both with the king, and Clanvowe was just ushering in Sir John Montague, Richard's seneschal, along with an elderly man dressed plainly in brown wool. Anxiety stabbed through Anne as she saw the worried look on the seneschal's face.

"No more . . ." she whispered, and felt Chaucer's steadying hand on her arm as he led her to a chair.

"My lord," Montague began, "this is the castle gaoler. He came to me this morning with a tale I think you should hear."

Richard, sprawled on cushions in the window seat, straightened and beckoned to the elderly man.

"Speak."

The gaoler shuffled forward and bowed clumsily.

"Begging your pardon, my lord," he said, "but it's that friar, Master Latimer. I can't stand by and see it done, even if it was by your orders."

"An honest man," de Vere murmured satirically.

Richard leant forward, frowning, and put out a hand to silence his friend.

"See it done?" he echoed. "See what?"

"I'll not lay tongue to it," the gaoler said. "Not in front of my lady. But they've killed him with their filthy games."

"Killed him?" Richard's voice had sharpened. "Who?"

"Sir John Holland, and some other gentlemen of the duke here." The gaoler ducked his head towards John of Gaunt. "They brought Master Latimer to the dungeons yesterday, and put him through the torments of hell to make him speak. When they'd done, I took him and lodged him decently, but I doubt he's long for this world."

The colour had drained from Richard's face as the gaoler spoke.

"I did not order this. Clanvowe, I sent him with you yesterday, to write down an account of what he knew. What happened?"

Uneasily, Clanvowe came forward.

"On our way from the garden, Sir John Holland met us and questioned us, and said that he would see to the matter." His voice rising in protest, he added, "He is your half brother, my lord! What was I to do?"

"I should have been told." Richard waved him away, and stood up. "Montague, send for my physicians. I will go to speak with Master Latimer myself."

He strode out, and the Duke of Lancaster went with him. De Vere looked as if he would follow, and then sank down among the cushions where Richard had been sitting. For once there was no amusement in his face.

Montague left with the gaoler, and Anne dismissed Clanvowe and the other attendants. Once they had gone, she covered her face with her hands.

"They will lay this vile thing at Richard's door," she said.

"No." De Vere made a small sound of contempt. "The whole world knows that Holland is a brutal lout."

"What we should ask ourselves," said Chaucer, "is whether he tortured Master Latimer to make him speak, or to keep him silent."

Anne and de Vere both stared at him.

"He's Gaunt's pensioner," de Vere said. "He'd not –"

"Nevertheless," Chaucer said sedately, "it might be well if you would go and speak with him, and try to discover what happened yesterday. He might tell you, my lord, when he would not deign to tell me."

De Vere broke into laughter.

"Holland will speak me fair when hell freezes over." He rose and bowed extravagantly to the little poet. "However, my wise friend, I will try."

He bowed more soberly to Anne, and went out.

Alone with Chaucer, Anne allowed herself a sigh of weariness. After a moment's respectful silence, Chaucer asked,

"My lady, do you believe these accusations against my lord de Vere?"

"No. Oh, Robert is ambitious – but he would do nothing to harm Richard."

"Or to harm my lord of Lancaster?"

"Perhaps." Almost against her will, Anne felt herself smiling. "But not this way. He would not leave so clear a trail to himself."

Chaucer stroked his beard thoughtfully.

"Then do we look for an enemy of Lord de Vere? Someone who would work his ruin?"

This time Anne could not restrain laughter.

"Master Chaucer, if you search through all the nobility of England, you might find one man – old, or pious, or wanting in his wits – who is not Robert's enemy. You heard them yesterday."

Chaucer nodded slowly. More hesitantly, he said,

"Then you do not believe what they say of de Vere and your lord the king?"

"I do not." Anne's voice grew sharper. "Master Chaucer, who should know better than I that those slanders are not true? These dukes and earls – they would have Richard a warrior like his father and grandfather. Because he is not, they call him coward, weakling . . . and worse. They do not ask themselves what he truly is, or what he might become."

She had spoken for once from her heart, unafraid that the poet would repeat her words, and she could not hide from herself the admiration she saw in his eyes. Protesting, she began, "But I do not –" and broke off, startled, as the door flew open.

King Richard stumbled into the room, and held out his hands to her.

"Oh, Anne, Anne," he said. "That such things are done in my name!"

He fell on his knees beside her, and buried his face in her lap, sobbing. Anne stroked his hair.

John of Gaunt followed the king into the room and closed the door behind him. For all his soldierly bearing, Anne thought there were tears in his eyes too.

"It's true, then?" she asked.

Gaunt nodded.

"Master Latimer has suffered unspeakably," he said. "He is dying. But he has said no more of this plot. I think he knows no more."

Richard raised his head, choking back tears, and sat on the floor, leaning against his wife's chair. Anne kept his hand clasped between both of hers.

"Master Chaucer, tell us what to do," he said.

Anne thought that for a moment Chaucer looked bewildered, but his face quickly cleared. When he began to speak, it was slowly, but with confidence.

"My lord, you are likely never to learn more of this than you know already." He raised a hand to forestall Richard's protest. "Unless you seek out the villain yourself."

Light sprang into Richard's face.

"Tell me how."

"Were you alone with Master Latimer?"

"Yes, except for my uncle of Gaunt. And the gaoler at the door."

Chaucer nodded, his eyes keen.

"Then you will tell your courtiers, my lord, that the friar spoke a name into your ear. A name that you alone heard. You will tell them that you will meditate alone in the garden, until you have decided what to do with what you know."

Fear coursed through Anne.

"But they will –"

"Yes, my lady." Chaucer was smiling. "We must make his enemy come to him."

"I shall have men hidden among the trees," Gaunt said. "We'll take him, whoever he is."

"But there will be danger, my lord," said Chaucer. "Have you courage?"

Richard was flushed, but calm now, his mouth firm. He did not answer the question; there was no need.

"And none of us," Gaunt said, "will speak of this to anyone."

"I must tell Robert," the king protested.

"No, my lord," Chaucer said. "Say nothing to my lord de Vere. Let him abide the test with the others." Richard sprang to his feet.

"Then you believe he is guilty too!"

Blinking a little, Master Chaucer looked up at him, and said mildly,

"No, my lord. I would give him the chance to prove his innocence."

Later that day, Anne was seated with Master Chaucer in the rose arbour, concealed by a trailing curtain of leaves. Sunlight dappled the grass; the only sound was the gentle sighing of the trees.

A little way away, Richard sat on the grass with head bent, golden hair shining. After a few moments, he reached out to pluck a daisy, and twirled the stem in his fingers. But for that, he was utterly still.

Very softly, Anne murmured,

"Did you learn any more from Sir John Holland?" Chaucer shook his head. His voice just as low, he replied,

"No. He was drunk when de Vere found him."

"Then you do not know –"

Chaucer gave Anne a sideways look, silencing her. Somehow, though he said nothing, she realized that he knew very well who would come into the garden.

Movement from the rose alley. Anne caught her breath, and felt Master Chaucer's hand laid warningly on her wrist. A tall figure appeared from behind the trellis, and paused briefly, outlined against the bright new growth. De Vere.

Anne whispered, "No." Close to her ear she heard the poet murmur, "Wait."

Robert de Vere called, "Richard!" and strode across the grass towards the king. Richard raised his head, and slowly rose to his feet to meet him.

"Richard, what is this nonsense?" de Vere asked. "What name did the friar speak? Why did you not tell me?"

The king did not reply. Wildly, De Vere caught at his hands.

"Is this a trick?" he said. "A trap? For me? Richard, do you truly believe that I could harm you?"

His face was fierce; his grip on the king's hands must have been painful. Slowly, Richard said,

"No . . . But they have accused you. They will take you from me." He shook his head helplessly. "I cannot protect you."

De Vere's face changed. He said, thickly, "Richard . . ." and caught the king into an embrace. They clung together; Anne's heart twisted at their desperation.

Running footsteps, and another figure burst out of the rose alley. He hurled himself across the grass, a sword in his hand. Chaucer let out a faint sound of satisfaction. The running man was the king's uncle, the Earl of Buckingham.

De Vere was aware of him first, and thrust Richard behind him, drawing his belt knife in one fluid movement.

"Get back," Buckingham snarled, with an added obscenity that brought blood to Anne's face.

De Vere stood firm, his tiny jewelled dagger no match for the earl's sword. Buckingham stepped forward, and at the same moment Richard raised his hand.

It was as if the trees spawned bowmen. Silently they moved forward, encircling the king and his assassin. One man, silhouetted against the dying sunlight, knelt on the wall, his arrow aimed straight for Buckingham's heart. From among the trees John of Gaunt strode forward, his hand on his sword hilt, and stood at his brother's side. Finally, Chaucer gave his hand to Anne, and drew her into the circle.

Laughing unsteadily, de Vere sheathed his dagger and stepped aside. King Richard faced his uncle.

"Can you tell me, my lord," he said, "why you come with drawn sword into the presence of your anointed king?"

As he saw the garden suddenly alive with witnesses, the earl's face had turned to a congested purple, his eyes staring. He looked at the sword in his hand as if it had turned to a serpent. Blustering, he said,

"I will defy anyone who dares speak slander of my brother of Lancaster."

John of Gaunt let out a snort of amusement. His voice high and quick, Richard went on,

"Your outrage comes late, my lord. For no one now speaks ill of the Duke, and though I own I believed it at first I know now that he means nothing but my good."

He had grown breathless, and he paused, a hand on his breast. Quietly de Vere came to his side and put an arm round his shoulders. Richard leaned against him thankfully.

"If I might speak, my lord," Chaucer said, stepping forward. At the king's nod, he looked around the circle of faces and continued, his voice and manner precise as always. "When I considered, my lords, why –"

"A moment, Master Chaucer," John of Gaunt interrupted. "If you intend stripping us naked, it might be as well to do it in a decent privacy."

He waved a hand, and the archers faded back into the trees. Gaunt nodded to Chaucer to continue.

"I thank you, my lord. When I sought the truth, I never seriously questioned that Master Latimer believed the story he told. Someone claiming to be a squire of my lord de Vere warned him that John of Lancaster plotted against the king's life. Master Latimer held to this through torture, and lies at the point of death without adding to it."

Richard winced and turned his face away. Buckingham spat out a blasphemy, and said, "You lied –"

"The friar spoke no name," Chaucer agreed. "But it seemed good to us to know who would fear that name, and try to silence the king before he could repeat it."

Buckingham sheathed his sword, and spun round.

"I'll listen to no more of this."

Before he could leave, John of Gaunt put a hand on his shoulder.

"Don't be more of a fool than you can help, Thomas," he said pleasantly.

Buckingham turned back, fuming, and Chaucer went on,

"A plot: but who was its target? King Richard? My lord of Lancaster might plot against his life, for he could make himself king in Richard's stead. But he has shown no wish to rule, and in all his doings he has supported and guided Richard as best he might."

Gaunt inclined his head a little, his eyes twinkling.

"I thank you for this testimony, Master Chaucer."

As far as Anne could see, Chaucer remained unembarrassed.

"I speak no more than truth, my lord. And with your loyalty established –" he picked up the threads of his argument again – "we might then assume that the plot was meant to bring you down. And perhaps my lord de Vere sent his man to pour this tale into the friar's ear, for it is no secret that you and he do not love each other."

De Vere shot a look at John of Gaunt, half mocking, half ashamed; Gaunt received it with raised eyebrows, not entirely hostile.

"But de Vere had no reason to fear any name that the dying friar spoke, for he stood accused already. And here in the garden he defended Richard against a man better armed. My lord de Vere, you may have to reconcile yourself to being a hero."

De Vere could not meet the poet's eyes, although Richard murmured something to him that made him flush bright scarlet.

"And then," Chaucer continued, "I gave thought to the Earl of Arundel. He might have plotted to strike two targets. He is a rival of my lord of Lancaster, and the whole of England knows how he hates de Vere. To bring one if not both of them down – yes, those are good reasons. And I own, my lords, I would not be surprised if it were the Earl of Arundel who stood here with us now."

He paused, and Anne felt her breath come short.

"Well?" Buckingham snapped.

"Well, my lord of Buckingham, it is not Arundel who stands here, but you. A man with reason to aim for all three targets."

"Three targets?" Buckingham's tone was scoffing. "Rubbish!"

"No." Still calm and prosaic, Chaucer ticked off the points on his fingers. "One. Though you claim to support your brother of

Lancaster, all men know that you resent him for being your elder, and you envy his influence with the king. You would not grieve if he were brought down."

Buckingham opened his mouth as if to protest, but Chaucer ignored him.

"Two. You hate and despise my lord de Vere. If the king had executed my lord of Lancaster, how long before Robert de Vere was blamed for it? A servant's confession, perhaps, or a missing letter conveniently found. And then the king would have had no choice but to condemn him for treason."

Anne could scarcely bear to see the look that passed between Robert and her husband. Their pain was almost tangible.

"Three," Chaucer went on. "With John of Gaunt and Robert de Vere both disposed of, King Richard would be stripped of his chief defenders. Vulnerable, my lord Buckingham, to anyone with ambitions for the crown. Can you honestly say, my lord, that your thoughts have never strayed that way?"

Once again Buckingham took breath to speak, but remained silent. King Richard stepped forward, looked him up and down with eyes that were suddenly searing, and said to John of Gaunt,

"Take him and have him executed."

"My lord, you cannot do this," Gaunt said.

"Cannot? You say that to me?"

"You cannot," Gaunt repeated. "Master Chaucer speaks truth, no doubt of that. But how will we prove it?"

"There is no proof." Buckingham had recovered enough to speak, a sneer in his voice. "It's a pack of lies."

"I think not." Gaunt faced his brother, hard and cold. "But your position protects you. My lord Richard, you cannot execute him without a civil uprising, that will harm you and your kingdom more than it will harm him. Be assured," he added grimly, "I shall watch him from now on."

Richard was white, immobile for a moment until he turned aside, with a sound of disgust.

"Get out of my sight," he said.

Buckingham stared at him, mouth working.

"I admit nothing." The words were choked out. "But could anyone deny I would make a better king than you, you . . . catamite?" When no one rose to the insult, he swung round on

Chaucer. "And you, master poet . . ." His tone made the words an equal insult, if not worse. "Pray that you never come within my power. Fine words won't save you then."

Chaucer met his eyes, gravely calm, and Buckingham could not hold the level gaze. Spitting a final blasphemy, he turned and strode off across the garden. Gaunt nodded to the king, and followed. Anne almost thought she could hear a shared exhalation of relief as the two men disappeared.

Richard straightened, drew an uncertain breath, and managed to smile. He pulled off a ring, a resplendent emerald, and placed it on Chaucer's hand. It glittered extravagantly against the poet's sober garments.

"Not payment, Master Chaucer," the king said, "but a token of my friendship, and my thanks."

Chaucer bowed to him, and the king withdrew, tossing a careless, "Come, Robert," over his shoulder as he went.

De Vere did not follow at once. He remained standing in front of Chaucer, gazing down at him with an intensity Anne had not often seen in that mocking face.

"Richard is my king," he said. "He delights to give, and I confess I rejoice to receive his gifts. But know this, Master Chaucer –" His voice dropped. "If he were the lowest beggar in the stews, I would sell my body or my soul to give him an hour's comfort."

The silence was broken only by the king's voice, impatiently calling, "Robert!" from the garden alley. De Vere still did not move, until Chaucer, smiling a little, inclined his head, in a gesture of understanding – almost, Anne thought, of absolution. Only then did de Vere spin round, and almost ran across the grass towards his king.

Chaucer held out a hand to Anne, to escort her, but before she took it she paused. The day was drawing to an end, the daisies in the grass folding their petals. She saw the last of the sunlight gathered around Richard's bright head, and the shadows lengthening across the garden.

Henry VI ❧

NEITHER PITY, LOVE NOR FEAR

Margaret Frazer

England has had its share of sad kings, but one of the saddest is Henry VI. He was the son of Henry V, the hero of Agincourt, and grandson of Henry IV, who had deposed our previous king, Richard II. Henry was nearly nine months old when his father died in France, so there was never a time in his youth when he was not expected to act like a king. He is the only king of England to have been crowned king of France, when he was ten years old. Henry was not well equipped for this responsibility. He rapidly lost most of his lands in France and became afflicted by an illness which caused him to have moments of depression and mental decline. It may well have been the same illness, porphyria, that affected George III. One of these bouts coincided with the birth of his only son, and Henry later claimed he had no idea how he came by the heir. This gave rise to rumours that his wife, the domineering Margaret of Anjou, had been unfaithful. It was because of Henry's weakness that power struggles broke out between his relatives, the rival factions of the Yorkists and Lancastrians which erupted into the long drawn out Wars of the Roses. Henry was deposed in 1461 and, after a period of exile in Scotland, was captured and imprisoned, defeated by his distant cousin, who became Edward IV. Henry spent six years in the Tower of London, apart from a brief period when he was restored to the throne in 1470. His mental condition deteriorated further and many believe he knew little about his final years. When Henry died, in May

1471, his body was displayed in order to prove there had been no foul play, and his death was attributed to "displeasure and melancholy". No one was fooled. But what did happen on that night in 1471 when Henry met his death? Here Henry tells his own story.

A room.

Quiet in its thickness of stone tower walls. Reached by several ways – stairs and passage and wall-walk – but all kept locked, to keep the room entirely to itself, a place apart in the fortress spread out all around it. A prison room but not a cell, its high-groined stone ceiling painted white and patterned with gold stars. Fifteen stars to each portion of the ceiling; there's been time enough and more to count them, know them, even to where the paint batch was made anew, the stars a slightly darker gold, there above the stairway door. *The walls hung with tapestries over the plastered stone for something against the draughts and boredom of plain walls: tapestries grown old in other rooms and so good enough for here, where comfort should be given but why bother with much, the man is mad?* But with wit enough to question who thought that tapestries, even faded, of lords and ladies laughing, talking, riding in a spring world of sky and trees and flowers was something to hang in a prison room I'm never meant to leave. *With on the floor a carpet woven intricately in red–green–yellow–blue–tangled patterns but, like the tapestries, a thing grown old in other rooms, used and reused in lesser and lesser chambers until brought down to this.* Very possibly a carpet that I walked on in my "better" days – its better days – without more than vaguely knowing it was there, while now, with its days and mine both faded and finishing, I know it well enough to trace out its patterns behind my closed eyes as I try for sleep in bed at night. *A comfortable bed, narrow but well-mattressed, with covers enough and the sheets cleanly kept. A table, too.* That a man may dine decently and have somewhere to set his books, few though they are, and write if ever there was need to but there isn't. *And two chairs.* Because though a man needs only one to sit on for himself, there do come visitors. Even here. Or there used to come, though mercifully fewer as the years have passed. The dead and the wise do not come visiting – the former for sufficient reason, the latter having better things to do. *A quiet room except for the quiet passing of his footsteps back and forth; and often and often, when his pacing stops and he kneels at the altar set below the narrow window with its colored glass of "Mary with Angel, Dove, and Lily" where on bright days the morning light falls in colored patterns, the murmur of his prayers . . .*

Henry, king of England by title, not by right.

That's how they say it now. King not by right but only title.

Succeeding to my father King Henry V as he succeeded to his father King Henry IV who succeeded by usurpation, greed, pride, and treachery to his cousin King Richard II's crown – succeeded by ways as far from "right" as can be compassed, and now, by greed and pride and treachery not my own, have I come here.

And here, I suppose, I'll die.

Kneeling, head bowed over breast-clasped hands, on a gold-embroidered crimson cushion in front of the green-clothed altar in the chapel made for him when this became his prison-room, his cell, his waiting-place these seven – or is it eight years now? – in the southeastward curve of the tower where a window embrasure widens through the thickness of the wall toward the river. A small chapel, not even twice the stretch of a man's arms at its widest, far less where the walls narrow in to the window's slit and the altar. But then, how much room does a man need to kneel and pray? Or try to pray, the murmur of his prayers shutting out other sounds – the stone-distanced sounds of people passing below the windows, through the gateway there or between the fortress walls that are double here between the river and the Tower of London's heart, coming, going, busy with their lives while he keeps busy with his death . . .

They've wanted me dead for a long while now, and with Ned dead, they can have their wish.

> Now Ned is dead,
> They'll have my head.
> Sing-song,
> Rhyme and wrong.
> Now Ned is dead . . .

A man worn to leanness by nature and will, his dark hair well-threaded with gray but his face gone ageless, out of the world around him into somewhere else. An aging man but far from old, forcing his mind back to his prayers.

Prayers that have been my shelter since I learned as a child that even my great lords hesitated to come between me and God when I was deep in prayer. My noble lords. Who never hesitated else to demand, drive, bully, insist at me to do whatever it might be they wanted done, to give them whatever they wanted to have, to be whatever they thought I ought to be.

Left king of England at nine months old when his father died, and so never a time he can remember not being king of England, all these almost fifty years.

And now at last all they want from me is my death.

Now Ned is dead, they'll have my head.

Because while he still lived, though it was surely trouble to keep me, a sometime-king, prisoner in my sometime-own Tower of London, it would been greater trouble to have me dead and my son declared king in my place, because my son in his young manhood and free and with all his wits about him would have been a far better rallying point than long I've been for anyone yet preferring the House of Lancaster to the House of York on England's throne. No matter the liability in having me alive, there was no profit in having me dead. No profit in killing a king, your prisoner, if it only makes his son, free, into king of England in his stead.

But now Ned's dead.

On a hot early summer morning in a squalid squall of battle outside a Gloucestershire market-town, his army unable to make the river-crossing to safety before the enemy closed in on them. Dead, left buried in the abbey there, already forgotten, done with life almost before he had begun it.

Edward, Prince of Wales.

Ned.

She hated when I called him that. His mother. My lady wife. The queen. Crying at me, "Edward! His name is Edward! He's not some peasant's 'Ned'!"

Despite she'd never wanted him named "Edward" either.

"Let him be called Louis," she pleaded on her knees before he was even born, before we even knew he'd be a son. "Or Charles or even

Henri." Sometimes begging it in French, forgetting her English. Henri. As if this son she so desperately needed would somehow be French, would somehow make up for everything she hated having left behind her to be queen of England.

Urging, "Let him be named Henri for you and your father."

Not understanding that was the plea least likely to move me.

She even tried, "If he were Louis or Charles or Henri, how much the more easily France will accept him for king when the time comes, yes?"

That was how great a fool she thought me, to try that, then, when France was already three years lost to any English rule and we were in the midst of losing Gascony. But in truth France had been lost to English rule before our war for it ever began, if ever anyone had cared to face the truth of it, because who but the war-mad, profit-proud hunters of glory in other men's blood could believe, even when my great-grandfather started his war these more-than-hundred years ago – or when my father opened it again, God save King Henry V, he and his piety rotting together in the grave he didn't come to soon enough – that England could actually take and hold all of France?

But I forget. It was God's will that France belong to England.

That was their argument, whenever there was question about the war, the ones who hoped to make a profit from it. They may even have brought themselves to believe it.

But if the war was God's will, it must have been his will, too, that France is lost.

And that Ned is dead and soon I'll be, now that the last reason for keeping me alive is gone . . .

God's will.

An answer that's no answer, that serves for comfort to those who want to ask no questions.

Or for those who want excuse for what they mean to do. Or for what they've done.

I wonder how they mean for me to die.

And who they'll send to do it.

Aware that behind him someone has come in, that he's no longer alone in the room where mostly, almost always, alone is all he is. And in a while, when nothing happens – not death or anything else – he crosses himself, rises to his feet, turns, finds . . .

My good Archbishop of Canterbury.

To use the word "good" loosely.

To use the word "my" most randomly.

Come on someone's purpose, though I doubt his, to see how I do. But not to be my murderer. There's no need for archbishops to be given that kind of task, though likely when it's done, he'll give absolution to whoever does it.

He was my archbishop for six years but turned easily from me to Edward of York when the power went that way and as easily turned back when Warwick re-managed matters to put me on the throne again, and now he's gone back to King Edward since Fortune's wheel has spun that way. He has power, wealth – betrays kings with impunity. Everything I've done and am are things that, judging by how he's lived his life, he despises in a man, and now here he is and what am I supposed to say to him, here in my prison room with all the gulf of who we are between us?

And why, when I say nothing, only stand here looking at him, does he find it hard to look back at me as – giving up waiting for me to speak first – he says stiffly, "It was thought you should know his grace King Edward is returned to London today."

As if I wouldn't have heard the cheering from the streets beyond the Tower's walls and known it had to mean King Edward and his glittering retinue of lords was returned, even if my keeper hadn't given me certain word of it along with dinner at midday . . .

My dinner. Poison. There's a thought I try not to have. They could kill me that way, easily. A swift poison or a slow, in one meal or by way of several, since they're sure of me here, either way. A simple way to be rid of a king, with an unmarked body afterward to show to the people and say, He fell ill . . .

My lord archbishop shifts uneasily and I realize that I've been looking at him without seeing him, thinking instead of answering him. He's high churchman of the realm and not used, my good archbishop, to being unseen, going unanswered. His kind need constantly to be seen, so they can constantly be sure that they exist, and even this warm summer's day he goes dressed in a richness of furs and velvet, his belief unabated in the necessity of being gorgeous for the world to see.

Do these great churchmen ever actually hear, ever think about the words they say in their services day in and out, through all the years of their churchly lives? About the difference between the outward poverty of Christ and the richness of spirit that brings salvation? If they ever hear, ever think, about that teaching, how have they come to live their lives in such outward richness and inward poverty? What do they think will come to them when they're done with the matter of the world and they have to live for all of Eternity with what little they've made of their spirits?

I remember, as I stand here in my plain black monk's habit, the weight and drag and bother of such richness as my lord archbishop wears. Remember it being as heavy as the world's sins. Remember particularly my first coronation, when I was seven years old and already seven years a king, that day a distillation of all my life till then – and most of my life to come, if I'd but known it – a seemingly unending necessity of royal robes and ceremony and men's expectations weighing on me, with no tears allowed me, no pleading for relief or pity, because I was *the king*. My shoulders aching at day's end from being *king*. My mind aching at day's end from being *king*. My heart empty from years of being *king*.

There are no words would reach to any purpose between my lord archbishop and me, and so I go on standing here, doing him the small courtesy of letting him see I see him, but he doesn't seem to find that easeful and stiffly says, "His grace the king asked me to come and see how it is with you. To see if all's well . . ." At least on that, my lord archbishop sticks a little. ". . . that all's as well as . . . may be."

As well as may be, considering I've been unkinged again, imprisoned again, and that my son is dead and shortly I'll be, too, as my good archbishop knows as well as I do.

But death won't come by his hand so he's no use to me and I turn my back on him, cross myself and kneel again and after a while hear him go away, to learn what he can from my keeper and guess at the rest and return to his king to tell him Henry of Lancaster, once King Henry VI, is as witless as ever – beyond feeling even the loss of his kingship or the death of his son.

Their trouble is that they think I ought to care.

That I *must* care.

Not understanding that my lord of Warwick drove too much of caring out of me a long while ago.

Not this earl of Warwick lately dead, called the "Kingmaker" though "Gravemaker" would be closer to the truth, unmade now into his own grave by one of us "kings" he thought he'd made. Not him. Nor the Warwick before him, who was my friend, a boy when I was a boy but given God's blessing to die before he much became a man. No. *His* father. The earl of Warwick who oversaw my bringing up from infancy to my young manhood. Who helped to make my bringing down by teaching me my deepest lessons of kingship. He was forever telling me in his utterly certain voice, "You are the king, my lord, you must do this," or else, "You are the king, my lord, you must not do that." Tossing "must" and "must not" around like coloured balls in a juggler's game to which everyone knew the rules but I. And when I tried to make my own rules to the game – I was the king after all; they kept telling me so – I was told most firmly that I *must not*. He ruled my childhood, ruled my youth, forced me into the shapes he thought I ought to be, until I was of too much an age for it to be seemly another man's will be set over mine, and then . . .

By then, when he had to set me free, he was grown old and ill and wanted only to be left to die in peace, among familiar comforts.

So I sent him to be governor of the war in France.

Forced him to go where he did not want to go. Forced him to be what he did not want to be. Made sure he understood, with no word said between us, that I did it purposefully. And left him there to die.

He did.

That was the first death that I managed.

But not the last.

And now, soon, will come my own.

How God must weep to watch the foolishness of men.

Or mayhap he laughs.

Or simply leaves the tears and laughter all to us.

Not that either makes any great difference in how things are, so far as I can see. I've cried and laughed enough, time and time about, and never found that either made much difference to anything.

Not even, any more, to me.

I wonder if my poor lady wife, my queen, my princess out of France has learned yet that all her surfeits of passion will never suffice to make the world the way she wants it to be. I tried to tell her sometimes, but why should she listen to me? No one else did, toward the last. Why should they, knowing what I am? Knowing me for a weakling fool who twice in his life slid into madness, slipped out of his senses into unreason and never recovered more than a corner of them. A witless, hollow man, *stulticiam*, fit only for what's come to him.

I wonder if anyone believes anymore that I meant to be a good king. Upon a time, I truly did.

But then, what else was there for me to be? I grew up with a brace of uncles and a pack of lords baying to govern me and England both. It wasn't only Warwick hounding me, though he led the pack. It was all of them. My lords of Winchester, Gloucester, Suffolk, Somerset, Buckingham, Northumberland, Canterbury, Chichester, Lincoln, Ely . . . I tried to be what they demanded because what else did I know to do? I tried to be their King but I wasn't my father and that was the King they wanted, not me. They fought who I was every step I tried to make, from the time I first began to make any. They fought that poor little boy to bend – or break – him into the shape they wanted.

If I'd been weaker it might have been the better. I might have bent, become the king they wanted. Instead . . .

Instead . . .

Instead I broke.

In a sun-rich summer garden, under a laurel tree, with the sound of a fountain playing somewhere near and his lady wife to hand, finally great-bellied with the child she's been so desperate to have but still not satisfied, always dissatisfied, wanting this, wanting that, wanting more, wanting him other than he is – and three lords with her, come to yammer over a score of things they insist he has to do, telling him that the French war is going worse, another English army has been lost, that somehow, somewhere, something must be done and he has to do it, do it now, do it . . .

His throat closing, his chest constricting, a blackness sweeping up inside his head, and . . .

Nothing.

For what became a long while . . . nothing . . .

Then a slow graying back toward . . . knowing.

Knowing, first, simply that he was. Then knowing who he was. And then aware that it was no longer summer but winter in a room with a fire on the hearth and frost on the windows and, he was told, Christmas near to hand. A Christmas more than a year from the summer he remembered, with the French war long since lost and a boy-child put into his arms. His son, they said.

I was still king but men walked wary of me after that, not certain, among their uncertain rivalries, what would happen if they "lost" me again.

I left them to their uncertainties. Why not? It gave me a little peace and I still had my game, the game I'd learned before my madness came on me and could still play.

It wasn't a difficult game, not when my lords all worked so hard to make it easy for me. All I needed to do was give them the chance to have what they wanted to have, let them take what they wanted to take – power, money, pride of place – and then watch what they became and what they did to one another.

If they came to their deaths because of their choices, how much of the fault was mine?

How much fault do we bear for the ends other men choose to have?

Or, in this matter, how much fault do I bear for the ends I helped some of them to?

As assuredly I helped my lord Bishop of Chichester.

Bishop Moleyns. A man who should never have been let near power or money, his desire for both standing out like sweat on him, too strong for there to be hope he'd ever make wise use of either. Therefore I let him be made clerk of the royal privy council, so near to power that his hunger for it nearly choked him. He couldn't help but reach for it, and when he did, I didn't stop him. There were so many I didn't stop when I knew I should, and most of them did as he did: grasped power to him, fondled it, crushed it, began to corrode with it, and – being far more greedy and corrupt than he was intelligent – made small attempt to hide what he was from anyone. St Eligius, but he made himself hated. Then, when the soldiers waiting at Southampton – unpaid, underfed, frustrated with delay at being kept from either sailing to the French war or else sent home – were known to be near revolt and someone had to go to tell them that somehow the money there should have been to pay them had disappeared, was gone, I saw to it my lord Bishop Moleyns was sent.

He was afraid to go. He had that much sense at least.

"Send a herald," he said, fear sharp behind his words. "Or a clerk. Someone out of the Exchequer. This isn't a matter for me, for a bishop to attend to."

Why not? I didn't ask, or point out he'd been most prominent among the lords responsible for the money, why shouldn't he be the one to go. Even then, they'd all come to suppose I was too simple to understand such things, too wrapped in prayers to know what my lords were doing. Why is holiness supposed to make you blind?

But blindness has its uses. I wouldn't see why my lord bishop should be afraid to go, and he dare not tell me why, nor anyone speak up for him, and so he went to the soldiers at Southampton and they killed him.

They mobbed him and beat him to death.

And somehow no one was ever brought to justice for his murder nor even much outcry made. A king's indifference can heavily weigh down what ought to be the course of justice, and if the king is as simple as everyone knew me to be, no one looks twice at him for having done it because surely he didn't know what he was doing.

Only the duke of Suffolk was never quite so easy with me after that. He felt, I think, that something was wrong but he wasn't clever enough to make out what, not in the little time he had left by then. Like Bishop Moleyns, he'd ridden his ambitions and his greed too hard and openly, and Parliament was demanding he be arraigned for treason. For his own safety, I said, I had him kept here in the Tower until, when it was clear that Parliament would settle for nothing less than his blood if he stayed in their reach, he willingly took my word that I would save him from them. He accepted exile in preference to a trial and I saw to it – he was most grateful to me – that he was helped to slip secretly out of London and able to take ship for France where he had friends enough to keep him in comfort until it was safe for him to come home again.

Now here's a puzzle I've never had answered. Why did no one ever question, then or afterward, how it came to happen that a royal ship, the *Nicholas of the Tower*, was waiting for my lord of Suffolk in the Channel, and its captain took him prisoner and oversaw his death and the throwing of his body and his head on Dover beach, and that afterwards nothing was ever done about any of it, despite so much was known?

I gave orders and he died, then I gave more orders and nothing was done about his death, and never once have I heard that anyone ever openly questioned any of it. It's as if, by then, I'd made myself so invisible of will that no one could see when I made a thing happen, could not believe I'd done it, even while my orders were obeyed, because . . . I didn't do that kind of thing. To all their thinking, I never did anything. I only let things happen to me while they, my noble lords, ruled England.

Men who couldn't even rule themselves.

Why is it that they always think someone a fool for not doing what they want of him, when it might just as well be they're the fools for wanting what they want?

Raising his head from clasped hands and the seeming of prayer to find that the westering light no longer slants through the window beyond the altar, that the day, like the world around him, is going away, leaving him to the dark. Sharply aware, though he doesn't show it, that someone has again come into the room behind him, that again he's no longer alone.

Here, where almost no one has come this month and more except my priest for Mass and my keeper with my meals. First my lord archbishop and now someone else not so subtle as the good archbishop, someone more heavy-handed with the door, more open in crossing the room to stand at my back. Close at my back. Letting me hope . . . hope . . .

But nothing comes.

And when nothing has come long enough for me to cease to hope that something will – if it's not to be poison, it's likely to be a dagger, leaving a wound fairly easily concealed when they have to show my body to the people to prove nothing was done to bring on my death – I turn my head and look to see who's there.

A tall and well-formed man, garbed not in armor but in a doublet of crimson velvet trimly held in to his fine waist by a wide blue-dyed leather belt, his hosen smooth to his long, well-muscled legs, his shining hair a little marked where the encircling weight of the crown bore down on him during his triumphant ride through London for the crowds to see him in his kingly might.

Though he's bare-headed now. The crown's an awkward thing to wear except at the most necessary times, even for someone who enjoys it as much as I think he does.

Edward of York.

King Edward IV of England by right of inheritance and force of arms. Come victorious from battle, leaving behind him most of his enemies vanquished, dead, presumably buried, with only me left, the last problem to be solved and my death the only solution there can be.

In all these years I've been his prisoner, he's never troubled to see me until now, and somehow I doubt he's come for courtesy's sake.

Unless it's the courtesy of actually looking on the man who's death he means to order – whose death he's probably already ordered.

And I have a sudden hope. What better answer could there be to the question of who should kill a king than the king who profits by his death? Send someone else to do it and the man you've sent to rid you of a trouble becomes a trouble in himself, maybe needing to be disposed of in his turn. But do the thing yourself and there's an end to it

He's even armed. Most men wear daggers and his right hand rests on his. Belt-hung on his hip, in an embossed and gilded-leather sheath, with jeweled pommel and gold-wrapped hilt, it's a kingly dagger. For a kingly killing?

But he only stands there, looking down at me, seeming uncertain of what he should do, faced with the man he's deposed, whose lords he's slaughtered, whose son he's killed, whose queen he holds prisoner. Whose crown he wears. The battle that gave him all that is nigh to three weeks behind him. All its grime, sweat, blood, stink – the stink of triumph, as I recall from battles of my own, smells much the same as the stink of defeat, except the living do not rot and the dead do – have long since been washed away from him, and there's only the small matter of me to be dealt with, but I begin to doubt he's here to do it and I stand slowly up, stiff-kneed from so long kneeling but enjoying as I turn to face him his surprise at finding we're almost of a height. He thought he'd overbear me in that as in all else because he's tall beyond the ordinary. But so am I.

And now what shall we do, one king in the presence of another and both of us King of England?

Not kill me, certainly, because I can see now his attendants – kings never go anywhere alone; it's one of the great tediums of being king – beside the door at the head of the stairs. You want more privacy than that in killing a king, and impatiently I move past him, making him turn to keep eye on me as I cross the room to the better of the two low-backed, curve-seated chairs beside the table, and there turn to face him again, and sit.

You do not sit in a king's presence before he gives you leave to do so and I make it worse by gesturing toward the other chair, giving him leave to sit, thereby insuring that he won't, because to do so now would be as if at my bidding. A suffusion of red starts up his face and he'd say something, but before he can, both of us knowing full well that it's discourtesy to speak to a king before he's spoken to you, I say, "It's most kind of you to come here, my lord, with all you must have in hand just now. You bring me condolences on the death of my son, I suppose?"

The colour of his face deepens – is he so unused to being crossed? – and I smile on him.

"And word of how my lady wife does in your keeping? She's well, I trust?" Knowing full well she isn't, held prisoner by a man she hates, with her only child dead and all her hopes with him.

I'd goad him more but he's regained his balance if not his temper and says in his turn, smoothly, "If you like, yes, I'll give you condolences on your son. Not for his death but because he was a traitor. And on your wife for good measure, because she's worse."

Fair enough, from his point of view, but why let it be that easy for him? I go on smiling as I say, "And you want to ask after my own health, surely. It's very well, I thank you." Blandly. Adding more blandly, still smiling, "You know I killed your father, don't you?"

At that the colour rises in his face again; but he's taken firm hold on remembrance that I'm a "mad" man, that most of what I say can go unheeded, and he answers, triumphing a little at having caught me out – but what triumph is there in besting a madman? – "My father died in a battle you weren't even at."

True. When my queen and her lords broke the Christmas truce and killed the duke of York in Wakefield battle, I was more than half the country away.

"But I made it happen," I say quietly, still smiling, certain and pleased and letting York's son see I am. "If I hadn't for years betrayed your father almost every chance I had, there would have been no battle for him to die in."

For one poised instant he almost believes me.

He should. It's true.

The duke of York was a part of that game I played. I was playing it when I let the earl of Somerset command an army into France despite I knew he'd make a disaster of it. He did, so much a disaster that afterwards he killed himself in shame. I doubly played the game that time, because the troops and money Somerset wasted should have been given to York, my governor of France then, who desperately needed and would have made good use of them. But all my courtly lords wanted York's power kept down, hating him – on my behalf, they said – because he might at any time try to claim the crown away from me.

They never added that his claim would have been a just one, grown from my grandfather unjustly seizing the crown for himself out of the right line of inheritance.

The odd thing is that York never made that much-feared claim until he had been pushed by more than twenty years of injustices from me, to the point where not to claim the crown would have meant the destruction of all his family. But then, York was always a different matter from most of my other lords. Foremost, he was as fair as might be in his dealings between men. For another, all he asked of me for years was to be trusted and to be treated justly. Instead, I acted on my lords' insistence that he was my enemy, knowing he wasn't, until I made him one, and then let my lady wife and lords destroy him.

But York's son has remembered that I'm mad and therefore a nothing, that almost everything about me can simply be dismissed, ignored, and he answers, angry anyway, "You don't know up from down or down from yesterday. My father died because your wife's a bitch and you're a fool and the world's well rid of both of you and your ill-whelped son into the bargain."

He enjoys he has the power to say that to my face, but I'm enjoying that he's angry, so no one's lost here. Except, if he's not to be my death, he's of small interest to me, already tedious, and easily, from long practice, I let my face go slack, cease to see him, focus my eyes vaguely on nothing somewhere between us.

After a startled moment, while he realizes that I've gone "mad" in front of him, he laughs and says, contemptuous, "I'd rather have you wherever you've gone than here," and makes to leave but stops out of sight behind me, near the door, I think, and turns back, to say, contempt and laughter and anger mingled all together in his voice, "But then there's this, too, isn't there? If my father hadn't died as he did, I wouldn't have become king so soon. If you'd indeed killed him, I suppose I'd somewhat have to thank you, wouldn't I? For that much at least." And finally he goes.

Leaving me to wish he was a lord of mine, that I might set his ambitions against his stupidities and watch while they brought him down.

But at least he's left me with no doubt he'll have me dead as soon as may be. It's only a matter of waiting out the time.

I'm so tired of time.

So tired of waiting.

I want to be done with both.

I want to know who'll come . . .

Warm day drawing into cool evening, the windows blue with twilight, the far curve of the room gathering itself into shadows, into quiet. Somewhere outside, close by but distant through stone walls and up curved stairways and through shut thick doors, the sounds of other people's living. Shod horses' hooves on cobbles under the gateway. Voices raised to a brief exulting shout. Laughter. None of it more than barely brushing against his mind, hardly heard because it's not what he waits for.

. . . to kill me.

But here's my keeper come instead, with lighted lamp in one hand, my supper bowl, bread soaking in whatever stew it is tonight, in the other, hurrying, head down to show he has no inclination or maybe time to talk but that makes two of us and doesn't matter. Nor do I want the food but the light is welcome and that's strange because the darkness hasn't bothered me before.

It's only as he's going out that I realize he didn't come alone. There's a boy standing just inside the door, and I have the momentary thought it's Ned, ghost-come to see me before I become a ghost myself; but my keeper bows low to him in going out, so I know he's really there and I see as he comes forward, more into the lamplight that he's not so much of a boy as I thought.

Slight-built, dressed with a richness that tells his rank as plainly as does the chain of gold and white-enameled roses around his shoulders and the surety with which he moves, as if he has the right to be wherever he chooses to be. Even here.

Though he and Ned must be much of an age. Young. Ned was, what, nine years old when I saw him last, how many years ago? Eight years?

Eight years of him being raised by his mother and her pack of lords in exile, all baying to be back in power at whatever cost and Ned their best hope of managing it.

He was grown a fine young man, I'm told. The earl of Warwick, called the Kingmaker, after he came to break my peace here, to haul me out and proclaim me king again as if that were something I must want and be glad for, kept telling me how my son was all a father could be proud of, how very bold he was, how very forward . . .

Now he's very dead, despite of that.

Dead probably because of that.

And with him dead . . .

This isn't Ned in front of me. But who?

For all his outward surety, hesitancy flickers in his eyes and I realize I've been staring at him, just staring, and lower my gaze, but the hesitancy is still there in his voice as he says, "My lord brother, when he was here, meant to ask you . . ."

That's who he is then. There were four York sons. The eldest is now king of England, and this isn't George, duke of Clarence who I had such regrettable chance to know these six months past, between the time he turned his coat from his brother and turned it back again. Nor, obviously, is this the one who was killed along with York – How odd. York was not quite fifty when he was killed and I'm not quite fifty now when I'm to die – So this must be the youngest son, Richard, duke of Gloucester.

My poor queen. Among the things, besides his royal blood, she hated most about the duke of York were his four sons. All she had was me – and I was proving worthless to her – and Ned, with all the whispers there inevitably were that he wasn't likely mine, that I was incapable of enough manhood to father a son and that she must have gone elsewhere to get him . . .

". . . he meant to ask you if there's aught you need or want for your better comfort here."

But I made his brother angry and he forgot, and suddenly, illsensibly, I wish there was indeed something I wanted besides my death. Even something as simple as a last walk in a garden or someone dear to me to see and talk with.

But there's nothing. Nothing beyond wanting to have it done with, and this boy isn't here for that. Are you, youngling? You're farther from being a boy than I first thought. Farther, at least, than years have anything to do with. You were in the battles that put your brother back on the throne, weren't you? You've killed and faced the possibility of being killed, as Ned must have done, but he's dead and you yet live and haven't come to kill me. You lack the look men have when they're set to kill. I've seen it on my lords before battles. You don't have it, but you know I'm going to die. That's why you're here, isn't it? You've come to see me so my death will have a face for you, even a voice, not simply be a death with a name and nothing else attached to it. You've come to see me so you won't have the profit of my death without the cost. My death will cost your brother nothing, not even a second thought, I suspect. But you . . .

I hear my voice, not in my head but in the room, and realize I've said all that aloud. Or enough of it. Too much of it.

Worse than that, this boy who's much Ned's age is more than looking at me. He's seeing me.

No one has seen me in years. Even before I was shut away here, men had long since stopped seeing me. They saw "the king". They saw "the madman". They saw a failure, a fool, a nothing, a puzzlement. Never me.

But he is. He's looking past what I leave out for men to see into where no one has been for years. Into the part of me I took into the blackness and never brought out again for anyone to know. The part I hid away when there was nothing and no one left for me to care about.

We mostly live by never seeing one another. It's hard enough to live within ourselves without living, even a little way, into someone else. Our each and own pains, hopes, hatreds, griefs, loves are enough to bear, and aside from that, men don't want to be clearly seen. They want their seemings seen, their pretences believed, not their truths. They hate those who see them as they are, and if this boy is after all a man who sees past other men's seemings into who they are, he's going to be hated. He's . . .

I sit back in the chair, sick and shuddering and hoping that I'm hiding it. I hate these seeings when they come on me. I don't want to know. This boy isn't Ned. What comes to him is no concern of mine, and I answer why he's claimed to come with, "No, I'm in want or need of nothing." Coldly, as if everything between his asking and now hasn't happened. And add, "Except to be left alone."

He goes on looking at me a moment longer. An endless moment longer. Then bows to me. A slight inclination of his head. A small bending at his waist. Giving me far more courtesy than a prince of the House of York needs give to a sometime-king of the House of Lancaster.

It's only when he's nearly out the door that belatedly I think and say, "My pardon, lord. There's one thing."

He turns in the doorway, waiting, the darkness of the stairway behind him.

And I ask, "Would it be possible for my lady wife to be brought to see me?"

Does he guess? He's beyond the reach of the lamplight, I can't clearly see his face, but he says, as quietly as I asked it, "I'll see to it, my lord," and leaves.

Now Ned is dead . . .

I'm praying when she comes in: on my knees in front of the altar again, in my own small holy place, readying myself – as I've been readying all these years past – for my next place, my even smaller place. My grave. I don't know how long it's been since Gloucester left. It doesn't matter. Night is night, and if I'm too far gone in prayer, I don't hear the watchmen calling the hours.

I used to find freedom in prayer from my great lords. Now prayer is where I go because where else is there for me to be? Besides, there's presently so much praying to be done, so many new-departed souls to pray for.

My son's among them.

I never betrayed I heard the rumors that he wasn't mine – I always heard more than my lords or my lady wife thought I did – but neither did I ever do aught to quiet them. I even sometimes, as if unwitting, said or did small things that added to men's doubts and took pleasure in my lady wife's raging discomfiture at anything she ever heard, even whispered hints, against her honor and her boy.

By then he was all she had to keep her life from being a waste.

And now he's dead . . .

She's here. Whoever brought her must have let her come the last way by herself and she's come almost silently, but I know she's here and my mind goes still, before I make one last whispered prayer, cross myself, rise to my feet, bow to the altar, and turn to face her.

There's little to be seen. Shadows are thick everywhere and she's standing past the table, the lamplight there behind her, while the lamp that always burns above the altar throws too little of its ruddy light to more than show the white shape of her face in the black surround of her mourning wimple and veil that blend in a single sweep of shadow with the mourning black of her gown.

I can hardly be more to her and want no more, but she comes forward the few steps needed to close the distance between us. My lady wife. Brought out of France to be my queen when she was sixteen years old because my lords said our marriage would bring about peace in the French war and because I thought her picture lovely and that here would finally be someone who cared more for me than for my kingship.

I was wrong.

And here in a shadowed prison room we look at one another with nothing to be said between us. Her mourning black and my monk's robe say most of it. Her face says the rest.

She's grown old.

She's younger than me by how many years?

Many.

But she's old.

And hates me still.

It's etched there in her face, along with the ravaging lines of her grief.

She fought for years against who I am and what I couldn't give her.

She's hated me for years because I failed to be the king she wanted me to be.

But then I was never the king anyone wanted me to be, not even myself.

Ned was the only heart's desire she ever gained from our marriage. And now he's dead. And I still live. And she still hates me.

What a pity it is that she's always had more passion than wit. That she's always *felt* what she wants without ever considering whether the thing she wants is a good thing or an ill. She *feels*. And supposes that's enough to justify whatever then she chooses to do.

I know what I must needs say to her. The knowing came to me a while ago and, smiling, I say it.

"My lady, I'm sorry your bastard's dead."

And turn my back on her and kneel to the altar again, bending my head to prayer, with no need to see more.

No need to see her take four spasmed steps forward, out of the shadows, into the chapel. No need to see her reach past him to seize one of the great brass candlesticks that flank the altar. No need to see her take a half-step backward from him, the candlestick in both hands now, and raise it up and back and swing it down with all her hatred, rage, and grief behind it . . .

According to an official report, King Henry VI died that night in the Tower of London of "pure displeasure and melancholy". The following night his body, with no wounds showing on it, was publicly displayed in St Paul's Cathedral, that people might be sure of his death, and then was buried at Chertsey monastery up the Thames, until twelve years later King Richard III, once duke of Gloucester, had it moved to St George's Chapel, Windsor, where what is left of it remains.

Miracles attributed to King Henry were reported at both at Chertsey and at Windsor, and the movement to have him declared a saint was cut short only by the English Reformation.

When his tomb at Windsor was opened in the early 1900s and the skeletal remains examined, the skull was found to be badly broken.

HAPPY THE MAN . . .

———————

Amy Myers

Now we turn to perhaps the best known of all royal mysteries – the fate of the Princes in the Tower. The Princes were Edward V and his brother Richard of York, the young sons of Edward IV. When Edward died, his heir was only twelve, and Richard two years younger. They came under the protection of their uncle, Richard, Duke of Gloucester, who very quickly had the children proven illegitimate, and usurped the throne as Richard III. Like King John, Richard III is so often portrayed as an evil villain, particularly in productions of Shakespeare's play. I'm not convinced Richard was so bad as he is depicted. By all accounts he was an excellent king, much liked by his populace, though there is no doubt that he was ambitious and cruel when the circumstances warranted. Richard's name has been linked with many royal murders, including that of Henry VI as well as the Princes in the Tower. It is the fate of the Princes that the following story explores.

I, known as Richard of Eastwell and the bastard son of King Richard III of late unlamented memory, being now in my eighty-first year and approaching my own grave, set my hand to paper in order that the true story of King Edward V and his young brother the Duke of York may be known at last, and my conscience rest the easier. When the terrible murder in the Tower took place, I was only a lad, and slight for my age; its memory haunts me still. Beatus ille, wrote Horace, happy the man who tills the fields of his ancestors, far from the machinations of men; and happy the man who may live peacefully on this fair Kentish estate of Eastwell. The tale begins in the middle of June in that fateful year of 1483 . . .

"Come, young Richard, I am bid to take you to the Tower."

"Shall I see lions and leopards and apes?" The menagerie at the Tower of London was famous, even the other side of the water at Southwark.

My lord the Duke of Buckingham laughed at the excitement he had aroused. He doffed his feathered cap in mock respect to a lad who then had no idea that he was the son of a king, but since the age of eleven had dwelled quietly with Master Jeremiah Thwaite for three years to be taught his books, believing that the nurse who had reared him was his natural mother. She had been glad enough to see the back of him, and although Master Thwaite was a fine Latin tutor, he was but little company for a growing boy.

"I will show you them all." Yes, and snakes and jackals also, he added as if to himself. "You are to meet a rich and noble gentleman, Richard."

Another rare event, another mystery! One at least was solved. Although his lordship came to Southwark once a quarter, with a purse of gold for Master Thwaite, his identity was unknown – until that day, when he declared it boldly upon his arrival.

At that age one steps lightly into dark alleys, which beckon so enticingly that safety and sense are left behind, in belief that nothing can do you harm. The duke's carriage awaited, and the dark alley was entered.

"The Tower, Richard."

The journey as the horses trotted over London Bridge had been wonder enough, but the last stage, rowed by the duke's boatmen along the River Thames towards the Watergate, crowned it all. The duke merely waved a casual hand at that massive fortress, but who could forget their first sight of this royal palace, menagerie, Royal Mint, public meeting place – and, for the unlucky, prison? In the outer ward, the public mill at their leisure, according to the ancient custom of such castles, and the roars of the strange beasts excite, rather than disturb.

As they did that day. Milord Buckingham seemed in little mood to pander to his charge's desire to visit the Barbican menagerie now, but hurried through Watergate entrance at St Thomas's Tower, under the portcullis, and into the inner area, where the kings of England had walked and lodged since the far-off days of William the Conqueror. To the right were grand timbered buildings of the last century, with an elegant turret soaring upwards. Ahead, abutting the turret, was a forbidding-looking massive square stone keep, built in olden times, and the noise of the animals suddenly seemed more fearsome.

"The White Tower, Richard." Even the Duke of Buckingham seemed quieter now, almost nervous.

"My lord duke!"

He turned to see who had summoned him so peremptorily. The man was half hidden by the shadows of a tree, in a hedged garden not far away, a man so huge he seemed an oak himself, dark-haired, and with dark eyes that missed nothing, a man as black as the ravens that, legend has it, guard the Tower and England from harm.

"Will Slaughter, Richard," Buckingham snapped, displeased, it seemed, at being summoned by a servant, and yet surprisingly he obeyed the summons. "They call him Black Will."

Dear Will, a true friend – it was not for your kind heart they called you Black.

"My masters would meet your young companion," Will growled. "Richard, is it not?"

He was not alone in the garden. There could have been little doubt of the identities of the two boys who ran up eagerly to join him, one a slender youth of thirteen, and the other some four years younger. Even Southwark had been agog with the news that the young King Edward V, son of the late king, had been brought to the Tower last month by his uncle, Richard, Duke of Gloucester and now Protector of the King and Realm. He was housed, it was said, in the King's Lodging, the timbered buildings adjoining the White Tower, as befitted his regal status, and his younger brother the Duke of York had joined him to prepare for his coronation. It was obvious they had been bowling along this garden pathway, their target an empty flagon; it seemed a poor toy for a king of England. Kings are the loneliest of men, and any newcomer of their own age must interest them.

"Wilt thou join our game?" It was said that King Edward's long fair hair was inherited from his mother, Queen Elizabeth of York, now in sanctuary at Westminster, for these were uncertain times.

"Oh yes, sire. Shall we play at skittles?" Master Thwaite did not approve of such light amusement, and there was none else to play with.

It was not to be. My lord duke bowed deeply to his king: "Sire, I would take Master Richard to the audience chamber. My lord Protector must not be kept waiting."

From the look that passed between Will and Buckingham, it was obvious they were in agreement, but the wait in the audience chamber proved long for a lad whose merriment had given place to nervousness. The room, decorated so grandly with brightly painted animals and the royal arms, suggested that my lord Protector must indeed have some great interest in a humble lad of Kent.

Buckingham paced up and down, seemingly nervous, until at last the doors were thrown open, and the rich and noble gentleman came in. No name was spoken but only a fool would not realize this was Richard, Duke of Gloucester himself. If Black Will did not deserve his name, then here was one that did. Yet this man looked no monster, as our Tudor kings would have it now. There was no hump upon his back, no withered arm. He was richly clad, small, and as it were, *coiled*, ready to spring, as full of energy as though he were a cannon ball ready to be fired. His eyes could flash you in anger to your death, and many was the good man whose head had tumbled at his order. Today, however, those eyes were soft; there was emotion in them, as he came forward at a rush, then suddenly halted, as though he must hold himself in check.

"Richard, my son."

Those were the only three words he spoke, and they were thrown to the wind, for he straightaway departed, leaving only ten gold pieces in the hand of a bewildered boy behind.

It was just over six weeks later when Black Will himself came a-knocking on the Southwark door, having, he explained later, bribed Buckingham's man to learn where Master Thwaite's lodging lay, and much had happened before this surprising and welcome visit. On 6 July the coronation took place, not of King Edward V but of the usurper Richard III, erstwhile Protector. Indeed, there was no

Edward V now, for his uncle had declared him bastard and his
brother with him, in order to gain title to the crown. Their royal
lodgings, it was said, had been exchanged for a Tower prison; the
princes were no longer to be seen playing in the garden, but
occasionally glimpsed behind bars high up in the White Tower keep.

"The two royal bastards, Richard, would have you as playmate,"
Will grunted. "Will you come?"

"But they are prisoners, sir." And he their warder.

"Edward is sickly, and his brother stays with him. They need
company to play at marbles and dice, to occupy their days." The eyes
were hooded, watchful, judging the reaction of his words upon the
listener. Then came a great bellow of laughter, a roar that befitted the
man's girth.

"Fear not, young Richard," he guffawed. "You will lodge with
me." This brought little reassurance until he added, "Mistress
Slaughter is a fine cook and being barren longs for a lad to cosset." A
large purse of money was passed over by Will to appease Master
Thwaite for temporary loss of his ward, and thus, Edward and
Richard were to be playmates.

"You are much of an age, Richard, and have blood in common, I
hear," quoth Will. "For sure there is something of the Plantagenets
about both of you, although you have more of your father, and King
Edward much of Queen Elizabeth. You have noble features, lad, and
your mother must have been of high rank if King Richard III spares
her blushes by not openly acknowledging her son as his own."

Will was at the moment the only companion – or gaoler – to the
two princes. King Richard had dismissed the other three, and so Will
must tend to the princes' needs by day and night, leaving Mistress
Slaughter alone with her new lodger. It was a happy time, spent in
the royal apartments in the White Tower by day, and in the small
cottage, one of many on the outer ring of the fortress, by night.

"Ah, Mistress Slaughter, I love thee well. If I could eat of your eel
pie all my life, I should not budge from this table."

"Get along with you, Master Richard," she retorted, but highly
pleased at the kiss upon her cheek. "You and your jokes."

It was not all merriment, for there were questions to be asked of
Will.

"Does the king know of this? Or my lord the Duke of
Buckingham?"

"There is no need, Richard. You are here only to keep company with the princes every day and carry their food to them. I would trust no one other than Mistress Slaughter to cook it."

"Why not?"

"Mistress Slaughter is a good cook," he answered evasively.

There was some evil in the Tower, and Will's answer less than reassuring.

"You get on well with Edward, do you not?" he continued.

It had been only two days, but dear Will was right. The time had passed quickly and merrily, with much to share, whether it be the Latin poets or chess and knucklestones; for exercise, there were skittles and bowling. The length of one room was hardly sufficient, and bowling was best played down and up a spiral staircase in the turret, which led down to the chapel below, and the King's Lodging adjacent to the White Tower, though the way to both was barred. With one a former king, another a young duke, and the other an unacknowledged love-child, there was much to discuss of life outside the Tower, and of how it had come to change. Bastards may be on equal terms, and nothing need be hidden. Even fears.

"Edward and his brother have nothing to worry about, Richard," Will said reassuringly. "Gloucester is crowned now. Why should he consider the late king's bastards a threat?"

"You would not deceive me, dear Will?"

He sighed. "My lord Buckingham has his eye on the throne, they say, as has Margaret Beaufort, who would have her upstart son, Henry Tudor, take the crown. These are dark days, and in dark days, one must trust only in our Lord. Who knows what evil may come upon us?"

Happy the man, far away from man's machinations, yet how could one ignore the chains of duty and love? Duty lay here, and now, so did love.

"Dear Will, let us go to the White Tower now. I would play at dice."

Within three days there was a dramatic change. Will Slaughter was joined at His Majesty's command by three other "servants", and I could see that Will distrusted these men. The worst was Miles Forrest, an evil-looking man and, it was rumoured, a murderer, from the north of England, which was loyal to King Richard. These men would play with us, hear all our speech, and watch our every movement. I had grown fond of my companion, so gentle and merry, but now scared, and growing pale and sick, while the young Duke of York was still ever bright, never believing there were black hearts in the world.

During those weeks of late July and August, a new Constable of the Tower was appointed, Sir Robert Brackenbury, a good man, Will said, but loyal to King Richard. There were important visitors from the north, and after they had left, Sir Robert had many a long talk with Will. He would be summoned to the Constable's lodging, and would return greatly disquieted. One day I thought I glimpsed my lord Buckingham, but Will said I was mistaken. He had quarrelled with King Richard, it was said, but had returned to his lands in Wales, and not come to declare his support for the rightful king. Talk, talk, while suspicions multiplied. It grew so bad, Will urged me to leave, but I would not. I might be needed, and my place was here. Will, being officially servant to King Richard, could not be seen to be too familiar with the prisoners. I began to feel a prisoner myself, however, and daily escaped into the fresh air to return to Mistress Slaughter's house, with a guilty relief that I was free and they were not.

At the end of August all seemed set for the investiture in York of King Richard's son Edward as Prince of Wales. After that, I was sure, there could be no threat to any of Edward IV's surviving offspring. But winds changed quickly in those evil days.

"In the name of the king, open!"

I saw a thin-faced man spring from his horse, as his manservant, as broad and square as Will himself, thundered on the door of the Constable's lodging, and both went inside. Not long after, Sir Robert himself came to Will's cottage, nodding to me. I took the hint, and went upstairs to join Mistress Slaughter, but fixed my ear to the floor where I could hear every word. Something unusual was afoot.

"Sir James Tyrell carried a letter from His Majesty bearing his own seal commanding me to hand over the keys of the Tower," Sir Robert said heavily. "What else could I do, Will Slaughter? Even now he and that knave John Dighton are with Forrest."

There were sounds as if Will intended to rush straight to the White Tower, but Sir Robert stopped him. "No. You are suspected, Will."

"Of what, my lord Constable?"

"Of too much compassion for your prisoners."

"I do my job well. I guard them close," growled Will.

"Too close."

I froze in fear and, as soon as Sir Robert left, I ran down to join Will.

"Will they take the boys away?" I asked. It would be a mercy if that were all, but in my mind was the terrible thought of the green that lay by the Tower, where so short a time ago the loyal Hastings had had his head struck from him.

"Perhaps, lad. But you must go *now*. This is no place for you."

"I shall not, Will. I owe them my loyalty at least."

Will said no more, but bid me stay with Mistress Slaughter. When he left the cottage, I followed at a distance, creeping into the Tower and up the steps that led to the royal prison, where the guards kept constant watch. I stopped half way up, for I heard shouting ahead, and recognized Forrest's thick accent.

"Get thee gone, Black Will, and quickly."

"Do you think you are the king that you order me away?" I heard Will yell.

A snigger, and a different, menacing voice. "It is the king's wish that you leave the Tower. Do you wish to try my dagger, fool?"

"I wish to see your letters of authority, stranger."

I shrank back, as from above came the sound of blows and a gurgling choking sound. It was followed by laughter, as Will, thrust headlong down the stone steps, tumbled at my feet, half strangled, and groaning in pain. I helped him up, and he rasped his fury that I was there, dragging me by the arm until we were safe back at home. There he stared at me with tears in his eyes, while Mistress Slaughter tended him.

"It's gone awry, Richard. I could not have foretold this. What shall we do?"

"Leave," Mistress Slaughter said sharply. "All three of us, *now*."

"No," I cried out in agony. How could we abandon those innocent prisoners?

"Then," Will decreed hoarsely, "we will take lodgings in a tavern in Tower Street."

It was strange to find myself in a tavern, for I had never been in such a place, and the noise and roughness scared me. Will sat by my side till I slept at last, and I stirred at dawn to find him still with me. "Richard, I shall go now to see if my wards are well."

"Then I come too, my valiant Will," I said, leaping up and snatching at my hosen. My eye met his. "No harm can come."

He was unwilling, but I would not be dissuaded. With heavy heart we walked through the Lion Gate as soon as the drawbridge was down, hearing the roars of the caged beasts so close to us in the Barbican. We completed our crossing of the moat, and approached the portcullis through which we must pass for the White Tower.

"Sir Robert's business," Will called easily, being known to the guard, and we were through.

We had no chance to escape notice, however, for at the entrance to the White Tower, stood Sir Robert himself.

"Get thee gone, Will," he said harshly, when he saw us, "or I must take you up, and Richard too."

"Take me first to see my charges, my lord Constable."

"I cannot. They are gone."

"How, gone?" I earned a look of displeasure from Will, but fear made me speak. "Are they taken by Sir James to another prison?"

"Gone," repeated Sir Robert, as though this word were from a lesson he had learned well." And Dighton and Forrest too. Sir James returned my keys, and he too has departed."

"Then take us to the princes' rooms," I piped childishly. Indeed the child in me would out, for I felt tears pricking at my eyes, through terror at some deep and dark mystery here. "I would have some memento of my friends."

"I cannot do so. They are empty."

"Then there can be no harm in our seeing them," Will said mildly.

Unwillingly, Sir Robert led us up the steps I knew so well. The apartments were indeed empty. No bedclothes, no mattresses, no clothing, books, nothing to show this had but yesterday housed two young boys. Yet there was no sign of blood either, and my deepest fear of all receded a little. I saw only the empty flagon we used as the jack in bowling, and a forgotten marble. I began to take heart. Maybe my worst imaginings were unfounded, and they had indeed merely been taken elsewhere.

"The chapel," Will roared obstinately. "They may have fled there for sanctuary."

"They have not," Sir Robert said hastily – too hastily, for we realized he was still nervous.

Nevertheless, he led us out down the main staircase to the chapel which was indeed empty. A sudden desire to see the steps where once we had played at bowling made me unbolt the door to take the other way out, however, and although Sir Robert tried to stop me, I sped once more down the stairs within the turret which adjoined the King's Lodging.

"It is bolted fast at the foot," Sir Robert shouted after me.

"No matter. I will return when I have done." I jumped the last few steps as had been our custom, and twisted my foot on a loose pebble. I looked down, to see some specks of sandy earth and tiny pieces of stone at my foot, and caught an elusive whiff of a sweet smell. Then it was gone. I would have thought little of it, save that Sir Robert, fast behind me, was very pale and would not meet my eye.

"Come, lad," Will said harshly. "Nothing to keep us here. For sure, they have gone to some other place." He too had seen what I had seen, and I realized then that the nightmare had returned. I took a vow that day that if harm had come to my dear companions, I would avenge them. We knew who would have carried out the deed, if cruel murder had been done, but who had placed the golden coins in the hands of Sir James Tyrell, John Dighton and Miles Forrest?

Within weeks it was openly said in marketplace and tavern that the princes were dead. Our English history has been fraught with untimely deaths and intrigues, and even the trail of blood left in the wake of King Richard III might have passed without rebellion; now, however, the people murmured against the murder of a divinely appointed king, for few had believed King Richard's claim that Edward V was not born in wedlock. Will and I went out from our lodging daily to listen to what was said. Master Thwaite saw his ward no more, and Will apprenticed me to a friend of his, a stone-mason. I worked hard and listened hard. My lord Buckingham was one of those who balked at the murder of a king, and now there was talk that he supported the claims of Henry Tudor. No bodies had been found, and the mystery of what had happened that evil night was a trail that had led nowhere, although what Will and I had seen suggested its ending would be dark indeed.

In October came the news of Buckingham's failed rebellion, timed to coincide with the landing of Henry Tudor in Cornwall. Buckingham ended on the block, and Henry Tudor, betrayed by the Channel winds from arrival at the expected time, returned to

Brittany. And still the bodies had not been found.

"It was Buckingham who had them slain," was Will's opinion, "to clear the way for Master Tudor."

"If he would not condone the murder of a king for Richard of Gloucester's sake, he would not do so for Henry Tudor."

"Richard, you had best be an attorney, not a stone-mason. Your wits are shrewd."

"They have need to be," I answered soberly. "Even the bastard son of a tyrant may have enemies. Moreover Tudor has the same motive as Richard III. He too seeks power and the throne, without hindrance of law."

"No one could have demanded the keys of the Tower save King Richard," Will pointed out. "Tyrell carried the king's letter, with his own seal."

"Is that so?" I asked "Pray, how do we know that?"

"Why, Sir Robert –" Will stopped, realizing what I meant. "Sir Robert is a good man," he snapped.

"And might well have believed the honeyed talk of Buckingham that Henry Tudor would save the princes' lives if they could be spirited from the Tower out of Richard's clutches. Perhaps he wished a better master than Richard."

"They say Sir Robert is being rewarded by the king for an evil night's work."

"King Richard may not have appreciated his motive. There is but one man can lead us to the truth, and he dwells in the Tower."

"Sir Robert?"

"No, Will, his priest."

I had at last identified that whiff of scent, so familiar, yet so out of place at the foot of a stone stairway. It was incense.

It was now harder for us to gain entrance to the inner ward, but we managed it by wearing the clothes of my new trade. Two stone-masons, in my master's cart, with a load of Kentish ragstone and flints, watched carefully for Sir Robert's departure and promptly bluffed their way in past the guards, claiming their task had been given them by the Constable himself.

The apartments I had known so well struck cold, and the air seemed heavy with menace. Even the flagon and the marble had disappeared now, and I knew if we descended the spiral staircase the same broom would have swept the ground clean long ago. I could not bear to do so, for I realized what must lie there buried deep. Instead we climbed down the steps only as far as the chapel through the door used only by kings.

The double-storeyed Norman arches gave this place of worship a grandeur and holy authority that even I hesitated for one moment before approaching that solitary figure, kneeling in his robes of office at the altar. Will had no such scruples.

"Father!"

The priest turned, and seeing two workmen of most unroyal mien, showed his surprise. "Would you make confession, my sons?" he asked doubtfully.

"No. We would hear yours," growled dear Will, never one for diplomacy.

"Of what?" He looked nervous for all his calm words.

"There is a grave in this tower, is there not?" I said. "Were you not asked to sanctify the ground, and conduct the rites of burial one early September night?"

"I cannot answer." There were tears in his eyes, as well as wariness.

"We saw the earth you scattered, smelled the incense you burned. Earth to earth, dust to dust, ashes to ashes."

"I still cannot answer. I am bound –"

"Not by the confessional, not by God."

He made no reply.

"It is no matter," I continued. "We will dig to discover the truth."

"No! It is holy ground."

In those few words we had our answer.

"Do not worry, Father. I know now whose hand rewarded those assassins for their evil night's work, and one day, when my opportunity comes, they will be avenged."

It was not quite two years before that day came, during which King Richard's legitimate son had died, leaving him without an heir. The spectre of Henry Tudor loomed ever closer. By now Will and I had moved with my master to Kent, where Will too took up the trade of stone-mason in the countryside near Ashford. I lived with Will and Mistress Slaughter, and we were as content as we could be until our unfinished business was complete.

In early August 1485 Henry Tudor sailed again, and this time we heard his army was marching from Wales towards King Richard unopposed. It was time for us to go. It took Will and myself five days to travel north to Leicestershire, where it was said the armies of the king and Tudor were now gathered, and we arrived at the small town of Market Bosworth to find that battle was expected on the morrow. I dressed myself, not as a stone-mason, but as befitted the son of a king setting forth for combat: in plated armour, vizored sallad and bavier. With Will as my man, we found the king's men encamped on a hill two miles from the town, and Henry Tudor's army in the valley.

Now that the moment had come, I was trembling, aware of what risks I took, but remembering my sweet playmates in the Tower who lay buried deep under the stones, I could not abandon them again. Hearts in our mouths, we made our way to the murderer's camp.

"Make way," Will shouted to the guard, "for Richard, Bastard son to the so-styled Richard III, King of England."

Shortly I was face to face with the murderer himself. "Why have you come?" The eyes were watchful, though the face was drawn and weary.

"To avenge the murder of two princes of tender years."

He showed no surprise, indeed he seemed indifferent.

"Only for you would Brackenbury have needed to clear away all traces of the murder, lest you be linked with it. Had Henry Tudor so eased his path to the throne he will surely take tomorrow, he would have proclaimed the murder to the world by revealing the bodies and declared you the obvious murderer."

He seemed not even to be listening, though his eyes were fixed fast on me.

"Take off your visor, Richard," he said slowly, a choke in his voice, "That I may kiss you as my son."

I must have seemed his dead child restored to him. I wanted nothing further, save the quiet peace of the English countryside. I needed no family, save Will's, nor had it need of me with Henry Tudor close at hand. I desired only time to pray God for forgiveness that by mischance I had been responsible for the murder of my playmates.

"My son," he murmured.

I opened my visor, then bared my head. Down tumbled the golden locks of the eldest male child of Queen Elizabeth of York.

"No, sire. I am your king, Edward V of England."

The tale I have related to you has not been mine alone: it began as dear Richard's, as we talked in the Tower of how he had come there. His story entranced me for he came of a world unknown to me, and I have recorded it here just as he re-enacted it for my brother and myself.

Before Sir Robert and my new gaolers including Forrest came to the Tower, five days after Richard's arrival, my dear Will, devoted to me, contrived to exchange me with Richard. I then dwelt with him and Mistress Slaughter, and they called me henceforth Richard. Dear Richard and I were like enough, and once Richard was clad in my rich apparel, the newcomers would assume him me, his hair though not as fair as mine, being very light in colour. Richard was most eager; he had great compassion for me, and there seemed no danger to him, for Will was there to reveal his true identity if the king's assassins should come. They would not dare to kill the king's son, and in the delay Richard would be whisked away to join me. My dear brother the Duke of York, too young to see danger, thought it a merry game, and I believed there would be no threat to him once I were away from the Tower. We could not have foretold that Will would be dismissed so abruptly, and yet the burden lies on me still.

After poor Will and his wife were dead, and myself ageing, Sir Thomas Moyle of Eastwell discovered me reading my poems of Horace in Latin; he questioned me closely, and I told him a little of my story, though not my true identity. He became my kind benefactor, granting me a cottage for the rest of my life.

Now I live close to the church in which I shall shortly be buried. They say those upon whom remorse lies heavy linger close to earth, and perhaps my restless ghost will haunt Eastwell where I have dwelt so contentedly save for guilt for the death of that sweet and joyous lad, for whom I am now called Richard of Eastwell.

God grant peace to my immortal soul, but even now I rejoice at remembering the look on that bloody tyrant's face at Bosworth, as he realized he had ordered the death of his own son.

BORGIA BY BLOOD

Claire Griffen

Although this collection concentrates on the kings of England and Scotland, it is difficult to overlook the murders and mysteries that surround so many of the European courts. One name that is synonymous with murder is that of the Borgias, particularly Cesare and Lucretia Borgia, children of the later pope, Alexander VI. They lived in the final decade of the fifteenth century, when Italy was divided into several kingdoms constantly at war with each other or in an uneasy alliance with Spain, France and Turkey. In the Papal States the flag of the Borgia Bull was flying. The Spanish Borjas had changed their name to Borgia and made Italy the arena of their ambition. The ruling Pope, Alexander VI, was Rodrigo Borgia. It was a matter of scandal that he openly acknowledged his children and advanced their careers. In 1497 an event occurred which changed the course of Cesare Borgia's life and launched him on a five-year conquest of Italy. In a parallel career there was another young man in Rome of mysterious origins whose star was also on the rise as a master-spy and "solutionist" of murders.

An hour after the news was out on the street that the Duke of Gandia had been fished up dead from the Tiber, the shield-bearers of Cardinal Valencia were beating on the doors of Don Alessandro Orsini.

With an air of languor, Sandro rose from his Spartan meal of bread, cheese and wine and fixed his dark, almond-shaped eyes on the captain of the guard with and expression of polite inquiry. His servant, Ugo Beppo, who had known Sandro since boyhood, was alert to every nuance and knew that his master's sense of survival was darting about like a fox in a trap.

At the age of twenty-six, Sandro Orsini was earning the reputation of solving the seemingly insoluble in murders both domestic and political. But he also had the same name as a certain noble family who were the traditional enemies of the Borgias and who had just bested them in a disastrous war. Was it his expertise Cardinal Valencia required or the skin off his back as a possible suspect?

He was summoned to the dread Castel Sant' Angelo. Many who crossed the *ponte* of the prison fortress were later discovered, floating corpses, in the Tiber.

Cardinal Valencia received him in the *salottina di audienza*, sprawled so carelessly in his high-backed ecclesiastical chair he looked as if he had been flung there, his scarlet robe an incongruous splash of color against the purple plush. Cesare Borgia had inherited the incredible beauty of his mother, Vanozza Catanei, never more intense than when his eyes were raw with grief. He had discarded his hat, which lay beside him on the floor. His hair, light in color, hung to his shoulders; in his vanity he had only the tiniest of tonsures.

He proffered his ring to be kissed and then gestured at a stool, which placed Sandro lower than his chair. It was the first sign of arrogance Sandro had noted in the twenty-two-year-old cardinal; he had hitherto been described as a youth of rare charm and humorous wit, as sweet-natured as his sister Lucrezia, but dwelling in the shadow of his flamboyant brother. Now there was an ambience of *something else*, as if his sibling's death had already marked him for some other destiny than the service of Christ.

"You've heard, of course, of the murder of the Pope's eldest son." It was not a time for preliminaries.

"May I offer my condolences, Your Eminence."

"I'd rather have an explanation of your whereabouts last night."

After a slight pause, Sandro said, "I visited the house of a courtesan."

"A convenient alibi. Whores are always ready to lie for their patrons."

Sandro took a deep breath. "If you want the murderer of the Duke of Gandia, don't look for him in my house. What motive could I have had to kill Don Juan? He was never my enemy."

"But were you his? You bear a name hateful to our house."

"Some would say my link with the Orsini name is a fragile one. I took it from my uncle who raised me when my mother died."

"And when her lover was slain leaving you nameless."

Sandro was silent. *Let's not discuss bastardy, Cesare Borgia. Mine is less public than yours.*

"I've heard you are nicknamed *Il Saracen.*" Cesare studied the black curling strings of hair that fell from under the toque with its upturned brim, the lean dark face above the pale colours Sandro affected, a satin doublet of a gold so dull it took on the green of verdigris in some lights, a square-necked shirt cut so low and of such transparent linen one could see the black hair curling on his chest. "You might dress as an Italian, but I'll wager there's more than one Turk in your pedigree. Do you spy for the Sultan Bajazet or for your Italian uncle? How else does a young man adrift in the world earn his living?"

Sandro smiled inwardly. *Not being a Pope's son, I couldn't expect to be a Cardinal from the age of eighteen.* Aloud, he said, "I've been called many things but assassin's not one of them. You may recall I've brought one or more murderers to justice.

"You may even recall how it began with the murder of my wife at the time Rome was sacked by French mercenaries. I was advised to regard her death as the work of a vandal, but I tracked the murderer to your household."

"Do you still bear a grudge, Don Sandro?" The question was asked so softly it was almost a plea.

Sandro shrugged. "Let's not open old wounds. Does Your Eminence desire me to conduct an investigation into the Duke of Gandia's murder?"

"In my own name, yes." Cesare's eyes glowed with a peculiar light; it was the first flaring of a passion for vendetta that would never leave him. "I want the vitals of the man who killed my brother and threw him like dung into the river."

"Where is Don Juan's body?" asked Sandro, gently. "That should be my initial examination."

"I've anticipated your wish." Cesare smiled wanly. "He lies in the next room. His body's been washed, but he's still naked."

"Washed!" Sandro frowned. "That was ill-advised. There might have been signs on his body that would have been useful. I trust you kept his clothes."

"Yes, his gloves were still tucked in his belt which contained a pouch holding thirty ducats."

"So the motive was not robbery."

Sandro entered a long narrow room with doors at each end, bare of furnishings but for a bier covered with a crimson cloth on which lay the body of a young man, blond of hair and beard and splendid of physique. Death's pallor was made more obvious by the rich color of the panoply. *Rigor mortis* had passed, his limbs had been composed and his eyes closed. Beside the corpse, the clerk of ceremonies Bernardino Gutteri kept lonely vigil.

"How many wounds?" asked Sandro, tersely.

"Nine. Would you like to examine them?"

"One in the neck. One in the chest. Either of which would have been fatal . . ."

"There's also one at the base of his skull."

"Two in his thighs, one in the lower abdomen, dangerously close to the genitalia but taking a different direction as if an assailant meant to mutilate him but one of his accomplices intervened, implying he didn't want a sexual motive suspected."

"You think there was more than one assassin?" ventured the clerk.

"Oh, assuredly. Mayhap five or six. Where are the other three wounds?"

"In his back."

"Deep wounds?"

"All from a stiletto."

"It was obviously an act of vendetta, but who among his enemies . . . ?"

The clerk shook his head, wordlessly. He looked shocked that such an illustrious, well-loved figure from the Papal Palace would be considered to have enemies.

"Where are his clothes?"

"I set them aside as the Cardinal instructed me. As you see, they were most gorgeous. The duke has dressed in the Oriental style since his friendship with Prince Djem. His undershirt and doublet of blue are both of silk. Ruined by water and refuse, of course, and all the blood-stains washed out, only the holes and slashes from the stab wounds remaining. Fastened to his shoulders was this cloak of figured gold brocade. His collar was made of pearls and his turban was also strung with pearls."

"All intact."

"Yes." The clerk frowned. "There was one strange factor. Look at his boots. The duke always wore tiny bells around the tops of his Cordovan boots. See, they've been slashed off. Why would such trifles be stolen and his money-pouch and precious ornaments left untouched?"

"To ensure his silence, Don Bernardino. But by whom? His murderers? Or did Juan desire discretion? He had quite a reputation as a *libertini*."

Bernardino Gutteri again put on an expression of shock at such a slur.

"Come," said Sandro, irritated. "We both know he was made for Venus not for Mars, especially after his disastrous attempts at conquest as Captain-General of the Papal States. He came home to follow his true vocation, the pursuit of women."

"The possibility existed that the Pope would have given his favourite son the vast tracts of land His Holiness had wrested from the Orsinis."

"So you personally believe the Orsinis are responsible for the duke's murder?"

The clerk was silent; he slid a furtive, but frightened glance at Sandro.

"You spoke of Prince Djem, the hostage held by the Pope but whom he was forced to yield to the French king when Charles invaded the Papal States three years ago. Prince Djem also died mysteriously and not long after he was delivered into the hands of the French."

"The physician diagnosed pneumonia." Two bright spots appeared in the clerk's cheeks.

"But there were rumours that Djem had been poisoned before he left Rome to prevent the French from enjoying the revenue paid by the Sultan for his brother's safekeeping."

"You surely can't believe His Holiness guilty of such malice. Djem was Don Juan's closest friend."

"It doesn't matter what *I* believe. It's what Bajazet believes. Has it occurred to you this murder could be revenge for his brother's death?"

Bernardino scoffed. "The Sultan would have breathed a sigh of relief at the news. His brother was a renegade who tried to take his throne and fled to the Knights of St John on Cyprus for sanctuary when he failed. That's how he fell into our hands. Now he's no longer a threat to the Ottoman Empire nor does his brother need to pay the revenue."

They were interrupted by a hovering in the doorway of a slightly built youth with long, light-colored, curling hair. His face above his green satin doublet was as pale as his dead brother's; he gazed at the corpse with an expression of stark horror.

"You must cover up these wounds," he stammered. "You mustn't let His Holiness see them. Already he mourns so piteously it's rumored he can be heard in the street."

"Don Joffre Borgia, Prince of Squillace," the clerk murmured to Sandro, "the Pope's youngest son." Aloud, he said, "We plan to dress Don Juan in military costume and at the sixth hour of the evening, accompanied by the Cardinals and his own shield-bearers, carry him in torchlight procession to Santa Maria di Popolo."

"Where he's to be interred?" the boy asked, eagerly. "And we'll never have to look on him again?"

"Fear not, Don Joffre. After I've tended him, he will appear to be sleeping not dead."

"But he'll never wake up." The boy touched one of the stiletto wounds with his fingertip.

"Don't touch him!" Joffre flinched as a woman glided through the doorway.

"Sancia of Aragon," murmured the clerk. "Don Joffre's wife."

She too wore green, dressed almost identically to her youthful husband, but with a long skirt and jeweled skull-cap which failed to keep in check her long, curling, auburn hair. Above her divided bodice with its criss-crossed laces, there was a mere wisp of a chemise revealing the upward thrust of her breasts. She emanated an aura of sensuality; she pulsed with fire like the twin emeralds on her forehead and on her bosom.

Joffre withdrew as Sancia approached the bier. Her eyes were glistening, either from tears or from the morbid curiosity some people had for the dead.

"You didn't keep your promise," she breathed, so softly only Sandro picked it up. She ran her fingers lightly along the full length of his body. "Such a waste."

This time Bernardino did not have to pretend shock. Sandro decided to withdraw discreetly.

In the *salottina di audienza* Cesare Borgia still sat in the ecclesiastical chair, gnawing sombrely on a fingertip of his scarlet glove. "Well?"

"I require from you, Your Eminence, the details of your brother's death, his last sighting alive, the discovery of his body."

"Yesterday Juan and I dined as is our frequent custom at our mother's house in Vincola. There were other guests. The weather being warm we ate in the vineyard. At dusk a masked man appeared among the guests. I saw him deep in conversation with Juan. As it was growing dark, I approached my brother with the suggestion we return to the Vatican with our little company of servants. I marked that Juan took the masked man up behind him on the crupper of his mule. I remembered then there had been talk of Juan being visited several times recently by a masked man."

"Did he speak?"

"No, he may have feared I would recognize his voice."

"And Don Juan offered no explanation of his identity."

"Nor did I ask. There are some who perpetually wear masks to conceal the embarrassing disfigurement of the French disease. I also considered it might have had something to do with a lovers' tryst." Cesare gave a hollow smile. "With Juan there was always some dalliance of the moment. As it happened when we reached the palace of Cardinal Vascanio, he abruptly parted from me. He was in good spirits and we parted on friendly terms, but he dismissed all his servants but one footman and with the masked man rode towards the Piazza degli Ebrei. When he had not returned to the papal palace by morning, His Holiness grew concerned and a search was conducted. On the evidence of a dealer who sells wood near the Ospedale of Schiavoni, one Giorgio Schiavi, who reported seeing a body flung into the Tiber at midnight, the boatmen and fishermen of the city were called together to use their tackle in the depths of the river. The body was discovered just before Vespers, weighted with stones . . ."

"And the footman?"

"Remains missing."

"May I ask if you have any personal suspicions?"

Cesare shrugged. "If not the Orsinis? A week ago Juan was invested with the Duchy of Benevento with the cities of Terracina and

Pontecorvo to be held by him and all his descendants in perpetuity. Some of the Cardinals protested, Cardinal Piccolomini most vigorously. I don't accuse His Eminence but the investiture gave rise to resentment among many people. Then, of course, there's the question of my sister Lucrezia's estranged husband Giovanni Sforza with whom Juan has quarreled bitterly and who is partly blamed for their estrangement."

Sandro studied him, thoughtfully. "Your Eminence, what I require from you is your authority to question whom I please, to enter any place, be it private dwelling or ecclesiastical precints that I might conduct my inquiry."

"I'll summon my secretary."

As if pre-empting his master's requirement the secretary entered and whispered in his ear. Cesare glanced at Sandro with a smile tinged with irony. "It seems we have word of the footman."

A man of the merchant class, Alfonso Caraffi by name, was ushered in. He was dressed soberly, florid of complexion, moist of eye and sweaty of brow. It was not only from fear inspired by the august presence in which he stood but by the presidio of Sant' Angelo, in some people's reckoning on an equal plane with Hell.

"What have you to tell me of the Duke of Gandia's footman?" demanded Cesare.

"Last night at about midnight there was a hammering at our door . . ."

"Where do you live?"

"In the Piazza degli Ebrei, Your Eminence. We were roused from our beds." *Sandro had a mental picture of the merchant tousled and shaky from broken sleep.* "By the time we got downstairs the knocking had become feebler and my servants admitted a dying man. He only had time to utter his master's name before he expired."

"Why didn't you call the city watch?" Cesare was scowling; he had gnawed a rent in the seam of his glove.

"Your Eminence, forgive me, I was afraid. It was past midnight. His assailants might still have been lurking outside."

"And this morning?"

"I was still afraid, because he was the servant of such an illustrious master. It did not cross my mind, I swear, that the duke had also been set upon. Only now when we learnt that he'd been found dead, oh, the profoundest of condolences, Your Eminence, did my wife prevail on me to come to you with our story. Tho' I don't know what assistance it will be to Your Eminence. He said so little before he died."

"Was he stabbed?" Sandro asked.

"And beaten over the head."

"Give me the directions to your house. I will call on you at another hour."

The man looked as deathstruck as if he had received this advice from the Devil himself. He was hurried away by the captain of the guard. Sandro was presented with the Cardinal's Authority and released to the outside world.

He found Ugo lurking anxiously across the Ponte Sant' Angelo. It was twilight, but still light enough to read his doleful expression. "Fear not," Sandro greeted him with a wry smile. "I live to hang another day."

"What befell you, master?"

"Cesare was after a scapegoat. He tried sticking his claws in to see how I'd respond."

"Like a cat with a mouse."

"Like a wolf with a fox. The Vatican's a den of wolves."

"What befalls *us* now?"

"First we return to the Piazza Venezione to saddle my Spanish mare and your mule and commandeer some footmen with torches and staves to safeguard our way, then we're off to the Ospedale of San Girolamo degli Schiavoni to buy wood."

"At this hour?" protested Ugo.

"I'm sure the good dealer, Giorgio Schiavi will still be about."

The body of the Duke of Gandia had been thrown into the Tiber near a conduit where there was a direct way from the Ponte Sant' Angelo via the Church of Santa Maria del Popolo, by which horse teams were accustomed to take their sewage and rubbish to dump in the river.

Not far from the conduit was a spot where Giorgio Schiavi had his wood offloaded from a ship. Here, he could be found rowing his boat up and down the river, keeping an eye on his produce to prevent it from being stolen. Sandro hailed him and after making a purchase of logs, which the disgruntled Ugo loaded into a barrow, the spy began a conversation with the wood-dealer.

"I understand an incident of great import occurred here last night."

Giorgio Schiavi was a cheerful, gap-toothed fellow, enjoying the celebrity status he had achieved from his role in the drama.

"Yes, indeed, signore, 'twas *my* evidence that led to the discovery of the corpse."

"Won't you tell *us* what you told the Pope's servants?"

"If you wish." The man appeared hesitant, despite his grin.

Taking the hint, Sandro dropped two more carlins into his outstretched hand.

"Thank you, signore. I'm a poor man who works hard for his living. Well, as I told the Pope's servants I was resting in my boat, watching over my wood, when I saw two men coming on foot down that alley to the left of the Ospedale of Shiavoni. It was about midnight. They walked along the public path, glancing cautiously about to see if anyone else was abroad. At that hour the area was deserted and they retraced their steps along the alley. After a while, two other men came from the same alley and repeated the actions of the first two. I had the good fortune, as I now realize, to miss their glance. Finding the coast clear, they gave a low whistle. Thereupon a rider appeared on a white horse with a body slung across its back, the group moved past the sewage outfall and there halted, the horse was turned with its back to the river, the body rolled off and taken up by the four men by its arms and legs and hurled into the river with all their force. The man sitting on horseback asked, *Has it sunk?* The others replied, *yes, my lord.* But then they noticed his cloak was still floating on the surface of the water so they threw stones to weigh it down. All five men, including the horseman, departed in the direction of the Ospedale of San Giacomo and disappeared from my sight."

"Why didn't you inform the city watch?"

The wood-dealer shrugged. "I thought nothing of it at the time."

"You thought nothing of it?" choked Ugo.

"My dear signore, it's plain you haven't lived your life on the river. In my time I've seen a hundred bodies disposed of in like fashion, cut-purses and cut-throats, the usual scum. Why should I think this was anything different? Let them sink their ill-deeds out of sight, as long as they don't hook me."

"The man on the horse, did he impress you as a nobleman?"

"They called him *my lord*, didn't they? Of course, I couldn't see his face."

"Was he wearing a mask?"

"Not that I can recall?"

"Was his voice deep or light?"

"It was light like a woman's. I thought it *was* a woman at first, but then what would a woman be doing there at night? And they did call him *my lord*?"

"Do you know where the body was actually discovered?"

The wood-dealer pointed across the river. "By that great palazzo."

Sandro peered through the darkness. "The house of Don Antonio Pica della Mirandola." He dropped another carlin into the wood dealer's hand and bade him goodnight. "Now we pay a call on the noble lord Don Giovanni Sforza, the husband of Donna Lucrezia Borgia."

"Must I trundle my barrow all the way to his house?" complained Ugo, and then was struck by a more profound dismay. "But he lives in Pesaro."

"He's presently living in Rome at the home of his uncle Cardinal Sforza at the command of His Holiness. There's a question of annulment brewing."

"I should think Don Giovanni would rejoice at being released from the Borgia *ménage* not plot murder."

"It depends how deeply his pride has been hurt."

The lord of Pesaro received them with ill grace in his uncle's *salottina audienza*. He sat behind a table of polished cedar, keeping a distance between himself and his interrogator. He was a tall man of about thirty, dark-haired and dressed somewhat provincially. His deepset eyes burned with resentment, he was seething with the humiliations he had endured and would still endure. *Good*, thought Sandro, *once he gets over his ill-temper with me, he'll spill everything out, his marriage to Lucrezia, the secrets of the Vatican, his quarrel with Juan.*

"Why does Cesare Borgia send *you* with a warrant, Don Alessandro? Does he suspect *me* of murdering Juan? God knows I have just cause."

"You know my name, Don Giovanni?"

"The whole world knows how you tracked your wife's murderer to Cardinal Valencia's household. I'm surprised you're still alive."

"I wonder at it myself sometimes," murmured Sandro, with a

disarming smile. He glanced about the room, sumptuous for so small a space with Turkish rugs and paintings. "Are you enjoying your sojourn in Rome?"

Giovanni sneered. "I thought you had a reputation for intelligence. What man enjoys having his manhood slandered because the Pope wants a more gainful match for the pawn in the Borgia power-play?"

"Your wife Lucrezia being the pawn." Sandro spoke gently; it was a statement rather than a question.

"My wife! They're trying to prove she was my wife in name only, that the marriage was never consummated, that I'm impotent and that's why there's been no issue in the past four years. My God, she was a child of thirteen when we were wed. A man has some decency. I held off for a year or so, but I swear as I've sworn before the College of Cardinals I've had her and there's nothing virginal about Lucrezia Borgia, including her morals. Did you know they wanted me to prove my virility on a whore in the presence of the papal legate from Milan? Of course, I refused. I hear Lucrezia's taken refuge in a nunnery, there to hide her blushes for the lie she's told . . ."

"I understand," interrupted Sandro, still gently, "that you quarreled with Juan. Was it over Lucrezia?"

"You've heard what is said of the Borgias. They need no one but each other. They are sufficient unto themselves. They are a House turned in on itself. They love only each other, they bed only each other. Yes, I quarreled with Juan. I accused him of seducing my wife. I suspect Cesare, too. I wouldn't put it past the old man himself . . ." He bit off the insinuation and gulped a mouthful of wine from the goblet beside him, but nothing could stem the tide of his bitter denunciation. "I'm no puling puppy like little Joffre who accepted it meekly when *his* wife Sancia and Juan openly flaunted their lust. Have you ever seen Sancia? She's no beauty but she has an unequaled notoriety for whoredom. And they wed her to a twelve-year-old boy! Sancia and Lucrezia were best friends, which should give you a clear insight into the situation."

"Thank you, my lord, for your candour and your cooperation."

Giovanni shrugged and took a deeper swallow of wine. "Juan even tried to persuade Joffre to accompany him on his escapades – *to make a man of him*. God, what a family! Someone had better cause even than I to murder that lecherous dog."

"Do you think the lord of Pesaro is guilty?" ventured Ugo as they made their way out from Cardinal Sforza's palazzo. "He's vindictive enough."

"But indiscreet."

"Did you believe his tale of incest . . . ?"

"It doesn't matter what *I* believe. It's what others believe," was Sandro's only reply.

"Where now do we hie, master?"

"I've often accused you of having the longest ears and the longest nose in Italy, my friend. What can you tell me of Don Antonio Pica del Mirandola?"

"That he has a face like a death's-head and the prettiest daughter in Christendom."

"Then we shall pay a call on Don Antonio Pica del Mirandola."

"I hope he invites us to supper. My belly's as empty as a leper's begging bowl."

"A nice comparison," rebuked his master, but added, "I shall get you supper later at the house of the turnkey Alfonso Caraffi."

"I thought Signore Caraffi was a merchant."

"We shall see what profession he's best at."

The house of the Mirandolas had so grimly forbidding a facade it was a castello rather than a palazzo. Or a mausoleum. Its master well suited the description of a living corpse. In a *libreria* lined with black marble and dark wood and stark of the most comfortable of furnishings he sat on a pew overlaid with leather under a closed casement. His face was the colour and texture of wrinkled parchment, his eyes deep-sunk in his head. Under his tilted baretta, lank wisps of hair clung to his bony skull. Despite the time of year he wore a long velvet coat with a sable collar.

"Living so close to the river I feel it on my bones," he answered Sandro's look.

Even his voice, thought the imaginative Ugo sounded as if it issued from the depths of a sepulchre. He wondered what ate at this Don Antonio, if it was a malignant illness or a deep-rooted rancour. Or both.

Don Antonio studied the Authority his Groom of the Chamber had brought him and then studied his visitor. "I don't understand why His Eminence sends you to *me*? Am I to blame because the rivertide carried the duke's body to my doorstep."

"It's the tide of events I've come to question, Don Antonio," replied Sandro. "Or perhaps you're expecting guests or dining out this evening?"

"I no longer entertain nor seldom go out."

"Were you acquainted with the Duke of Gandia? Was he ever a guest in your house?"

"What enjoyment would a profligate such as Don Juan find in the company of a dried-up old intellectual?" Mirandola permitted himself a smile, showing yellowed fragments of teeth.

"You may have possessed something that appealed to him. I understand you have a daughter, Don Antonio, whose beauty wins the admiration of all who behold her."

The sunken eyes looked suddenly as malignant as the disease that consumed him. "My daughter is an unmarried girl and therefore remains cloistered from the sight of men until her wedding day to a suitor I shall choose."

"Servants gossip. Curiosity is fired. Especially the curiosity of a libertine. I must request an interview with your daughter."

"And I must refuse it."

"Then you leave me no alternative, Don Antonio, but to enforce my Authority. I mean the girl no harm. Her duenna may remain with her at all times."

The corpse suddenly came alive with basilisk's venom. "Bastard son of an infidel Turk! You're nought but the vassal of the bastard son of a Catalan Pope who barely speaks Italian. All Rome knows you're the spawn of the hostage Ahmed, uncle of Bajazet."

"How enterprising of all Rome to be present at my conception," murmured Sandro. "I would say any man's guess is as good as mine. *Now will you send for your daughter?*"

His lids had dropped over his almond-shaped eyes and his mouth was a straight steely line. It was a look Ugo knew and feared. Don Antonio was suddenly seized with a fit of coughing which seemed to drain him of resistance if not malevolence.

The girl was summoned. Despite the fact that she looked close to death with fear of her father and her eyes were swollen with crying, she was remarkably beautiful with black, lustrous hair and the white skin sought after by so many Italian women. As in many European dynasties she had been given her father's name.

"Donna Antonia, will you sit here?" Sandro led her to a second pew across the room. Mirandola seemed determined to stay, but the spy strode back to him, reclaimed the Borgia Authority and waved him from the room. The duenna, a somewhat vapid woman, plain and plump, he placed at the door, out of earshot of their conversation. He returned to the girl and sat beside her.

"You are distressed. And afraid. Is it because of the death of the Duke of Gandia?" She stole a pleading glance at him and remained mute. "Did you know him? Had he ever come to visit you here in your father's palazzo? Did you see him on the night he died?"

She shook her head and glanced nervously at the duenna. Sandro followed her gaze. The duenna too looked agitated, constantly entangling her hands in a fold of her dress, as she watched the proceedings.

"But he was your lover, was he not?"

"No!" Antonia tried to flee, but Sandro caught her hand. The duenna made no move to prevent him. She seemed mesmerized in awe of the Borgia agent.

"Antonia, I don't wish you hurt or disgrace, I only want to get at the truth. Were you in love with Juan of Aragon?"

She nodded miserably. "I used to watch him from my balcony as he rode by. He was the most handsome of all the princes. I wove fantasies of him in my mind like the legends in the tapestries I stitched. Then one day he looked up and saw me. My father was very angry; I was never allowed to go out on the balcony again. But Juan sent his servant to negotiate with Bianca, my nurse. We exchanged letters, his were full of poetry," her eyes glowed softly; Sandro could imagine how the lonely, isolated girl virtually imprisoned by her father's stern authority had conceived from this blatant seduction a chivalrous romance. "He begged me for an assignation. At first I was afraid, but then I longed for him as he wrote he longed for me . . ."

"And of course all palazzi, especially those close to the river, have secret doors and secret stairs. Don Juan was smuggled to your bedchamber."

Sandro could imagine the connivance of the duenna, living vicariously through her young mistress the breathless excitement of a clandestine tryst she could never hope to experience herself.

Antonia blushed and avoided his glance. "It was more than I intended, but he was so ardent, so masterful . . ."

"How did your father find out?"

"We were betrayed by one of the servants. He called me a whore of

Babylon." She looked at him then. "My lord, I am not a whore. Tomorrow he sends me to a nunnery where I'm to spend my life."

"Did your father swear vengeance against Don Juan?"

"At first he ranted and raged, then he fell silent. His silence frightened me more than his rage."

"Did you ever see a masked man in your father's presence?"

She gave him a strange look as if her thoughts had suddenly turned inward. "Only last evening. They were in the courtyard. My room leads out to a terrace with a balustrade overlooking the courtyard. I saw them in conversation."

"Who?"

"My father and the masked man. And a woman dressed as a man. I found that very curious. What would a woman be doing dressed as a man and in my father's home. Tho' I've heard some prostitutes dress as boys during Carnival."

"How did you know it was a woman?"

"By her slight build and long curling hair."

"My thanks, Donna Antonia," he carried her hand to his lips, "and my best wishes for your future."

"My future!" she showed the first flash of spirit. "What future have I in a nunnery?" She looked at him, consideringly. "Do you think my father murdered Juan? I hope he did. I hope they take him and cut off his head!"

Sandro and Ugo retraced their steps to the Piazza degli Ebrei in silence. The spy sat slumped in the saddle of his Spanish mare. Ugo caught a glimpse of his face once in the torchlight. It was a look that frightened him, the look of a man who hated the world and all who lived in it.

The house of the merchant Alfonso Caraffi was more comfortable and extravagantly appointed than the palazzo of the noble lord Mirandola with its tapestried wall hangings, Turkish rugs, Murano glass and family portraits. But the merchant appeared to find no enjoyment in his luxury that night. His large, noisy family were gathered together in the dining hall. Sandro despatched Ugo to the kitchens as promised and allowed Signore Caraffi to usher him into a sala for privacy.

Caraffi had the mien of a man whose worst fears had been realized. "I was dreading your visit, Don Alessandro," he confessed, candidly, while he served the malvasy wine. "I'm sure you have no cause to question me further. I told Cardinal Valencia, and in your presence, all I know."

"Not quite all you know, I think," replied Sandro, as he leaned back in a black velvet chair and sipped appreciatively from his goblet.

Caraffi gave a start of alarm. "Am I to blame that Manuel Diaz chose my door to beat upon in his extremity?"

"No one seems to be to blame for anything," murmured Sandro, "yet someone's to blame for the footman's murder." He watched the merchant over the rim of his cup. "So he had time to tell you his own name. I thought he only told you his master's name."

"Oh, well, I had forgotten that, the house was in such turmoil. And to have the man die on our divan of Genoan velvet . . ."

"Did he bleed much?"

"There was only one knife wound, but his head had been split by a cudgel. We did give him succour, I swear. But he died before we could send for a physician."

"What other name did he utter? What put the fear of God into you?"

Caraffi hesitated. "It was a Spanish name. I didn't catch all of it. It could have been Valdez. He said . . ."

"Yes?" Sandro watched him keenly.

"*I recognized him even under the mask.*"

"What made you too afraid to tell Cardinal Valencia that? Because of something more Diaz said. What was it?"

Garaffi turned the colour of candle-tallow. "Don Alessandro, you'll be the death of me."

"*What was it?*"

"*Brother against brother.*" He looked as forlorn as if he had written his own death warrant.

"Diaz and Valdez are *both* Spanish names. It's possible he meant it was a betrayal to be slain by a fellow Spaniard."

The merchant's expression brightened considerably. "Is that your interpretation? Oh, thank you, Don Alessandro!"

Sandro put down his goblet and rose. "I enjoyed your hospitality, signore. I don't think I need trouble you again."

While he waited for Cardinal Valencia to join him in the Appartamento Borgia in the Vatican, Sandro wandered about the room studying the frescoes by Pinturicchio, depicting among others the Family Borgia. Pope Alexander, stout, bald and large-nosed, clasping his hands in prayer. Lucrezia with a jeweled cross on her forehead, a sweet-faced girl displaying her famous golden hair. Juan, Duke of Gandia, mounted on a white horse, his face in profile almost hidden by his huge turban. Cesare, bearded then, crowned, sceptred and enthroned, wearing doublet and shirt of figured gold. And the bridal pair. Sancia of Aragon, illegitimate daughter of the King of Naples, and Joffre, Prince of Squillace, the Pope's youngest son. It was difficult to tell at first glance which was the girl and which the youth; both had delicate features and long curling hair.

Sandro was interrupted from his scrutiny by the arrival of Cesare Borgia. Although the hour was late, the Pope's second son was keen and alert. He preferred night to day, conducting most of his business affairs by candlelight and sleeping at noon.

He had laid aside his Cardinal's robe and wore doublet and shirt of black silk.

"Do I see you so soon? You have been assiduous in my service."

"I have traced the Duke of Gandia's murderer to the palazzo of Don Antonio Pica della Mirandola. Mirandola has a pretty daughter your brother Juan had seduced. Both the wood dealer Giorgio Schavini and Mirandola's daughter reported seeing a woman dressed as a man, Schavini at the site where the body was dumped, Donna Antonia earlier that evening in her father's courtyard. The masked man was also seen at Mirandola's palazzo. He was not present at the riverside, but he was in the Piazza degli Ebrei where he slew the footman Diaz. Diaz recognized him despite the mask, a fellow-Spaniard Valdez."

Cesare stood beyond the circle of light from the corona overhead. His face was unreadable in the shadows.

"Who else would resemble a woman but a pretty youth?" Sandro sauntered back to the mural. "Like your brother Joffre. I believe that Joffre conspired with Don Antonio with Valdez as the go-between to lure Juan to a second tryst with Antonia. This second assignation needed more stealth, more subtlety because this time Juan was taking Joffre along to participate as a spur to his manhood. I only hope Antonia was never aware of her lover's perfidy.

"But Joffre had another plan. He and Mirandola's servants set upon Juan and stabbed him to death, then cast his body in the river.

Valdez was sent to murder the footman Diaz in fear that Valdez might have recognized his fellow countryman on the ride back from Vincola. Do you know a man by the name of Valdez? I see you do. Is he in the service of the Prince of Squillace?"

Cesare strode to the door and flung it open. "Have my brother Joffre brought to our presence."

"Do you need a motive?" asked Sandro, when he returned. "Juan and Sancia had cuckolded him and openly flaunted their affair, a slap in the face to any immature youth with a high-spirited, loose-moraled wife. I fancy Juan even promised Sancia to *make a man* of her little husband."

"*Joffre!*"

"That puling puppy? Cubs grow up to be wolves, Your Eminence. If it's any comfort to you I'm sure he's remorse-ridden. I don't think he even meant to kill Juan, but to castrate him. It was Don Antonio who had another fate in mind."

"I'll drag that high and mighty lord out of his castello and burn him alive in St Peter's Square." Cesare's face was working with rage; he ground his teeth as he spoke making his words almost unintelligible. In his extremity, he picked up a poker from the hearth and bent it double with his bare hands. Sandro became aware for the first time of the physical power this young Borgia possessed.

"Heed my advice, my lord. Mirandola is a man being devoured by day and night by a slow death. If you want to hurt him more than death, have His Holiness personally grant Donna Antonia a dowry and choose for her a personable husband."

"Valdez must die. He'll suffer many mutilations before they fish him out of the Tiber. As for Joffre." Cesare flung himself into a tapestried chair and gazed moodily into the fire. "Blood of my blood. Brother to me as Juan was brother. His Holiness mourns one son who meant more to him than life. Would you have me deprive him of another on some misjudged supposition? No, you are mistaken, Don Alessandro. You've come to a false conclusion. I don't believe Joffre took any part in the murder. A sixteen-year-old boy! 'Twas the henchman Valdez who conspired with Mirandola."

The door opened to admit the Prince of Squillace. If Cesare needed proof of guilt he needed only to read the boy's features. Joffre was abject with terror, glancing from Cesare to Sandro and back to his brother.

"It seems Don Alessandro has again traced a murderer to the household of a Borgia." Cesare spoke softly, but his tone made Sandro's skin crawl. "Your man Valdez. I'm afraid you'll have to sacrifice him. Have you any objections?"

Joffre shook from head to foot. "N-n-no," he stammered.

Cesare held out his hand dismissively. As Joffre knelt forward to kiss his ring, his brother suddenly seized him by the throat and spat a torrent of Spanish at him. Sandro understood not a word that he said, but he suspected from the expression that washed over Joffre's face that his soul was being been flayed alive. When he had finished he kissed the boy fiercely on the mouth and threw him aside. Joffre took to his heels and fled.

"I can see I was misguided in my conclusions," Sandro conceded, suavely. "But I would not allow it to be published abroad that Valdez is guilty. It might be traced back, mistakenly, to Joffre. And I would call off any investigation instigated by His Holiness even if it should give rise to suspicion."

Cesare studied him with a deep bitterness. "You're a cunning fox, *Il Saracen*. A prince of foxes. And now you know too much about the House of Borgia. Mayhap you'll wake tomorrow to find your tongue nailed to a prison door."

"Then Your Eminence would lose a good lieutenant," replied Sandro, lightly. "One who has a still tongue and a short memory."

Cesare laughed softly, crossed to a credence and poured wine from a silver ewer into two goblets. "Are you brave enough to share a cup with me?"

Sandro tossed off the wine without hesitation.

Cesare returned to the fire, picked up the poker and straightened it. His face was moody in the glow of the fire. "I must forsake the service of Christ for the field of war, a course better suited to my temperament then it ever was to Juan's. Whatever I achieve it will be because Juan was murdered. The pity of it is, history will say I did it, and of this, if nothing else, I shall be innocent."

Henry VIII and Anne Boleyn 🍇

THE CURSE OF THE UNBORN DEAD

Derek Wilson

Although Henry VIII is regarded as one of Britain's most successful monarchs, and certainly one of its most powerful, as a man I find him obnoxious, spoiled, vindictive and callous, and certainly a far nastier monarch than either John or Richard III. His treatment of his wives Katherine of Aragon and Anne Boleyn, and to some extent of Katherine Howard, was contemptible. Derek Wilson became intrigued with why the king suddenly and unexpectedly discarded the woman he had been passionately in love with, the woman for whose sake he had risked the enmity of Spain and his Catholic subjects and had severed the English church from Rome. As Derek Wilson comments, this story is more a whydunnit than a whodunnit!

I heard of it first from that malicious, midden-mouthed, lecher and gossiphound, that self-important, salacious slobber-tongue, Daniel Ludge. He could not wait for me to set foot in his decrepit Stag's Head Inn but must trundle out into the yard rubbing his greasy hands on his apron and holding the mare's head as I dismounted. That uncharacteristic courtesy alone should have prepared me for some new unpleasantness but I was still fog-headed from the May Day revels, and paid even less attention than usual to his words.

"Morning, Master Ned" – curse the villain for his familiarity. "I was so sorry to hear about your father."

I ignored the fellow. It took all my thought and energy to stop my legs buckling like rushes as I leaped to the cobbles. Sauntering into the inn, I left Ludge bellowing for his boy to come and look after the horse. The room, which reeked of spilled ale and smoke from last night's fire that still smouldered in the wide hearth, was as yet deserted. There was no sign of Matt, Hugh and Roly – still, no doubt, sleeping off the party or entangled in the arms of their night companions. So there was no escaping Daniel Ludge, who waddled in after me as I slumped onto a bench.

"Yes, Master Ned, real shocked I were and Master Henry so high in His Majesty's favour – *as was thought*."

I leaned forward across the table and slumped my head on my arms. It made no difference to my loquacious host.

"There's many folk around here not sorry to see the back of the French whore but 'tis a shame she should take Henry Norris with her."

The words entered my head slowly, like a blunt knife cutting through plum pudding. I resisted them because I loathed the innkeeper's gossiping and the relish with which he always imparted ill news. Yet dully I realized that here was something I could not ignore. Without troubling myself to look at the man, I mumbled, "What nonsense are you on about today, fellow?"

"Why, only what Master Secretary's messenger told me when he changed post horses here, first thing; that the Lady Anne is to the Tower and her lovers with her – including Master Henry, your father."

I lifted my head long enough to glare at the man. "What idiocy is this? Get about your business and stop hawking stupid tales of your betters."

"Why, Master Ned, I was sure you would know of this already." Ludge's face showed shock and concern but his voice smiled. "Of course I'd not have believed it myself had it not come from Cromwell's own man and he in so desperate a hurry to reach Oxford. I declare his horse was ready to drop; lathered all over he was. You can see him for yourself in the stable."

"All right, all right!" I pushed myself up to my feet again. Whatever garbled piece of court gossip Ludge had picked up I would have to listen to it; sift out any grains of truth, if my fuddled brains would answer to it. John and Henry Norris were among the king's closest companions; our family fortunes depended on that friendship. It was ridiculous to imagine my father falling out of favour so suddenly. "Now then, you worthless blabbermouth, what is this tale . . ."

"Bread and cheese, *now*! And some for my friend!"

I turned my head to see Hugh Godwin's tall frame crouching in at the door. He was fresh-faced and well groomed as ever and showed no signs of the previous night's excesses. As Ludge turned away with an obsequious bow Hugh gave me a half smile.

"You look terrible. Come on, let's see what cold water will do." He took my arm and half dragged me out to the stable yard trough beside the well. Hugh, nineteen and still at Oxford, had regarded himself as my older brother since as long as I could remember, and especially since my mother had died three years earlier. My father liked him to keep an eye on me so that I did not drink away the income from the farms and tenements. Now Hugh stood over me while I ducked my head in the trough.

"Better?" he asked as I wiped my face on my sleeve.

"A little."

"Good, you will need all your wits about you today. I imagine our fat host has been telling you the news from court."

"He said something about my father and the Tower but none of it made sense."

"Whether it makes sense or not 'tis true. After the tournament at Greenwich, yesterday, Henry Norris was taken up river to the Tower. Had you slept in your own bed last night you would have heard it from the king's own men sent to seize Ockwells."

"But what ridiculous . . . There must be a mistake . . . how do you know? . . . Surely someone is playing an ugly joke . . ." My confused brain tumbled out foolish responses.

Hugh took my arm and led me back to the inn. "Food first to soak up what remains of last night's ale and while we eat I'll tell you what I know."

Thus the direful details of my father's disgrace were opened to me by a friend as we broke our fast on Ludge's meagre fare. Everyone had heard the rumours that our king had tired of his second wife and was seeking diversions elsewhere and few were sorry of it. Many were loyal to the memory of Queen Catherine and to the Princess Mary. My uncle John, for all he was a member of the king's outer chamber, secretly favoured the old queen but that may have been because my father always supported Anne Boleyn. Henry Norris had been one of Henry Tudor's firmest friends for over twenty years and was close to Queen Anne, also. All this I knew. What Hugh now told me was that the king had struck suddenly, unexpectedly – or rather that Secretary Cromwell had. Some of the queen's household had been arrested and put to torture. On the rack a man will say anything, betray anyone. So it was that names had been named – men supposed to have committed adultery with the queen. One of those names was "Henry Norris".

"But the king would never believe that!" I protested to Hugh. "He knows how much my father loves him."

Hugh frowned. "Whether he believes it or not no man can say. What is certain is that Henry Norris ran several courses in the May Day tournament, cheered on by the king and that afterwards the king took him on one side and spoke softly to him. Your father was heard to exclaim aloud several times, 'No Sire!', 'Not so, Sire!' Those that were there saw him fall on his knees but His Majesty walked away and ordered Sir William Fitzwilliam to convey him to the Tower. Ned, it grieves me sore to bring these tidings but better you hear them from a friend than twisted by malice from the lips of a man like Ludge."

"But why, Hugh, why? There is no sense in it. The king will not have my father put to the rack. He cannot." I looked to my friend for reassurance.

Hugh too hurriedly agreed. "I doubt not but the king intends only to frighten those who have been too close to the queen. Your father will be free again in a few days."

My head was clearing slowly but as it did so all I could see were questions. "But you say he has sent men to take our home. He did the same to Wolsey when he was disgraced. The Cardinal failed him over the annulment. How has my father earned his disfavour? The king cannot believe that Henry Norris, his longtime friend, would cuckold him. He just cannot . . . it is too absurd. This must be Cromwell making trouble."

At this point my miserable ramblings were interrupted by the arrival of Matt Willoughby and Roly Vane. It was immediately plain from their faces that they had heard the news.

"Ned, this is terrible." Roly straddled the bench beside me with an arm round my shoulder.

Matt stood looking down and tweaking his wisp of beard. "What are we going to do? We must make a plan." Matt was ever the practical member of our troupe. "We go to Greenwich, of course. Find out exactly what is happening. Do whatever is necessary to help your father."

As I recall, I said not a word; the others did the talking. Within minutes all was decided. Within an hour we were on the road. We reached London by nightfall and stayed at Hugh's father's house. He is a sergeant-at-law and has a fine dwelling close by the Temple. I think a man never had better friends; there's few would stand by a family with the Tower curse upon it but my companions never so much as mentioned the disgrace that had suddenly, inexplicably befallen the Norrises. As we rode they did their best to distract me with talk of different things. For my part I kept thinking of other times, better days. I remembered the king visiting us at Ockwells when I was ten and taking me on his knee and telling me I must be his page at dinner and how nervous I was serving him at table and how he and my father laughed and joked all the way through the meal and how the king gave me a noble before leaving. And now my father was accused of adultery with his queen! By all the saints, no man would be so stupid – certainly not my father. And would the queen? It took much believing. What we learned from friends in the City was yet more incredible. The place was alive with gossip: the Lady Anne (as many folk still insisted on calling her) had a cluster of lovers at court and she and they were now all in the Tower.

That night in our shared chamber the four of us tried to make sense of all the tales we had heard.

Roly lay fully clothed on a truckle bed by the door and stared at the moulded ceiling. "They say Harry has been wanting to be rid of his second queen for months, but this time there is no question of an annulment so some other way must be found."

"For what purpose? So that he can bed Mistress Seymour? I'm told she's no great beauty and not half as intelligent as Queen Anne." Matt crouched by the fire, prodding the logs with a poker.

I paused in unlacing my doublet. "But there is no need to kill a queen to bed a maid. Harry can have the Seymour woman for a mistress. She would not be the first."

"Aye but any son she bore would not be legitimate and His Majesty is impatient for an heir," Matt said.

Hugh was already between the sheets on one side of the wide bed. "There's no sense to that argument. Anne is young enough to bear many sons. Just because her only child after three years of marriage is Princess Elizabeth is no reason to be rid of her."

Roly yawned. "My uncle's wife bore him seven daughters before she had a son. Marrying them all off near ruined him."

Matt stood up and stretched. "Harry need have no fear of that, not with all the land he's taking from the monasteries."

"Haply he'll make better use of it than all our fat, lazy monks," Hugh scoffed. Since starting at Oxford he had taken up many fashionable ideas about religion.

I rubbed my aching temple. "They say the queen has thrice miscarried."

"What of that?" Hugh asked, turned towards me.

"I know not. I know nothing. Nothing! By the mass, where is the sense in all this?"

My friends gathered round and Matt dropped onto the bed beside me. "Ned, take heart, we'll save your father – even if we have to rescue him from the Tower ourselves."

The next morning we took boat downriver. I wanted to go straight to the Tower but the others persuaded me that it would be better for me to seek out my uncle at Greenwich while Hugh and Roly found out all they could at the royal fortress.

I expected little of my uncle and was not disappointed. I sent a message to him in the palace which was carried by one of the court flunkies and waited for a reply in a waterman's inn by the river stairs. I waited all that day and half the next before I was summoned to a small antechamber near the royal chapel. I knew the courtyards and inter connecting rooms well enough – having often visited my father there – in earlier years – to realize that the meeting place had been chosen to ensure maximum privacy. After another hour of frustrating inactivity my uncle entered the room in a swift movement, closing the door rapidly behind him. He stood looking at me for several seconds and I returned his gaze. John Norris's thin frame was garbed in a black unadorned doublet of severe cut.

"What good do you think to do by coming here?" he demanded.

"Where else should I be with my father in trouble."

"*In* trouble!" He sneered. "Why your father *is* trouble. Now you see what comes of encouraging the king to cast us adrift from the Church for the sake of a Frenchified whore. I warned him. I told him God would never forgive those who urged His Majesty to abandon his lawful wife and defy the holy father but . . ."

"Uncle, please!" I contained my anger as well as I could. "Spare me the sermon. My father, your brother, is accused of the most horrible crime. We both know he is not guilty and we have to save him."

"Save him?" John Norris uttered the words through clenched teeth. "Your father's folly and heresy may destroy us all. I was close questioned for four hours by Master Secretary's henchmen and had a hard task of it to extricate myself. I may yet be banished from the court, if not worse. And you talk of saving *him*!"

"So you disown him?" I shouted. "It was not so when he was the king's friend and spoke for you. You owe him everything – your position at court, your lands, your . . ."

At that moment there was a knock at the door. A liveried page entered and whispered something to my uncle who immediately made to leave the room. At the door he turned and I detected the fear and anger in his trembling voice. "I am called for by His Majesty. You will wait here till I can see you safe out of the palace."

Waiting was furthest from my mind, though what to do instead I could not conceive. Go to the king and plead for mercy? I would never get near him. Find some powerful friend of Henry Norris to whom his majesty would listen? They would all be, like my uncle, putting as much distance as possible between themselves and my father. Perhaps my companions would have better news or ideas. I had left Matt at the inn and we hourly expected the arrival of the others. I stepped out into the courtyard, my mind still in turmoil.

The cobbled square was filling with people and I had to elbow my way through the throng. Finding myself pressed against a fellow of my own age, I asked what was afoot.

"Master Secretary is coming to the privy stairs to board his barge."

It was all the explanation necessary. Wherever Cromwell, the second most powerful man in England, went men and women gathered – to press petitions, to offer gifts, or just to be seen and recognized. Perhaps if I could force my way to the front of the crowd I could gain a word, an audience. Then, on the instant, I thought of a better idea. I squirmed along the wall to the passageway which led to the privy stairs. It was, of course, guarded by a halberdier but he was busy keeping a pathway open through the surge of people and I was able to slip past and run lightly to the steps leading down to the staithing. At the top flight I paused. The barge was all in readiness drawn up to the wharf, the rowers with oars aloft and the bargeman talking with two royal guards. At any moment they must look in my direction. I cast around for a place of concealment, saw a door and slipped through into a dark storeroom filled with casks and boxes.

For several minutes I waited in my place of concealment. Then I heard approaching feet. Peering through the gap in the ajar door, I watched two yeomen of the guard march down the steps followed by a man in a fur-collared gown and black velvet cap. I had never seen Cromwell but knew that this must be he. Yet, how could I get to him? There were now four soldiers surrounding him. They descended to the staithe where Master Secretary was greeted by the bargeman and stepped aboard. For some moments they stood upon the deck talking. Then Cromwell turned to take his place under the stern canopy. The bargeman cast off and the boat began to ease out into the river. My chance was lost.

Or perhaps not. I saw the four soldiers, their task done, form up and march back up the stairs. The moment they had passed my hiding place I ran out. I leaped the steps in two bounds. The barge was an oar's length as I reached the edge of the wharf. I put every ounce of strength into a flying leap. I landed with my arms over the gunwale and my legs in the water.

There were shouts of alarm from behind and before. I stared up into the open-mouthed face of the bargeman. Then he leaned forward and grabbed at my jerkin to prise me away from the vessel and force me into the river. I struggled against him to lever my body aboard. We tussled for several moments, then I heard a shouted command and found my adversary no longer pushing but pulling. I tumbled onto the deck and was roughly hauled to my feet. While the man berated me, his assistant seized the dagger hanging from my belt.

"Bring the fellow here!" The order came in a gruff, authoritative voice and I was pushed towards the stern where Cromwell sat in a cushioned, armed chair. Intelligent eyes set in a fleshy face scrutinised me closely.

I immediately knelt. "Your servant, Sire."

Cromwell laughed. "And what service is this that you offer me?"

"The loyalty of one who is his father's son. My name is Edward Norris."

"So!" There was surprise and a trace of alarm in the monosyllable.

"Shall we throw him overboard, Your Honour?" the bargeman asked, clapping a hand on my shoulder.

"Sire," I begged, "let them cast me in the Thames or hand me to the guard, whatever you wish, but suffer me first to speak a few words with Your Honour."

Cromwell waved a hand at the bargeman. "Set your men to rowing. I wish to catch the best of the tide. I will look after Master Norris here."

I gazed up at the man half the realm hated and the other half loved for freeing England from the shackles of Rome. "Thank you, Sire."

"Stand up, Master Norris, and let us hear your 'few words', though I must tell you that if you come to plead for your father you will need to be a better orator than you are an athlete."

"My Lord, you cannot think . . . it is not possible . . . My father would never . . ." I felt panic rise within me like a schoolboy who looks at the master's cane and knows he has not learned his lesson.

"What, tongue-tied already? Then let me see if I can translate your mutterings. You want to assure me that your father is innocent of the crime of adultery with the queen of England." Cromwell spoke with a lawyer's terse economy.

"He has served the king – and the queen – faithfully for years. No one who knows him could believe him guilty of such a foul sin."

"His grace the king believes it."

"Perhaps his grace believes what others persuade him to believe."

"By others, I suspect you mean me."

"No man is better placed than your honour to convince the king that he is misinformed about Henry Norris."

"I fear you overestimate my power. I am like a boat without sail or oars floating on the tide of His Majesty's will and favour. To strive against the tide is hard, bootless and perilous."

"But why does the king want his queen dead, and my father and other loyal men who have served him well?"

"Even if I knew the answer to that I could not tell you. His grace has reason enough, you may be sure, else must we think him bewitched, who would give such orders – and that were treason, indeed."

"Then, all you can tell me is that the king is determined my father shall die and because even the greatest in the land refuse to come to his aid, which out of Christian love and all honesty they should do, he cannot be saved."

Cromwell stared past me and the faintest of smiles touched his lips. I turned and saw the bargeman edging towards us, head bent to catch our words. The king's secretary motioned me to stand closer and leaned forward. "One thing is sure about the tide: it will turn. Those who know whither they would go are more likely to succeed by waiting for the ebb."

I clutched at this wisp of hope. "So my father will be restored in His Majesty's good time. May I see him and tell him that?"

Cromwell shook his head. "He is kept a close prisoner on the king's orders. That means no visitors."

I went down on my knees again. "Master Secretary, I beseech you, let me have this one small favour. Just a brief meeting; it is all I ask."

He frowned and bade me with some impatience to stand again. "What you ask is no small thing." He fell silent for some moments, then said, "If I grant your request you must do something for me – though in truth it is more for your father."

"Name it, Your Honour."

"Tell your father his only hope to save himself is to confess that which he is accused of and ask the king's mercy."

I sighed. "I think he is too proud to swear to an untruth to save his head."

"Tell him he is foolish to swim against the tide."

I agreed and Cromwell promised that when we reached the Tower he would give instructions for me to be permitted access to my father. As we approached the busy wharf crowded with sea-going ships I could see warders running from the fortress onto the landing stage. The unexpected approach of an important visitor had been noted. As the barge nudged the stonework and I was set ashore while the captain of the guard approached and saluted Cromwell who called him aboard to receive his orders.

As the oarsmen once more bent to their task and Master Secretary continued upstream the captain ordered me to follow him. My feelings were mixed as we passed through the Watergate or St Thomas's Tower into the outer ward. I had never been inside that forbidding place of which so many gruesome tales are told and could scarcely avoid a shiver of apprehension. But I was about to see my father and that pushed other thoughts from my mind. I wondered in what condition I would find him and what I would find to say to him. The captain led me along the outer ward to a tower with a raised portcullis. When we had passed this I was alarmed to find that we were on the bridge crossing the moat. I turned to ask where I was being taken only to find my arm gripped tight by the guard. He half-pushed, half-dragged me through the middle tower, across the barbican and so to the outer gate through which I was thrust.

The captain laughed as I turned to glare at him. "Message from Master Secretary," he announced. "He says 'Go with the tide. If you interfere further in things you do not understand he will not be so lenient next time'."

"What monstrous, Machiavellian, deceit! 'Tis clearly true what everyone says of Cromwell!"

It was the following day (5 May) when I met up with my three friends again at the sign of King David cook house, hard by Queenhythe. They were appalled by my account of Master Secretary's double-dealing and Roly's outburst spoke for them all.

Hugh, as usual, was calmer in his appraisal of the situation. "When the king's closest adviser is driven to such demeaning duplicity he must have something to hide. This whole affair has a worse stink of fish than Billingsgate."

"According to Cromwell," I said, "it is all the king's doing."

"Well, we know how much we can trust Cromwell," Roly sputtered through a mouthful of coney pie.

Mat swallowed a draft of strong shipman's ale and belched. "No he spoke true on this. I talked with several court people down at Greenwich. The common bruit is of an estrangement between the king and queen which began suddenly in January at the time of the queen's last miscarriage. They say our Harry was in such a frenzy of rage and worry that no man durst go near him. They say he was at Mass every day which is a rare thing indeed."

Hugh nodded sagely. "Aye and there's a strange story around the inns of court where I have been discussing the case with some of the law students. Apparently Archbishop Cranmer is to pronounce the king's marriage to Anne Boleyn null and void."

"What is of interest in that?" Matt scoffed. " 'Tis becoming a habit with this king."

"The interest is this," Hugh explained patiently. "The queen and her alleged lovers are to be tried for treason, since treason it is to commit adultery with the king's wife. Now, if the royal marriage is voided then Anne Boleyn never was the king's wife. *Ergo* there can be no treason."

"But that is wonderful, Hugh!" I saw, at last, a chink of light. "It means the queen and her accused lovers will be found 'not guilty'!"

Hugh shook his head. "No, Ned, do not raise your hopes. I fear you will not find a legal mind in London which believes any court will bring in a verdict against the will of the king. All that this muddled proceeding reveals is that his majesty is determined her majesty shall die. All we can hope is that mercy will be shown to her supposed lovers."

"But why, Hugh? Why?" I pushed my wooden platter away, the pie smashed into a dozen untasted pieces. "If we knew that perhaps we could find some way to use the information."

"That could be dangerous," Matt said, then, looking around at his friends, quickly added, "Not that I care for danger."

Now Roly added the results of his research. "I have been talking with two of the queen's ladies who are allowed to attend her and are often to and fro the Tower on errands. They are very distressed, as you can imagine and they have been warned to speak to no one about Her Majesty's business."

Matt laughed. "But you have ways to loosen a maid's tongue as well as her gown, eh?"

"Aye, as you well know. Not that Margaret Candish is an easy mark. I had to work hard to gain her confidence. We shopped together in Cheapside, where she went to buy trifles for the queen. But she was much in need of a sympathetic ear and . . ."

Hugh interrupted. "Spare us the details of your power over women, Roly. What did you find out?"

"That is what I was about to tell you. Have you finished with this?" Roly pulled my discarded trencher towards him and attacked the pie with his dagger. "Margaret says that it did all begin with the miscarriage. When the king heard that Anne had been prematurely delivered of a dead boy child he went into a frenzy and would not see his wife for days."

"Then it is, as some men say, all to do with our Harry's need for an heir," I suggested.

"Margaret does not believe so, nor do any of the queen's household."

"What then?"

"There are strangenesses about this mis-birth. For one the physician and the two women who attended Her Majesty were straightly sent away, some say with much gold to buy their silence."

"Nothing odd in that," Hugh observed. "Catherine of Aragon's miscarriages were covered up, and this queen's earlier miscarriages, too. Of course, the truth came out but it was despite attempts at concealment."

"And that is the other strange thing," Roly said with a look of triumph. "This sad event was *not* hushed up. All the queen's household were brought together and given exact details. That is how everyone knew that Queen Anne was delivered prematurely of a perfectly formed man child."

"Now that *is* odd," Hugh mused. "If the king intended the full facts to be known why did he send away the only people who could have supported those facts?"

Matt thumped his beaker down on the table. "Because they were *not* facts!" he shouted. "That must surely be it. Everyone who knows the truth about the queen's miscarriage must be silenced. Servants can be bought off but not the queen herself. Some other means must be found to stop her mouth."

Roly shrugged. "But what truth can possibly be so terrible?"

We all fell silent and watched Roly finish his second dinner. A half-memory was fluttering in the thickets of my mind but I could not identify it. It was something that Cromwell had said. After a few minutes I gave up. If it was important it would come back to me. "We need to find the physician and his assistants. Roly, is there any chance . . ."

"The doctor is French and has gone back to Paris. As for the women, I think Margaret knows where they are to be found but she is too afraid to speak."

"Then you must work your charm on her." Hugh said. "I'll wager you already have another assignation planned."

Roly grinned and nodded as he wiped the platter with a wedge of bread.

Everything now depended on Roly's persuasive powers. There was little we could do but wait. The rest of us tried to find ways to get me into the Tower but it was an almost impossible task and my anxiety mounted as the day of my father's trial drew nearer. I wrote messages to him and Hugh delivered them at the Tower gate but no replies came and I had no means of knowing whether my father received my letters.

It was nearly a week later that Roly returned excitedly to our lodgings late one night. He threw himself onto the great bed and looked at us with a grin of triumph on his face. "Trussington," he announced.

We stared down at him with vacant faces.

"Trussington," Roly repeated. " 'Tis in Warwickshire – a poor place by all accounts but that is where you'll find Meg Archer who was one of those attending the queen in January."

"Well done, Roly," Hugh said and Matt and I added our congratulations.

We discussed what to do and agreed that Hugh and Matt should set out for the country next morning while Roly and I stayed in London to keep up with news from the Tower and the court. My father's trial had been fixed for the following day and I had to be in Westminster Hall for it.

It was, of course, a comedy of a tragedy. The queen had already been tried in the secrecy of the Tower and found guilty. How then could her supposed paramours claim their innocence? They did, most ardently, my father especially. It was harrowing to see him, manacled, haggard and unkempt, pleading for his life. Yet he did so with dignity. I longed to break through the crowds and the cordon of soldiers and stand alongside him. But to have myself arrested could not help him. His only hope, slender as it was, lay in my discovering something that I could use as a medium of barter with Master Cromwell.

I had to bite hard on my tongue as those around me in the packed hall cheered and jeered when the verdict was announced. "Death to the French witch and all her familiars!" a crone in front of me shouted and several others caught up the refrain. "French witch!" "French witch! French witch."

Roly tugged at my arm and together we shouldered our way through the screaming crowd.

I slept little that night or the next, but turned feverishly back and forth in the bed, the taunt "French witch" shrieking in my brain whether I was awake or not. Each morning I made my way to Whitehall to which the court had now moved. It was my intention to ask Cromwell again for permission to see my father. Surely, now that he was condemned, there could be no reason for Master Secretary to deny me. Each day I waited in an anteroom with scores of other suitors and then returned to Master Godwin's house for another troubled night. Try as I might I could not banish the word "witch" from my mind. It was towards dawn on the third morning that I remembered other words, words spoken by Cromwell, words that I had registered as strange when he spoke them but had later forgotten: "else must we think him bewitched, and that were treason".

I leaped out of bed, woke Roly, rushed in to my clothes and bade him do the same. In the courtyard I had our horses saddled and bridled before my friend emerged, demanding whether I had taken leave of my senses.

I had not, although, the strange euphoria I felt was a kind of madness. As we rode westwards through the waking villages of Acton and Ealing and so to the Oxford road I explained my idea to Roly. Or rather, I tried to explain it to myself; tried to turn a conviction – a revelation almost – into logical reasoning. All my friend would say by way of response was "Hm!" and "I see" and "I grant 'tis possible".

"Roly, I know it is right, or something very like it. Nothing else makes any sense. And if we can prove it Master Secretary will have to listen."

We reached Trussington by nightfall where inquiry after our friends revealed that, finding nowhere in the tiny village to stay, they had ridden into nearby Warwick. There we found them at the sign of the Adam and Eve.

"Have you found Meg Archer?" I demanded as soon as Hugh and Matt had recovered from their surprise.

"Aye, we found her – and terrified her, I think," Matt said.

"She certainly has come by what is for her a great deal of money," Hugh explained. "She and her brother have bought the freehold of their tiny farm and are in the process of adding to it, buying up any fields, meadows and barns they can persuade their neighbours to sell. 'Tis the talk of all the country around. No one knows how they came by their good fortune and, of course, they will say nothing. As soon as they heard we were from London and were inquiring for Meg they locked and bolted themselves inside their house for fear. I suppose they thought we were come from the court to take back the gold the king had given them."

Matt took up the story. "We stood outside that house all afternoon, calling and shouting. At last they opened up to us and we explained that we meant them no harm. I know not whether they believed us but they would say nothing. Meg insisted that she had been sworn to secrecy by one of Master Secretary's men on pain of imprisonment and death."

"I'll warrant she has much more than that to be frightened of," I said grimly and explained my theory. I was relieved when they took it rather more seriously than Roly had done.

It was mid-morning when the four of us rode into Trussington the next day. The Archers' farm was half a mile from the centre of the village, a tidy cluster of house and barns set amidst well-husbanded fields. Meg was in the wide yard behind the house feeding the chickens with corn from a brown pot. At our approach she started so violently that she almost dropped the vessel and grain spilled out in a deluge which set the fowls clucking and fluttering wildly.

"Calm yourself, Mistress Archer," Hugh said.

We dismounted and I introduced myself. At the mention of my name she turned pale. "Then, Sir, you are . . ."

"Henry Norris's son. My father is in the Tower of London awaiting execution."

She gasped. "And the queen?"

"She too."

Meg wailed and crossed herself. "Oh, the poor, dear, sweet lady."

"I think you can prevent it," I said, deliberately stepping close to her.

She backed away until she was pressed against the side of the barn. "No, sir. I durst not."

"Mistress Archer, all I want is the truth. Tell me that and I promise to leave you in peace. Hold your silence and I will denounce you for a witch."

"No, Sir, no, please, I beg of you. I meant it only for the best."

"Tell me about Her Majesty's miscarriage. The dead child she bore, it was a son was it not?"

She nodded and moaned.

"But not a handsome, well formed boy; it was misshapen, like the devil's spawn."

"Oh, no, sir. 'Twas as pretty a poor thing as you could ever want to see."

Her answer shook me. I had been so sure of my theory. "Have a care, woman. Only the truth can save you from the stake."

She slid down the wall cowering against the building and still hugging her pot. "We meant it only for the best, sir. It was the physician's idea. He was a close friend of the queen. She was that distressed at miscarrying of a boy. She knew the king would be angry."

I knelt beside the distraught woman, trying to catch the words which came between her sobs. "So you tried to help her?" I coaxed.

Meg nodded. "The queen never saw the child. We wrapped it up and took it away for burial. And the doctor he had to tell the king and he wanted the king to realize that 'twas not his wife's fault."

"So he decided to say that the queen had been bewitched?"

The woman nodded.

"That the child was hideously deformed?"

"Yes, sir. He rehearsed us in the story. We were to describe the child in detail if asked and, for good measure, I was to say that straight after the delivery I had seen the devil leave the room in the shape of a big black dog."

"What did you think the king would do when he heard this story?"

"We thought he would be sorry for the queen and send priests to say prayers over her."

"But that is not what happened, is it?"

The woman shook her head.

"The king believed your story and he was terrified. He really did think his wife was bewitched and that she had bewitched him. But he could not let people know that he had sired the devil's offspring. So he paid you to keep silence and sent you away." I stood up and turned to the others. "I was almost right. As soon as the 'truth' was covered up Cromwell was instructed to save the king's reputation. Just imagine what would happen if people believed the king and queen were in league with the devil and that was why he had broken with the pope. It could mean rebellion and every good Catholic in the country taking arms against the bewitched fanatic. The first thing Cromwell did was concoct a story about the queen being delivered of a perfectly formed male child – and ironically that was true. But he could never be sure that the other version would not leak out. So he made it possible for the king to deny that the child was his."

"By making his wife an adulteress?" Mat suggested.

"Exactly. And with four other men. Having gone that far he had to have those men – and the queen – permanently silenced." I helped Meg Archer to her feet. "I pray God may find it easier than I to forgive you. Good day, Mistress."

We remounted our horses and trotted down the lane.

"What do we do now?" Roly asked.

Hugh answered. "We set everything down in writing and send it post haste to Master Secretary. When he realizes that there are four of us who know the truth, he will have to treat with us."

We rode towards London, staying the night in Hugh's rooms in Oxford in order to compile our message for Master Secretary. When we had completed our task and Hugh had read the final version to us and we had agreed it Roly said, "Why did Cromwell make everything so complicated – the story that the queen's child was perfect; the story of her bedding *four* men; having her and her supposed lovers tried for treason; *and* having her marriage to the king annulled."

Hugh rose from the table where we were all sitting and stood before the hearth, warming himself. "Master Secretary is a genius who can think in bigger terms than most men. Breaking with Rome, tearing down the monasteries – he conceives things beyond the wildest imaginings of others. The great Cardinal Wolsey fell because he could not rid the king of an unwanted wife. Cromwell knew well that failure to dispose of the latest royal marriage problem would mean *his* ruin. To save himself he was prepared to sacrifice the lives of innocent men and of the queen. And he will not scruple to deal in the same way with us – unless we can outthink him. We may secure the release of Ned's father but we must not think that Cromwell will leave the matter there."

With that sober admonition in our ears we retired to our beds. We reached Westminster around noon the next day and went straight to Whitehall. Within minutes we heard the latest news: at nine o'clock that morning Henry Norris and the others had been beheaded on Tower Hill.

Thus, after all our endeavours our letter remained undelivered; our story untold. As Master Cromwell had said, it is hard, bootless and perilous to struggle against the tide.

TWO DEAD MEN

Paul Barnett

If the fate of the Princes in the Tower is England's best known royal mystery, then perhaps Scotland's is the death of Henry Darnley, the second husband of Mary, Queen of Scots. Mary's whole life and eventual fate under the hands of her cousin, Queen Elizabeth, has long held the fascination of many. In the following story Paul Barnett considers Mary's reign and considers not one, but two, or even three murders.

I first saw her as a child, although this is something little known. She must have been no more than six or seven, with her pinched, earnest little Scottish face. Very frightened she was, torn from her home to be at the court of the great king Henri II – a man widely regarded among his countrymen as both a saint and a butcher. Mary was betrothed to his son François. who was even younger than she, but this would not protect her from Henri's wrath should she fall foul of it. All that would stay his hand would be the thought of the succession: should she die childless. Scotland would be France's – and later, perhaps, England might be as well.

Childless? She was a small child herself when I saw her in the park. Whichever attendant had been charged with looking after her must have slipped away for an assignation or some less lofty reason, for she was entirely alone. In the middle of a clover-laden lawn she was dancing sombrely, her arms stretched out from her sides, her plain white frock belling in the wind that brought her high singing voice to me but had kept mine away from her. Her dark hair hung loose, dancing to a far more rapid rhythm than its owner.

I paused by a yew tree and watched, fascinated, the song long gone from my lips. I had seen a spider in amber before this time, and that is what this beautiful, engrossing child reminded me of. The stiffness of her movements as she performed the formalities of her dance made her seem as if she had been plucked from a different, earlier time. Of course the truth was that, in a sense, she had: the Scots had yet to attain the sophistication of the French court – but this I did not then know. I did not even know, as I looked entrancedly upon her, that she was a Scot. She could have been a wild child from the woods, dressed in better than rags because of a whim of some high-blooded courtesan who, becoming bored with her new toy, had set her loose again.

There are many forms of love between men and women, and not all of them are impure. I have no notion of the number of times I have enjoyed such impurity – women have always looked on me fondly, for no reason that I can ascertain – but the carnal sensations have never lingered in my memory long . . . as if I had drunk good wine one night, and then too much of it, so that in the morning my throbbing head could remember nothing of the taste, only that the wine had indeed been good. But in the real sense of the word "love", there is only one who has ever captured my heart.

She was that child, dancing amid an aura of innocence, the trees behind her, tossed by the wind, seeming to perform some anxious counterpoint.

I fell in love with Mary – Marie, Maria Stuarda – then and there. Had I known that I would kill for her, I would have turned away and fled off through the prim plantings that Henri II had decreed for his park. Instead. I stood stock-still and covertly watched, my heart stolen by a thief who knew nothing of the crime she had committed . . . and nothing of the blood I would one day have on my hands.

I don't know if she ever noticed me as she grew through childhood into an ungainly adolescence, and then into the beauty of her womanhood, losing the coarse, unmusical grating of her Scots accent as she did so. There were attendants in plenty – a flock of peacocks, I always thought them – at the court of Henri, and I was just one more peacock among them. But I was never unaware of her presence, even when she was not within eyeshot, and I kept a guardian watch upon her. Many times I gazed at her again as she danced through the gardens, growing more at ease with herself and shedding her childhood fixity of concentration. Once I saved her life, but that is another story: she heard nothing and saw nothing of the Guise assassin and his demise.

The Dauphin was growing up as well. I liked what I saw of him enough, but he was a frail youth. Although it was hard to believe that he had tackle between his legs, he learned to look on Mary fondly and to speak with her courteously. She was wary of him at the age of ten, tractable at the age of thirteen, and deeply pleased by his presence at the age of fifteen. A year after that they kissed for the first time – a clumsy peck at each other's lips as they danced, for now he was always with her on those garden expeditions.

Their betrothal made my life a hell.

I was not so many years older, after all, than my darling, than the shining crystal who illuminated and was the focus of my life. Sometimes as I lay in my hard bunk at night, at the time between wakefulness and sleep when one can still control one's dreams, I fancied the youth would die and that then she would turn to the one who had loved her for longer years than he. Other nights I would be with a serving girl or some petty aristocrat from an obscure family of the far south and I would have to clamp my lips tight shut for fear of murmuring Mary's name. Not that I wanted her in any carnal sense, you understand; just that I desired her always to be close to me.

But she married her betrothed, and still I was just another among the cloud of attendants surrounding her.

I was right about the sickliness of her husband. Henri died, and then for a few months Mary was queen of the French alongside her husband François. Then, in turn, he died. It came as no surprise to anyone, except to those who had not expected him to live as long as he did.

It came as no surprise to *me*. For some weeks the more credulous gossips around the court hazarded that the wee Dauphin might have been, shall we say, sped on his way, but no one with a brain in their head, myself included, paid them any mind. Had I known then the violent way in which my Mary's second husband would be sent to his ungodly Father by a hand that is still unknown to the world, I might have needed them better; I might have learned from their chatterings.

Only weeks after François was put into the ground, I was sold – any other word would be a euphemism – to a different court. As the hills and plains of France reeled past me, I let my heart begin to know that I would never see my Mary again. Not she, but the accident of our different births and stations, had betrayed me.

Yet there was some joy left, a joy of memory. Those skinny hands of François had violated her nakedness. It had been good when he had died. And he, unlike myself, had never looked upon the earnest-faced young child who danced alone in her white frock among the clover, when she was loved by no one but myself. Ah, watching the lassie had been an act of love more pleasurable than any to be found in the bed.

I did encounter her again. I like to think of she and myself as two lodestones, pulled together inexorably by the currents of life, the eddies that shape the passage of time. Some years later my French master took me to the bleak court of the Scots, and I entertained the couthless nobles well enough that they agreed with him that I should remain once he had gone. As soon as he had departed, though, I was relegated to the role of court buffoon, something – not someone – to be mocked and kicked if there was nothing better to do. Their pleasures were as uncivilized as the rest of their lives: in their badly sewn garments they spent their days killing animals or each other in the country all around. While at night as the wind shrieked through every crevice of that grey stone place, they warmed themselves by fucking toothless peasant women, beating the thin-boned waifs senseless beforehand if there was no other way to achieve consent.

I have said that the place was grey. All the colours there were muted, from the stone of the undraped walls to the tiresome greens of the roughly woven woollen garments the men wore and the pallid ashiness of their unsunned faces. It was as if God had picked up the entirety of the Scottish court and wrung it between His hands until all the colours had bled out.

With one exception.

There was my Mary. Whenever she was nearby God gave the colours back to the world.

The first time I saw her here, she saw me as well. There was only the slightest trace of recognition in the glance she gave me, but it was clear to me she saw something in my face that she remembered. It was above a lady of her status to smile at a mere servant, but she gave me a half-smile anyway. It was more than she had ever done in France.

The days and the months went by, and I counted my bruises in the times when I was not watching her. As we both grew older, the years that separated us became smaller. Had I not been a commoner and she not a Queen . . . As it was, I had to make do with becoming her favourite amongst those whose task it was (and it was no task to me) to brighten her days with light thoughts that would help her forget the loss of the French boy.

The more it became clear that she enjoyed my company, the less often her crude courtiers beat me. She was a slight figure and her voice was soft, but she was their queen. And she had the lealty of a man called Bothwell, who was big and dark-bearded and built with the shoulders of a bull. It was clear to all that he would allow no one to displeasure his lady.

I know he loved her almost as much as I did myself. He, too, had been at Henri's court, drawn there initially by Mary of Guise, and had fallen for my Mary not long before the French whippet died. I did not resent his love for her, nor the sly smiles she sometimes gave him, but all the same I was guiltily pleased when he was imprisoned on a charge trumped up by the other nobles of plotting to kidnap her. If there had been any such plot, then she might have been a willing participant – as years later she would be. As it was, for three years or more there was no Bothwell: the hierarchy of the court floundered on somehow.

I was often with Mary then, and she told me in confidence of matters that were unqueenly. I shall not break that confidence even now, even to these voiceless sheets of dingy parchment. She trusted me.

We sang together sometimes. Have I mentioned that? I stole tunes from others and wrote new words to them, lovesongs which I would teach her. Sometimes she wondered aloud who the object of my affections was, but I never dared tell her. Even when she and I were close together and alone, I was gazing at her from afar.

There was a newcomer to the court, and he was different from all the others – or, at least, he seemed to be. To look at him, you might have thought he was from France, or Italy, or another of the cultured lands. This man was Darnley, his given names being Henry Stewart – he was a legitimate great-grandson of England's Henry VII, whose seed be for ever cursed. Darnley's face was clean-shaven except for a silly wee beard on the tip of his chin. His voice was, after my Mary's, the purest that I have ever heard among the Scots. He had charm. He had presence. She did not like him much, but she was drawn to him. She was a woman, and the men around her were like swilling pigs compared with the elegant Henry.

She never loved him, I think, but she needed him. And he needed her – not for her companionship or all the other things that can pull two people together, but because of his ambitions. One day, when he was old enough, he would be proclaimed king.

Mary married him. I wept. There was so much unhappiness to come, I knew. What I did not know was that, for me, there would also be a time of happiness.

Two days after the marriage, I saw Darnley sodomizing some poor girl from the town. Finished, he went to his wife's bed. The soldiers threw the girl out into the street. One of them tossed a coin after her. Her tears of pain still loud, she looked at it with revulsion and contempt, but then, just as she was about to limp away, she turned, picked it up from the paving stone, and tested it with her teeth.

I remember, clear as moonlight, the night that Riccio died – Riccio, who in his fancy Continental way pretended that his name was spelt Rizzio, because the ladies liked it more. But Mary always called him Riccio when she had to speak his family name, although more usually he was simply Davy to her, or David if her mood was sharp. As sharp it increasingly was, for Darnley, having attained a part of his monarchical ambition and certain he would gain the rest in time, was treating her neither as her lover nor even as her husband. By day he hardly needed her as he swaggered around Holyrood, strutting like Chanticleer: by night, if he were not tupping a courtly hen, he would sit up drinking and playing cards with milord Bothwell, now pardoned at the behest of our fair Queen: Bothwell was a most unwilling cards- or drinking-partner, if truth be told, but must obey the demands of the man who was almost king . . . and, besides, if Darnley were drinking with Bothwell or swiving a diddyhead then at least he was not in Mary's bed.

Bothwell did not hear – or chose not to hear – the sounds that came from the queen's bedchamber sometimes when Darnley retired from one of their monstrous drinking sessions. One morning the queen did not descend all day from her apartments, and the following day it was still hard for her ladies to paint over the bruise beside her eye. She ate supper that night seated beside Darnley but in truth many miles apart from him; and she left the company for her bed again as soon as the meal, at which she had but picked, was done.

Bothwell's hands trembled on the edge of the table that night. He had married a few weeks earlier – married, despite his Protestant vows, Jeannie Gordon, the papist sister of the Earl of Huntly – but it was plain to all but her, whom he treated kindly enough, that the love that set his heart and passions aflame was that for Mary. Darnley knew this too, and perhaps this was why he was so unkind to the queen and stayed so often from her bed with Bothwell as his companion. He, Darnley, was her husband, and the only one who could rightly be in her arms: that he chose to reject her allures in favour of those of the wineskin and the staggering and vomiting it caused him, and that he chose to do this in the presence of Bothwell, must have caused the noble earl great torment – and calculatedly so.

A light gleamed that night in Darnley's eyes, and it was easy enough to read what he was thinking. Bothwell, with the rage painted red above his beard, was enchained by his virile love for Darnley's wife. So, in a quieter and much more covert way, was Riccio, and Darnley – who for all the fact that he was a cockscomb and a fool, was shrewd and sly – knew of this as well. And he knew that their love was not entirely unreturned, for both were like to being her brothers. Without seeming in any way to do so with intention, he could have great merriment tonight by taunting both of those whom the queen held dear.

So, when the court and the servants were dispersing to their various destinations, he called Bothwell and Riccio to him. The lord would help him drink some wine that was new in from France. The queen's secretary and minstrel would serenade the drinkers as the cards chattered in their hands. Lady Bothwell entreated her husband with her eyes, but there was nothing he could do to disobey his master, for all that he wished to – I have said that Bothwell was kind to Jeannie and, if he could not give her his love, was always full certain to give her his affection and his tenderness. The lady was the last to leave them, except for the servant who lit the gloomy stairs ahead of us as they climbed to a private sanctuary, called the Queen's Supper Room but in fact the place where by day Darnley dealt with such affairs of state as he could abide.

The candles and the fire were lit, so that the cold room at least appeared to be warm. Darnley and Bothwell drew up chairs to either side of the table, from which the man who would be king impatiently swept documents and books and pens in a cascade to the floor, where dark ink spread across a rug that had been brought all the way from Italy as a gift to her husband from the queen. The rough goblets were filled, and the servant returned with two further jugs of decanted red wine. Riccio was given a pewter cup of wine to keep his throat moist, should he be required to sing as well as play; he was sat down in a corner on a stool, slightly behind Darnley so that, as the almost-king said with a loud shout of laughter, Darnley would not have to look upon his ugly face as he scraped his fiddle.

The cards began to fall even before Riccio had fully finished tuning his violin.

Darnley, as he had proclaimed, could not look upon Riccio's face without turning, but Bothwell could, and Riccio could look upon Bothwell's. Though not a word passed between the two men, they spoke in a language of expression and mien that, while invisible to the queen's husband, was perfectly comprehensible to them both. In a way they were rivals, but there was no rivalry between them: Bothwell was a husband, and had sworn oaths that it seemed he had full intent of obeying – rare at Holyrood in those days and maybe still – and Riccio had long ago resigned himself to the role of the Queen's dearest lapdog. The soundless tongue spoken by these two rivals who were not rivals, then, was the vernacular of hatred, and the object of that hatred sat oblivious between them, unaware – as he slopped more strong red grape into his goblet with an unsteady hand – of the fullness of the air.

Riccio, tuned at last and his bow rosined, strikes up a lively air, one to bring good cheer to the soul and set the feet a-tapping.

Bothwell seems to like it well enough, although he can read Riccio's eyes and see bitterness that belies the jaunty phrases, but after a few minutes Darnley gives out a growl – he is losing at the cards – and, without turning his head, tells the minstrel to cease that vile and devilish noise and play something more in keeping with his mood.

With a shrug for the benefit of both himself and Bothwell, Riccio plucks his bow away from the strings and pauses for a moment, selecting from among those in his mind a strain that might be in accordance with his master's humour. Too long a moment, for Darnley snarls at him, again without looking around, that this servant is here to play music and not to play in the garden of his own silent thoughts. Riccio at once begins to stroke a solemn melody of his own composition, one to which some years later, after the murder of the Queen's half-brother, a balladeer will put words –

> Lang may his lady look fae the castle doon
> Ere she sees the Earl o' Moray come soonding
>   through the toon

– and claim as his own. But this, too, does not please the temper of the divil who bruised Mary's face, and he shouts at the player to desist from this dreich dirge and play something with regal pomp for is he not in a palace? Darnley draws his skean from his belt and places it ponderously on the table in front of him to show the world – or at least the two from it who can observe him – that his almost-royal ire is rising.

Bothwell, feigning conviviality, chuckles and tells his fellow-bibber to be more patient with a poor musician who is but trying to please, but Darnley will hear none of it. Ascending into a high rage in the passage of a mere instant, he leaps to his feet, throwing backwards the chair with his legs so that it flies from the stained rug, falls on its back and skreeks across the black polished floor to crash against the wall.

Bothwell is on his feet in almost the same moment, and reaching out to stay the man's arm, but Darnley already has the skean in his hand, its handle darkly glittering between his fingers and its blade an evil slice of dead light as he turns, shaking himself free of the noble's clutch.

Riccio cringes away from him, holding the now and forevermore mute violin up before his face for the protection it can offer.

With a roar Darnley advances, but once again Bothwell seizes hold of him, this time by the shoulder.

Darnley whips around – he is stronger and quicker than he has appeared, even with the wine inside him – and holds the point of the skean directly under Bothwell's beard.

Who does Bothwell obey? The consort of the queen or some scrofulous queeriosity brought in from a foreign court where the young boys walk agley for the pain in their airses? Who – all in a roar, as the quavering knife-point now parts Bothwell's beard-hair – is the master and who is the servant?

Darnley is the master. Riccio is the servant. Bothwell, no less a servant for all his greatness in the world, must needs submit. And yet, as the nearly king thrusts with the skean and the fiddle flies to break its neck on a firedog, Bothwell tries one last time to wrench aside his master's arm.

And fails, for blood pours like an eager tide over the ink that was spilt earlier, so that now the rug which Mary so loved that she gave it to her young groom is doubly stained and useless except to go on the stone floor of a cook's assistant or some such vermin.

There is an antechamber, little more than a cupboard, off the study and Darnley, wiping the spittle from his lips with the sleeve of one wrist and shaking the blood off his skean with the other hand, gestures to his lordly servant, who is shaking with wrath yet white with shock, that Riccio's body should be hurled in there – to be out of sight, so that the room is no longer untidy. Bothwell does his master's bidding, and also throws the splintered fiddle on top of the sprawled puppet that only minutes before was giving it life.

By the time Bothwell returns to the table he has his hot temper under control. Darnley has shuffled the cards and starts to deal out another hand for them both. Bothwell fills his lord's goblet for him once more, with hardly a tremble as he pours.

I like to think that it was then that Darnley died, although he would not breathe his last until almost a year had passed.

Those lords who care little for the lives of other men seem not to know that those others may come to care little for the life of their lord. Darnley was no soldier to lead his troops to burn villages and spit babes, or even to challenge rebels on the field of battle, but tales of his petty cruelties, of the servants he sent to the gallows for imagined sins, of the women he disgraced – all were soon the common talk of the citizens of Edinburgh, and from there were carried by merchants to Aberdeen and Glasgow, to Dundee and Arbroath and even to France and England and Ireland. Scotland was then in a ferment, with the Papists at the throats of those who had given their allegiance to the new Church, and the people of the new Church as bad as the Papists. This was a new thing, for only a few years before there had been an easy peace between the two faiths – as there still was among the poor folk. But lords are greedy: what price is friendship worth if you covet the lands and the wealth of another and can claim you go to war because your neighbour speaks to his God in a tone of voice different from the one you use? What the kingdom needed was firm rule, to put an end to all this. But Mary was only a woman, and could not be expected to stamp out the flames or stop the slaughter, while her husband cared not for others' sufferings except when he sought to rejoice in them. Hers was a weakness she could do nothing to change: his was a weakness which he cultivated, as if it were a precious plant, and glorified in. Bothwell became Mary's right hand in trying to bring peace back to fair Scotland, but he was not a king – he was only a lord among other lords, who saw no great need to rally to his flag.

At the same time, harmless madwomen were being dragged from their homes to be hanged or burnt or pressed for having converse with the Devil.

It was a poor time for the tales concerning Darnley's cruelty to be spread all over Scotland and to further parts, and I confess I did my share of the spreading. More than my share.

This I did for Scotland, my adopted country, the country whose queen I cherished beyond all other women. If there was a rising, it would be against Darnley and not against his royal wife, who was much loved, and indeed pitied, by those who had sworn their fealty to her. If Darnley were dead, then soon she would be able to wed the Earl of Bothwell – a fitting wedding with a fitting groom, who would be a fine king to reunite a rent nation.

But there was more that drove me than great thoughts about the Game of Thrones. Should I have been allowed to choose anyone to press to death for dealing with Satan it would have been Henry, Lord Darnley, for he was evil through and through, from the tip of the long curly feather in his hat to the toes of his pointed, fancified shoon. His death, and his subsequent descent to the embrace of his own Master, would cause rejoicing among the angels in God's Heaven. Each breath that he took before that time was a breath stolen from the lips of dying children and their mothers and fathers. He sucked the life from those innocents as surely as if he were leaning over them to take their sighs from them.

Darnley, in a drunken moment, had succeeded in making Mary pregnant: he took this as a token that he had fulfilled his consortly duties to her and to the land, and disturbed her slumbers no longer. Indeed, he hardly saw her, for he spent much of his time in Glasgow from this time on, where it is said (and *was* said by me, often, in Edinburgh's drinking houses) he entered plots with his kin the Lennoxes, who were avid to see the end of Mary's reign and desirous to set Darnley on the throne in her place: Darnley, they perceived, would as a king be weak-willed enough to act according to their desires. Mary remained in Holyrood with her newborn babe while her husband was afield flattering himself that he was a fine conspirator, a high diplomatist.

Then came a time when the man fell sick of the smallpox. On the news reaching Edinburgh there was general, if quiet, rejoicing among the folk. But Mary, who was aye aware of the duties imposed by the marriage bond, appeared to forgive her absent husband much that had gone before, and journeyed from Edinburgh to Glasgow with her entourage to persuade Darnley to return to Holyrood, so that she would have him under her eye until his health was restored. To Holyrood he would not come, nor even to Craigmillar Castle, hard by the city; instead, he consented to bide in a private town house beside the church of St Mary in the Field, not a mile from Holyrood.

It was a foolish thing for the man to do. In Holyrood, where the walls were thick and the guards abundant, he would have been safe: and the same would have been true of Craigmillar. Perhaps he was afeared that in both places he would be in Mary's thrall, and at her mercy – perhaps he was afeared of those very guards, in that she might order them to take his life. Darnley, like so many of his kind, assumed that others thought as deviously as he did himself.

Nae matter: he took up his place in his town house and surrounded himself with those he believed he could trust, plus lassies whose task was to bathe him often to ameliorate his sickness but who in fact – if the reports I heard be true – were frequently called upon to perform other services for himself and his cronies.

February of this brand-new year had not long begun, and Riccio's blood had not had a full twelvemonth to dry, when one night the whole city was aroused from its beds by a sound that seemed to tear the cloudy sky in two. People ran to the quadrangle of St Mary in the Field to find that the old kirk still stood but that Lord Darnley's proud townhouse had become a pile of stones, with fires raging and adding their smoke to the remains of that caused by the gunpowder.

Darnley was dead, and alongside him most of his lassies and his henchmen. I and several others whose names will form no part of this account repaired ourselves to a drinking-house not far from there and raised a sad toast to the memories of the lassies, who had not deserved to die – who had but been caught up in greater events. Then we drank a noisier toast to the fact that the wee shit who sought so much to have been our king was dead as well.

Though my head throbbed the next day, I had to take the silly smile from my face before I dared venture out in the streets to fetch myself a loaf of bread and a herring.

Mary was by now pregnant again – some said by Bothwell, although I have never been able to believe this myself: in all that I saw, he seemed at this time to remain steadfastly loyal to his Jeannie, in body if not in passion. It is my mind that in Glasgow Mary used physical wiles to coax her husband into returning to Edinburgh. Whatever the truth of the matter, it is of no concern: the fact is that she was with child, and the wee baby James would have a sibling by the autumn.

Bothwell was suspected of Darnley's murder, and here my knowledge is more secure. He was haled up for trial by a panel of his peers, but as they were all his own or Mary's men his prosecutors were told he was an innocent man made by circumstances to look guilty. In fact, in fairness the judges should have found his case Not Proven, for although he played no part in the conspiracy he well knew of it yet said nothing either to Darnley or the queen. Even had he done so, it would have made no difference: there were so many other bruited plots on Darnley's life that the report of one more would have caused little remark.

In the weeks after he was declared guiltless there was great drama indeed. Mary was again a widow, and the country sair needed a king.

Bothwell was eager for the throne, almost as eager as he was for the warmth of her bed and the sound of her laughter. She, for her part, now openly acknowledged that she had for years been smitten by him. They could not wed so soon after the unmourned death of the man she had married scant years before, and besides Bothwell was still married to Jeannie, yet both the lovebirds were too impatient to wait until a fitting time had passed.

And so he and an 800-strong band of his men, of whom I, David Macrae, was by now one, seized their queen as she travelled by the Bridges of Almond and carried her off to Dunbar Castle. Never can there have been a calmer abductee: she told her own entourage that she wished no bloodshed and that thus they should not resist Bothwell's men, and her face was all smiles as she allowed him to hand her back into her carriage and then climb in beside her. It was put about that he had come to the Bridges of Almond only because he knew of threats to her life in Edinburgh and wished to take her to the safety of distant Dunbar, but I was there and I saw what I saw. This was no liege act any more than it was an abduction: it was a lovers' tryst.

Lovers they did indeed become behind the craggy walls of Dunbar Castle. Neither in France nor in Edinburgh had I ever seen Mary so happy, and the lines in Bothwell's face – formed during years of frustrated rancour – softened and flowed as he beamed at the lassie he had finally won.

A happy finish to a love story? No, for the story itself is too besmirched by blood to be ended in gladness. Jeannie Gordon allows her husband a divorce, despite the teachings of her own Church: she justifies the act through continuing to maintain that she is still married to him, although he is no longer married to her. In the middle of May Bothwell and Mary are married at Holyrood, with all due formal celebration, and with bonfires and drunkenness in the streets – for at last Scotland believes there is a strong king on the throne. The bulge of Mary's belly goes consciously unnoticed. Master, mistress and all who cling to them settle down to enjoy the long, calm, soothing twilight of the tale.

And it is not to be.

The ceremony of marriage changes everything between those two. The little love-jokes, the banter, the playfulness which made even glum Dunbar Castle seem to smile – all these are gone, and in their place are stiff silences and formal conversations that lead nowhere. It is as if the lovers were Mary and her swain, but that the pair who married were a queen and her soon-to-be king: they are political allies thrust into the same bed by force of circumstance.

I remember the wee girl with the sad, lonely face who danced in the gardens of Henri's estate. Now I am seeing her again.

For his part, Bothwell knows there is something wrong yet he does not know precisely what it is nor what he can do to change things. He has taken to seeking out my advice, for he has decided that I am wise, yet whatever counsel I give him he completely ignores, preferring to batter his way through life like an enraged bull rather than use the merry knock-kneed stealth of the puppy, who through cumbrous guile wins over even the steeliest heart. Bothwell shouts at Mary that she no longer looks on him with favour, and it is plain that sometimes she is scared to be in his company. He cuffs the servants and even some of the noblewomen at the slightest pretext. Some say that Mary's coldness is beginning to unsettle his mind, and I am inclined to credit their gossip, for sometimes his wild ferocities are akin to those of a madman.

I am drinking one night on my own in my small room tucked under the attics, the candle guttering to remind me that I am tired and a wee bit drunk and should have been in my bed an hour gone, when there comes a pounding on my door. Even before it is thrown ajar I know who the pounder was, for those fists could belong to none other than Bothwell. He has been drinking, like me. Although he has doubtless been supping of the sweetest wines while I have been swigging from a jug of the rawest usquebaugh, we are no drunker nor less drunk than each other: yet our different indulgences have affected us differently, for his face is red yet again with ire while I am looking upon the world in a dreamy contentment.

My room may be a small one, but it has a chair: this is not a boast that every man in Holyrood can claim. Bothwell kicks the chair into the centre of the floor and throws himself down on it with such force that I am afeared the weight of his body will shatter the carpentry.

He looks at me, and loudly admires my long, tangled beard – a symptom of my wisdom, he proclaims. Then he tells me that no two men in the world, not even if they are twins, have eyes the same as each other. He takes one of my hands, grown calloused these days but with its nails still bitten trim, as of old, and tells me that it is the hand of a musician, not a soldier . . .

And I know that he knows me for who I am.

I am David Macrae, Davy to most, but David Macrae is not yet two years old – a veritable babe – whereas I am now in the middle of my years.

Fumbling often in his speech, Bothwell tells me most of my own story, although I help with the pieces he cannot have known before he came thundering up the stairs to my room.

Davy Riccio died in the antechamber off the Queen's Supper Room, stabbed by his master's skean . . . but stabbed only in the shoulder, for Bothwell's strength made sure of that as he deflected Darnley's arm from its elected target. There was blood in plenty from the wound – enough that the would-be king, already drunk as he was, believed he had murdered, however slight he regarded his crime. Bothwell, making a great rumpus in the little antechamber, in truth laid the body gently on the floor there, and was rewarded when Riccio opened his eyes, smiled painfully, and winked at him.

But that was not the real time of Riccio's dying, which came but a few moments later, when Bothwell tossed the wreckage of his violin towards him. Never afterwards would Riccio pluck or pipe or bow or strum or blow so much as a note, far less a tune: he would not so much as sing, even as he stood in the back of the kirk and all around him were singing. The musician was slain by Darnley, indeed, who had broken the musician's fiddle and thus ended his life. The body in which the musician dwelt, however, lived on.

I was not made to lie in my agony long. In the darkness I sat up and did my best with my fingers and a kerchief to staunch the blood. Outside, in the Supper Room, Bothwell plied the nearly king with wine – I heard him call the servant to bring more because the card-players had finished what was there, and I will warrant that the earl's own voice was clear. There was a bump as a head hit a table-top, and then the sound of choky snoring.

Bothwell threw open the door to the antechamber and asked me if I could walk: I answered him yea, though I was less certain of this than I made my voice sound. He threw his own cloak about my shoulders, and pulled its hood low over my face so that none would recognize me if they saw me in the candlelit passage.

Indeed, we encountered few and, as I staggered along with his arm about me, they must have thought merely that Bothwell was escorting one of his drunken cronies to the man's bedchamber before seeking out his own couch.

Mary's private apartments were, as fortune would have it, not far from Bothwell's, so no one looked at us askance as he half-dragged, half-walked me there. He knocked on the door and one of the four Marys who attended the queen opened it, looking fair fetching in the looseness of her night attire. In his forthright way Bothwell quickly explained my plight, and I was ushered into the receiving room, where he told the woman the tale at greater length and in more detail. The only place in all Holyrood I would be safe as I recovered from my injury would be here, he said, in the queen's own rooms. He would send out a man in the morning to search the streets of Edinburgh for a corpse – these were not ever too hard to find, for the nights in my adopted land were gye chill – and another's body would be buried in my name.

By now the queen, having heard the racket through the door that led to her bedchamber, was with us, a shawl of plaid fastened tightly around her so that she was modest. She pulled the cloak away from my shoulders and hissed when she saw all the blood. She spoke rapidly, and in instants one of the Marys was laying me down on a bed in a wee box-room and cutting away the fine satin of my puff-sleeved purple jerkin, speaking soothing noises to me all the while. She and the queen took soft cloths and warm water to bathe the puncture Darnley's skean had made, tugging away the caked blood with their fingernails. At the last they tied a bandage around my shoulder and pulled sheets – clean linen sheets that had not been slept in before – and blankets up around me.

The pain did its best to keep me awake, but I did manage to sleep in fits and starts through the night. Whenever I opened my eyes I saw, sitting in the candlelight beside me, the figure of the woman who for so long had been at the centre of my world: and she would, seeing my wakefulness, soothe my hot forehead with her own cool hand and whisper tender words to me until I slept again. She was the fondest nurse that ever a man could know, and as days and nights followed each other, and I became persuaded that this was not a dream (for full many a time have I seen her face in my dreaming), I could easily have countenanced the notion that I had indeed died and had been transported by God's angels to Heaven.

As for Bothwell, it would seem that he lost all interest in me once he had assured himself of my salvation, for in all the weeks and maybe months that I skulked in the queen's apartments, growing stronger by the day, he never came near the place, and he was not there to greet me when finally the new-born David Macrae was escorted by Mary Fleming down the long steps and through the quiet passages of a sleeping Holyrood to be ushered out past the guards into the streets of Edinburgh, a bag of coin at his belt and a sword in his scabbard to help him make his own way in the world.

But now Bothwell is sitting in my small room, and once more has become interested in me. He calls me Davy, for that was Riccio's name and is now Macrae's.

My tale is at an end, I believe, but he carries on to tell me more of it: I hear him out in silence. He knew of Morton's plot against the life of Darnley, he says to me: while he did not participate in it beyond giving Morton some money to pay the men who would place the explosive charges, neither did he do anything to foil it.

How his knowledge came about was this. It was by sheer accident that one day he came across Morton, the almost-king's sworn foe, speaking in a low voice to some scruffy rapscallions in the street: as they dispersed on Bothwell's approach he saw something familiar in the aspect of one of them and, despite Macrae's heavy beard and long tangled hair, knew me for who I was. Thereafter, he tells me, he kept an eye on me and my progress, sending spies of his out to make reports on all my activities. Almost before the poisoned words were out of my throat he knew each of the tales I was telling to the detriment of Darnley. He knew when I, guised as a miller's man, persuaded the servant at Darnley's dwelling that he needed to provision the household with a dozen barrels of flour, and he knew of the powder that I and my fellows put in eleven of the barrels in place of that flour. As clearly as if with his own eyes, he had seen me take the opportunity of a dark night to sneak past the guards to light the long fuse that led down into the cellar where the barrel's were stored . . .

After he has finished speaking he takes a long gulp from my jug of usquebaugh, one that brings water to his eyes and makes his forehead sweat.

I say nothing until he asks me if what he has said is not the truth, and then I acknowledge that, save for the very finest points of detail, he has it all aright. Aye, I killed Darnley – the very hand that now trembling a little brings the jug to my lips is the one that lit the match that lit the fuse that lit the powder that blasted Darnley's evil soul to Satan. I ask Bothwell if, once he has had me hanged for my crime, as surely he must, he will ensure that my good right hand be cut from its arm and preserved for future Scots to revere.

But he does not want to have me hanged. Bonded irrevocably to him as I am by our shared secrets, he desires me to be his closest servant and confidant in the years that are to come. He tells me that he will be able to trust me in all matters, for he has but to mention a mere part of what he knows about Davy Macrae for my neck to be streetchit on the nearest tree.

He shakes my hand to signify that, if we are not equals, then we are at least bonded partners; and then he turns away for the door.

Once he reaches it, though, he pauses and looks back at me. Darnley, he tells me, was not the first man to be murdered by my hand, was he?

I begin obediently, blurting my words, to tell him a different and a longer-ago story, of a sickly prince in a foreign land, and of the beautiful Scots princess who was made to wed him for the sake of their parents' ambitions. I inform Bothwell of the love that I had for that young exiled lassie – love that I still hold, for all she has now married thrice – and of the wicked old woman who sold me a herb that would slowly make the dauphin yet sicklier until death came to claim him. It was not hard for me to administer these herbs, for they did not taste of the bitterness they contained and I volunteered myself whenever possible to act as Mary's taster – her bowl so close beside the dauphin's own.

Bothwell nods as if this, too, he has known all along but wished to hear from my lips.

Then he slams the door behind him and I am left alone with my usquebaugh, my memories and my guilt and my tears.

What more is there to tell? A great deal, but it shall not be told here, for the cold and damp of this grim Scandinavian prison are leaching the life from me almost as I watch.

Not long after my interrogation by Bothwell the rebellion of the nobles that had been so long simmering boiled over, and Mary, now very big with child, was seized at Carberry Hill and imprisoned.

Bothwell fled with me in his train for France, where he hoped to raise an army to invade Scotland and restore his lady, but a storm blew our ship off-course and we were forced to take refuge on the Norwegian coast. Alas, news of my master's arrival in their country soon reached the ears of some of those to whom he owed money from earlier Scandinavian sojourns, and also the powerful kin of a lassie whom he had swived and then deserted. He and his followers, myself never far from his side, were arrested on a nonsense charge and haled to Bergen, where a crooked court tried him and found him guilty. The others of his retinue were deported back to Scotland, to retrieve their lives as best they could: only I, his lealest servant, remained in Bergen with him.

King Frederik II, monarch of Denmark and Norway, soon heard news of his distinguished prisoner, realized there might be political gains to be had by securing him more closely, and determined that he should be brought to Copenhagen, where Frederik held his court. When Bothwell learnt of this he became wild-eyed with excitement for, while his incarceration in Bergen was in no ways onerous – having a sufficiency of money, he could afford all the best there was of food and drink, and his bed was a feather one, as befitted his status – he was weary of it. Moreover, were he once outside cold stone walls and strong iron bars, he might be able to elude his captors and head for the coast, where he might buy passage on a ship bound for home.

I had a better plan, and I explained it to him the last night I visited him in his cell in Bergen. In the morning he would be put in a carriage and sent with a heavily weaponed escort to Copenhagen – where, let it be noted, there dwelt no one who would know his face. Indeed, if someone else should take his place before the journey commenced, it would be no great task to personate him. Did I not owe him a life, twice over? He had saved me from Darnley's murderous stab, and he had saved me from dangling on the gallows to which he should have consigned me. It was full time that I should give him back a single life in return.

I took off my hooded cloak and gave it to him, all the while minded of how I had worn *his* cloak when I had staggered along by his side through the halls and passages of Holyrood towards the sweetest infirmary that God ever created.

So Davy Macrae came to visit Bothwell one last time, and Davy

Macrae left into a night that was clouded and dark despite the moon, and if Davy Macrae were larger and stockier when he departed than when he had arrived none of the stolid Danish sentries noticed a thing of it. Mine was the more dangerous commission, for one or other of the warders might chance to catch sight of my face as I ate my supper that night or broke my fast on the morrow, but by dint of helterskelter ruses I was able to maintain the subterfuge.

And, as I had predicted, in Copenhagen there was no one to recognize that I was not Bothwell . . . Sooner or later, once the situation in Scotland had steadied, there would be a call for "Bothwell" to be brought back to his native land, and I would be released to walk free in Scotland with the knowledge that my king was in my debt.

I had not reckoned with the English bitch. Mary had been forced to abdicate in favour of her brat, James, who ruled in name alone with the Earl of Moray as his Regent. Imprisoned in Lochleven Castle, she escaped and rallied further troops to fight her cause: but these were humbled at Langside by Moray and there was nothing for Mary but to flee to England and cast herself upon the mercy of her father's cousin, Elizabeth I. But the English bitch did not have such a quality as mercy, and had this desperate relation of hers thrown forthwith into prison. The bitch claimed that, so long as Mary remained alive, her own throne was unsafe, but the truth of the matter, so far as I could ascertain it, was that Elizabeth, whose selfishness is famed for having no bounds, felt that there was room for but a single female monarch to be worshipped by the people of England.

Of Bothwell I have heard nothing. He may have died aboard ship back from Scandinavia to Scotland, or he may have decided, on returning home, to forsake the gaudy life of power and glory to find serenity in some remote cot, where he can till his plot of land by day and sit by the river to catch fish of an evening. My preference is for the latter, for it would satisfy me if at least one of the players in this tale of tragedy and death should find the tranquillity that God has not seen fit to bestow upon the rest of us.

Still, there is a dream that comes to me every few nights, and I believe it to be a true dream. I dream that the English bitch has at last decided that Mary must be put to death. As the pious and the mighty gather around the executioner's block to watch the deed being done there is one among them who is rather more rustically dressed than a nobleman should be, although he carries himself with all the airs of a man of the blood. He gives his name in a soft voice as the Earl of Macrae: although none recognize him nor even his title, he goes unchallenged.

There is a roll of the drums, and Mary is led out onto the green: she has forsworn a blindfold, for she wishes to clap her eyes for one last time on the sky that the Good Lord created for us all. She lets her gaze scan around the faces of the folk who have come to watch her death – some prurient, some in tears, some stern in the false knowledge that they are here merely to see justice done. When she sees the face of the man who calls himself Macrae she starts, and stares fixedly at it. She says but the six words before she resumes her regal progress to the block where her life shall end:

You! Bothwell! You *murdered* me, James . . .

And she sighs.

But it is I, Davy Riccio or Davy Macrae or, now, James Hepburn, Fourth Earl of Bothwell, who am the murderer – the murderer of two of her husbands and, should the sorry day I see in my dream be indeed a true vision, of my queen, despite the fact that I have loved her – that I have had interest in nothing *but* her – for all these years.

Yet somehow my tears start to flow only when I think of that other dead man, Riccio the poet and musician, the bright little canary who brought smiles to Mary's long face. What might he have become had Darnley not lashed out in drunken fury? What might he have been *allowed* to become had not all those around him been playing the cruel Game of Thrones?

I am very frail now, and the night has grown gye cold: the shoddily built walls of this provincial gaol, the last of a long series I have tenanted, offer little protection from the Norseland's biting winds. I think it unlikely I will live to see another dawn.

Soon, very soon, I shall die for the second time and, as James Bothwell, go at last to meet my Maker.

Elizabeth I ❦

A SECRET MURDER

Robert Franks

The Elizabethan period is too fascinating to pass by without exploring the scope for two further stories. In this one Elizabeth teams up with Sir Walter Raleigh to solve a murder and a missing map.

The "best-hated man in England" gazed proudly at his cabinet of curiosities. It contained two of everything: buckskin quivers bristling with feather-tipped arrows, exquisitely arched longbows, glossy beaver pelts, headdresses displaying a spectrum of colored plumage and sinister tomahawks whose dangerous blades gleamed in the flickering candlelight.

Six months ago, Sir Walter Raleigh (for such was the name of the "best-hated man in England") had requested the captain of a Virginia-bound ship to return to London with two stalwart braves. By bringing the Indians to Queen Elizabeth's court, Sir Walter hoped to rival or even surpass the sensation caused years ago when Martin Frobisher introduced Londoners to their first Eskimo.

The presence of the Indians would be a marvellous publicity gambit for Raleigh's fledgling colony. Virginia was only a toehold now, but Sir Walter had dreams of stout English boots stamping the soil far beyond the coast of the New World.

When the ship returned to London, Raleigh, wishing to surprise the court and queen, had ordered the captain to stow the Indians on board until nightfall. Under cover of darkness the Indians were transferred to Raleigh's private coach whose curtained windows hid them from curious eyes on their journey to the palace. Covertly, they were smuggled up a secret staircase and into Raleigh's rooms.

The next morning Raleigh asked the queen to invite the court to a noontide presentation of his devising which, he explained, would be most amusing and instructive. Tantalized, Elizabeth agreed.

The Indians' entrance was electrifying. Clad only in animal skins, brandishing tomahawks and longbows, Manteo and Wanchese strode over the polished floor to the queen's throne. Three ladies-in-waiting swooned. The guards, clutching their rapiers, edged closer to Her Majesty. But Elizabeth was made of sterner stuff. Boldly she left her throne to greet the Indians, who bowed as Sir Walter introduced them. Then as Raleigh had arranged beforehand, they performed an elaborate war dance. The palace walls reverberated with blood-curdling howls and spine-tingling ululations which galvanized the astonished audience. After this mesmerizing performance everyone at court was won over, except for the queen's Italian jester and two dwarves, who scowled at these pagan interlopers.

Being of a scholarly bent, Raleigh realized that the Indians' attendance at court offered a unique opportunity to study the Algonquin language. Therefore, the Indians were given their own rooms where they worked with the gifted linguist, Thomas Harriot, in the compilation of an Algonquin dictionary. Knowledge of the native tongue would be indispensable to new settlers.

To advertise the Indians further, Raleigh commissioned the royal artist to paint their portraits while the royal carpenter was asked to construct a glass-fronted cabinet to house their exotic paraphernalia. Sir Walter himself catalogued and arranged their weapons and habilements.

As he stared this evening at their unique belongings, Raleigh found himself especially fascinated by the tomahawks.

Manteo's consisted of a stone blade lashed by leather thongs to a haft of brass-studded hickory. This blade was sharpened to a flesh-lacerating edge. At the butt of the haft, a braided leather strip, drawn through a hole, was knotted around the shaft of an eagle's feather and a clutch of porcupine quills. In contrast, Wanchese's tomahawk was a unique combination of weapon and pipe. The bowl which held the tobacco was affixed above the metal blade. The smoker was treated to a pewter mouthpiece and five small holes had been drilled into the polished handle to allow the smoke to escape.

Raleigh's gamble had paid rich dividends. Investors, who had been wary of the New World, suddenly became interested in Virginia and beseeched Raleigh to grant them an audience. Fortune was smiling upon him, but even though he dabbled in alchemy, Sir Walter could not foresee that on the morrow the Indians would be implicated in a terrible crime or that Manteo's tomahawk, now a harmless exhibit for children to wonder at, would revert to its original purpose – the swift and painful onset of death.

Unconscious of the tragic events that were about to unfold that day, Raleigh had been in his own rooms at matins, admiring himself in a full-length mirror. He was dressed in a wheel ruff of enormous dimensions, a white satin pinked vest, brown velvet doublet, white trunk hose, satin-fringed garters, and buff coloured shoes decorated with jewels. With a rapier at his hip and a cloak sprinkled with pearls draped over his shoulders, he looked magnificent.

There was a knock at the door and his manservant entered with a note. Raleigh turned from his dazzling reflection and opened the paper. He recognized the crest and florid hand of the Duke of Nottingham. What the devil did Nottingham want with him now? Another favor from Her Majesty, no doubt. The note urgently requested Raleigh's presence. Sir Walter sighed. He tolerated the duke only because they shared a common passion for exploration.

After a last appraising glance in the mirror, Raleigh left for Nottingham's rooms. Perkins, the duke's man, opened the door and ushered Raleigh into the book-lined library. Raleigh was surprised to see that the duke was not alone. Seated next to him was Sir Roger Peele. A fabulously rich patron, Peele had given Raleigh financial assistance in the founding of the Virginia Colony.

The duke checked that the door was locked then returned to his guests. He bade Raleigh sit and pulled up a chair close to them. After waiting for a few moments and listening intently, he leaned forward and whispered, "Gentlemen, walls have ears and halls have tongues."

He listened again, cocking his head, then confided in low voice, "What I am about to tell you both is of the utmost secrecy. The three of us have for years sought the land of El Dorado. After untold disappointments," he sighed, "I have at last found the key to unlock that golden door. I have in my possession," his hand closed into a fist, "a map which will lead me – I mean us – directly to the city of gold. But I require your assistance in turning the key."

Raleigh looked at Sir Roger, whose eyes bulged.

"I will show it to you." The duke left the room.

"Is it possible?" Sir Roger asked in hushed tones.

"Anything is possible," Sir Walter said.

For years the three men had been entranced by the fabulous legend. Over the centuries, near the sacred lake of Manoa, the Indians of Guiana had anointed their king with oil and fragrant gums, then blown gold dust through hollow reeds over his entire body, transforming him into "El Dorado", or "The Golden One". Sprinkled with gold, the king boarded a raft which transported him to the middle of the lake. After intoning ritual prayers to the gods, the monarch dived in, washing off the aureate integument. This great king ruled over a vast city where every object, no matter how humble, was fashioned from gold. (At one point the city had adopted the name of its king.) The Spaniards had been searching for "El Dorado" for decades but were confounded by the riverine maze of the interior. Was the duke's map the Ariadne's thread they needed to reach their goal? Could the English better the Spanish?

The duke returned, carrying a rolled piece of parchment. After closing the door, he again made certain it was locked. He approached Raleigh and Peele and untying the red ribbon, slowly unfurled the parchment.

"Early this morning," the Duke began, "an agent of mine brought this map to me. It was drawn by a Spaniard named Abuljar. The sole survivor of an *entrada* into the jungle, Abuljar was half dead with fever when an Indian scout from 'El Dorado' came upon his emaciated body. Having never seen a white man and thinking him to be a god, the Indian restored him to health with miraculous herbs.

"When Abuljar had recovered the Indian put the Spaniard into his canoe and they travelled deeper into the jungle. After weeks of hardship, the canoe reached a huge lake on whose shores lay 'El Dorado'.

"Abuljar remained in the gilded *ciudad* for six months. He was treated like royalty, offered concubines and enjoying such delicacies as hummingbird and parrot stew. However, he was a man after my own heart. Abuljar was secretly plotting to relieve the citizens of their wealth. When the opportunity arose, he fled at night from the city in a stolen canoe. As he navigated this craft down the labyrinthine rivers, he drew this priceless map. He reached the coast after a hellish journey. A few months ago he finally returned to Spain. My agent caught wind of his incredible story in Seville and managed to secure this parchment before Abuljar was able to sell it to a wealthy *hidalgo*."

Raleigh saw a brownish stain in the lower left corner of the parchment.

Noticing his glance, the duke said dryly, "I did not inquire into my agent's methods. It was his task to bring me a map."

The map's detail was incredible. It not only displayed the Orinoco but named the numerous tangled tributaries and highlighted a southern effluent that led directly to Lake Manoa. No other maps contained such particulars. To hide their ignorance, geographers invariably populated this *terra incognita* with Amazons, cannibals and a strange tribe called the Ewaipanoma, whose eyes were in their shoulders and mouths in their chests.

"It is a marvel," Sir Roger whispered.

"I congratulate you, Nottingham," Raleigh said, attempting to keep envy out of his voice. "However, you are aware that the queen does not favor such rash ventures. It took all my powers of persuasion to convince her of the viability of the Virginia expedition."

"That is precisely why I asked you here, Sir Walter. You have the ear of the queen."

The duke had heard that Raleigh possessed more than this part of the queen's anatomy. But as Raleigh was the queen's favorite, the duke kept his own counsel.

"You must convince Her Majesty that we can reach 'El Dorado' before the Spaniards can."

"It is as good as done. But as you know, Elizabeth has been in a melancholic humour of late. The morrow would be a more suitable time to lay siege to her breastworks. May I take the map with me?"

The duke bristled. "I cannot possibly let it out of my sight. Come to me when her black bile has receded."

"Who else knows of this map?" Sir Roger asked in a concerned tone.

"Only my agent. He is on his way to the Continent."

"Conceal it well, then," Raleigh admonished the duke.

"I have an admirable hiding place," Nottingham boasted.

"Let it remain so. That map is worth a queen's ransom. On the morrow gentlemen, I will plant the legend in the queen's mind, and in a few short days it will bear fruit." He smiled. "Golden apples of the sun."

The three men laughed conspiratorially.

That afternoon, Raleigh sat in his study, composing an ode to the queen. Sweet words and rhymes always soothed her; she especially favored honeyed expressions of sorrow for supposed acts of treachery or infidelity. Dipping his quill in ink, he wrote and rewrote until he was satisfied. After an hour's work, he read:

> Distrust doth enter hearts but not infect.
> And love is sweetest seasoned with suspect.
> A secret murder hath been done of late:
> Unkindness found to be the bloody knife,
> And she that did the deed a dame of state,
> Fair, gracious, wise as any beareth life,
> Wounded am I but dare not to seek relief . . .

A knock at the door interrupted his reading. His servant entered with another note. This also bore the duke's crest, but the shaky writing was not Nottingham's. It was barely legible and ink spattered the bottom of the paper like drops of black blood. With difficulty Raleigh read, "Sir Walter, please come at once. A great tragedy has befallen the duke." It was signed Bartholomew Perkins.

"I had just stepped out for a few moments and when I returned I found him . . . like this, Sir Walter," Perkins moaned. "At first I could not believe my eyes. That tomahawk in his neck and the blood . . . I . . . I did not know what course to follow . . . If only I had been here . . ."

The servant's eyes welled with tears. Raleigh led him out of the bedchamber and seated him in a chair.

"You did the proper thing, Perkins. Remain here." Perkins buried his face in his hands.

Raleigh walked back to the bedchamber. The Duke of Nottingham lay on his back, three feet from the canopied bed. The tomahawk blade was lodged up to its hilt in his neck and his ruff and doublet were steeped in blood. Raleigh averted his gaze from the horrible staring eyes.

He immediately recognized the tomahawk's feather and porcupine quills. Around the body lay other objects which silently mocked his ambitions. A blood-tipped rapier lay by the duke's shoulder. Near its hilt a length of red ribbon snaked across the carpet. Just beyond the bed a corner of this carpet had been folded back revealing a small trap-door. Its hinged lid was open but even before peering into it, Raleigh knew it would be empty. He had been a fool to let the duke keep the map. Now all his splendid plans were smashed. Cursing himself bitterly, he returned to Perkins.

"Where were you when this happened?" Raleigh asked roughly.

Perkins hesitated.

"Come, man, this is murder. Speak!"

His face contorted by grief, the servant spoke haltingly. "His Grace asked me to deliver a confidential epistle to a . . . a certain lady this morning, just after you and Sir Roger left . . . I . . . I was gone only a short while. When I returned I found the duke . . . like this. I was so stunned that it took me a few moments to see that his hiding place was empty. Next I espied drops of what looked like blood leading into the duchess's boudoir. Fearing that the murderer still might be lurking about, I picked up the rapier and slowly crept into her room. Thank God, Sir Walter, it was as empty as the hiding place. But the duchess's bureau had been raped and her jewels stolen. I replaced the rapier, on the floor."

Suddenly Perkins rose from his chair and glared at Raleigh. "It must be your heathen savages. You should never have brought them here, Sir Walter, never! They will pay for this, and pay dearly, believe me."

Raleigh was startled by this outburst. "Under the circumstances, Perkins, I will excuse your insolence," he said haughtily. "Murderers can also wear powdered wigs and ruffs and speak the queen's English. Now tell me, what was in his hiding place?"

Perkins sat down wearily, his shoulders sagging. "Please forgive me, Sir Walter. Only letters of a private nature were hidden there. Last summer when the duchess was in Venice, the duke had workmen construct the secret trap-door. He confided in me in the eventuality that I might have to hide letters for him."

Raleigh knew, as did the rest of the court, save apparently for the duchess and Lord Carrington, of the duke's liaison with the lovely Lady Carrington. As the duchess had left a few days ago for her country estate, the duke was free to resume his amorous escapades with his *inamorata*.

"You saw nothing else in the hiding place this very morning?"

"No, the duke had gone out for a few moments. I was dusting the drawing room when he returned. I only saw him later when he gave me a note to deliver to Lady Carrington. If only I had not left him –"

"Never mind that," Raleigh snapped. "How did he seem?"

"Very pleased, yet restless. But he was always in such a mood when the duchess left for the country."

"What was in this note?"

Perkins sniffed. "I was not in the habit of reading the duke's letters."

"I wish my man was so virtuous. Do not leave the room, Perkins. I will send a guard to share your vigil."

On his way to her royal suite, Raleigh wrestled with the most satisfactory way to describe the afternoon's tragedy. He realized that at court, truth was as rare as a unicorn. Subterfuge, lies, machinations and intrigue were the court's coin of the realm. Telling the unvarnished truth made him feel like a counterfeiter.

Queen Elizabeth was playing the virginals when Raleigh was led into her privy chamber. He dreaded adding discord to her sweet harmonies. When she turned on the bench, she knew immediately from his troubled countenance that something untoward had occurred. Her hands lifted from the keys.

"What has happened?" she asked in a hollow voice.

"Tragic news, Your Majesty." As he recounted the theft and the duke's murder, the queen's mouth hardened and her delicate, bejewelled fingers closed into fists.

When he had finished she slammed her hands on the keys. With the chords still ringing in his ears, she barked, "As captain of the guard, is it not your duty, sir, to protect me and those around me? Is my court to resemble the last act of *Hamlet*, where the stage is strewn with corpses?"

"Only one corpse in this case, Your Majesty."

"Your jest is ill-timed." Her blue eyes, set in a white mask of lead, powdered eggshell, poppy seed and borax, blazed fiercely. "Why was he murdered? Was it for the incriminating letters?"

"Possibly, Your Highness." He paused. "But I believe it was for the map."

"What map? Make yourself clear, man! I cannot abide conundrums!"

He enlightened her about his meeting with the duke.

"And why was I not told of this?" she burst out. She rose from her bench and paced back and forth, the pearls on her magnificent gown glowing like remote stars.

"I know how you feel about such ventures," he said consolingly, "and thought that you would be displeased. I awaited the return of your good humour."

"My good humour has been banished, sir, as you may soon be," she snapped. "Was the thief after the map? Why not the compromising letters or the jewels? Was the theft merely a ruse committed by someone who harbored a personal grudge against the duke? He may have forced the duke to reveal his hiding place and merely took whatever it contained."

"That is plausible," Raleigh said, but the queen realized that his mind was fixed on the map. "Howbeit," he continued, "it seems coincidental that the robbery and murder occurred this very morning. The thief must have seen the map and purloined it."

The queen, following her own train of thought, pursed her lips. "The tomahawk obviously points to your Indians," she observed. "Do you believe them innocent or are you merely protecting your investment?"

"They know nothing of maps, Your Highness. Besides, they are not fools. They would not kill with the one weapon we associate with them."

The queen's pacing slowed. Her anger, though smouldering, was gradually giving way to curiosity.

"Who were the duke's enemies?" she asked.

"They are legion. He has ground his heel into many faces. The most recent victim was Dawson, the court artist."

"Ah, yes, Geoffrey Dawson. A talented man, but flawed by a violent temper. Only last week, the duke pleaded with me to dismiss him. Dawson had painted such an unflattering portrait of the duke that Nottingham refused to pay him. Heated words were exchanged. Dawson even threatened to kill the duke."

Raleigh shook his head. "The man is impossible. A fortnight ago I asked him to paint a portrait of the Indians. He had the gall to tell me that he only painted 'civilized' Englishmen, not savages. The offer of a princely sum finally convinced him. Still, after all this time he has barely begun the faces and torsos."

"His faults do not make him a murderer."

"But, Your Highness, he despises the Indians. In some fashion he learned of the map, stole the tomahawk and killed the duke. I am convinced of it."

"And what of this blood-stained rapier?"

"Perhaps the duke wounded his assailant before he was killed himself."

"These speculations are bootless. The murderer may have run the duke through. When the duke was forced to lead him to the jewels his lifeblood leaked out, drop by crimson drop. Did you examine the body for other wounds?"

"No," Raleigh admitted shamefacedly. "I assumed –"

"One cannot assume anything. We need facts." She stamped her foot on the floor. "Hard facts, not speculations that vanish like smoke. I must assist you in your investigation."

Raleigh gasped. "But, your Highness, it is hardly proper for the queen –"

"Damn propriety! I crave a diversion from the stultifying round of palatial politics. An investigation into a murder will be a welcome divertissement."

"But this is a dangerous undertaking. One man has been slain –"

"Have you ever known me to avoid danger? Listen, I will make you a wager. If you find the murderer before me, I will issue the letters patent, enabling you to find your precious 'El Dorado'. And if I win, which is of course inevitable, I will never let you forget my triumph. But time is of the essence, otherwise a scandal may ensue. Agreed?"

Raleigh smiled, recalling their most recent wager. He had boasted that he knew so much about tobacco that he could weigh its smoke. Wanting to deflate his pomposity, Elizabeth bet that he could not. With a hint of a smile, Raleigh called for scales. He pinched some tobacco from his pouch onto them, weighed the amount needed to fill his longstemmed pipe and tamping it into the bowl, smoked it. Next, he weighed the ashes. Subtracting the second weight from the first, he paused, then triumphantly proclaimed the answer. Elizabeth was so delighted by his demonstration that she commented. "I have heard of men who turned gold into smoke, but Raleigh was the first who turned smoke into gold."

Sir Walter excitedly agreed to this newly proposed wager, and left the queen's presence.

Hoping to reclaim the priceless map, Raleigh set to the task required of the captain of the guard. Deciding to first investigate the theft of the tomahawk, he cautiously approached the cabinet. As he opened the glass doors he saw the gleaming blade of Wanchese's tomahawk. Manteo's was conspicuously absent, but Raleigh knew well its location.

While Sir Walter was scrupulously searching the cabinet, the queen began her inquiries by visiting the duke's rooms. At the sight of the queen, Perkins nearly fainted. Only by holding on to the guard's arm did he remain vertical. The queen offered her condolences, then asked the guard to accompany her into the bloodied bedchamber. The sight of the severed throat shocked her. Her heart pounding violently, she gestured to the guard to remove the duke's doublet. As he did so, she approached the body, being careful of the spattered blood, which was visible just under the head, like a fringe of red lace. Though she owned 2,000 gowns she refused to stain this one.

His body was free of other wounds. Next, she examined the trap-door and then followed the sanguinary track to the duchess's rooms. Satisfied that the jewels were gone, she inspected the drawing room to ascertain if Perkins had dusted it as he claimed. This was the case. The queen returned to Perkins, offered her sympathies again and departed.

As she walked to the Indians' rooms, she attempted to picture the servant driving the tomahawk into his master's throat. Had he seen the duke hiding the map and, wishing it for himself, committed the murder? Yet what would Perkins do with the map? He had no resources to travel to Guiana. Besides he was an old family retainer and was devoted to the duke and duchess.

Still, she reminded herself, one should not assume anything. Men were such violent creatures; hideous demons slithered beneath saintly exteriors. Elizabeth ventured down the hallway towards the red men's rooms. She was eager to learn of their whereabouts at the time of the murder.

Her knock was answered by Thomas Harriot. After the initial shock of the unannounced royal visit, Harriot bade her enter.

She noted at once Harriot's heavily bandaged hand.

Following her suspicious glance, Harriot promptly explained, "It is nothing, Your Majesty. During my weekly fencing match with George Farqhar, my attention strayed and I was slightly injured." He led her into an adjoining room.

The pungent smell of smoke burnt her nostrils. Alarmed by the thought of a conflagration, Elizabeth looked at Harriot with concern. Then she espied Manteo and Wanchese sitting cross-legged on the floor, smoking long clay pipes. As they rose to welcome the queen, their taffeta suits rustled.

From a distance no wounds were visible, but their clothes could have hidden a myriad of gashes. She proceeded to tell Harriot of the murder by tomahawk but left out the map. Astonished at the news, he translated for the Indians. Their solemn faces did not change, but Manteo replied to Harriot in a cacophony of harsh gutturals. Was the savage confessing to the murder? Harriot said to the queen in a shaken voice, "Manteo wants to see the cabinet for himself."

The bizarre quartet marched down the tapestry-covered hall. Elizabeth watched the brave's face as he opened the doors. His bewilderment at the absence of his tomahawk seemed genuine. The Indians had visited the cabinet only yesterday to dust it, Harriot told her, and nothing was missing.

The only time the weapons had left the cabinet, Harriot elucidated, was when Dawson had borrowed the tomahawk and longbow last week. The court painter had insisted on using them as props in his painting. When he had finished with them, the Indians replaced them in the cabinet.

The three of them had been working in their rooms all day on their linguistic pursuits and were not aware of any disturbance. Harriot himself had left only for a quarter of an hour, around sext, to fence with his friend, then returned promptly to the Indians' quarters. Harriot turned to Manteo and Wanchese, rapidly uttering incomprehensible syllables. The Indians nodded in assent, a gesture they had only recently learned.

"You see, Your Majesty, that none of us knows anything about this appalling crime. I can personally vouch for my charges, as they for me."

The queen said reassuringly, "Of course, both Sir Walter and I believe in your innocence, Mr Harriot, but you know that rumours spread like smallpox." Then she added firmly, "By royal command you are henceforth under quarantine."

When she left, Elizabeth felt doubts nagging at her like an aching tooth. Though the Indians appeared innocent, what did she know of Thomas Harriot? He was a brilliant naturalist and linguist and an old friend of Raleigh's, but what of his relationship with the duke? She seemed to recall that he had once had a falling out with Nottingham. Could his alibi be trusted? In addition, could he have mistranslated, using other words which would have elicited nods of assent from the Indians? The cut on his hand was certainly suspicious, but would he have flaunted it? Gloves would have concealed any incriminating marks.

She also chastised herself for not observing Wanchese's face when the cabinet was opened. Could he have wielded Manteo's toma-hawk?

The queen left off in her ruminations. Although Mr Farqhar would undoubtedly have to be interviewed, first she wanted to gauge Sir Roger Peele's reaction to the tragic news. He was the only other one, besides the duke and Sir Walter, who knew of the map. Turning into another corridor she proceeded to his chambers.

When he heard the devastating news, Sir Roger bounded from his chair and exclaimed, "God's Wounds! We are ruined. We must find that damned map!"

"That is my intention, sir. Where were you early this afternoon?"

"So I am a suspect, too? I was in the yard." He smiled wryly. "Your Majesty was seated next to Walsingham."

She nodded. "Yes, bear-baiting always exhilarates me. But I did not see you. What animals were present?"

"Ursus was indisposed. A pack of greyhounds and an ape were substituted. I pitied the poor simian, though, being torn to pieces."

"You seem to regret the ape's demise more than the duke's death."

"I desire a kingdom, not a mere dukedom."

"Who would want the duke dead?"

"By the beard of Merlin, he was a cruel, arrogant varlet who broke many men as he amassed his fortune. Of course, any one of these could have killed him. A ruined rival mayhaps or a gambling crony who wished to wreak revenge on the duke for too great losses. Some accused him, behind his back, of cheating. Yet I believe the duke's agent is the one to seek. I have had similar dealings with such vermin. My advice, my Gloriana, is to search for this mysterious agent. I can see the vile, weasel-like knave bribing his way back into the palace, and creeping down the halls until he beholds the lethal edge of steel. I suspect that shedding blood was not new to him. There was a stain which looked like blood on the map. With one blow of the tomahawk the agent could regain the map and sell it again. A clever ruse."

"Ingenious, Sir Roger, yet I remain plagued by doubts. Why, if the agent wanted the map, did he not kill the duke immediately after receiving the gold? Why risk returning?" As an afterthought she asked, "By the way, you are not injured, are you? No, I can see not." With these words, she swept out of the room, heading to George Farqhar's chambers.

She knew as little about Sir Roger as she did of the Indians or Harriot. He was undeniably forthright in his desire for a kingdom. Would he have murdered for his "El Dorado"? Had he really been in the yard or had he merely sent a servant to see what was occurring and report back to him?

While the queen was thus occupied Sir Walter, having found nothing in the cabinet, paid a call on the ravishing Lady Carrington.

He found her lying seductively on a settee, fanning herself. Solely in the interests of his investigation he let his eyes rove over her porcelain shoulders and barely concealed bosom. No severed skin was visible, thankfully.

Without preamble he asked about her whereabouts this afternoon. "Did you receive a communication from the duke today?"

Lady Carrington hesitated. "I was in bed from prime to sext. I only just dressed," she said saucily. "Perkins brought a missive to my maid not long ago." Boldy, she added, "The duke and I have a rendezvous tonight." She purred, "While the cat is away –"

"I am afraid, my lady, that the male mouse will be unable to attend your nocturnal tryst."

"But he assured me in his note that he anxiously awaited me. Are you his emissary?"

"Nottingham's hourglass has run out of sand. Rather than an emissary, I shall be a pallbearer." He studied her lovely face and let his eyes roam over her charms. Then he added brutally. "He was found murdered."

She gasped and lay down her fan. "Murdered? Did that old harridan poison him? Did she find my letters?" Her fingers seized Sir Walter's wrist. He was surprised at their strength. Raleigh released her grasp with some effort.

"As far as I know, the duchess has not returned. But the letters, my lady, are missing."

"You must find them," she wailed. "If they fall into the wrong hands –"

"My hands will be the only ones to secure them. What did he write in his note?"

"I have it next to my heart." Reaching down into her decolletage she retrieved a folded paper and passed it to Raleigh. "My adorable Columbine, I count the hours til we meet. Love, Harlequin."

Raleigh arched an eyebrow. Certainly Nottingham was not guilty of usurping his place in the history of English letters.

"My lady, do you have any idea who could have murdered your –" he cleared his throat, – "Harlequin? A former beau of yours, perhaps?" Raleigh ventured.

She shrugged her beautiful shoulders. "Men are such fools. But the letters, Sir Walter?"

She pressed herself against him. He could easily have succumbed to her charms. After all, only by disrobing her could he be absolutely convinced of her innocence. But this was neither the time nor the place. He imagined repeating this scene just before he sailed for "El Dorado". The denouement would be different. Then, abruptly he stood up and, to her amazement, stalked out of her room.

As he headed for the palace gates, his face was grave. Could she have killed the duke? Her hands were strong. Or had she seduced one of her many admirers into acting as her accomplice?

At the gates, Raleigh questioned the guard on duty. The man told Sir Walter that he had indeed let the stranger into the palace early that morning. A tall, gaunt, clean-shaven fellow in a hooded black cloak, he bore a letter of introduction signed by Nottingham. He spent only a short time in the palace then left by the same gate. As far as the guard knew, he had not returned.

While Raleigh was questioning the officer, the queen came up. "Our paths were bound to cross, Sir Walter," she teased. "Have you inquired about the duchess?"

"I was just about to do so. James, has the Duchess of Nottingham returned?"

"Not to my knowledge, Sir Walter. She is due back in a fortnight."

"Well," Sir Walter said, following the queen back into the palace, "we can assume that the duchess did not effect a permanent divorce from her cheating spouse. She is one playing card that can be discarded from our hand."

"As I have said before, Water" – her affectionate sobriquet for Raleigh – "one cannot assume anything. The duchess may have been in disguise or she may have slipped up a secret stairway, like the one you used, if you recall, to smuggle the Indians into the palace."

Sir Walter grudgingly admitted this, then to recover his ground, asked in a taunting voice, "Any progress on other fronts, Your Majesty?"

"The murderer is one step closer to the scaffold," she smiled.

"Ah, it's a man, then? You have seen Lady Carrington?"

"I have yet to see her. However, I know you have."

"How?"

"That long blond hair adhering to your cape."

"You *are* a sleuth," he laughed.

"And what of you?"

"My lips are sealed. But you know of my prowess in alchemy. I will soon transform the duke's spilt blood into the hemp of the hangman's rope. But I cannot afford to waste time, lest time waste me."

Raleigh headed in the opposite direction he intended. When he saw the queen turn a corner leading to a staircase, he doubled back to Dawson's atelier. He prayed that she had not already seen Dawson. He wanted to pluck this goose himself.

The studio door was open. Redolent of turpentine, linseed oil and paint, the studio was cluttered with canvases, props, frames and plaster casts. Against one wall, Raleigh saw the controversial portrait of the duke. Indeed, it portrayed his vile character eloquently. Small wonder the duke had been incensed by it.

Along the south side a temporary wooden platform had been constructed to hold a dozen large earthenware pots containing plants

from Virginia. These formed the botanical backdrop for the Indians'
portrait. Dawson was working on that very canvas and when Raleigh
entered he saw to his surprise that both the faces and torsos of his
native showpieces were completed. The portraits were magnificent;
Dawson had brilliantly captured their primitive nobility. Wanchese
held a longbow and Manteo grasped his tomahawk.

"Good day, Mr Dawson," Raleigh said with false geniality.

"Sir Walter! This is a pleasant surprise." Dawson replied with an
edge to his voice as sharp as the palette knife he held in his hand.
"Observe our Indians. What is your opinion?"

"Superlative," Raleigh confessed.

Dawson grinned. "I will soon need those beaver pelts from your
cabinet, Sir Walter, to complete the portrait. The Indians have been
wearing blankets around their privates thus far. I must admit that
your Algonquins are excellent models. Their ability to remain
immobile must stem from their hunting skills."

Raleigh stroked his beard. "Yes, they approach their quarry
downwind. Their victim is totally unaware of their presence.
Suddenly they pounce. The kill is swift."

Raleigh watched as Dawson applied the knife to the canvas. His
paint-flecked hands bore cuts, but none were fresh.

"It is unfortunate that you will never finish the painting," Raleigh
said slowly, "as the Indians will not be available for future sittings."

"Not available? Are they returning to Virginia so soon?"

"No. They have been arrested."

"Arrested? For what?"

"Robbery and murder."

"You are jesting."

"Mr Dawson, have you been here all day?"

"Why, yes, except for a few moments. I was conversing with
Thomas Harriot when a servant brought me a note from Lady
Marchbanks. She asked to see me immediately about an urgent
matter. I left Harriot here and went to her, but when I arrived she
was in fact not expecting me. She professed no knowledge of the note
whatsoever. Curious, is it not?"

When Raleigh only stared at him, Dawson said in an uneasy voice,
"You do not believe that I am involved in this murder?"

"You did threaten the Duke of Nottingham's life."

"Nottingham, is it?" Dawson laughed sharply. "Good riddance."

"The murderer also stole something that was mine."

"I know nothing of it."

"Are you sure?"

"Sir Walter, I resent your insinuations. If you think I am involved in this, then find what belongs to you! Tear my studio to ribbons if that will satisfy you! Meanwhile, I have a painting to finish."

"You may have to finish it in the Tower," Raleigh said, "if I find what I am looking for."

"Threaten me all you like. I defy you to find anything! I am an artist, not an assassin."

Raleigh glared at the painter and turned on his heel. Searching the chaotic studio was going to be a daunting task, but Sir Walter was determined to find the map.

He started his quest against the south wall where dozens of rolled up canvases lay on a table. After discovering nothing there, Raleigh continued searching, becoming more destructive as his anger and frustration mounted. In his obsessive search he virtually ransacked the studio, until at last, breathing heavily and sweating profusely, he reached the stage.

Furious and exasperated, his jewelled shoes stamped up the stairs. He stopped when he noted clumps of dirt scattered on the floor behind one of the pots. The rest of the stage was spotless. Raleigh also saw, as he crossed the creaking planks, that the other pots had been watered, while the one with the dirt by its base was bone dry.

Raleigh's heart pounded. He could smell the tropical vegetation and see the shore of Lake Manoa and the shining roofs of the golden city. He thrust his rapier deep into the dry soil. It struck the branching roots, but when he thrust again it hit something hard. Withdrawing his rapier, he leaned it against the pot, and began to dig feverishly with his fingers.

"This New World plant has strange roots, Mr Dawson," he shouted. Dawson's brush was still as Raleigh's aching fingers scrabbled at the dirt. Suddenly he stopped digging. Wedged between the roots, Raleigh felt a small flat metal box. He dug with renewed fury and wriggled the box from the soil. Cleaning it off, he opened the lid and took out a folded parchment, a small packet of letters and a velvet bag.

"Eureka! Well, Mr Dawson, can you explain this?"

He opened the parchment, smiled, then withdrew a handful of sparkling jewels from the bag.

Dawson's jaw dropped.

"Nothing to say, Mr Dawson?" Raleigh held up a pearl necklace, This necklace will become your noose," he intoned. Raleigh held up his rapier. "In the name of the queen, I arrest you, sir, for the murder of –"

"Sir Walter!" the queen's shrill voice resounded through the studio like a trumpet fanfare. "I have found your map." The queen stood framed in the studio's doorway, exultantly holding a parchment aloft. Firmly planted behind her stood a royal guard and next to him, Thomas Harriot.

Sir Walter's jaw dropped.

As the queen, the guard and Thomas Harriot advanced towards the stage, Sir Walter stammered, "But, Your Highness, *I* have the map. And look, here are the jewels and the letters." He regained his composure. "Dawson is the murderer. You see, *I* have won!"

"No, Sir Walter, you won our last wager but this one you have lost," the queen retorted. "Mr Harriot has confessed. The map you hold in your hand is a merely a forgery planted by Mr Harriot. It is an illegitimate progeny. This is the duke's map. *I* have won!"

Dawson's fierce eyes locked with Harriot's. "That explains why I was called out of my studio! Harriot wrote that note, not Lady Marchbanks." Brandishing his palette knife, Dawson stalked threateningly towards Harriot, but the guard, armed with a halberd, intervened.

"Let me see both maps," Sir Walter said excitedly.

He bounded off the stage, strode to a cluttered table, swept paints and jars off its surface and grasping a square of canvas, lay his map upon it. The queen placed hers next to his.

"They are identical," Raleigh whispered, pointing with a trembling finger. "Even to the blood stain in the lower left."

The queen said, "Observe your stain closely. It is a burgundy color, yet on mine it is more brownish. Burnt umber, isn't it, Mr Dawson?

Dawson nodded, restraining his temper in the queen's presence.

The queen continued, "The burgundy stain is undoubtedly fresh blood." She glared at Harriot. "Is it yours, sir?"

Harriot exclaimed defiantly, "Yes, I have shed my blood. And I would shed more to possess that map."

"Thomas –" Raleigh began.

Harriot cried, "You were not the only one who desired fame and gold. For years I have been shunted aside as an impoverished scribbler. And what am I now, a schoolmaster to brutish savages. With the discovery of 'El Dorado' I would be respected, honoured and fêted. What right had that devil Nottingham to the map? I wanted," – his eyes brimmed with tears – "above all else, to be a bold maker of history, not its lowly reader. Thomas Harriot, the discoverer of El Dorado! Yes, I murdered him. I proclaim it!"

"Take him away," the queen said with a flourish.

Later that day, Raleigh read Harriot's confession with a heavy heart. Harriot wrote:

"My knowledge of the map of El Dorado was entirely serendipitous. At matins I was in the palace library searching the tall bookcases for a volume of Ovid. As it was still quite early, I was the only patron. Standing behind a tall bookcase I suddenly heard the door slowly creaking open. I peeked around the side of the case and saw two men enter furtively, close the door quickly behind them and bolt it from the inside. As their manner suggested something villainous. I remained hidden and mute.

"I recognized the duke, but the other man, a tall cadaverous fellow in a black hooded cloak, was unknown to me.

"The duke hissed, 'Well, where is it, man, where is it? Quickly! I must see it!' The other man, who stood in profile, smiled evilly. His face was a macabre, grinning skull. Slowly reaching under his cloak he removed a parchment tied with a blood-colored ribbon. As the duke grabbed for it, the man pulled his hand back and tucked the parchment in his doublet.

" 'First, the gold,' he growled.

"The duke threw back his cloak. In his hand he held a burlap sack, fastened at the top with cord. The duke smiled and lifting the bag, shook it to emphasize its weight. The stranger snatched it from his hands, fumbling at the cord with skeletal fingers then plunging one hand into the sack. His hollowed eyes blazed with greed as he immersed his bony fingers in the coins. He withdrew a gleaming gold doubloon and scrutinized it closely. Charon, receiving his obolus to ferry the dead across the river Styx, could not have looked more evil.

" 'The map!' Nottingham repeated. The duke seized the parchment from Charon and, with trembling hands, undid the ribbon.

With Charon grinning at him contemptuously the duke unrolled it. 'El Dorado,' the duke breathed. 'At last, it's mine. El Dorado.' He pressed the parchment to his heart.

"My body tensed. I knew of the duke's obsession with El Dorado. Years before I had worked for him briefly, cataloguing his personal library. However, finding him to be a contemptible blackguard I soon left his employ. But I still remember the tantalizing references to the location of 'El Dorado' in Leon's *Cronica del Peru*, Gomara's *Historia General de los Indias*, and Thevet's *Singulaterez de la France Antartique*.

"After a moment, the duke, still clutching the map to his breast, realized that Charon was still there, letting the coins run through his fingers.

" 'You have your lucre,' the duke snarled, 'now get out!' Charon sneered and tying up the sack, tucked it under his cloak. Turning sharply he undid the bolt, opened the door, poked his black hood out and exited with feline swiftness. Rebolting the door the duke looked rapturously at the parchment. Then carefully concealing it he too left the library. As the door closed behind him I came out of my hiding place.

"Suddenly I was seized by a fit of the ague. Trembling and feverish, I saw myself plunging a dagger into the duke's breast and stealing the precious map. With the words 'El Dorado' flaming in my brain like a whitehot jar fired in a kiln, I left the library.

"In my rooms, I paced back and forth, evolving my murderous plan. What right had Nottingham to the glory and the gold? Though temporarily mad, I also had the cunning of the mad. I must throw the blame, like a gladiatorial net, upon someone else. Thoughts of the vile duke, recalled to me his quarrel with Dawson and this thought engendered another about the Indians. Only last week I had seen Manteo and Wanchese replacing their longbow and tomahawk in their cabinet. A tomahawk would be a perfect weapon. I could feel its blade biting into the duke's flesh.

"I left my room and dashed to the cabinet. The hall was empty and it took but a moment to remove the tomahawk. I raced back to my rooms and practised striking with the tomahawk. Then I realized that if Sir Walter, as captain of the guard, investigated the duke's murder, he would not be long fooled by my subterfuge. His partiality to the Indians was well known. I needed a second scapegoat. Dawson's face rose up before me. Still trembling, I sat down and planned my strategy. (This must have been the time, as I later learned, when Sir Walter and Sir Roger were viewing the map.)

"At last I was ready. Hiding the tomahawk under my cloak where I could feel its cold metal against my anguished heart, I crept to the duke's rooms.

"Dame Fortune was with me. The duke himself opened the door, meaning that his man was out. I had no time to waste, so I immediately demanded the map. He was shocked and professed that he had no map. Was I mad? I threw back my cloak, revealing Manteo's tomahawk. When I brandished the razor-sharp blade in front of his vicious face his bravado disappeared. Like all bullies, he was merely a coward.

"I followed him to his bedchamber. Kneeling by the bed he fumbled with the corner of the fringed carpet and lifted it. A trap-door was revealed. Grasping the metal ring, he opened the door and reached in. He removed the precious parchment and with great reluctance, he gave me the map. As I untied the ribbon, he suddenly dived to the wall and seized a rapier, which was hanging by the bed. The duke lunged at me and I dodged, but his rapier cut me on the hand. Furious, I knocked the rapier from his hand and smote him, bringing the heavy tomahawk down on his soft neck.

"He dropped like a felled tree. Though my hand was bleeding, I had to work with dispatch. From the trap-door I took out a small bundle of letters. I would read these later. First I had to find the duchess's jewels. I dashed to her room. I knew that she had likely taken some of her baubles with her on her journey, but as the roads were plagued by highwaymen, she probably left the most valuable ones here. At last I found them in a bureau. I looked at them as greedily as Charon had gazed at the doubloons. These jewels would ferry two savages across the river of death. When the good lords and ladies found the duke murdered by tomahawk they would accuse the Indians of stealing the duchess's precious stones. I prayed that even Raleigh's support of them would be of no avail.

"Staunching my bleeding hand with my handkerchief, I fled. Back in my chambers, I bandaged my cut, then examined the map. It was everything I had dreamed of: a royal road to a fortune. The letters from Lady Carrington I could use later for blackmail. Lord Carrington, who was fighting in Ireland, might be interested in their contents. But now I needed an alibi for my cut. I was concerned that Sir Walter, who would, in all likelihood, be called in on the case, would see the blood-stained rapier and realize that the murderer had been wounded. I then realized that I should have taken the rapier with me.

"Then I remembered my weekly fencing match with Farqhar. I hid the plunder, put on gloves and fenced with Farqhar in his rooms. I always enjoyed these matches, as I was a far superior swordsman and always defeated my mediocre opponent. Today he would help save me from the gallows. I let him wound me, but I bungled it by turning too sharply. He sliced me above the wrist, instead on my gloved hand. After he bandaged me, I returned to my rooms, changed my blood-spattered shirt and rolled the sleeve of a fresh one down over the wound. Then I sat down to copy the map.

"Because of my cuts and fever, my task took longer than I wished. When I was done, I reopened the wound on my hand and let a drop of blood spill onto the parchment. It was not exactly the same as that on the Duke's map, but I believed that if Sir Walter should investigate he would think this was the original.

"Now I had to deal with the court painter.

"I wrote a note addressed to Dawson, then called for a servant. He was to report to Mr Dawson's studio in ten minutes, bringing the note with him. I found a small metal box, placed the spoils in it and tucking it under my cloak, headed for Dawson's studio.

"I sat down on a chair and when Dawson was not looking, hid the box in a rolled canvas. After conversing with the painter for about ten minutes the servant came in. Dawson read the note, and excused himself. This gave me the opportunity to hide the box. But where? Then I saw the large pots. Noticing that all of them were dry, I liberally watered the plants with a can I found on the stage. But the one nearest the stairs I did not water. After burying the box in the dry soil, I purposely left some of the dirt I had scooped out remain on the stage. Then I wrote a note to Dawson, informing him that I had forgotten an important appointment.

"Back in my room I was content. When Raleigh found the map and jewels, Dawson would certainly be arrested and tried for his crimes. By that time I would be on the high seas.

"I was working with the Indians in their rooms when there was a knock on the door. Was it Raleigh? I opened the door to the queen, a guard and Dr Templeton, the royal physician.

"She greeted the Indians then said in a friendly, concerned tone,

" 'I told Dr Templeton of your wound and he asked to see it. Such wounds can become inflamed,' she said. I demurred, claiming that it was only a scratch.

" 'Mr Harriot, you are too valuable a man for me to lose. I insist. Doctor?'

"Templeton stepped forward and undid my bandages.

" 'Royalty has miraculous powers of healing, You know of scrofula, also called the "King's Evil". It is cured by royal touch.' With her slender fingers she palpated my wounded hand, while firmly gripping my forearm with her other hand.

" 'You are very hot, Mr Harriot. Have you fever? And what is this swelling?' She felt the bandage under my sleeve. 'Yet another wound?'

" 'Yes,' I confessed, 'but I was too embarrassed to admit it. Farqhar was a devil with his rapier today.'

" 'You are lying, sir.'

" 'What?'

" 'I have just come from George Farqhar. Remembering that one should never assume anything, I asked Farqhar exactly where he had wounded you. I fully expected that he would reply "on the hand." But when he told me that the wound was on the forearm, I knew that you had lied. Why? Did this lie conceal a greater crime?' The queen slowly rolled up my sleeve. 'This wound was from the Duke's rapier.'

"I denied this vehemently.

" 'Look at me, sir and tell the queen of England that you are not the murderer.'

"I hesitated.

" 'I did not mean to kill him. I was mad.'

" 'I will be the judge of that,' the queen said."

Raleigh put down the confession and sighed deeply.

That evening the queen, basking in her triumph, invited Sir Walter to her rooms. Despondent over having been duped by an old friend, and embarrassed at losing the wager, he presented a gloomy prospect.

"Be of good cheer, Sir Walter," the queen exclaimed. "I can do nothing about Harriot's fate; he is guilty of murder. However, I have changed my mind about the wager. I have decided to issue the letters

patent. All the ships and crews you require for your voyage will be at
your disposal. 'El Dorado' will be yours!"

Overcome, he knelt before her.

"I have only one condition."

"Your Majesty?"

"When you return, laden with gold, also bring the king himself. I
should rather like to meet this 'El Dorado'.

Ferdinando, King of Man 🦅

THE GAZE OF THE FALCON

Andrew Lane

This Elizabethan story includes one of our forgotten kings, and a tragic one at that. For centuries the Isle of Man remained a separate fiefdom with the sovereignty of the island bestowed upon the Earls of Derby. They were originally called Kings of Man but in later years, in deference to the Tudor monarchs, they renounced the title and were called Lords of Man. Amongst them was Ferdinando Stanley, who was also descended from Mary Tudor, the sister of Henry VIII, and thus had a distant but genuine claim to the throne. Ferdinando, however, was staunchly loyal to Elizabeth and this was his undoing. His fate is the subject of the following story.

I must include, though, an interesting aside. In this story the "detective" is none other than William Shakespeare. There are those who believe Shakespeare did not write the plays ascribed to him and suggest many other contenders. Amongst them is William Stanley, the brother of Ferdinando, who succeeded him as Lord of Man. If you are interested in stories involving William Shakespeare or related to his plays may I unashamedly recommend my two companion volumes, Shakespearean Whodunnits *and* Shakespearean Detectives.

*   *   *

4th April, 1594

As the cold, Lancashire wind ruffled his hair and sent freezing fingers questing through the gaps in his doublet, William Shakespeare realized he was being watched. It was an unmistakable feeling, like the pricking of a fur collar at the back of his neck. Working for Sir Francis Walsingham in the conspiracy-ridden environs of the Court sharpened a man's senses. Somewhere close by, someone dangerous was observing him.

He turned suddenly, gazing up at the windows of Lathom House. Somewhere in the darkness behind that leaded glass perhaps? His gaze flicked from window to window, trying to pick out the pale glow of a face or the glint of morning light on watching eyes, but he could see nothing. The more he looked, the more he doubted himself. Not on the fact that he was being watched – the sensation was too strong – but on the location of the watcher. That pitiless vision was not emanating from the house.

He turned slowly, his eyes scanning the sculpted gardens and low hedges that formed the setting for the perfect jewel of the Earl of Derby's manor house. He *knew* he was being watched, but he could see no one. The servants were in the house, setting out breakfast; the Earl and his followers were out hunting. Shakespeare was the only living creature in the vicinity.

He glanced toward the dark line of forest that surrounded the house. If the watcher was there then he was too far away to do Shakespeare any harm. The land still belonged to the earl, and did for many miles, so if he was there he was either a trespasser or one of the earl's own men. And given the way the earl had rode out to the hunt that morning, surrounded by retainers armed with crossbows, any trespasser would be unlikely to face a magistrate.

And yet . . .

And yet the watcher wasn't in the forest either. Shakespeare had the distinct feeling that there was a direct line of sight between them, not something broken up by the boles of trees and by the low bushes that buffered the house from the forest. Puzzling. Very puzzling.

A faint chime of bells from above made him flinch. He glanced up, raising an arm reflexively as if to ward off a blow, and then laughed.

Far above his head a falcon hovered like a scrap of black rag on the wings of the wind, the brass bells around its leg signalling its location to its master. What he had sensed had been its finely focused predator's gaze as it scanned him and decided whether or not he counted as prey. As he watched, it folded its wings and plummeted through the air, vanishing behind the line of the forest, and the sensation of being watched vanished with it.

There was such a thing as having senses that were *too* finely honed.

Still chuckling, he walked on, through the rose bushes that the earl's gardeners were training and clipping into a maze. It would be many years before the maze was high enough to shield its design from the eyes of its walkers, but the earl was a man who thought ahead.

As he turned the corner of the house, Shakespeare caught sight of one of the earl's gardeners bending low over a mass of silvery leaves. The mingled smells of sage, lavender and mint made his nose twitch and his stomach rumble. "How goes it?" he asked as he approached.

"Back-breaking work, young master," the gardener sighed as he straightened. His wispy white hair blew around his eyes, and he reached up to brush it away with a hand that was as gnarled and as brown as a tree root. "But I've spent my life in this garden, I have, in the service of the earl and of his father before him, God rest his soul, and I wouldn't have it any other way."

Shakespeare nodded. "Now it is the spring, the weeds are shallow-rooted," he said. "Suffer them now and they'll overgrow the garden and choke the herbs."

"That's true enough." He gestured at a pile of weeds on the path beside him. "Although life would be simpler if we kept the weeds and pulled up the herbs, they grow that fast." He held his hand, palm out, toward Shakespeare. The skin was blistered and red. "Nettle-rash, young master. Dock leaves help take the sting out, but there's a precious sight more nettles in these beds than there are dock leaves."

His mouth half-way open to make some rejoinder, Shakespeare suddenly noticed a patch of brown fur, half-hidden by the sage bushes. Bending, he pushed the stems aside. The stench of maggoty meat swamped the smell of the herbs, making his gorge rise.

Lying on the ground beneath the bush was a rabbit, about the size of Shakespeare's hand. The fur around its muzzle was stained black, and parallel gashes marked its back. Its eyes had already decayed back into sticky sockets.

Involuntarily, Shakespeare's gaze flicked upwards to the clear blue of the morning sky. "Hunting must be good around here," he said, "if the earl's falcons can afford to leave their discarded kills lying around for days on end."

"Aye, young master," the gardener said, but there was a note of uncertainty in his voice. "Yet that creature wasn't there an hour ago, I swear it."

Shakespeare straightened up, frowning. "From the smell of it that animal has been dead for three or four days. Falcons don't pick up carcasses and throw them down willy-nilly. They only catch live prey."

"I know." The gardener shook his head. "I know. But look at the marks of the claws in its back."

For a moment he couldn't see what the gardener was referring to, and then a shiver ran through him as he noticed.

The gashes where the falcon's claws had ripped into the rabbit were filled with fresh blood, coagulating into purplish clots around the edges.

Shakespeare stared at the rabbit for a few moments more, at the bright red blood on its back and the sunken sockets of its eyes, and then walked away rapidly, his empty stomach suddenly burning with acid. He could feel the gardener's gaze on the back of his neck, prickling like that of the falcon, but he didn't turn back. He did not understand what he had seen, but there had to be an explanation. Everything had an explanation.

He kept walking, his breath steaming in the chilly morning air, until the gardener was lost around the corner of the house.

After a while, Shakespeare thought he could hear the sound of raised voices out in the depths of the forest. He turned his path toward the front of the house, and as he approached the main doors a small group of horsemen and accompanying hounds broke from the trees and cantered toward him. Most of them had hooded bastardes or sakers resting on their outstretched arms, their leather jesses preventing them from flying off. One of the horsemen was riding close beside another, supporting him in the saddle. Shakespeare halted and watched them approach, concern blossoming in his breast.

"My lord!" he cried as the identity of the supported horseman became clear. "What has befallen you?"

"My brother has been taken ill," said William Stanley from his position supporting the Earl. He was burlier than his brother, and concern furrowed his staunch, honest face.

"A pox on that," snapped Ferdinando Stanley, now the Fifth Earl of Derby, but still Lord Strange in Shakespeare's mind. He was ashen faced, and there were traces of dark vomit staining his jerkin. "I should have –" He paused and bit his lip. "I should have known better than to hunt on an empty stomach. A cramp, that's all. It will pass."

"No doubt, my lord," another man said. He supported a bastarde and the earl's own falcon on his gauntletted forearm. "But the sooner we get you to bed and a doctor attending you the better. Especially –" He paused, and Shakespeare noticed a guarded look passing between some of the hunters. "– Especially considering how worried Lady Alice will be," he finished weakly.

Shakespeare helped support the earl while William Stanley dismounted. Ferdinando Stanley leaned closer and murmured, "My apologies for this inconvenience, Will. We will have to talk about the new season's plays and the disposition of the Company at some later time."

"I am at your lordship's disposal," Shakespeare murmured.

"It was a fine hunt – a *damn* fine hunt. Have you ever gone falconing, Will?"

"Never, my lord – although I do know a falcon from a heronshaw."

Weykin draped the earl's arm around his shoulders, and together he and Shakespeare manhandled the earl into the house. The servants flapped around helplessly like a flock of rooks, but together the two men half aided and half dragged the earl to his bedroom where the beautiful and regal Lady Alice shooed them from the room.

Ferdinando Stanley, Fifth Earl of Derby, formerly Lord Strange, died twelve days later.

16 April, 1594

Shakespeare saw the earl once more, on the very day he died. The sharp, sweet smell of decay lay over everything and, as he was ushered into the darkened bedroom, Shakespeare had to quell his churning stomach.

The earl was almost unrecognizable. His skin was blistered and bloody, his beard caked with bile and the bony edges of his skull showed beneath the thin sheet of his skin, but his eyes were alert. He watched as Shakespeare approached the bed.

Doctor Case moved from the bed to intercept him. He held a clove-studded orange beneath his nose. "God will embrace the earl to His bosom before the day is out," he said quietly. "Knowing this, he asked to see you."

"Has he –?"

Case shook his heavy head. "He has kept nothing down since the hunt. Not solids, not liquids, nothing. We have bled him and purged him, we have tried him with poultices and with tinctures, we have given him bezoar, pearls dissolved in wine and the heart and liver of a viper, but to no end. He sinks lower, minute by minute."

Fighting his way through the miasma of putrefaction, Shakespeare came to the edge of the bed and stared down at the face of the man he had loved as his patron. Gratefully he accepted the handkerchief that was pressed into his fist by one of the other physicians. Holding it up to his face, he breathed deeply of the lavender scent.

The earl's lips moved. The dry skin cracked as Shakespeare watched, and a clear liquid seeped out and down his chin. "Leave us," he breathed. His breath stank like a draught from the very mouth of hell.

Obediently and, Shakespeare sensed, with some relief, the physicians withdrew to the open window.

"Will, as you love me, you must help me."

Shakespeare opened his mouth to frame a reassuring reply, but Ferdinando Stanley spoke again.

"I know I am beyond any mortal help now," he whispered, his voice as soft as the wind in the trees, "but listen to me. This was no accident. I have been poisoned."

"Murder most foul!" Shakespeare murmured.

"Listen closely, Will, for only you and my brother will know of this. I wrote to William Cecil before I left London, having learned of a conspiracy to murder the queen and replace her with a Catholic monarch. Kit Marlowe discovered something of the plot last year, and warned me of it before he was done to death."

"Why warn *you*?" Shakespeare asked, keeping his voice low so that the group by the window did not overhear him. "Why not warn William Cecil?"

The earl's mouth stretched into a thin parody of a smile, sending fresh rivulets of fluid trickling down his cheeks. "Because the secretary of state would immediately have imprisoned my father and myself as chief suspects. Kit knew we were not involved, and wished to protect us."

Shakespeare nodded slowly. It made a horrible kind of sense. Henry, Fourth Earl of Derby, had been rumoured to have been a closet recusant and Catholic sympathizer, and as the great-nephew of Henry VII he would have had a good claim on the throne of England, had Elizabeth died. "And what of your father's death?" he asked. "Has this matter any bearing on that?"

Ferdinando Stanley blinked slowly: probably the closest he could come to nodding. "I believe he was approached by the plotters and sounded out as figurehead for their schemes. He would have refused: he loved the queen, as I do. Rather than have their plot exposed, they killed him."

"And how do you know all this?" Shakespeare asked, already knowing the answer.

"Because they approached me last month," the earl whispered.

"And you refused them?" Shakespeare said urgently, unsure even as he said the words whether he was inquiring or demanding.

"I did," Stanley sighed. "I love the queen, and would not see her come to harm." He laughed suddenly: a dry, racking sound that convulsed his body. "Often did I tell her that I would give my life for her. Now it looks as if I have."

"You fear you have been poisoned by these papish plotters?"

"As with my father before me, they fear exposure now that they know where my sympathies lie."

Shakespeare leaned closer, daring the rancid odours of Stanley's body. "Who are they? What are their names? You know I will not rest until I bring them to justice."

"Richard Hesketh, Will Houghton, John Garside . . . My brother William has the list. Talk to him. I would ask him to avenge me, but he knows little of intrigue. I know you have worked for Walsingham in the past as an agent of government: you have experience in these things. For the love you bear me . . . see my murderer to the gallows."

A movement to one side made Shakespeare look up. Doctor Case was approaching the bed, his face wrinkling as he moved away from the fresh air by the window. He held the clove-encrusted orange to his nose and talked around it. "Master Shakespeare, I pray you do not tire the earl. He will need all his strength for the trial ahead."

"I am dying, sawbones," Stanley snapped with something like his old fire. "Let me at least say my piece before I go."

Case retreated with remarkable speed to where the group of physicians were talking, heads together. Shakespeare gazed at them for a long moment, not actually seeing them but casting over in his mind what the earl had said. Something about the whole affair tugged at the back of his mind. Like the gaze of the falcon twelve days ago, he was bothered by something but could not pinpoint its location.

"If you knew that this Hesketh and his minions would try to do you harm," he mused, "then what precautions did you take against their plotting?"

"You saw the group that went a-hunting with me – all trusted men, and all armed. I have travelled nowhere without them. And my food has all been tasted by my servants and my brother before I ate it for months now – I watched them do so." He grimaced, and the sight was so much like the bare grin of a skull that Shakespeare had to look away. "I am not a cowardly man, Will, you of all people know that, but I was determined to live to see their traitorous heads on Tower Bridge. And yet . . . And yet they found a way to kill me. If I had not all the charms and amulets that Doctor Dee could provide, I would almost believe it to be witchcraft." His stick-thin arm moved up his chest, his hand like a bundle of twigs grasped feebly for something beneath the coverlet. "Look," he said, holding a brown object suspended on a length of silk around his neck out to Shakespeare, "a spider in a nutshell, lapped in silk. Proof against all kinds of devilry."

Shakespeare was not looking at the nutshell. He was more concerned with the weeping, black-edged holes in Stanley's wrist. They looked as if someone had taken a corkscrew and jabbed it several times through the skin.

"Enough of this talk," Stanley murmured, his eyes closing. "I grow weary. Tell me of the Company, Will. How fare Lord Strange's men?"

"We continue to be successful, and a credit to your name, my lord. Kit's play *The Jew of Malta* went down well again last month, going some way toward reclaiming his reputation, and we have been asked to perform several comedies before the Queen at Christmas."

"And you, Will? I trust you are writing for the Company now that Kit is no longer able to provide?"

Shakespeare shrugged, knowing that Stanley could not see him. "I am attempting a short comedy about the war in France, my Lord, entitled *Love's Labours Lost*."

"Good. Good." Stanley frowned slightly. His eyes were clouded now, and his face knotted in confusion. "You know what I require of you, Will? You do understand? We have shared secrets together, Will. Remember the School of Night? Remember the oaths we spoke? I pray you, avenge me."

Shakespeare glanced nervously over at the physicians, but they were too far away to hear Stanley's weak voice. His membership of the School of Night was not something he wished bandied about in the hearing of others. Walter Raleigh's little group of atheists had come in for some rather unpleasant scrutiny over the past few months. So far Shakespeare had managed to keep his name from William Cecil's notice and he wished to keep it that way. The earl would not normally have spoken of it in the company of others: his illness – or his poisoning – had made him clumsy. Shakespeare could only hope that he had not already said too much within the hearing of others.

Stanley suddenly convulsed on the bed, his chest rising and his limbs jerking wildly. Bile and a trickle of dark, tired blood splattered down his chin. Doctor Case rushed to Stanley's side from the window, closely followed by the other physicians. They gathered around Stanley like crows around a carcass, and Shakespeare found himself pushed back, away from the bed. He was not unhappy at that. Death had been hovering over Stanley for days, like a pitiless falcon, and if it chose now to attack he would rather not be in the room when it happened. Quietly, unnoticed, he left.

In the twelve days that Ferdinando Stanley had lain ill, Shakespeare had paced what felt like every inch of the house, the grounds and the nearby forest. He knew the location of every portrait on every wall, every rose bush and hollyhock, every lightning-blasted trunk and mossy oak. Ferdinando Stanley had been his friend and patron since Shakespeare had joined Lord Strange's Men at the Shoreditch Theatre as an actor and general dogsbody. Stanley – Lord Strange in those days – had encouraged him to write plays for the company, first in conjunction with Kit Marlowe and then by himself. Shakespeare owed him everything.

And now it was all thrown into chaos by one of the interminable and endless intrigues that bred like lice in the dark recesses of Elizabeth's court.

His footsteps turned, as they had tended to do more and more over the past few days, toward the garden. The weather was warmer than when he first arrived, and there was less of a wind. The trees whispered gently. A flock of seven magpies chattered as they flew overhead to alight on the eaves of the manor house.

The old gardener was busy with a spade, planting a small shrub in the shade of what appeared to be a nettle bush. Shakespeare had often passed the time of day with him in his peregrinations, and so deliberately walked over to where the old man stood.

"I thought you were removing all the weeds from the garden," he called, "and yet you are ignoring the biggest one I have seen since I arrived."

The old man looked up and grinned toothlessly. "The strawberry grows underneath the nettle," he said, indicating the bush, "and wholesome berries thrive and ripen best neighboured by fruit of baser quality. Sometimes there is wisdom in leaving weeds where they be."

"And gentler on your hands, I'll be bound," Shakespeare rejoined.

"That's not something I need worry about any more." The gardener raised his arm, and Shakespeare was struck by the sight of the single leather glove that he was wearing on his left hand. More of a gauntlet than a glove, it covered most of his forearm as well. The material was singed around the top, but it was still a fine piece of apparel.

"Found it on the bonfire," the gardener said with pride. "Fits me perfectly, it does." Seeing Shakespeare's expression, he added defensively, "I didn't steal it, for t'was being thrown away."

"Yes," Shakespeare said quietly, remembering the birds that Ferdinando Stanley had been hunting with the day he was taken ill. "But why was it being burned?"

"There's some tears in the cloth here, young master," the old man said, eagerly turning the wrist of the glove to display four holes that had been punched through the tough leather. "I reckon that whatever lord found this damage to his fine glove, he decided straight away to buy himself a new one, so he threw this one out."

"But why *burn* it?" Shakespeare mused. "And why burn just one?"

The old man looked so crestfallen that Shakespeare patted him on the shoulder. "Ignore me. You keep the glove. You deserve it, and nobody can deny that."

"You sure nobody will mind?"

"If anyone complains, send them to me," Shakespeare said with some bravado. He was suddenly feeling giddy, as if he had drunk a goblet of warm sack on an empty stomach. Things were beginning to fit together in patterns he had not been expecting. "Thank you, my friend," he said. "You've been more help than you know."

Later, Shakespeare was at a loss to say where he had walked after leaving the gardener. He was so sunk in his thoughts, assembling the elements of a fantastic plot against the earl in the same way that he would assemble the dramatic elements of a play, that he paid no attention to his surroundings. Eventually, with the characters, their various driving forces and the props they would have needed all assembled in his mind, he found himself at the back of the house.

All he lacked now was a denouement.

The stables were busy with farriers and grooms, and he noticed almost automatically that all the horses were present in their pens. There was nobody present in the darkened stone building that housed the various birds – the falcons, the bastardes, the sakers and sacrets, the lanners and the lannerets. They watched him with glittering eyes as he passed along the row of wooden bars. The sharp smell of bird lime, like *sal ammoniac*, made his nostrils twitch and his eyes water.

The last but one cage was empty. Odd that he remembered all the cages as having been filled seven days before. One bird was missing, and as all the horses were present it was unlikely that anyone was out hunting. And that meant –

"Master Shakespeare."

He turned rather faster than decorum would have allowed, his heart fluttering within the cage of his chest. "My lord."

The burly form of William Stanley stepped forward into the small building. The light was behind him, shadowing his face. "I understood you not to hunt."

"Not with birds," Shakespeare said carefully. "But I was wondering what happened to this one." He indicated the empty cage. "The earl's falcon: a fine specimen, as I recall."

William Stanley's voice was calm, but Shakespeare was used to actors and their ways and could hear the tension underlying it. "Alas, the poor creature broke a pinion. We had to have it destroyed."

"Burned perhaps, like Lord Stanley's gauntlet?" Shakespeare ventured without thinking, and then cursed himself beneath his breath.

William Stanley stood watching Shakespeare for a moment, hands clasped behind his back. The meagre light penetrating the slats of the roof illuminated his eyes, making them glitter watchfully. "You are an intelligent man, Master Shakespeare," he said eventually. "Your plays are popular in London, I understand. When my brother dies, I shall inherit the title of the Earl of Derby. I am sure that it has crossed your mind that your Company, so well patronized by the present earl, might be at risk. That risk might be . . . mitigated . . . if you were amenable to conveying certain messages through the plays the Company puts on – placing what might seem to be unpopular opinions in the mouths of your more heroic characters, or basing your plots around the more neglected areas of our history. Do you understand me?"

Shakespeare gazed into William Stanley's eyes for a moment. "Playwrights are oft accused of ambiguity and excessive wordiness, so let me be absolutely clear. I will not use my plays as vehicles for your abhorrent papist dogma. I serve and love the queen."

William Stanley pursed his lips and nodded. "As I expected. We have had little luck with our approaches this year, I fear. We will have to select those we approach more carefully in future. Might I ask what gave us away?"

Shakespeare shrugged. "Would it make any difference if I enlightened you?"

"It might delay your own demise for a few moments longer."

"A fair point, and one exceptionally well made. In point of fact, the matter that indicated your guilt is the amount of time that your brother is taking to die."

William Stanley frowned. "Explain yourself."

Shakespeare took a deep breath, feeling himself slip into the frame of mind he used when on stage at the Shoreditch. This looked as if it might be the performance of his life. "If we assume that the earl was poisoned in order to stop his mouth," he began in a deliberately uninflected tone, "and ignoring for the moment the mechanism by which it was delivered, then why choose a poison that takes so long to kill? The answer is obvious – because the assassins *wanted* it to take that long. Why? Again, the answer is simple once the right question is asked – because they actually *wanted* the victim to talk. Whatever the victim said must, therefore, be discounted. And what did the victim say? He named his murderers."

William Stanley nodded as if in encouragement. "Go on."

"The earl suggested I consult you over the names of the people he wished to be brought to justice – Richard Hesketh, John Garside and William Houghton. Once I decided they were, in fact, innocent, I had to look around for another murderer. That was when I realized the significance of the glove and the falcon. The earl knew that he was the target of base and foul murderers, and was taking precautions. His food was tasted – by you, as well as by his servants – and when riding he was always accompanied by armed guards. Therefore, another method of introducing this slow-acting poison had to be found. I saw the marks of what looked like claws on the earl's arm earlier, just where a falcon would land when called, and I also noticed that a glove with similar holes had been disposed of. That suggested to me the earl's falcon was involved. Its recent disappearance would serve to confirm my supposition. You had to ensure that the claws penetrated the glove – I presume that the leather was somehow weakened to ensure the bird's claws penetrated – and as only an earl can fly a falcon, you could be sure that the bird would return to him and only to him. But the bird managed a catch before it returned, didn't it? A rabbit that it dropped in the gardens?"

"It may have done. Why does that concern you?"

Shakespeare remembered back to the moment when he had seen the dead rabbit, its eyes decayed but the blood still fresh on its back. That moment had led inexorably to this, like links in a chain. "The rabbit was freshly dead," he explained, "but the body had already begun to decay. When I looked at your brother I see the same process – the dissolution of the flesh while he is still alive, the stench of the grave hanging about him. That speaks to me of foul poison. When he is dead, I would wager that his body will rot within hours. That seems to be a characteristic of the poison you have used."

Stanley's right hand appeared from behind his back. He was holding a bodkin. Noting Shakespeare's horrified gaze, he smiled slightly. "Yes, and as you have surmised, this blade is coated with the same poison – albeit a much stronger decoction. Obtained from the Spanish ambassador, who would love to see a Catholic heir to the throne of England. With my brother dead and the queen's life imperilled, I will be that heir."

He took a step forward.

Shakespeare couldn't tear his eyes away from the bodkin. "That poison. From the Americas I assume?"

"So I believe. The natives use it on their arrows when they make war on each other." He shook his head. "Enough of these pleasantries. Let us bring this to a close." He stepped forward, raising the bodkin. Shakespeare tried to raise a hand to defend himself, tried to move his feet, but his limbs were clumsy and slowed by terror.

Light gleamed on the blade. The last inch was coated with a rust-like brown stain.

The falcons fluttered wildly in their cages.

William Stanley's hand flashed forward, too fast to stop.

The small room was filled with a sound like a muffled bell. Stanley seemed to rise from the floor, his eyes wide and amazed, before he crumpled to the feather-encrusted ground.

The bodkin slipped from his fingers and rolled across the dirt to Shakespeare's feet.

Behind where William Stanley had stood was the old gardener, the light spilling round his body like water. His gnarled fingers clutched his upheld spade.

"I came to ask you if I should put the glove back on that bonfire, like its owner wanted," he said. "Then I heard what his lordship was saying. A damned papist! I never would have credited it if I hadn't heard it with my own ears!"

Shakespeare walked past the gardener to the door of the building and gazed up at the back of Lathom House. His mind worked quickly, shifting logical arguments. Somewhere in the manor house, God willing, the fifth earl was still clinging on to the shreds of his life. If his mind was still intact, and Shakespeare could get to him in time and explain what William Stanley had attempted, he could rewrite his will, disinheriting his brother. He could also dictate and sign a letter to William Cecil, the secretary of state, outlining the papist plot to put William Stanley on the throne. The word of an actor and playwright would not count for much against the son and the brother of an earl. The word of the earl himself would. Dead, William Stanley would be another martyr to the papists. Alive, he could be . . . persuaded . . . to list the names of his fellow plotters from here to Kingdom come.

And, if he showed any reluctance, Shakespeare would be perfectly happy to help loosen his tongue.

He turned back and gazed into the building. Feathers fluttered gently in the shafts of sunlight. The falcons all watched him, their eyes cold and measuring.

The gardener gazed curiously down at the body. "Is he dead?" he said, a trace of worry in his voice as if he had only just appreciated what he had done.

"I hope not," Shakespeare said.

"Why's that?"

He smiled. "Because sometimes," he said, "there is wisdom in leaving weeds where they be."

James I 🍇

THE MYSTERIOUS DEATH OF THE SHADOW MAN

John T. Aquino

When Elizabeth I died in 1603, with no direct heir, the throne of England passed to James VI of Scotland, the son of Mary Queen of Scots. For the first time Scotland, England and Wales were all ruled by the same king, although it would be another century before legislation officially called it a United Kingdom. James VI travelled to Westminster and thereafter paid little heed to his Scottish kingdom, instead delighting in the ostentation of the English court. Not everyone wanted James as king of England. The most famous assassination attempt was that later known as the Gunpowder Plot, for which Guy Fawkes and his fellow conspirators were arrested and executed. The following story takes place seven years after the Gunpowder Plot and shortly after the death of James's eldest son Henry, Prince of Wales. Henry had purportedly died of typhoid, but is that what really happened?

The four rows of robed Peterborough friars formed a tidy packet framed against the stones of Westminster Abbey. Dawn hung just beneath the world's rim, and so the band of brothers moved quickly, carrying the three decade-old casket from the darkness without to the darkness within.

Like children following a trail of corn, the procession walked in the echo steps of canons who knew the cathedral's way without light. Silently and secretly, the coffin was brought to its place of rest and placed on the mossy marble floor.

It was only then that tapers were lit and only then that the forty monks saw one another. They did not see the shadow man in the corner, tall and lean as if sewn to the darkness.

He did not speak but only watched the archbishop say the words of the rite faster than anyone had ever said them.

The man knew that this was because the dead woman had died a Catholic and did embrace the old faith defiantly and triumphantly even as she laid her head on the block. She had also died a queen, not of England – in spite of her best efforts and those of others – but of Scotland – and had lain in fitful peace in Peterborough Cathedral for thirty years. She had been moved here finally only because her son was now king.

But the king had stayed home. His son was the shadow.

The rite wound down, and the procession with no corpse left quickly, leaving their unknown audience behind, and finding baby shadows outside to welcome them. Shadow man had come because he had to, and coming at this hour was not difficult since he had not been sleeping. Henry, Prince of Wales, steadied himself by pressing his hand into Westminster's walls and wiping the blood from his nose with the other. "I honor your memory, grandmother," he whispered, "just as I despise your faith. But I will honor your memory. And I will make you proud, just as your own son has not."

He gathered his strength to leave, turned, and in his full sight loomed a woman's shape, the walls clearly visible through her body, and her demon eyes embracing the prince in their hold.

In six weeks, in November 1612, England mourned the death of the Prince of Wales, their ideal king, even though he was barely eighteen years old. But sadness was short-to-live as the royal wedding of his sister Elizabeth to Count Frederick of the Palatinate was quickly celebrated.

Bagnet smiled at the echo of Shakespeare's *Hamlet*, who complained of his mother's haste in remarrying so soon after his father's death. Bagnet, sometime-agent of Lord Salisbury, the king's chamberlain, had met William Shakespeare during his investigation of the powder plot in 1605. But Shakespeare, perhaps shaken from the experience, had weaned himself from plays and politics, and retired to Stratford. The powerful but crippled Salisbury had finally passed away shortly before Prince Henry. It is ending, thought Bagnet – Elizabeth's England. It lingered for a while through the early days of stodgy James. But now it was gone.

Almost with Bagnet's thought of his former master, two of Salisbury's servants were at his side and firmly led him by pressure to the pits of his arms and through routes that doubled and tripled themselves on one another until it left Bagnet without a touchstone in the city he knew so well. Soon, he was standing alone in a room whose ceiling carried stars against a backdrop of blue. "The Star Chamber," Bagnet whispered to himself and remembered the tales he had heard of the court that was held in this room. It conducted trials in secret outside of the normal course of common law and equity.

Suddenly, a door squeaked open, and he heard a voice he recognized say, "Four men's work – four men's work that is not well done is not worth the work of one man's that is. So find me one good man. Now off with you." The voice was followed by the figure of Sir Francis Bacon, who had just been named attorney general, and by the jiggling sound of someone running away. "Oh, it is you, Bagnet. Thank you for coming. As you will see, it is important."

Bacon walked briskly to another door and knocked once and then again. It opened slowly and, in a surprisingly shy way, in shuffled King James himself. "Yes, yes," he said distractedly. "Well, here we are." Even after nearly ten years away from Scotland, the king's burr made his speech difficult to endure let alone understand. His face was doured by his Presbyterian upbringing as well as by his recent grief. "Well, Bagnet, I wager you never thought you would end up here with an even-money chance of getting out alive. Yes, yes, well. Salisbury – late departed – thought highly of you."

"I had not seen him since –"

"Since the plot. I know. That wretched plot. He told me of your help with that, never you fear. You stopped the papists from blowing us up. And they may again. They may again. Threw my attempts to tolerate them in my face and moved to kill me and my family! But we have other, more recent plots to turn over to you to – unravel. My son –"

Bagnet instinctively turned his eyes to the floor as a sign of respect. "You have my sympathies, Your Majesty –"

"My son is dead. And I think he was murdered –"

"Murdered, Your Majesty? I had been told –"

"As I was, as I was," the king paced stiffly and abruptly under the painted stars. "The doctors bled him and covered him with warm cocks and pigeons newly killed and after he died told me that it was some new disease that infected the blood and poisoned the brain and that no one could have cured him. But I know," he suddenly spoke hoarsely, "I know he was murdered. I know of death. My father was murdered in front of my mother when I was still in her womb and I felt him die, I felt it, do you hear. And my – mother – dead on the block. Hundreds of miles away, and I felt her head leave her body. And now my son. All killed. Not a natural death among them. I know he was murdered, Bagnet. I feel it. Find those who did it. Find them for me, Bagnet. Or the next time you come here, you will not leave alive."

Bagnet's open-mouthed staring was interrupted by Bacon's touch on the crease of his arm and his taking him to the door. As he was led away, Bagnet looked over his shoulder and saw that the king was still pacing and mumbling.

"Tell me what to do," Bagnet said to Bacon once they were outside. "I do not –"

"You will investigate and report to me. Whatever you find, I will attempt to present it in the best light – for you."

Bagnet assessed Bacon's tone to mean that he was truly on his own. Consequently, he realized that he would have to get us much information out of him as he could – now. "Is there any evidence that the Prince was murdered and did not die from this disease?"

"I do not know," Bacon said airily and made as if to walk away.

"But, sir, you are known for your analytical reasoning, in your writings and speeches. Can you think of anyone who would have wanted to kill Prince Henry?"

"My duty is to serve the prince, Master Bagnet. I cannot discuss policy with you."

"Sir Francis, is the King –"

"Mad?" Bacon turned and finished for him. "With grief. With shame. He was envious of his son's popularity. Envy is like witchcraft. There is no cure, except removal. Also, he did not understand his son." Bacon moved closer to Bagnet, trying, analytically to explain. "When they were hunting once, the young Prince, disgusted with the bloodiness of the hunt, started to ride away. The king raised his whip to strike the Prince and would have – had others not held his arm. He had wanted to share his love of hunting with his son and then grew angry when he could not."

"So the relationship was not a loving one?"

"I do not know. The joys of parents are secret, and so are their griefs and fears. It may have been. He does not show love well," Bacon said, walking away again.

"I understand that he did not attend the prince's funeral."

"No surprise in that," as Bagnet attempted to keep up with him. "He did not go to Salisbury's either, or his mother's reinterment. Henry went, ill as he was. As he lay dying, Henry claimed to have seen her there – delirious, no doubt. But he took it as a warning. No, the king was not at his son's funeral," Bacon said, putting his hand in front of Bagnet to signal he was leaving him behind. "He is afraid of death. All men fear death as children fear the dark. But, given his history, the King fears it more. Who can blame him? And he does not – know what to do with grief or pain or – love, and at funerals, nothing else is present."

"Sir Francis –" Bagnet shouted at his back. The attorney general stopped with a shrug of annoyance and stood – pointedly – with his back to him. Bagnet searched his mind for anything pertinent to ask – while he could. "What was the last thing that the prince ate or drank?"

"Ah," he hesitated as if opening drawers in his mind. "A drink – from Sir Walter Raleigh, who is in the Tower, as you know, for attempting to kill the king. The queen had asked Raleigh to mix up a curative that he had given her once and that had proved effective. Even though he is a prisoner, the king has allowed him a laboratory in his cell. The queen knew Raleigh would do this because of his affection for the prince."

"Raleigh and the prince were close?"

Bacon strode away with a deliberate stride that showed that he would not stop again. "Yes, very close. The prince was heard to say that Raleigh was like his second father."

When Bagnet needed to clear his head, he went to the Mermaid's Tavern, where the players would meet. He was sitting alone over a mug of ale when stout Ben Jonson, actor, play-maker, and author of court masques, sat with him.

"You look bemused," said Jonson.

"Tell me about Prince Henry. You knew him," said Bagnet. "What was he like?"

Jonson grinned and shook his head as if clearing it. "I wrote a masque about Oberon that was performed at Whitehall, and Prince Henry played Oberon – just as the queen and princes and princess are wont to take parts. Not the king – he could barely watch plays let alone act in them. Prince Henry had no lines but stood there while others spoke about him." Jonson closed his eyes and recited from the masque:

> He is the matter of virtue, and placed high.
> His meditations to his heights are even,
> And all their issue is akin to heaven.
> He is a god o'er kings, yet stoops he then
> Nearest a man when he doth govern men,
> To teach them by the sweetness of his sway,
> And not by force

"It was difficult, I may add, to praise the prince so while the king was sitting there and still – well, king. But Henry was, well, a wonderful young man, a shining beacon for a generation, which, sadly, will never see it."

"They will only see his shadow. Was he headstrong?"

"Yes!"

"Biting in his wit?"

"Yes!"

"Is it true that when the king compared his study habits unfavorably to those of his brother Charles, Prince Henry said, 'Well, when I am king, we will make Charles Archbishop of Canterbury and the good news is, the long robes will cover up his lame leg.'?"

"Yes. I actually schooled him on his wit. I thought that when the time came the country would benefit from a more interesting king. All for nothing." Jonson shook his head again and then drank again to cloud it.

"Such comments could cause some people to hate him."

"Perhaps. He was quite blunt in his remarks about how he despised Catholics, papists. And yet, on the other hand, he had agreed to be married to Anna, the third daughter of the Duke of Savoy, and a papist. His mother is Catholic, and so was his grandmother. He attended her reinterment."

"And so," Bagnet said, trying to take it in, "papists could hate him for his remarks, and Protestants could fear that his Catholic marriage would bring the old faith back to England."

"Yes," Jonson nodded with his cup to his lips. "In fact, the prince told me once that he feared for his life, that he would be seen in England like King Henry of France was, who converted to Catholicism in order to become king. And when King Henry was murdered three years ago, the prince said to me, 'I have lost my second father'."

"His 'second father'?" Bagnet repeated. "How many 'second fathers' did this young man have?"

"What?" Jonson asked, his eyes half closed.

"Nothing. So," he said aloud, "his contradictory signals about religion, especially his announced marriage, could have caused Catholics and Protestants to act –"

"And his mistress."

"His mistress? Who was she?"

"Elizabeth Howard."

"The Earl of Essex's wife?"

"Yes. The wife."

She was seated alone in the ante chamber, her auburn hair caressing her shoulders like an evening cloak. It was noon, and the sun was clear and bright. But Bagnet had never seen so many candles lit in such a small place.

"If you had not mentioned Sir Francis Bacon's name, I would not have agreed to see you." Bagnet could not be sure if the red glow in her eyes was reflected from the candle glow or was part of pigment and soul.

"I come on a delicate matter. I understand that you were – friends with Prince Henry."

"Speak frankly, man. We were lovers. He was potent, my husband was not."

"Potent in more ways than one. He would one day be king, the most powerful man in the country."

"But jealous. He objected to my liaison with Robert Carr while he was away."

"Carr, the king's favorite and the Prince's rival for the King's affection?"

"Hmm," she purred and leaned back to push her breasts forward.

"And so, where was it left? Were you with Carr or Henry?"

"I was with Henry as he lay dying, and he welcomed me. But now that he is gone, Carr is the king's favorite – and mine."

Bagnet tried not to let his amazement and morals show in his face. "So, a bird in the hand is worth two in the bush. Pardon my proverb, Lady Essex, I have been with Sir Francis Bacon, who uses them a great deal. You say you know him?"

"He knows my husband."

"Ah, but I do know someone you knew, Lady Essex. I attend the Globe Theatre and have found myself sitting more than once next to a man by the name of Simon Forman. I remember especially discussing with him Shakespeare's *The Winter's Tale*, about a father whose jealousy costs him his wife and son, and an old play *Friar Bacon and Friar Bungay*. I remember especially the sound of bells in that one, which were used to summon the power to make a magic head talk. Forman was very interested in the latter because it was about an alchemist and Forman said he had some familiarity with alchemy and the dark arts. He also said he knew you, that he did business with you."

Elizabeth Howard purred again and stretched as felines do. "Poor Simon. He died, you know, last year."

"Yes, he drowned in the Thames on the same day he said that he would die – although many say that he killed himself to make the prediction come true. But did you –"

"Yes, we did business together. He would bring me potions for my skin and hair. Now that he is gone, I must rely on Mrs Turner, a widow of a doctor of physics."

"How long do you think your husband will tolerate your lovers?" The lady shrugged, and Bagnet kept on. "Divorce is so difficult to obtain. And it is the staple of the plays I attend that illicit lovers will poison husbands so that they may marry."

If Bagnet had intended to provoke her, he did not. "I do not go to the theatre, Master Bagnet. My schedule does not allow it. But unlike the theatre, reality requires proof."

Sir Walter Raleigh was at his laboratory when Bagnet arrived, accompanied by Sir Gervase Elwyn, lieutenant of the Tower. The cell was larger than rooms at some inns where Bagnet had said. Raleigh shared the cell with his wife and son, but they had evidently been allowed to roam. The gallant knight who was already sung in children's history for his part in the fight against the Spanish Armada and his voyages to new lands, was scraggly of beard and slack in his cheeks and forehead. White was his shirt from frequent washings, but also frayed as a result. Raleigh was at his laboratory and continued working while Bagnet spoke.

"I understand that you sent the prince a mixture that was the last thing he tasted before he died."

"Pearl, musk, hartshorn, bezoar, stone from the intestines of ruminants, mink, borage, gentian, mace, sugar, and spirits of wine. The queen requested it. And I am told that it had a positive effect at first, but that he was too far gone."

"Are you positive that the concoction was beneficial?"

"As opposed to not?" Raleigh smiled as he poured a blue liquid into a bowl. "You asked that because I am imprisoned here for plotting against the king. If you offend this king in any way, he will make you pay. And Bacon and Salisbury plotted against me, made up offences to the King, and here I am. But I would never harm the king, let alone his son. I loved the boy."

"He told people you were his 'second father.' But then he also said that about Henry of France."

"He was searching for one. I do not know that any of us measured up, surely not his own."

"Meanwhile, the king searched for a 'second first son' in Robert Carr – Charles being only twelve."

"I am prisoner here, Master Bagnet. I know nothing of politics."

"Yes, I see how you are deprived here. Did you know Simon Forman?"

"The astrologer? No. I have heard of him, though."

"And Elizabeth Howard?"

"I know her husband. I knew him long before he became Earl of Essex, after my friend, the real Earl of Essex died."

"For attempting to seize the crown from Elizabeth. You will forgive me, Sir Walter if I notice a pattern here."

Raleigh emptied a white powder into the bowl and mashed the mixture with a pestle. "So you say. We were very young, Master Bagnet, and did foolish things."

"Such as practising in witchcraft, which is what Salisbury also accused you of at your trial?"

Raleigh's eyes never wavered from his work. "As I said, he made up charges for the king. But, as for the occult and the dark arts, they were the things of youth," he repeated.

"Elizabeth Howard has an interest in the occult as well. Has she ever asked you to help her?"

"I told you I have never met her."

"Is that true?" Bagnet asked Sir Gervase.

"Oh, it is true, sir," the lieutenant of the Tower answered at once. "She sends a messenger."

Bagnet searched out Forman's dwelling to see if he had left any notes or records. What he found were rooms filled with broken glass and shattered wood. The sheriff told him that vandals were ransacking empty houses for sport.

"And that is where we are," Bagnet told Bacon. "It is possible Elizabeth Howard poisoned the prince to ensure that she and her lover Robert Carr would not suffer from her previous affair with Prince Henry. She had access to poison from Forman and from Raleigh. Or it is possible that he was poisoned by Catholics who were angry at Henry, or by Protestants who attempted to prevent his marriage to the Catholic Anna. Or by the Earl of Essex, who was jealous of the royal lover of his wife."

"Or by Walter Raleigh?"

Yes, he had the opportunity, if not the motive. Or by the king –"

"Watch what you say, Bagnet. I am, after all, the attorney general of the kingdom. There are things that I cannot –"

"A king," Bagnet persisted, "who was envious of his son and who is known to punish those who displease him. But he is also a king who is afraid of death and leaves it to others to do his work."

"I see," said Bacon after a moment. "Is that what you will tell the king, that he killed his son?"

"No," Bagnet said softly. "I am telling you that you did it."

"I?" said Bacon without anger or surprise. "I murdered Prince Henry?"

"You caused it to happen, Sir Francis. When I first saw you at the Star Chamber, you were saying, 'Four men's work if not well done is not as good as one man's that is.' You changed what you were saying when you saw that I was standing there. What you were saying was, 'Forman's work must be destroyed.' You said that to Mrs Turner, the widow of a doctor of physics, who has taken his clients. When she left, I heard the jingle of her occult bells. And the next day, Forman's dwelling was destroyed."

"Hardly proof, Master Bagnet."

"You had access to all things connected to the Prince – his daily schedule, his servants. You even had some knowledge of poisons, being descended from Friar Bacon, the alchemist. And you had a motive. The prince was indeed going to marry the Catholic princess of Savoy, despite your best efforts to prevent it. In spite of his personal convictions, he was going to honor the faith of his mother and grandmother and, when he was king, offer religious acceptance to papists. This, you could not allow, you, the author of *Advice to Queen Elizabeth*. Twenty-five years ago you were telling the queen to be intolerant of Catholics. Over the last few months, you tried to dissuade the prince. And when he would not listen, you arranged for the daily administration of poison. But it is difficult for a loyal subject to kill a prince. You even sent Elizabeth Howard to meet the Prince at the reinterment of his grandmother, to give him one last chance."

"I barely knew her!"

"She only saw me because of you! You even took the opportunity to seal the fate of your rival Raleigh, whom the king imprisoned but for which the death warrant had not been issued. You had Elizabeth Howard ask him for a poison to kill her husband. Raleigh would not murder the king or the prince, but he would gladly help a fellow devotee to the occult murder her husband, who, incidentally, had taken the title of his good friend. He sent her poison by messenger. You planted the clue, leaving him for someone like me to find. But the poison you used by Foreman – he was more expert. And that is why you ordered his workrooms destroyed."

"I see. This sounds quite – terrible. Why would I do this, Master Bagnet? Why would I arrange to poison Prince Henry?"

"Because you are a reader of Machiavelli. You said earlier, 'My duty is to serve the prince.' You did not mean Prince Henry. You meant 'prince' in the way the Italian Machiavelli used it – the king, the ruler, the sovereign, for whom you would do – anything. You have an analytical mind, Sir Francis. And the analysis was very simple. Prince Henry must die. That is what happened. That is the truth, is it not, Sir Francis?"

Bacon nodded in admiration but, rather than agree, said, " 'What is truth, asked jesting Pilate, and would not stay for an answer.' You said that you are familiar with my works, Master Bagnet. Surely you know that essay. As for Prince Henry, he was a lovely boy. If there were not so much competition for the title, I would say that I was his 'second father'. But I could not allow him to do what he planned to do. It would have torn this country apart. Well, I am attorney general. What do you think I should do with this report?"

"Analyse it, Sir Francis. It is what you do. And report it in a way to the king that will not bring me back to the Star Chamber. I have put the report in writing and given it to a friend who will release it on my unexpected death."

Bacon sighed and rose. "What a waste of my time. I am back where I began. Ah, well. I imagine I will have to learn about the new type of infection that the doctors think the prince died of and then convince the king that the doctors are correct. Goodbye, Master Bagnet."

As Bagnet started to leave Bacon's office, he paused. "I am, as you said, familiar with your work, Sir Francis, some of which I have seen in manuscript. You only quoted the beginning of your essay, 'On Truth'. It ends, 'There is no vice that doth so cover a man with shame as to be found false and perfidious.' Did you save England, Sir Francis? You say that Prince Henry thought that he had seen the ghost of Mary, Queen of Scots, and that it was a warning. Perhaps it was."

Bagnet left Bacon and walked to the Mermaid's Tavern. He sat down with Ben Jonson and asked him to give back the sealed letter he had left with him that morning. Bagnet took it and tossed it in the fire.

"What was that?" Jonson asked.

"Nothing. Sir Francis Bacon and I have one thing in common. We want the best for England. What will happen to me, will happen."

Jonson and Bagnet raised their mugs to the dying embers of the burnt parchment.

Elizabeth Howard did obtain a divorce from her husband, with the help of the king and Sir Francis Bacon. She and Robert Carr married in 1613 but in 1615 were accused of having poisoned Carr's friend and rival Sir Thomas Overbury, who had been confined to the Tower. They themselves were sent to the Tower and released after five years to die in obscurity.

Mrs Turner and Sir Gervase Elwyn, however, were executed for having assisted Elizabeth Howard in her poisoning of Overbury.

Sir Francis Bacon was appointed lord chancellor in 1618 as a reward for his loyalty and service to King James. But in 1621, he was found guilty of bribery and other forms of corruption. His power removed, he retired on his release from the Tower and died in 1626.

James, having lost his first son and then his second first son, selected George Villiers as his new favorite – only to be disappointed yet again and to die virtually alone the year before Bacon.

With this foundation, young Charles became king, and twenty-five years later, he was beheaded and the monarchy was abolished – for a time.

The ghost of Mary Queen of Scots is still occasionally sighted standing near her tomb in Westminster Abbey.

Medical history records that Prince Henry of England died of one of the first recorded cases of typhoid fever.

Bagnet never saw the Star Chamber again.

Napoleon Bonaparte ♥

THE DAY THE DOGS DIED

Edward D. Hoch

Although the French revolution of 1789 put an end (at least temporarily) to the French monarchy, it did not stop Napoleon Bonaparte declaring himself Emperor in 1804. The following story is set during Napoleon's rise to power, shortly after he had conquered Egypt and established himself in Cairo.

Each morning during his three weeks of imprisonment Garrison had been awakened by the barking of dogs, and this day during late August of 1798 was no different. He awakened from a dream of his wife back in England, rolled over on the hard cot, and opened his eyes. The morning sunlight was already hitting the bars of his cell window, and awareness of the growing desert heat made him shed the blanket and sit up, scratching at the beard he'd grown during his captivity. Then he carefully inspected the dirt floor for scorpions before setting his bare feet on it.

Garrison stood up and stretched, considering the barking dogs of Cairo. There were hundreds of them just in the area of the prison, and his guards told him they barked at the unfamiliar odor of the French troops. When the troops marched out to relieve the night sentries each morning, the dogs barked. The same thing happened in the evening. The people of the city were always alerted to the movement of the troops, and it was the people along with their religious leaders who offered the most resistance to General Bonaparte's army. Already the word was that the French had converted a ruined mosque into a fortress to defend themselves against attacks.

The clanking of the cell door interrupted his thoughts and he turned to see the French guard named Paul standing there. "The prisoners will assemble in the courtyard after breakfast," he said, speaking English for Garrison's benefit. "You will be privileged to see a spectacular demonstration of French power. A large hot-air balloon will be launched from just north of the city. We will have a good view from here."

"A hot-air balloon? Will Napoleon be giving a speech along with it?"

The guard turned and left the cell. Garrison decided that at least the balloon flight would break the monotony of the day. There were about a hundred of them in the old prison, men of all nationalities. A few were British like himself, but most were Cairo residents who had resisted the invasion with more determination than that shown by the Egyptian army. But in fairness he reminded himself that the Egyptians had only just driven the Turks from their land when Napoleon's fleet appeared. It had been a tumultuous summer for them.

After breakfast that morning all were assembled in the walled courtyard to watch the balloon fly high over the city. It was respect that Napoleon desired, Garrison decided. Respect was something he hadn't gained when he landed forty thousand French troops from three hundred ships off the Egyptian coast a month or so earlier. He had conquered the army but not the spirit of the people.

"There it is!" someone shouted, and Garrison could see a tiny dot rising in the northern sky, gradually growing larger as it drifted toward the city. The balloon was up.

But even as the prisoners and guards watched, the top of the balloon seemed to collapse inward. It stayed aloft for another few seconds and then spiraled downward to crash into the ground. The watching prisoners were silent for the space of a heartbeat, as if to be certain of what they had seen. Then a spontaneous cheer went up. It seemed to echo from beyond the prison walls, as if the entire populace of Cairo had joined in to ridicule Napoleon's fiasco.

For a few moments, until the guards herded them back to their cells, it was the best Garrison had felt since they pulled him out of the Bay of Abukir three weeks earlier.

He was dreaming about that, dreaming of the ship shuddering under his feet as the French guns launched a last desperate salvo, when he awakened the following morning.

He knew at once that something was different. But what?

He lay on his cot without stirring, listening for something that wasn't there. Finally he opened his eyes and saw sunlight on the barred window as usual. It wasn't sunlight that was missing. It was the barking of the dogs. There had never been this silence before.

When the jailer named Paul brought him his meager breakfast Garrison asked, "Where are the dogs this morning? I don't hear their barking."

"The dogs are dead," Paul said simply.

"Dead?"

He placed the piece of bread and cup of water on the floor near his prisoner. "They barked at our soldiers. The order came down to kill them with poisoned meat."

"Napoleon's order?"

But Paul would say no more. He left the cell and locked the door behind him. Garrison tried to peer out the barred window, but he could see only the eternal blue sky and the top of a nearby mosque.

The day passed uneventfully, like most previous days of his imprisonment. It was not until after his evening meal, when the summer sun was low in the west, that Paul reappeared at his cell door. "Come!" he ordered.

"Where to?"

"Interrogation."

His hands were tied behind his back and he was led up the stone steps to the prison office where two uniformed French officers awaited him. "You are Lieutenant James Garrison, ship's doctor aboard the British man-of-war *Marlborough*?"

"I was until your navy blew the ship out from under me."

"You are to come with us," one of them said.

"Where to?" Garrison asked again, but the French officers did not answer. They took him out of the prison through the front gate, where a carriage awaited. His hands were still tied, and as they helped him up into the carriage he noticed the initial N on the door. He hardly could believe this might be the personal coach of the commander of the army. The streets of the city were alive with people, even though it was almost dark. Here and there he could see dead animals, sometimes being cried over by their owners. One man, a Turkish shopkeeper, must have recognized the passing coach. He lifted the body of a small dog and hurled it at them with what was surely a curse.

They came in time to a fortress that served as a military headquarters of some sort on the bank of the Nile River. Garrison could only imagine that it had been the command post during the long years of Turkish rule. In a way it was the Egyptians' revolt against the Turks during the past two years that had encouraged the French under Napoleon to seize the country in hopes of cutting Britain's trade routes to the east.

Once safely delivered inside the fortress his wrists were freed and he rubbed some circulation back into them. A grey-haired officer wearing a major's insignia entered the room. "You are Lieutenant Garrison?"

"Yes, sir."

"Major deLoy of the commander's staff. He wishes a private audience with you."

"With me? Napoleon wants to speak with me? There must be some mistake."

"No mistake. Come this way."

Garrison followed him into quarters at the end of a long corridor where armed soldiers stood guard. A short man, barely five and a half feet tall, rose to greet him and in that instant he realized he was face to face with the famous general. Garrison was surprised at the man's youthful face, remembering then that Napoleon was not yet thirty. Even at that age he had strong, commanding eyes, with long chestnut hair that fell over his forehead and shoulders. "Come in, Dr Garrison," he said in French, not bothering with the military rank. Garrison at once suspected he had been summoned as a physician rather than as a British officer.

"It is a great honor to meet General Bonaparte face to face."

Napoleon waved his hand in dismissal. "Take a seat, please. Are you comfortable speaking French, Doctor?"

"Certainly."

"Very well, let us proceed." He stared into Garrison's eyes, weighing his next words carefully. "I understand your ship was damaged on 1 August at the Battle of Abukir Bay." He allowed himself a slight smile. "Or, as the present revolutionary government would have it, the month of Thermidor in Year VI of the Republic. Believe me, if I should ever be crowned emperor we will return to the old calendar!"

"Emperor? That is a lofty ambition."

"Far in the future. For now let us speak of Cairo and the present." He produced a small snuffbox and inhaled a dab of powdered tobacco from it. "How much have you heard about the battle?"

"Very little, General. I know the French suffered heavy losses."

"My fleet was destroyed by Admiral Nelson. Only two of seventeen ships avoided capture or destruction. I have conquered Egypt with forty thousand troops and now we are virtual prisoners here!"

"The fortunes of war," Garrison replied with a shrug. "I can feel no pity for you when many of my friends were killed."

Napoleon was silent for a moment. Then he said, "You were the ship's doctor."

"Ship's surgeon is probably a more accurate title. There are always a few cases of scurvy to be dealt with, but in battle my main concern is with amputations."

"How much do you know about poisons?"

"I have a general physician's knowledge. Why do you ask?"

Napoleon rose and began to pace the floor, his hands clasped behind his back. "We have conquered this ancient land but not its people. They are turning against us just as they turned against the Turks. I am stranded with my troops and forced to remain here for many months. This time can be spent in helping them if they will but give me an opportunity. I want to bring in scholars to study their heritage, and abolish the system of serfdom to guarantee their basic rights."

"How can I help you in any of that?"

"This is another matter, though it bears on the general unrest. Yesterday, following the destruction of our hot-air balloon, which was cheered by the people in a show of disrespect toward France, Brigadier General Lanz issued an order, without my knowledge, that every dog in Cairo was to be put to death immediately. His nominal reason was that the animals barked at French soldiers and thereby revealed the movement of troops about the city."

"How were the dogs killed?"

"Poisoned meat was thrown to them and left in the streets overnight. By this morning barely an animal survived."

"What poison was used?" Garrison asked.

"I believe it was some form of deadly nightshade, purchased locally from a trader, fatal within fifteen minutes. But that was only the start of it. General Lanz himself was stricken and died shortly after eating his afternoon meal. That is why I have summoned you, to tell me if he was poisoned like those dogs."

"Surely you have doctors of your own that could tell you this."

Bonaparte shook his head. "He died in the officers'' mess. If he was poisoned, the killer could be someone assigned to this very building, someone I see and trust every day. If an investigation needs to be conducted it must be done by an outsider."

"I understand, but I am no investigator, only a ship's doctor. And an enemy besides!"

Napoleon smiled slightly. "Because you are an enemy you are the only one I can trust."

The deceased General Lanz had been taken to his room and laid out on the bed. Major deLoy accompanied Garrison to view the body, while making it clear that he did not approve of a British officer's involvement in the affair. "There are certainly enough trusted French doctors who could examine the general. Do you have special skills in this area, Lieutenant Garrison?"

"General Bonaparte apparently believes so." He entered the sparsely furnished room and approached the body on the bed. General Lanz was fully clothed in his military uniform, with his hands stiffly at his sides, fingers bent like claws. "Were you present when he died, Major?"

"I was. It was a terrible death. He went into convulsions shortly after finishing his meal, and the body stiffened as soon as he died."

"Were those the same symptoms suffered by the poisoned dogs?"

"Yes," Major deLoy confirmed.

"Tell me who else was present."

"The general's aide-de-camp, Colonel Clary, and Major Rosen."

"Only the four of you?"

"Yes. The other officers had eaten earlier."

"No one else came or went?"

"Only the young African woman who served us. I questioned her, of course."

Garrison lifted the eyelids and poked around at the body. He'd seen such stiffness before, after death, but usually it took several hours to set in. "I am fairly certain he was poisoned," he told the French officer. "But I can't be sure until I find the source of the poison. How many troops were assigned to killing the dogs?"

"I believe there were sixty-four, all enlisted men. The officers supervised distribution of the poisoned meat."

"I need to see the person who procured the poison for this use."

"That would be Colonel Clary. I can take you to him."

"If you would, Major."

Clary was on the promontory overlooking the Nile, standing in the dusk as he supervised the unloading of grain from a flat-bottomed native boat. Major deLoy saluted as they approached and introduced Dr Garrison. "The doctor is examining General Lanz's death, on direct orders from General Bonaparte."

Clary was a stocky man, obviously older than the others, wearing a full uniform complete with sword. Garrison thought he could have been Napoleon's father. "You are one of the British prisoners," he remarked, perhaps recognizing Garrison from the time of his capture.

"I am."

"Hardly the person to be investigating the death of a French officer."

"General Bonaparte felt he needed an independent physician to determine if there has been a poisoning."

"There have been many poisonings this day. Simply look at the bodies of the dogs. They are everywhere."

"I intend to do just that. In the meantime I understand you were instrumental in obtaining the poison locally."

"I was, on orders of General Lanz. The French army generally has no need for it among our provisions."

"I wish to speak with your supplier. I'm interested in the exact type of poison used, and if it's likely the same poison was used on General Lanz."

"The poison is a colorless crystalline powder supplied by an Indian trader named Ibn Tulun. He told me it was especially effective against rats, and when General Lanz ordered the dogs killed it seemed the proper poison to use. You can find Tulun in the Bazaar of the Three Maidens almost any morning."

"Will General Bonaparte allow me to go there?" Garrison wondered.

Colonel Clary pointed over Garrison's shoulder. "Do you see that man in the white burnoose? His name is Maximilian Fey. He has been assigned to follow you at all times. If you attempt to leave Cairo or go into hiding, he will kill you." The colonel gave him a slight smile. "But perhaps General Bonaparte neglected to mention that."

Garrison slept in his usual cell that night, but he noticed that the guard did not lock the door behind him. When he awakened at dawn it was still unlocked. He dressed in prison pants and the tattered remains of his old uniform jacket and went into the corridor where Paul was on duty. "May I leave?"

"My orders are that you may come and go as you please," the guard told him.

"May I take a carriage to the Bazaar of the Three Maidens?"

Paul shook his head. "You must walk or ride a mule. The streets in that area are too narrow for carriages."

Garrison went quickly up the worn stone steps to the courtyard, then crossed it to the open gate. The soldiers on duty there paid no attention, perhaps because they could see the man in the white burnoose following him. He'd walked about ten minutes when he realized he had no idea which street would take him to the Bazaar of the Three Maidens. He stepped into a doorway and waited until Maximilian Fey appeared, walking fast and scanning the streets for his quarry.

"Hello," Garrison said, stepping out beside the tall man in the caftan. "Can we walk together? I've lost my way."

Fey made a motion toward some weapon beneath his garment, then thought better of it. "Where are you going?"

"To the Bazaar of the Three Maidens, to speak with a trader named Ibn Tulun."

"Come with me."

They rounded a corner, then moved by a circuitous route through narrow streets into a large open square filled with merchants selling their wares. Many had mules tethered by their owners' stalls, and even a few camels were visible. "This is the bazaar?" Garrison asked. moving along the aisles of merchants selling everying from clusters of dates to camel hides.

"Yes. Ibn Tulun is usually in that corner, selling goods from India."

Garrison found him easily enough, a scrawny little man in a fez, with a wispy gray beard and bony hands that were constantly in motion. "India!" he shouted, trying to make himself heard above the other stall keepers. "Medicines and remedies from the Far East!" He spoke in Arabic and French, but switched to English when Garrison approached in his old uniform jacket.

"I am a ship's doctor," Garrison explained. "I need to know what sort of poison you supplied the French for killing those dogs."

The bearded merchant glanced nervously to his right and left, fearful of being overheard. "I know nothing about the dogs! Go away!"

"I was told by Colonel Clary that you supplied the poison. Shall I tell him you deny it?"

Ibn Tulun glanced from Garrison to the tall man by his side. "It was a legal transaction. I have a bill of sale for the supplies."

"I want to know what poison was used."

Still nervous that their conversation might be overhead, he told Garrison, "Come inside where we can talk."

They entered the corner building facing the bazaar. Windows in the opposite wall let in enough sunlight so Garrison could see a young Arab woman working over a large sack of dried leaves, separating them into smaller individual sacks. "This is my daughter Fanta," he said by way of introduction. "She helps me on days when I need her."

Fanta gave Garrison a quick smile without pausing in her work. "You are British," she observed. She had black hair and soft skin not yet darkened by too much exposure to the sun. She wore a necklace of beads and a blue sapphire ring on her left hand.

"I was captured by the French when my ship was damaged at Abukir Bay. Now they have asked for my help in a medical matter. What can you tell me about the dog poison? Is that what you are sorting?"

Fanta gave a quick laugh. "These are hemp leaves for smoking."

"A narcotic," Ibn Tulun explained, rubbing his bony hands together. "The poison you ask about comes from the seeds of the dog button plant, grown extensively in southern India. The fruits are abundant in March, resembling a mandarin orange with seeds as large as a small coin, like velvet-covered buttons, that supply the plant with its name."

"This poison causes convulsions and death very quickly?"

The tradesman nodded. "Usually within ten to fifteen minutes. The body stiffens quickly." He added, "I speak of animals, not humans."

Certainly the symptoms matched those of General Lanz. "Did you deliver this poison to anyone else at French headquarters?"

"No one."

"Anyone else in the city?"

"Not recently. I sell it to farmers who wish to kill pests. One man told me enough of it would kill a crocodile."

"Is there an antidote for it?"

"None that I know of. It kills too swiftly."

Garrison thought about that. "One more question. Where did you deliver the poison to General Lanz?"

"I didn't. He sent a carriage here to pick it up. General Bonaparte's own, with the initial N on the doors."

Garrison left the man and his daughter and returned to the bazaar. He had learned very little, but the morning was still young.

Garrison's fondest hope was to see his wife and small daughter back in England someday soon. He wondered if that day would come quicker if he solved the mystery of General Lanz's poisoning or if he failed to solve it. Did Napoleon really want the killer brought to justice? Whatever the truth of the situation, he knew that he must pursue the investigation. His fate was entirely in Napoleon's hands.

"Where would I find Major Rosen at this time of day?" he asked the big man who had become his constant shadow.

Maximilian Fey looked toward the sky as if studying the position of the sun. "Why do you wish to see him?"

"There were three men with General Lanz when he died. I have spoken with Colonel Clary and Major deLoy, but not with Major Rosen."

"For that you must have the permission of General Bonaparte."

Garrison frowned. "Why is permission required?"

The big man stared down at his feet. "Major Rosen was arrested and confined to quarters this morning. I do not know the charges against him."

Garrison hurried back to the fortress headquarters of the French army. He found Major deLoy in his office, staring out the window at the small boats on the river. "Major –"

The grey-haired officer turned abruptly at the interruption. "What are you doing here, Dr Garrison?"

"I understand Major Rosen has been imprisoned. Do the charges against him concern the poisoning of General Lanz?"

"I cannot speak to that. Lanz was arrested on direct orders from General Bonaparte himself."

"Then I must see the General."

"He is in conference with his advisors."

"I can wait," Garrison replied.

Major deLoy sighed. "Remain here," he said and exited the room.

Alone, Garrison scanned the bare walls, thinking that the French had done little to bring a touch of home to this strange country. They had not planned to stay long, and now the British fleet had trapped them here. Was it a victory or defeat for Napoleon? That was a question only history could answer.

By the time the major returned some fifteen minutes had passed. "General Bonaparte will see you," he said stiffly with a hint of disapproval.

He hurried to Napoleon's office where the guard on duty admitted him. The general stood with his back to the window, his right hand inserted in his vest. "What is it?" he asked abruptly. "Have you solved our little mystery?"

"I am only a doctor, General Bonaparte. I can tell you that the poison used to kill the dogs almost certainly killed General Lanz. The symptoms were the same. However I have not yet spoken with Major Rosen and now I understand he is under arrest."

"Correct." Napoleon's face was an icy mask.

"Does it concern Lanz's death?"

"No, no! A separate business entirely."

"Nevertheless, I need to know about it if I am to get to the bottom of this matter."

Bonaparte considered his request and finally answered. "We have been here but a matter of weeks and already the major has discovered a method of augmenting his meagre army pay. He purchased a quantity of dried hemp leaves for smoking. They are a narcotic which he planned to resell to men under his command. I have ordered him confined to quarters."

"I would like to speak with him. If you really desire my help, it is necessary that I talk to all three men who dined with the victim."

Napoleon gave a wave of his hand. "I will have him brought up to the officers' mess where General Lanz died. It is time for the noon meal and he must eat, even as a prisoner."

The small officers' mess was down the hall from Bonaparte's office. When Major Rosen entered some thirty minutes later, Garrison was surprised to see a short man with wispy hair and odd, square eyeglasses. He must have been in his early fifties, wearing his officer's uniform but without the sword. "You wished to see me?" he asked.

"Yes. I have a few questions."

"It is unusual to be questioned by an enemy officer who is a prisoner of my government."

"These are unusual times, Major. I am acting on the direct orders of General Bonaparte himself, investigating the death of General Lanz."

Major Rosen seated himself at the table. Almost at once a dark-skinned serving girl wearing shiny bracelets and rings brought them napkins and utensils for the noon meal. She returned with a pitcher of palm wine, leaning across Garrison to fill their cups. "What does my arrest have to do with Lanz? Does Napoleon believe I played a part in his death?"

Before he could answer they were joined by Colonel Clary and Major deLoy. The major immediately called for some palm wine though Clary declined. The stocky colonel seemed more subdued than on the previous evening, though after a few moments he did ask Garrison how his investigation was proceeding.

"Have you spoken to Ibn Tulun?" he asked, running his fingers nervously over the empty cup in front of him.

The name seemed to startle Major Rosen. He turned and said to Garrison, "So you have been to the Bazaar of the Three Maidens."

"I have, early this morning. It is an interesting place."

"They hate us there. It is where plots against the army are fomented."

"There are many of those," Clary agreed. "One had only to observe the reaction when our hot-air balloon went down to realize how much we are hated."

"Conquering armies are always a subject of hatred," Garrison said.

Major deLoy joined in. "Today I heard a small boy say we had blown the nose off the Sphinx with our cannon. People should know that happened over three hundred years ago when a religious sheik sought to demolish the entire statue. Old paintings of the Sphinx all show the nose to be missing."

When the food arrived it was good by military standards, and to Garrison it was a special treat after the meager prison rations. As he ate, he heard Colonel Clary inquire again about Ibn Tulun. "He supplied the poison for killing the dogs. Was that same poison used to kill General Lanz?"

"I believe so," Garrison acknowledged, repeating what he'd told Napoleon. "The symptoms were the same."

Clary turned toward Major Rosen. "And if I remember correctly, you were opposed to the dog poisoning."

Rosen slipped the square eyeglasses from his head. "Am I to be charged with the general's murder too?" he asked, his uncovered eyes wide with emotion. "These eyeglasses were given me by the former American minister to France, Benjamin Franklin. I have had them for thirteen years. General Bonaparte was still a child then, barely fifteen years old. He is the commanding general now while I am still only a major, passed over for promotion. I have been made the scapegoat before, but I will not sit quietly by and suffer these attacks again! I was once a decorated officer with a bright future, an honorable man. Will Bonaparte ruin me for a few leaves of hemp?"

Both Clary and deLoy seemed embarrassed by his outburst. After a moment the colonel said quietly, "Return to your quarters, Major Rosen."

Rosen rose without another word and departed.

Major deLoy frowned, looking uncomfortable. "It is a difficult situation. Rosen has been my friend since the day I graduated from the *Ecole Militaire* in Paris."

Colonel Clary shook his head sadly. "The order to confine him to quarters came from General Bonaparte himself. A quantity of hemp leaves was found in his possession. Unfortunately this arrest only adds to Rosen's growing resentment of Napoleon."

Garrison was reaching out for a piece of bread when he noticed a dark brown smudge on his sleeve. He was trying to remember where it might have come from when there was a shout from the corridor outside. A physician's life had trained him to move fast. He was at the door before the others could react. Down the hall by Napoleon's quarters the guard was sprawled on the floor, apparently unconscious. Major Rosen, armed with a single dueling pistol, was just entering the room.

"Rosen!" Garrison shouted. "Don't be a fool!"

He hurled himself at the man's back, not waiting to see if his words had any effect. Rosen's pistol fired into the ceiling as he went down. Garrison had a quick glimpse of General Bonaparte's horrified face beyond the door. Rosen gave a cry of frustrated rage, then rolled free of Garrison's grasp and struggled to regain his footing.

Colonel Clary was there in an instant, drawing his sword. "This is tyranny!" Major Rosen shouted.

"This is treason," Clary replied, and ran him through with the sword.

After Garrison had treated the injured guard and established that Rosen was beyond help, General Bonaparte called them into his office. "I owe you my gratitude, Lieutenant Garrison," he said. "More than that, I owe you my life. What can I give you in return?"

"My freedom."

"You have it," he said with a wave on his hand. "There is a Spanish trader sailing from Alexandria tomorrow. You will be on it. Major deLoy, let us have some wine to toast my survival."

The major called for the dark-skinned serving girl and gave the order. She returned in a few moments with a bottle of fine French wine. Colonel Clary was speaking as she filled Garrison's cup. "I think we can safely assume it was Major Rosen who poisoned General Lanz. I suppose he resented the killing of the dogs."

"Rosen didn't kill him," Garrison heard himself say. He saw the dark wrist in front of him and grabbed it. "Here's your killer!"

The serving girl tried to break free, but Colonel Clary was on his feet, grabbing hold of her. Garrison seized a napkin, dipped it in white wine and wiped it across the girl's face. "Let me introduce you to Fanta, Ibn Tulun's daughter."

"This is one surprise after another," Napoleon said. "Please explain it, Dr Garrison."

He finished rubbing the rest of the brown stain from Fanta's face. She'd ceased to struggle but remained silent. "In addition to the poison for the dogs, she and her father supplied Major Rosen with hemp leaves for smoking. I imagine they saw it as the start of a profitable business, with forty thousand French soldiers stranded here indefinitely. Somehow General Lanz found out about it. Perhaps a packet of hemp was accidentally included with the poison. I imagine he threatened to imprison them both, so Fanta used some of the poison on him."

"How did you know all this?" Napoleon asked.

"When I asked Ibn Tulun where he delivered the poison to General Lanz, he said the general sent a carriage to the bazaar to pick it up. This was manifestly untrue, since the streets in that area of the city are too narrow for carriages. I asked myself why he should lie about such an unimportant fact. It could only have been to conceal the actual delivery system for the poison. Today I realized it must have been his daughter Fanta who brought the poison here when she came to work. She disguised her identity with dark brown pigment, perhaps because an African might move more freely among the French than an Egyptian. But when she brought our food I recognized a familiar ring on her finger, one I'd seen only this morning on Fanta's hand. When she reached across me to pour our wine she left a brown smear on my sleeve, from the vegetable dye she used to darken her skin. Of course if someone had poisoned General Lanz she was the logical suspect. She had actually served him the poisoned food!"

General Bonaparte nodded and turned to the prisoner. "Do you wish to confess, young woman?"

She spat at him.

His expression never changed as he wiped his chin and said quietly, "Put her in a cell and arrest the father too. They will both be tried by a military court in the morning."

Later that afternoon Napoleon bid goodbye to Garrison at the door of the French headquarters. "This carriage will transport you to the ship," he said. "She sails with the morning's first light."

"Thank you, General." Garrison gave him a salute.

"Someday I will meet the British on the field of battle, Doctor. I hope you are not among them."

Garrison turned and hurried down the stone steps to the waiting carriage.

George IV 🍎

NATURAL CAUSES

Martin Edwards

For some reason George IV is remembered more fondly than his father, the so-called mad George III. The colourful period of the Regency, when the Prince Regent (before he became George IV) lavished money upon his pet projects and dominated Society, particularly in London and Brighton, has a strong romantic appeal. In fact, the Prince of Wales was a spoiled, irrational and irresponsible individual with no scruples or morals. The continuing scandal of his day was his treatment of his wife, Caroline of Brunswick, whom he despised and whom he was determined would not be crowned queen. This scandal was more than equalled by Caroline's own lifestyle and adventures. Their relationship was tailor-made for this book.

"I am afraid for the Princess of Wales," the thin, dark man hissed. He spoke with the nervous intensity that was his trade mark.

Lord Hutchinson frowned. They were standing together in a dusty recess of Westminster Hall, keeping their voices low so as not to attract attention. "She is a strong woman. Formidable. I do not doubt that she can take care of herself."

"She has needed every ounce of that strength. Her husband never loved her. Now, I believe, he hates her."

"What can he do? She is popular, he is not. Besides, he still has the other lady. The one he loved long before his marriage – and still does."

"The people adore her, yes. But she has many influential enemies. Above all, the heir to the throne."

"You must concede that her behaviour has been scandalous," Hutchinson said. "The evidence gathered by the Milan Commission is damning. Whilst she has been travelling on the Continent she has allowed a succession of foreign gigolos to cuckold the son of the king."

Henry Brougham said coldly, "You disappoint me, sir, if you rely upon the tittle-tattle of dismissed servants, discarded flunkeys. The authorities loathe Caroline. Ever since she travelled from Brunswick to marry Prince George, they have done their best to discredit her. Ironic, given his continuing infatuation with Mrs Fitzherbert."

Hutchinson grimaced. Nominally, he shared Brougham's political affiliations and was opposed to Lord Liverpool's administration. But he was close to the king and thus to many of the king's ministers. Whereas Brougham – well, he suspected that Brougham's first loyalty was to himself. "His Majesty is gravely ill. Do you expect that Caroline will return to England soon? The whole of London has been buzzing with rumour ever since she left Italy. You realize that if she comes back, the Prince Regent will insist that proceedings are instituted against her?"

"She may be headstrong, but she is also brave."

"Then why are you afraid for her?"

"Because her courage is careless. She has no sense of danger – whereas I have an acute instinct for it."

Hutchinson raised his eyebrows. "And your instinct tells you – what?"

"That if she comes back to England, her life may be at risk."

"Let us suppose for a moment that you are right. Surely it would be better to persuade her to remain abroad?"

"No words of mine could influence her, once the decision is made. All that I can do is to seek to discover the truth about whatever threats she may face."

Hutchinson leaned forward to speak in Brougham's ear. "Candidly, your concerns seem far-fetched to me. But if you were right – you would yourself be playing a dangerous game, would you not?"

Brougham looked him in the eye. "Perhaps. But as you know, when I play – I play to win."

In a small hotel at Marseilles, a pretty Swiss maid was holding up a mirror to enable the princess of Wales to judge whether her face was sufficiently rouged to conceal the signs of a bilious attack she had suffered the previous evening as well as to suit the colouring of her dark wig and thick black eyebrows.

Caroline nodded and laid down the bottle of cosmetic preparation. "What news of your sister, Mariette? Is she still in England?"

Mariette Bron started. "I believe so, milady. I understand that she is living under an assumed name. She calls herself the Comtesse Colombier."

Caroline guffawed. "A fine title for a former maid and secretary!"

The girl's face reddened. "She has brought dishonour upon our family."

Caroline touched the maid's hand. Her guttural voice was for once tender with concern. "Do not let it concern you, Mariette. So many have betrayed me. What difference does one more make? Besides, I always liked Louise, you know. I did not want to dismiss her from my service."

"There was nothing else you could do, milady. I understood it perfectly. She was a scandalmonger."

"And a thief's accomplice, don't forget! She abetted that rogue Sacchini when he stole my gold napoleons! Are they still together?"

"I believe so, milady. He now styles himself the Conte Milani."

Caroline raised her eyes to the heavens, then sighed. "Why your sister remains with Sacchini, I cannot conceive. For all that, I was sorry to dismiss her. She had spirit. It saddens me to think that if I do return to England, she may be bribed to testify against me."

Mariette said impulsively, "Why should you go back? It is not your native land. You were never happy there."

"That is true, but there is a complication. I have received news of my father-in-law. He is very sick."

"The old malady?" Mariette asked, with as much delicacy as she could muster.

"No, no. It is not merely a question of his mind now, but rather of the frailty of his body. He caught a cold at Windsor and now it has gone to his lungs. Do you realize what it means, Mariette? On his

death the royal annuities will lapse. I shall be queen – oh yes, I shall!
– but if I do not persuade Parliament to award me a suitable income,
I shall be a beggar too. Now, the headdress with pink feathers, do
you think?"

"The queen for ever, the king in the river!" someone cried.

The crowd outside the house of Alderman Wood in South Audley
Street was growing larger with every minute that passed. George III
was dead and Queen Caroline had at long last returned to the capital,
where they believed she belonged. They had been cheering her until
their voices were hoarse. Brougham, newly appointed as the queen's
attorney general, noticed Mariette at a window; she was smiling
down at the mass of faces, exchanging a wave with a pretty young
girl whose face seemed somehow familiar to him. Brougham rubbed
his chin thoughtfully.

"Take your eyes off the queen's maid, Henry," whispered his
companion, Thomas Denman.

Brougham allowed himself a smile. "I was intrigued to see – ah
well, no matter. The queen received you this afternoon, did she not?
Was she in good spirits?"

"Certainly," Denman said. He was Caroline's solicitor general.
"She even made an appearance on the balcony of the house. I
thought she could scarcely credit the adulation which she had
inspired."

"She was nervous?"

"Uncharacteristically so, yes. Of course, she has not been well for
several weeks. She simply bowed to her supporters, but that gesture
alone was enough to send them wild with delight."

"Fascinating." Brougham bit his lip. "Yet I sense that the mood of
this gathering is volatile. Tempers might easily fray."

"I agree. It would take only a spark to ignite a fierce fire of rage
against the authorities. Shall we go in?"

As the two lawyers shoved their way through a group of ruffianly
looking fellows, Brougham heard the mob jeering at a householder in
a building opposite the Alderman's.

"Illuminate for the queen!" one man roared.

"Lights! Lights!" demanded another.

The householder disappeared. If he valued his safety, he would be
searching out a candle to put in his window in honour of his new

neighbour. It was not wise, on this of all evenings, not to demonstrate love for Queen Caroline. Although the evening was warm, Brougham found himself shivering as they reached the door of Wood's house.

A minute later they were in Caroline's presence. After a few pleasantries, Brougham asked, "Your Royal Highness has fully recovered from the illness that you suffered after leaving Rome?"

"Thankfully, yes, although I am still rather fatigued. I was struck down whilst we were crossing the Alps, you know. The most dreadful spasm in my stomach. No matter. I need to know how to claim what is rightfully mine. My husband persists in treating me like some unwelcome adventuress. Why was there no royal vessel to convey me from Calais? For how long must I be cut out of the people's prayers? And when will the coronation take place?"

"As to the last, I suspect that it will be postponed until a decision has been taken as to whether to launch judicial proceedings."

Caroline gave a bitter laugh. "For my alleged adultery? George would not dare! He has too much dirty linen of his own."

"Nevertheless, I fear that the risk of a trial is all too real. My surmise is that the Lord Chancellor will opt for a Parliamentary Bill of Pains and Penalties."

"It sounds reminiscent of a form of medieval torture. What, pray, would it achieve?"

"You would be stripped of all your titles, Your Majesty – and then forced to leave the kingdom."

The queen sat hunched up in her scarlet chair in the House of Lords, waiting for the next witness to be called to give evidence against her. Brougham glanced at her squat, miserable figure and gave her a half-smile of encouragement. He knew that behind the thick white veil, her face was pale, her eyelids sunken. To the people gathered in the streets outside, she remained a heroine. Inside, however, their waving handkerchiefs and shouts of support were easily forgotten.

Caroline had listened to hostile testimony from a succession of former confidants about her supposed affair with the Italian courier-turned-chamberlain Pergami. Sly hints about used bedclothes, immodest clothing and the couple's enjoyment of an obscene dance by Mahomet the Turk had not been the worst of it. A waiter and a cellarmaid had described snatched embraces and indecent stroking in a curtained carriage. When her former servant Majocchi had emerged to take the stand, the queen had cried out and stumbled from the chamber of peers. The drama of that single incident had persuaded many onlookers of her guilt. Her sickness had returned and that night she had been copiously bled. Since then, she had spent much of the time in her robing room, but she returned to watch Louise Demont betray her.

Brougham wrapped his gown tightly around himself as Louise told her story. He studied her closely: an attractive woman with a determined set to her jaw. He sensed she had a sharper brain that her sister Mariette; her weakness was greed. He knew that, during her time with the princess of Wales, Louise had been no angel. She had slept several times with a servant to Caroline's vice-chamberlain and ultimately had conspired in theft with another lover. But one could not escape the fact that she had been privy to her mistress's confidences. Discretion had never been Caroline's strong suit. The next few hours could destroy the queen, perhaps the monarchy itself.

At last he rose to question her. An advocate embarking on a crucial phase of cross-examination has two choices. He may start quietly, seeking to lull the witness into a sense of false security, securing damning admissions before the poor wretch has realized what has happening. Or he may launch into a ferocious counter-attack from the outset. Brougham was at heart an actor. He did not hesitate in opting for the latter course. Faced with a barrage of questions about matters of fact which had been omitted from her evidence-in-chief, the woman fell into the trap and claimed a faulty recollection.

"*Je me ne rappelle pas.*"

Brougham refused to let her off the hook. He reminded her that her sister remained devoted to the mistress whom they had both once served. He teased her with the letters which she had written to Caroline after her dismissal, pleading for forgiveness.

Louise coloured. She said they were a *double entendre*.

Brougham's lip curled. "There is a shorter, Anglo-Saxon word which better describes your evidence, is there not?"

He glanced at Caroline. The queen, he thought, was forming the word with her lips. *Lies!*

Not for the first time on a particular November evening, Denman raised his glass. "To Henry Brougham, the finest orator in England!"

Brougham thumped the dinner table in delight. "We showed them, Thomas!"

"I must say that your submissions were masterly. 'Save the country, my lords, from the horror of this catastrophe . . . She has the heartfelt prayers of the people. She wants no prayers of mine.' I tell you, Henry, I have heard it said that even their Lordships' House has never heard such sustained eloquence."

"I trust that she will remember how much she owes to her lawyers," Brougham said dryly. "I suppose that she will insist on attending the coronation. Yet it is difficult to imagine how George could tolerate her presence at Westminster Abbey."

"How can he prevent it?"

"Who knows?" Brougham's face darkened. "I am troubled, Thomas. It has occurred to me that our glorious triumph may have an unexpected consequence."

Denham was puzzled. "Which is?"

"It may be that Caroline is now in even greater jeopardy than before."

Denham waved his hand dismissively. "Forgive me, Henry, but at times your mind is too ingenious. You search for complications where none exist. Let us savour the moment. I shall refill your glass."

"Thank you," Brougham said. But under his breath he added: *Yet I am sure that I am right.*

On the day appointed for the coronation, Brougham made his way down Constitution Hill, wondering anxiously what dramas the celebration would bring. The king had made it plain that his wife would not be allowed to spoil the day that he had anticipated with relish for so long. Caroline, however, had let it be known that she was determined not only to attend but to be crowned herself. The city was awash with speculation; some said that if she dared to show her face at the Abbey, the king would have her seized by force and shipped down the Thames to be incarcerated in the Tower of London.

Eventually, he caught sight of the queen dismounting from her carriage in Dean's Yard, close by the Abbey. She and her attendants were dressed in all their finery: she wore muslin, with a purple scarf and befeathered diamond bandeau. Yet for all the elegance of her attire, he thought that age and sickness were taking their toll at last.

She had often complained to him of her stomach problems and he noted that her features today seemed more sunken than ever. His sense of foreboding had never been so strong. He was well aware that, in the eyes of many, his fate was inextricably linked with hers.

Arm in arm with her chamberlain, Lord Hood, she led her party up to the door of the west cloister. The chamberlain waved a piece of paper, but then Caroline said something and the attendant shook his head. She gestured impatiently, then tossed her head and led the way to the door which gave on to the east cloister. The pantomime repeated itself.

Brougham saw Caroline flinch at her rejection. "Hood has contrived to acquire a ticket," he said to himself, despairing at the evidence of his own eyes, "but she declines to proffer it to gain admittance. She is insisting that she be allowed inside by virtue of her status as wife of the king."

The queen called for her carriages. Grim-faced, she climbed inside and was driven round to Poets' Corner. Brougham followed in her wake, listening as the onlookers in the public stands shouted words of encouragement, while the gentry watching down from the roof of the House of Commons kept crying, "Shame!"

Suddenly she dismounted and headed with her chamberlain towards Westminster Hall. Hood knocked on the door and bellowed, "The queen – open!"

A porter opened the door a fraction. Looking inside, Brougham could see a group of young pages, dressed in red, gathering round. Their faces were pink with excitement.

Caroline stamped her foot. "Let me pass – I am your queen!" she demanded. "I am queen of Britain!"

Like everyone else in the crowd outside, Brougham held his breath, unsure what would happen next. He could imagine the urgent whispered consultations taking place within the Hall. Would the king relent?

Then he heard a stentorian voice from inside. "Do your duty! Shut the door!"

And as Caroline stared at the little pages, the great wooden door was slammed shut in her face.

Long after midnight, Caroline asked Brougham if he had stayed to watch the procession after her humiliating departure from the scene.

He inclined his head and said in a neutral tone that the whole business had, beyond doubt, cost the country a great deal of money. It would be cruel to marvel in her presence at the pomp and ceremony which the king had arranged.

All through the evening meal she had put on a show of unconcern, laughing and talking vivaciously. She had kept her companions in conversation so long that Brougham guessed that she dreaded going up to her bed alone. He sensed how deeply wounded she must feel and this impression was reinforced when she said that she had heard that the onlookers at the coronation had cheered her husband with affection for the first time since his ascent to the throne.

"If they did not cheer him on the day of his coronation," Brougham said, struggling to conceal his dismay at the day's events, "things would have come to a pretty pass."

"I shall never let him win!" she cried. Tears began to trickle down her cheeks. "I have support aplenty in Scotland, I shall travel to meet the people there. They have no brief for my husband. They will take my part."

Brougham flinched. "Your Majesty, have a care! Do not expose yourself to a charge of treason!"

Suddenly she seemed to be gripped by a spasm of pain. "Mariette!" she called. "I need water and a drop of magnesia with laudanum!"

Brougham caught the maid's eye. Her face was white. As she passed him, she gave an anxious shake of the head and muttered something under her breath.

He rather thought she had said, "My Lord Brougham, I fear she will kill herself."

A fortnight later, Brougham stood with Denman outside the queen's bedroom. "The will is prepared?" he asked.

Denman produced a document tied with pink ribbon. "Its contents have been most carefully checked." He paused. "She says she wishes to be buried in Brunswick. Her tomb should bear a solitary inscription: 'Caroline of Brunswick, the injured queen of England.' "

Brougham winced. "And the doctors' diagnosis?"

"Those who accuse lawyers of loving to sit on the fence should consider the antics of the medical profession," Denman said with a shake of the head. "She has been attended by a host of doctors. Holland, Warren, Ainslie the king's physician. They seem unable to agree about anything. One man says she is suffering from acute inflammation, another claims that there is an obstruction in the bowel. A tumour, a disorder of the gastric system, there are as many opinions as there are medical men. She is nauseous all the time and in constant pain."

"Have they bled her?"

"More than once, but to no avail. Henry, I am sure that she is dying." Denman sighed. "Shall we go in?"

Mariette ushered them into the queen's presence. Caroline was sitting up in bed and Brougham's first fleeting impression was that she might be recovering. Her eyes seemed brighter than in the recent past and when she greeted him her voice was firm. He read out the contents of the will and she listened with every appearance of understanding. The witnesses were called in and she reached out of bed and, taking the pen from Brougham, signed with a steady hand.

"I am going to die, Mr Brougham," she whispered. "But it does not signify."

"Your Majesty's physicians are of quite a different opinion," he lied.

"Ah, I know better than them. I tell you I shall die, but I don't mind it. I am so fatigued. Leave me now."

After all that she had endured, Brougham believed her. At the door, he paused and took a last look at her. Her head was resting on the pillow. Already she was asleep. As he gazed back at the royal bed and the table next to it, a bleak suspicion began to form in his mind.

Half way down the corridor, he paused and clapped his hand to his forehead. "I forgot my pen! Thomas, I shall rejoin you in a moment."

Before Denham could say a word, he hurried back into the royal bedchamber. This was no time for observing the proprieties. Caroline was snoring gently. Biting his lip, he moved to her bedside. Soon he would learn whether his apprehensions were misplaced; and, if they were not, he would have to decide what to do next.

On 15 August 1821, Caroline's body was taken on board the frigate *Glasgow* in the busy harbour of Harwich for the final journey to Brunswick. The sun was high, the sea calm and the crowd sombre. At intervals a gun was fired and all the while a naval captain who had served the queen long and faithfully sat on the pier and tried without success to control his grief.

Denham turned to Brougham and said, "So you decided not to accompany her to Brunswick?"

Brougham hesitated. "Well, Thomas. It is a fact that I was her close adviser. But I was never so much for her. I am a patriot, when all is said and done. My first loyalty must always be to the king. If I were to sail with the coffin, it might create the wrong impression."

"George has the last laugh after all," Denman said with a frown.

"I always feared it," Brougham said.

A week later, Brougham dined with Hutchinson at Westminster and when the meal was over he lit a cigar.

"So how fares the king, now that he is a widower?"

Hutchinson was guarded. "His Majesty was, naturally, affected by the death of his wife. Despite their – estrangement – he was not without sympathy for the difficulties which she encountered in the final years of her life."

Brougham raised his eyebrows. "You surprise me. At the very least, I would have thought that the king would have been relieved to learn of the news. Even if not surprised."

Hutchinson stared at him, as if trying to fathom whether there was a deeper meaning to the lawyer's words. "It was common knowledge that Caroline had been ailing for some time. I gather that even before she reached England she suffered a period of sickness during her passage across the Alps."

"Do you know," Brougham said, leaning across the table, "that within two hours of her death, the queen's body was swollen and black?"

"What of it? Presumably there was an infection of the blood."

"Impossible to tell. The queen left a specific instruction that her body should not be opened. The cause of her death is guesswork. The guesses, of course, are plentiful: everything from death caused by an excess of magnesia to the same disease of porphyria that so afflicted the king's own father, her uncle."

The waiter refilled their tumblers. Hutchinson nodded. "We shall never know."

"No," Brougham said, before adding quietly, "But my own guess is that she was murdered. Killed by the administration of poison."

"What?" Hutchinson banged his glass down, spilling whisky on the table.

"I have been thinking long and hard. In addition, I have studied any number of learned tomes. As you know, the law is not my only interest. Amongst many other things, science fascinates me."

"You are known as a man of many parts," Hutchinson said grimly.

"I am grateful for the compliment. Well, the queen's symptoms tally with the conventional indications of arsenic poisoning. Vomiting, diarrhoea, fainting fits. The poison can have a cumulative effect, so that in the end, a very small dose can suffice to kill."

"Do you realize what you are saying?" Hutchinson hissed. "It is quite monstrous! Who could have wished Caroline dead – and yet had the means to achieve the end?"

"His Majesty," Brougham said, "is a man determined not to be denied his inheritance – the throne. Look what has happened to those who seemed to stand in his way. His father – consigned to the madhouse, allowing the son to rule as Regent for a decade before his proper time. His estranged wife – dead at fifty-three."

"And you accuse him?"

"I am a loyal subject." Brougham's tone was ironic. "I know where my allegiance lies. As I said earlier, I am only indulging in guesswork. Call it fantasy, if you like."

Hutchinson's eyes narrowed. "What form does this fantasy take?"

"Picture a man who is about to inherit the kingdom of England yet who is burdened with a troublesome wife. His government is desperate to make sure that the woman does not threaten the security of the state. There are grounds to believe that her adultery may entitle her husband to a divorce. Damning evidence has been taken from a dismissed servant, Louise Demont. The authorities take care of Louise – they pay handsomely to bring her to Britain and keep her sweet. But they are rightly cautious. They know that Louise's sister is still in the queen's service. Let us say that they make contact with that sister covertly, bribe her to keep them informed of her mistress's movements and whether she means to return to England. The girl, Mariette, appears to be devoted to Caroline, but has a greater loyalty to her sister. They were united by blood. I suspect that lust for money – and ruthlessness – ran in the family."

"Go on," Hutchinson said grimly.

"The trouble is that even when Caroline tells Mariette what she intends to do, she is apt to change her mind at a moment's notice.

Thus Mariette's value as an informant proves to be strictly limited. So the authorities hatch a darker plan."

"Indulging you a little further, what does this darker plan entail?"

"Mariette is persuaded to start feeding Caroline with arsenic. She is told that the dose should not be fatal, but rather just sufficient to prevent her from returning to London. Caroline duly falls ill on her way home, but the plan fails: she is not deterred. She makes ever more mischief. Mariette feeds her more arsenic. Caroline is ailing, but intransigent. When she arrives back in the capital, Louise keeps her distance, but their half-sister acts as a go-between." Brougham jabbed his finger at his companion. "I saw Mariette waving to her from the window at Alderman Wood's house, but at first I was reluctant to draw the obvious inference. There had never been a question about Mariette's integrity. Only after the queen was dead did a logical explanation for much that had perturbed me finally occur to me."

"As you said," Hutchinson muttered, "you have been allowing your imagination free rein."

"Court proceedings were inevitable. George was insistent. But – thanks, in no small measure, to excellence of advocacy – Louise was discredited and Caroline acquitted. The inital scheme had proved a catastrophic failure. An alternative solution had to be found."

"Namely?"

"Mariette was kept in place. The authorities were hoping that she would help to encourage Caroline to surrender gracefully, to take a pittance and leave the kingdom. It was an impossible objective. She was intent upon being crowned. The farce at Westminster Abbey was the final straw. George knew he would never be free of her whilst she remained alive. But if she died . . ."

"You are suggesting – what? That this maid killed her?"

"Mariette Bron, yes." Brougham coughed. "I took the liberty of taking a bottle of cosmetic preparation from Her Majesty's bedside table. Analysis confirmed my suspicion: it was laced with arsenic."

"You have been treading on dangerous ground."

"Indeed." Brougham sighed. "And before you make the point, let me say that I recognize that nothing can be proved. The powers-that-be are not so foolish. I believe the peasants of Styria in Austria regularly use arsenic for cosmetic purposes. For all any of us know, the lady from Brunswick might have had the same risky taste for it.

Besides, if there were a breath of suspicion, I expect that Mariette would meet a regrettable accident. Her death might be passed off as the suicide of a devoted servant unable to cope with the loss of her beloved mistress."

"Of course," Hutchinson said in a careless tone, "if there were any merit at all in these treacherous ramblings, the life of the man who sought to expose the evil conspiracy might itself be at risk."

Brougham looked into Hutchinson's eyes and said steadily, "Believe me, that precise thought has much occupied my mind."

Hutchinson leaned back in his chair. "Your theory is, frankly, absurd. But I appreciate that there are enemies of the government who would find it amusing. Tell me candidly: is it your intention to spread rumour, seek to destabilize your political opponents in the hope of securing personal advancement?"

Brougham shook his head with vigour. "My wish is to bury past misunderstandings. I am loyal to the king. Moreover, I am immodest enough to believe that at some point, perhaps not too distant in the future, I shall obtain preferment on the only basis that appeals to me. On merit."

Hutchinson said slowly, "That would, certainly, be the honourable course."

"Although I have spoken freely with you, I recognize how much mischief could be done by any loose repetition of my idle fancy. I do not propose to discuss the queen's tragic demise with anyone else. No good could come of it, especially since the doctors in attendance – one of them was the king's physician, was he not? – were satisfied that Caroline died of natural causes. Who am I to challenge the verdict of specialists in their field?" Brougham smiled. "Incidentally, perhaps you could tell me whether my hopes for the future seem to be ill-conceived."

"I think I can reassure you on that." Hutchinson returned the smile. "Your ambitions seem to me to be eminently reasonable. The future of a man who is not only gifted but also discreet must be bright. Confidentially, I understand that there may soon be a vacancy on the Woolsack. And I have no doubt that you have the acumen to be one of this country's most distinguished lord chancellors."

"You are more than kind. I am glad we understand each other. With that, perhaps we can drink another toast." Brougham raised his glass. "To King George IV – long live the King!"

THE MODERN CYRANO

Stephen Baxter

The following story scarcely needs an introduction. Suffice it to say that you are about to discover Queen Victoria: Detective.

[Editor's Note: *Queen Victoria (1819–1901) maintained a Journal from the age of thirteen. After Victoria's death, at the Queen's wishes, a selection of this material was transcribed (and edited) by her youngest daughter, Princess Beatrice. The original ms. was destroyed. The following account – based on Journal fragments said to have been retrieved, imperfectly burned, by Osborne House servants – must therefore remain apocryphal.*]

Balmoral. September 3rd, 1849.

. . . Albert has a new enthusiasm.

He has proposed what he calls a *Great Exhibition of Science & Industry*, a convocation of the industrial flair of this Nation & others, to be held perhaps in 2 years. It will be a monument, he says, not just to the new Machine Age, but to what the Ingenuity of Man can accomplish for Good. My dear husband, with his usual energy, has already called a Royal Commission with such luminaries as Mr J. Paxton [*Joseph Paxton, the architect and gardener to the Duke of Devonshire*], & Mr J. S. Russell [*John Scott Russell, engineer*].

Myself somewhat surprised to note the exclusion of Mr I. K. Brunel, the one name above all others to stir the imagination of those of the Public who follow such issues – I only have to witness the mighty transepts rising above Mr Brunel's new Railway station at Paddington to see *that*.

[*This is, of course, a reference to Isambard Kingdom Brunel (1806–59), perhaps the greatest engineer of the era. His achievements included railway systems, bridges and stations – including Padding-ton – and the iron-clad "Great Britain". But Brunel was beset by financial difficulties, rivals and opponents, and at the time of this writing was about to become immersed in his most difficult – and only partially successful – project, the "Great Eastern".*]

. . . Albert himself disappointed by this, but Mr Brunel is well represented on the Commission by his friends Messrs P. & R., and will no doubt shape the Exhibition mightily. & besides, says Albert, Mr B. is becoming absorbed in some new research into Rocketry.

As a child my mother took me to see a display of Congreve's War Rockets – great ugly iron tubes of gunpowder – but that was superseded by developments in cannon and other artillery pieces, and Rockets are rather old hat. But Albert is excited. Perhaps Mr Brunel is planning to use Rockets to power a carriage, or even some form of aerial Phaeton! – how *intriguing*, if improbable.

A Great Exhibition! Such projects, I know too well, are fraught with ambition & division, especially in these difficult times [*probably a reference to the dispute between the Free Trade advocates and the Protectionists, a dispute which had already threatened the royal family's own position*]. Already we have had a taste of this with a visit from Col. Sibthorpe, who maintains his usual blanket disapproval of all things Modern. [*Colonel Charles Sibthorpe, reactionary Member of Parliament for Lincoln, was well known to the royal family; he it was who moved the amendment in the House – even before Albert came to England – that his stipend should be reduced from £50,000 to £30,000.*] My Poor Angel! He is as blond & *handsome* as when I first met him, 15 yrs and 7 children ago, even if the burden of care he has assumed make him look rather older than his 30 yrs. His enthusiasm for his Exhibition is fired, of course, by his desire to be loved by his adopted country – a desire which, I counsel him daily, may lead him into danger if he speaks too freely on political issues. But it is endlessly endearing, nonetheless. Glad that George A. is working with Albert on this. [*George Anson, appointed Albert's private secretary on the prince's first arrival in Britain, later treasurer; the two men became close friends, sharing loves of hard work, chess, billiards, shooting, coursing with greyhounds and hunting.*]

[*The royal family spent September 1849 at Balmoral, as was their custom.*]

Windsor castle. October 13th 1849.

George A. [*Anson*] is dead.

Can scarcely believe those words, even as I shape them on this page. My poor Angel is devastated.

This bad news came after we had all had *such* a time at Balmoral. George A. left with us on September 27th, but because his wife – who is heavy with child – was not at all well, George sought Albert's permission to stop in Derby and visit her at her parents' home in Staffordshire. He would combine this, he said, with an Exhibition meeting with Mr I. K. Brunel, who was in the area attending to some railway project or other, and none other than Col. Sibthorpe, who was travelling the other way, to Scotland.

And it was there – so we heard a day after the event – at New Lodge in Neewood Forest, that George A. was found dead in his bed, on the morning of Tuesday 9th October.

My Albert is distraught. He often said he had but 2 friends in this country, George and Sir R. Peel [*Sir Robert Peel, Tory Prime Minister, 1841–6*]. And now the closer of them is gone. Admit I was concerned for Mrs A., who is one of my Bedchamber Women.

And as for Albert, I am afraid that such weeping appears unmanly to all.

Both of us travelled to Staffordshire to comfort the family. Our visit was unannounced; no desire to draw stares at such a time.

The family of Mrs A. met us, distressed and distracted, in their small and rather plain house. Col. Sibthorpe was there – a portly, *corrupt*-looking man with that florid complexion that comes after a lifetime of hunting and excessive indulgence. He habitually wears a silver high-pitched hunting-dog whistle around his neck. A *hateful* man, not at all *sympathique* at such a time.

And there was poor George A., laid out in his finery in the parlour; even as we visited he was being measured by the undertaker, a shy boy who could barely meet my eye.

The house was rather cluttered, in fact, with some obscure Equipment Mr Brunel had been demonstrating [*Brunel had left the previous day*] – pipes & tubes & cylinders of Gas and the like. Some of these Gases were noxious, and Albert showed me a protective mask Mr Brunel had urged him to wear.

[*Brunel's own notebooks shed a little light on this meeting. Brunel had been testing the energetics of rocket propellants, and had become frustrated at the low efficiencies of solid gunpowder as a propellant. Therefore he was beginning to experiment with combinations of liquid propellants, such as ether or alcohol burning with liquid oxygen. He showed Anson and Sibthorpe results from a small test stand he had erected near Morpeth, Northumberland. His purpose in meeting Sibthorpe seems to have been part of a campaign by the prince's friends to win over opponents of the Exhibition.*]

. . . Albert was distraught anew over the body of his friend, & he began to insist, rather *impracticably*, that he would refuse to appoint a new Treasurer . . .

. . . And it was then that Col. Sibthorpe began to whisper, for the first time, his poisonous accusations against Mr I. K. Brunel – *who he claims has Murdered George A.*!

Col. S. produced a cylinder of some Gas, and demonstrated that it was empty. This was part of the collection of apparatus produced by Mr Brunel, and left here. Col. S. claimed that it had been found beside the body of George – and that was confirmed by the maid.

Col. Sibthorpe's contention is that Mr Brunel, that last evening, entered George's room. Mr B. opened his Gas cylinder and departed the house; the Gas, hissing out, poisoned poor George as he slept. The doctor who visited confirmed that George's death was consistent with a kind of *suffocation*.

There you have it: Mr Isambard Kingdom Brunel, *Murderer* of the Keeper of the Queen's Privy Purse!

Albert and I could scarcely believe this wild nonsense. But Col. Sibthorpe insisted on its consistency and truth. Mr Brunel is unstable, he claimed, like all engineers; he had done in poor George as revenge for imagined slights over the Exhibition. & who else would have had the cunning or opportunity to deploy the Gas cylinder in such a fashion?

We agreed there and then that we would speak of this no more. Poor George is lost; it would do him no good, and the Nation a deal of damage, to have such a scandal dragged out in the pages of *The Examiner*. We shall consider the matter quietly, and consult those who might handle the affair with some *discretion*.

So hard to believe. Mr I. K. Brunel, *a Murderer!* And yet, who else? . . .

. . . Will record here some details of the scene that I found odd. [*Victoria sketched frequently and prided herself on her eye for detail.*] This business of the Gas cylinder, for example.

George A. – his tearful wife confirmed – was a light sleeper. He might have slept through the entry of some Malfeasant into his bedroom, even the setting up of the cylinder. But the escape of the Gas would cause a *hiss* which would surely wake the soundest sleeper. And yet George – we are assured – slept peacefully, until he entered the deeper Sleep from which there is no waking. What could suppress the hiss of escaping Gas?

Another thing. While the undertaker was measuring George, I could not help but notice that his arms *protruded* – just a fraction – from the sleeves of his jacket. And yet this was, of course, his finest dress suit. Why should it fit poorly?

Took the liberty of inquiring after George's height from a puzzled undertaker, and compared his result with the recollection of his wife. According to the functionary, George A. in death was a *good half-inch* taller than in life! . . .

Windsor Castle. December 25th 1850.

A charming Xmas morning. Albert's tree, decorated in the German style, looks delightful, and the children much excited . . .

A gift from Mr I. K. Brunel. It is a small Dewar flask, engraved with Mr Brunel's crest. On opening the flask Albert extracted – with some care – a small glass bottle of Porter. The Porter was self-evidently liquid – once could shake the bottle and see so – but but when Albert had it opened, *the beer immediately froze.*

Albert, who has always been intrigued by such things, bombarded me with explanations: higher Pressure induces the beer to stay liquid at lower Temperatures, & so forth; all deeply uninteresting. Mr Brunel has evidently been experimenting in the application of Liquid Air, and so has learned the rudiments of Refrigeration and Cold Storage. What is the *usefulness* of Liquid Air I cannot imagine. Perhaps this has something to do with Mr Brunel's search for new Fuels.

At any rate, such a light-hearted Gift scarcely seems to me the action of a Murderer! Albert still distracted by the loss of George A . . .

I too on this best of days find my mind has turned to poor George A. – or at least to the odd business of his ill-fitting suit.

Bertie will often seem a little taller in the morning than in the preceding night; I noticed this yesterday by the riding up of his pyjama legs as he ran about the morning rooms. (Though I confess my attention was more concerned with controlling his *rowdiness* than any physiological studies.) At first I put this down to a spurt of childish growth overnight. But today I measured myself carefully and found I grew a *full half-inch taller* overnight! – which, for a person of 5'2", is a blessing sadly lost. Perhaps it is something to do with the compression during the day of those discs which make up the spine, or other postural anomalies.

Could this explain the strange measurement of dead George A.?
. . . My head spins!

[*Brunel's journals show that during the winter of 1849–50 his rocketry research continued. He was considering the use of what he called "cosmic trains" – rockets designed to achieve greater altitudes by being stacked one on top of the other. And he was investigating the "problems of vertical launches in air". Most of this experimentation took place in seclusion on the moors of Northumberland, but there was a small-scale public trial in Hyde Park – a series of rifles and small artillery pieces fired straight up in the air. The team sheltered under a metal carapace, and when the firing was over, they sought out the bullets and shot where they fell. At the time of the incident described below Brunel himself was in Northumberland.*]

Buckingham Palace. March 18th 1850.

A bleak, unseasonably raw day. Spring seems far . . .

Our mood is bleak, like the climate. It seems scarcely creditable. I have to record here the untimely death of *Sir R. Peel* – the 2nd of my husband's *dearest* friends, and supporter of his Exhibition.

And, once again, Mr I. K. Brunel – named as an unlikely *Murderer!*

I will not pretend I care so keenly about Sir Robert, who has always seemed to me a *poor* Tory substitute for Lord M. [*Whig Prime Minister Lord Melbourne, who guided Victoria in her early years; Victoria remained instinctively a Whig supporter*]. I shall record the incident – not as seen by public, nor even the *Illustrated* [*The Illustrated London News*] – but as reported to us by *A Witness* (I shall *name* later!).

Sir R. was exercising his horse Peter in Rotten Row [*the path which skirts the south side of Hyde Park. Peter, a favourite of Peel, was himself something of a celebrity, for he had several of his teeth – smashed in a fall – replaced by metal posts, screwed in the jaw!*].

Now Mr Brunel's Aerial Experiments in the Park have been gathering a good deal of attention – much of it unfriendly – and Sir R. stopped by the area allotted to the engineer's assistants. It is all, Albert assures me, to do with measuring such ethereal concepts as Air Resistance and Terminal Velocity. The criticism has come, not unreasonably, from neighbours of the Park who fear having their windows shot out. For myself I suspect this is all a *bit of puff* by Mr B.

Sir Robert waited – on his horse, in a place he was told was safe – while a rank of rifles was fired in the air. Down came a shot (so our *Witness* says) which slapped Peter's rump.

The horse reared and Sir R. was thrown. He was a big, heavy man, and he smashed his collar-bone and shoulder-bone. I know he had an acute sensitivity to pain, and it took him 3 days of *agony* to die.

Our *Witness* had come to the Park to berate with Mr Brunel's minions over the Aerial experiments. In fact he had invited Sir R. Peel to be there – and he even had time to feed Sir R.'s horse (before the accident) with a lump of sugar. And he was so close to the drama he found the lump of deformed shot which (it appears) startled the horse.

And now, once more, Mr I. K. Brunel has been accused of Murder – and *this time in public*. For the Witness claims that Peel's horse was *deliberately* targeted by Mr Brunel's unfortunate aerial shot!

And the identity of our Witness? – *it was Col. Sibthorpe*.

I need scarcely summarize the effect of all this on Albert, who is now, he says, *friendless* and *desolate*.

It scarcely helps his mood that his Great Exhibition is coming under renewed attack, from the newspapers, the Protectionists who drove Sir R. Peel out of office – and in Parliament, by Col. Sibthorpe himself. [*At the time Sibthorpe was pushing for a vote of censure over the use of Hyde Park for the Exhibition.*]

Mr Brunel is riding out the scandal over Sir R. Peel's death. Col. S. is (happily) not a very credible witness. Nevertheless Mr B. must be damaged. My Albert's Exhibition, with its 2 greatest supporters lost & its greatest potential champion wounded, looks imperilled . . .

. . . Yet my jackdaw mind is caught by oddities. For in *The Times* – amidst all the acres of print devoted to Peel – there was a brief paragraph devoted to his poor horse Peter, who had, it seemed, a small piece of silver lodged in his artificial teeth! . . .

Osborne. June 21st 1850.

Yesterday was my Accession. 13 yrs already! . . .

There was much celebration in the capital . . . [including] . . . spectacular fireworks in the Park . . . [*This display featured several of Brunel's "cosmic train" experimental multistage rockets.*]

Albert remains obsessed with this business of Mr Brunel and Sir R. Peel. In his usual methodical way he has begun experiments to determine if the tragedy of the falling bullet could have unfolded as Col. Sibthorpe *claimed* – & if so, if Mr Brunel could have been responsible!

Albert has fired a variety of hunting guns vertically in the air, his own John Manton muzzle-loader and his Greener-type rifle included. He times the bullets' fall, and then he has the poor gillies run about collecting the spent shells . . . [*Albert was a natural countryman, as well as a keen amateur scientist; this account is plausible.*] The gillies insist on wearing thick books on their heads! . . .

Osborne. August 21st 1850

I am awaiting George Combe, expert in Phrenology, who is to examine Bertie's skull; meanwhile Arthur is proving a handful [*Arthur, later Duke of Connaught; Victoria's new-born fifth child*] . . .

In Albert's experiments, none of the bullets landed within 100 yds, and some as much as $\frac{1}{4}$ mile away, and others were lost altogether.

A bullet will reach a height of more than 1 mile in 15 sec., but because of the Resistance of the Air the bullet spends much of its fall at low speeds ("like a mouse in a mineshaft", as one of the gillies told me – *ugh!*), and is susceptible to lateral movements by the wind. And thus is explained the dispersion.

One must conclude, then, that although it may have been rather *irresponsible* for Mr Brunel to mount his experiments in a public Park, and although it is *possible* that poor Peel's horse may have been struck by a falling bullet, it is all rather *unlikely* – and certainly, concludes Albert (& I) could not reflect *deliberate* intent by Mr Brunel!

It is all rather puzzling . . .

. . . Meantime I have, in spare moments, been performing some small experiments of my own.

I remembered the poor horse of Sir R. Peel, found with a scrap of silver lodged in its peculiar metal teeth. I myself have more than 1 dental cavity filled with Amalgam, or Mercury, or whatever those fellows use. In the privacy of my Bedroom I reached into my mouth with a small silver coin and touched a filling with it.

Pain *sharp* enough to make me jump! (I imagine it has something to do with Electricity flowing between the dissimilar metals.)

There is every reason to believe that Peel's horse may have suffered just such a jolt, when that lump of silver touched its metallic teeth. And that would surely suffice to cause it to throw poor Sir R. Peel. No falling bullets required! – just a fragment of silver . . .

Osborne. August 30th 1850.

Albert came to me in a great agitation today, for he claims to have been informed about what Mr I. K. Brunel is up to! [*The prince's informant may have been John Scott Russell, whom Brunel regarded as a rival.*]

Albert now believes Mr Brunel is planning to build – and fly – a gigantic Rocket of a new type, fuelled by Liquid Air and alcohol! This explains the Rocketry studies, Refrigeration on a grand scale, & c.

The old War Rockets of Congreve had a range of a mile or 2. But with a large enough Rocket one could throw a load as far as one wished – so far, in fact, that one could evade the horizon and *circle the Earth altogether*. It would be an Artificial Moon!

Albert, who has studied a little Astronomy, finds this idea fantastic. But I have read my de Bergerac. [*This seems to be a reference to Cyrano de Bergerac's "Voyage Dans La Lune" (1649), in which Cyrano wrote (with satirical purpose) of a flying machine powered by rockets.*]

Quite a *firework* to commemorate the Exhibition! – Mr Brunel would be a Modern Cyrano, outshining his rivals and opponents.

But Albert is deeply distressed by the prospect of this exciting new form of machinery.

In the world of Futurity, Albert says, War will be different. It will be fought on a massive scale, Nation pitched against Nation, with *every* resource devoted to the conflict. If Britain and France were to go to War, for example, it would become essential for each Nation to strive to *eliminate* the Industrial capacity of the other . . .

. . . And that is precisely, says Albert, the purpose of Mr Brunel's Rocket machine. By carrying tons of explosives 1000s of miles through the upper Air, it would become possible to destroy, for example, the industrial towns of England – & the people who work there. Every human being, man, woman or child, would become a potential soldier!

It is indeed a horrific prospect . . . [*Horrific to one of Albert's sensibilities. Albert took a keen interest in the welfare of the working classes of Britain; in this he showed a better developed social imagination, in the new urban Britain of 1850, than Victoria, who simply feared revolt.*]

. . . Albert is determined, he says, to write to Mr Brunel outlining his suspicions, and to insist that he cease his destructive programme at once.

I have rarely seen Albert so agitated. I tried to calm him . . .

Osborne. September 4th 1850.

. . . I am secretly excited!

I believe I have an answer to the peculiar anomaly of release of toxic Gas [*which killed Anson*]. How could its hissing not have woken George long before his fatal succumbing?

A leaf through my Journal brought to mind recall an evening long ago with my dear Lord M. [*Lord Melbourne, then Prime Minister*] and Herschel [*Sir John Herschel, the noted astronomer*]. I fear the science of the discussion – something about an immense telescope being erected in the Southern Hemisphere, & the *exotic* possibilities of travel to other worlds – rather passed me by, & I must have seemed rather stupid! [*Victoria's science education was poor.*]

But Sir John was kind, and he showed me a curiosity he had learned in America from a Professor Leconte (as I recall). Sir John set up an open Gas flame (taking apart a lamp to do it), and a Music Box nearby. The noise of the flame diminished – *and the flame danced and curtseyed in response to the music!* I am afraid I clapped in girlish delight at this display. Sir John tried to explain how the sound can smooth out disturbances in the flow of Gas, lit or unlit, & make it quieter – but I absorbed little of this.

Could this have something to do with poor George's death? – but surely any Music Box would *itself* have woken George.

But after much meditation I think I see a solution. *Penser, c'est voir.*

Much food for thought! – and *must tread carefully*.

Osborne. September 15th 1850.

A beautiful Indian summer's day. Bathed. But tiresome disputes with Pam [*Lord Palmerston, Foreign Secretary*] over the French issue . . .

Called Col. Sibthorpe to visit me, here at Osborne. Col. S. has kept up his campaign of noisy opposition to my husband, and the Exhibition. In the interests of Albert – and the Nation! – I have decided to *confront* the issue.

Received Col. Sibthorpe in my Sitting Room.

This was deliberate. I sat at my writing table, with nearby (though unoccupied) Albert's table – just a little higher than mine, for he is taller – a *Symbol*, I thought cleverly, of he who is wronged in this affair. And I also had set up a Gas lantern, on a small occasional table.

I had Col. Sibthorpe sit on a hard-backed chair, and I am proud to say he looked *extremely* ill at ease – in fact, rather *absurd*, with his florid complexion & his affectation of a dog-whistle around his neck.

First confronted him over his continued opposition to the Exhibition, and I was treated to the ranting which has become a feature of Col. Sibthorpe's work in the House. "I would rather meet a highwayman or see a burglar on my premises than a railway engineer!" & so forth.

I held up my hands to stop this nonsense. "Let us," I said to him rather Grandly, "consider specifics. For some months you, sir, have been mounting a campaign of accusations against Mr Brunel, the engineer – accusations that he was responsible for the *Murders* of Mr G. Anson and Sir R. Peel."

"And so he was," said the defiant Colonel. "The engineer is a madman and a criminal."

"I put it to you," I said sternly, "that there were indeed 2 Murders in this sad situation. But the true Murderer was – *you*, Col. Sibthorpe!"

He had the grace to look startled; then a look of cunning came into his eyes. "Ma'am, there is no proof of that."

"*Au contraire.*" For answer I produced the silver pellet which had startled the horse, and killed Sir R. Peel. "It was *this* which caused that horse to bolt, sir – not some falling bullet! And I put it to you that the only way which that horse could have received this silver is *in the sugar lump which you fed it moments before Peel's death*."

I thought I detected guilt on that ludicrous old face – but he still brazened it out.

But now I turned to the 1st death, of poor George A., and the peculiar business of his height discrepancy – for I believe that discrepancy is evidence that George had died in the *morning he was found*, not the night before!

We are all at our tallest after a night in bed. George A., when found, was a $\frac{1}{2}$ -in. above his average height. But that must mean that he slept through that last night of his life and died *in the morning*, after his body had recovered his overnight tallness. But we have the testimony of Mrs Anson's family that Mr I. K. Brunel departed the house *the night before*!

I admit I am rather proud of my deductions.

"So you see," I said to Col. S., "that Mr Brunel could *not* have opened that Gas cylinder – for, by the morning, he was long gone!"

Col. Sibthorpe blustered. "But even so you have no proof that it was I. Anyone in that household could have committed the crime."

I smiled. "Colonel, would you turn on the gas lantern on the occasional table?"

With much bad grace he lofted his portly frame out of his chair, and complied. The lantern hissed noticeably, even unlit.

I said to him, "I was puzzled by the fact that George – a light sleeper – was not disturbed by this noise. Colonel, would you bend close to the jet – *and blow your dog whistle?*"

He made to refuse, but I mentioned that at the touch of a porcelain bell-pull I could summon the Pages, not to mention several burly manservants.

He bent to the flame and blew his whistle. It was a small silver piece, one of those devices which emit sound of such Pitch that only dogs can hear.

I heard no sound from the whistle – but I could hear the dogs bark, in other parts of the house.

And the noise of the Gas jet was suppressed, to the softest of whispers.

"I admit it would take a little ingenuity," I said, "to find a way to work the whistle through the protective mask of the type Mr Brunel provided. A valve, perhaps . . ."

The Col. slumped back on his chair. Now his voice was a mere hoarse rasp. "Progress, ma'am. It is the very devil. Everything we have fought for and cherished in this country is in flames. And it is the likes of Mr Brunel who wield the torch! . . ." & so on.

"And so you sought to destroy the Exhibition, and Mr Brunel with it?"

"Will you summon the Peelers, ma'am?"

"I will not."

He seemed surprised at what he saw as my leniency. I was *shocked* by the deaths, and the evidence of malice behind them. *But I am Monarch*; I have no wish to see the Nation damaged by scandal. None of it would bring back Sir R. Peel or George A. I told him I wish only that my husband's Exhibition be a success – and that Col. Sibthorpe should withdraw his opposition forthwith. To save my Albert from further distress, Col. S. should also withdraw his allegations about Mr B. – the unfortunate deaths of George A. and Sir R. Peel would be attributed to natural cause. And Col. S. should preferably, retire from public life.

For a noisy *buffoon* like Col. Sibthorpe, enforced anonymity for the rest of his days will be justice enough.

So there it ends! . . . But so exhausting. Tonight I shall sleep the *sommeil des justes* . . .

[*Sibthorpe withdrew his opposition to Albert, and did little to come to public attention for the rest of his life. The death of Peel was simply attributed to the fall from his horse, while Anson's was attributed to a "paralysis or fit".*]

Windsor Castle. May 1st 1851.

A magnificent day!

It has been the Opening [*of the Great Exhibition*]. Albert's dearest name is immortalized with his conception, and my own dear country showed she was worthy of it: a monument to Albert's patience, temper, firmness & energy . . .

[The opening] took place in Paxton's giant building of iron and glass, erected in Hyde Park – not so very far, in fact, from the place poor Sir R. Peel lost his life. We stood on a stage beneath a gigantic, airy cupola, with an acre of red carpet laid over the grass, & the multitudinous exhibits and fountains and *trees* all around us. Never have I felt so out-of-doors in a building!

The people came in their 1000s. There have even been special trains to bring the Workers of the industrial towns. It was remarkable to see the people *en gala*, neatly dressed and well-behaved – quite evidently *citizens* of our new Nation.

The Opening itself was a Procession of some pomp, headed by myself and Albert, with a great March of Engineers, Churchmen, Nobility & Parliamentarians to follow.

I observed a drab, rather squat figure as high as 4th from the front, in solitary state. He wore a baggy frock coat, a battered top hat, and from his mouth protruded a large & vile-smelling cigar. Somehow I would not have been surprised to see machine oil splashed on his solid hands.

It was, of course, Mr Isambard Kingdom Brunel.

In the end his contribution to the Exhibition was rather modest. He did have a rail engine, called *Lord of the Isles* – a broad-gauge flyer, whatever that might mean – mounted on a plinth in the Engineering Hall, and rather fine it looked too. And he also had a rather terrifying Rocket motor, with large "Centrifugal Pumps" to feed Liquid Air & fuel into a giant Burning Chamber. But that was all . . .

. . . After the ceremonial I took a moment to meet [Brunel]. He was affable, and he returned my gaze with a direct intelligence I rather admired.

"It was a rum affair, this business of Col. Sibthorpe," I said.

He shrugged with a Philosophical air. "I have spent my life plagued by Fools and Thieves and other opponents to Progress, ma'am."

"You do not look like a Murderer of Populations, Mr Brunel."

He looked shocked.

"My husband believed your giant Rockets would be used to bombard the French or the Germans."

"I sought only to achieve a great spectacle," he said.

"An Artificial Moon?"

"In any event I am done with Rocketry. I have no Rocket on the face of the Earth, and will build no more."

I was *suspicious* of this *ambiguous* reply! – for Mr Brunel is a stubborn man, who would not back away from a challenge until he had Proven his Point. Is it possible he has *already* achieved his goal?

I was, of course, neglecting my wider duties, and I prepared to move away. But I had one final question for him. "Tell me, Mr Brunel. If you *had* made a new Moon – what would it look like?"

He assured me it would appear as a star, circling the Earth in 1 hour and a $\frac{1}{2}$, and so crawling steadily across the sky. "But that is a vision for another century, ma'am."

"But *British* engineers will fulfil that vision, Mr Brunel."

He bowed.

And so we parted. We agreed that it would be best for *all* if we did not speak of this affair again . . .

Osborne. May 2nd 1851.

A welcome return to the Isle. The children were rather fractious after the excitement of [the Exhibition] . . .

In the night I spent some time wandering in the gardens. I hoped to study the sky, looking for a wandering star. For I am suspicious of Mr I. K. Brunel!

But it was cloudy.

I put the incident from my mind, and found dear Albert, & we turned our minds to our plans for the extension of Balmoral . . .

[*Albert's Exhibition was a great success, attracting six million visitors. Its profits were used to fund the construction of the great Museums in Kensington.*

There is probably no way to verify the queen's remarkable closing speculation. Is it possible Isambard Kingdom Brunel sent a satellite into Earth orbit a century before Sputnik 1?

Certainly the surviving evidence hints of developments by Brunel that anticipated by seventy years the work of such rocketry pioneers as Robert Goddard and Wernher von Braun. But Brunel's accounts show that his expenditure in Northumberland ceased soon after Albert's letters of protest of August 1850. The test rig, whatever its purpose, was dismantled completely and the moor land allowed to revert. No sign of rocketry was left for inspection.

There were local tales, however, of a great event on one of Brunel's final nights on the moor – a "noise like a door slamming in hell" and "a rising liquid light like the Sun at midnight" (JK Kensal, "Legends of the Northumberland Moors", 1956). But there is no proof. These stories – like the rest of this account – must be considered apocryphal.

Like Victoria herself, we shall never know.]

Edward VIII ❧

NEWS FROM NEW PROVIDENCE

Richard A. Lupoff

In recent years we tend to look back upon the Abdication Crisis of 1936, when Edward VIII forsook his crown for the love of Mrs Wallis Simpson, as something romantic and idealistic. In truth Edward (or David as he was known by his family) never cared much for pomp and ceremony. He was selfish and desired to follow only his own caprices. Even after his abdication he could not stop interfering in foreign affairs and subsequent revelations about his involvement with the Nazis up to and during the Second World War paint a very different picture of this king besotted with his lover. It is this Edward, Duke of Windsor, whom we encounter in the following story.

His royal robes were heavy, heavy. And so hot! Why was it so hot in the Cathedral? It was only June. Why could the Archbishop not complete the crowning and the anointing, the blessing of the monarch, the placement of scepter and orb? Then he would present his queen consort to the nation and the empire and be damned to the PM and the rotten dog-collared clergy, that bloodless superannuated fool Cosmo Lang, and –

– and suddenly he was looking up at the high ceiling above his bed, where the broad blades of a slowly-turning fan could do little more than stir the hot, moist air of this damned backwater island. The dream was gone, the dream that had come and gone so many times, and he was king no longer. He was governor-general of a string of rocky protuberances that poked out of this Caribbean backwater and gave home to a couple of thousand colonial expatriates, white chicken farmers and black fishermen.

And his aide was standing just inside the doorway of the bedroom fidgeting like a schoolboy and clearing his throat desperately to get the duke's attention.

He pushed himself upright in bed. His silk pyjamas, the lightest pair he owned, were stained with perspiration. The tropical sun beat through window curtains and turned the room into a blaze of daylight.

The duke reached for a cigarette, struck flame from a lighter embossed with his coat of arms, and drew in a deep draught of smoke. "Yes, Deering?"

"Something terrible, sir." Deering shifted his weight from foot to foot. He still carried the rank of colonel in the guards but he maintained a wardrobe of mufti at the duke's suggestion. "Something terrible has happened."

"Well?"

"It's Sir Walter, sir, Sir Walter Maples. At The Tradewinds, sir."

"Thank you, Deering, I know quite well the name of Sir Walter's home. The duchess and I stayed there at one time, you will remember."

"Yes, sir."

The duke drew on his cigarette, waiting for Deering to go on. The dream came every night now, or so it seemed. It left him high-strung and unrested each morning and a cigarette helped to calm his nerves.

"Sir Walter, sir –"

"Spit it out, Deering."

"He's dead, sir."

The duke hesitated for a split second. Then, "Who knows?"

"His houseman found him, sir."

"Oh, that fellow, yes. What's his name?"

"Plum, sir. Stolid black chap. Not too bright an individual. Skin the colour of his name. Marcus Plum, I believe it is."

"Who else?"

"Sir Walter was alone, sir. Lady Margarethe is off the island. In Canada with her daughter. The only other white man in the house was Mr Harrel. Plum fetched him and –"

"The duchess has not been disturbed, I hope."

"No, sir. As soon as Mr Easton –."

"You didn't tell me that Easton knew."

"Beg pardon, sir. It seems that Mr Harrel telephoned the commissioner as soon as Plum sounded the alarm. Mr Easton felt that the governor-general should be informed at once."

"Well, very rightly so, Deering, very rightly so."

"Yes, sir."

The duke climbed out of bed. He drew one final puff on his cigarette and crushed out the butt in a massive cut-glass ashtray. He smoothed his rumpled pyjamas, running his hands down the silken legs.

"Close the door, will you, Deering? No need to waken the household."

"Yes, sir." Deering complied.

The duke stepped into his lavatory and doffed his pyjama shirt. "All right, Deering, I can hear you from in here. You were saying –?"

While his aide spoke, the duke filled a glass with fresh tap water, wetted his toothbrush and sprinkled tooth-cleansing powder on its bristles. He gave his teeth a thorough brushing. Having rinsed his mouth, he instructed Deering to provide a step-by-step review of the sad events at The Tradewinds.

"It's unfortunate that we have to rely on the negro's version, sir."

"Nevertheless, Deering, nevertheless."

"Yes, sir. Yes. Well, apparently Sir Walter indicated that he wanted to spend the day fishing."

The duke shook his head. "Indicated how, Deering? To whom? You must be specific."

"I apologize, sir. I assume that Sir Walter would have spoken with Plum the previous evening. Last evening, sir."

"Are you unaware, Deering, that Sir Walter hosted a small dinner last night in honour of the duchess and myself, at The Tradewinds?"

"No, sir."

"No?" The duke raised an eyebrow. "No, you were unaware? Or no, you were not unaware?"

"Sorry, sir. I meant to say that, no, sir, I am not unaware of that fact. That is, I am quite aware that the governor and the duchess dined at The Tradewinds. As I recall, sir, the guest list was quite small, just Sir Walter Maples, Mr Harrel, Count Grenner, and Sir Walter's son-in-law, M. Delacroix. The duchess was the only lady present."

Of course. The duchess was at her best surrounded by male admirers who sought her favour and attention. She did not care for female companionship; it smacked inevitably of competition.

"Yes, M. Delacroix," the duke said. "Why the Vichy authorities didn't slap him in irons, I shall never understand. Or turn him over the Germans. The Gestapo would know how to deal with M. Antoine Delacroix, you can rest assured of that, Deering."

Deering ran his finger around his collar uncomfortably. He wished he could switch to clothing more suited to the climate of these islands, but the duke was adamantly opposed to the relaxation of Britannic propriety. More likely, Deering thought, it was the duchess's iron will rather than the duke's adherence to tradition that was at play.

He suppressed a sigh.

The duke asked, "Who else, Deering? You said that Commissioner Easton, Harrel and this negro, Plum, know about Maples. Who else?"

"That's all, sir."

"Well, why the devil didn't Easton telephone me? Why didn't he come straight to Government House and inform me? Who does he think he is, some ha'penny gumshoe? Who does he think I am?"

Deering bit back an impulse to answer the question and instead waited for the duke to continue. But the duke emerged from the lavatory wrapped in a heavy chenille robe.

"Damned place, damned job, can't even get a reliable dresser to tend to my needs. Deering, fetch me an outfit from the wardrobe and be quick." The duke gestured, then waited for Deering to select a medium tan silken shirt, regimental tie, pleated trousers and light linen jacket. He dressed carefully but swiftly, knotting the tie in the pattern he had himself invented and that bore his name world-wide – his personal contribution to sartorial posterity.

"One thought that His Royal Highness might see fit to take a personal hand in the case," Deering ventured.

"Yes, certainly, capital idea. I shall want to speak with Commissioner Easton first."

"Yes, sir. And I thought His Highness might wish to question Mr Harrel and the houseman, Plum, as well."

"Why in the world would I want to – oh, you did say that he found Sir Walter's, ah, remains, did you not? Well, I suppose it might be a good idea. Deering, you'll have to learn to order your thoughts, don't you know? You're much too confused to deal with a crisis such as this. Well, get Easton on the telephone. Have him come here at once. Bring Harrel, of course, and that black fellow. Where is he? Where is Easton? I suppose I must break the news to the duchess. I don't know how she's going to take this."

Deering stepped out of the duke's path, bowing slightly as the duke brushed past him.

The duke tapped gently on the door to the duchess's boudoir. He pressed his ear to the tropical wood. Was that a slight stirring? He tapped again. "Are you awake, my darling? May I enter?"

After a lengthy silence he heard her muttering. He scampered back to his own quarters. Deering was using the telephone. The duke signaled to his aide. Deering uttered a few more syllables and lowered the instrument. "Yes, sir."

"See to it that the duchess has her tea and toast. I don't understand this household, can't keep up the most elementary level of service."

Deering flushed. "At once, sir."

The duke waited outside the duchess's chambers until a servant approached bearing her breakfast tray. "I'll take that." The duke carried the tray into the boudoir and placed it carefully on the bed, its folding legs holding it at a level comfortable for his wife.

She sipped at the tea, swallowed and lowered the cup. The china was of course imported from England and bore the ducal crest. "Now, David, what is the fuss?"

He looked around for a chair, asked permission to be seated, drew it close to her bedside. "I have dreadful news, my dear. Sir Walter Maples is dead."

The duchess raised her chin. "Walter? What happened?"

"His houseman found him in his room this morning. Called Chris Harrel, he was staying over at The Tradewinds. Harrel phoned Ray Easton, then phoned here. Deering gave me the news. I hope you won't be too upset, my darling. If there were a way to spare you this I should have done so."

"But that's terrible, David." The duchess nibbled a corner of her toast. "Absolutely terrible." She washed the toast down with another sip of tea. "You've got to tell me everything."

Before the duke could answer, Deering rapped his knuckles on the duchess's door. "Beg pardon, sir. Madame. Commissioner Easton is here, sir. And Plum."

"Have them wait in my office downstairs. I shall be there as soon as possible." He turned back toward the duchess.

"Has anyone told Margarethe yet?" the duchess asked. "She has to know. Poor thing. All their years together. And she put up with so much from him. You know, David, he was not an easy man. Not easy at all."

The duke looked away. "I shall send your maid up to dress you, my dear."

"Yes, please."

As he descended the broad flight of stairs he wondered what his brother was doing at this moment. Adjusting for the difference in time, it would be late in the day in England. The Nazis had refrained from bombing Buckingham Palace for more than a year after the commencement of hostilities, and they might never have attacked – might never have *needed* to attack, had the duke remained upon the throne. Had he not allowed himself to be shipped off here to this lonely exile. New Providence, Grand Bahama, the rest of the islands of his Lilliputian realm – they might as well be Elba and St Helena.

Ribbentrop had been quite reasonable, after all. And his boss, Herr Hitler – well, a decidedly peculiar chap. Not a pleasant person, very poor manners. But then what could one expect of an individual with his lowly origins? But their ideas had not been so far apart after all. They recognized the twin perils to Mankind, Bolshevism and Jewry. Why should the great Nordic peoples, the Anglo-Saxons and the Germans, be at each other's throats while the lesser races stood by waiting to pick at their carcasses?

It didn't make sense, and he'd tried to make the politicians see that it didn't make sense, but Baldwin and Chamberlain and Churchill were all such a gang of stiff-necked fools, they either could not or would not recognize the reality that confronted them – and England.

Deering held the door for him as he entered his study. Ray Easton,

Christopher Harrel, and the negro, Plum, had preceded him, per his instructions. When the duke entered the room Easton sprang to his feet; Harrel rose lazily to his. Plum was already standing. Easton was a big-boned man. He affected a tropical linen suit and plain black tie. Harrel was attired in a colourful shirt, rough trousers and sandals. Hardly proper attire. The negro wore not a houseman's outfit of black trousers and white jacket but a fisherman's faded trousers and open-necked shirt. He held a battered fisherman's cap in one hand.

The duke shook his head in despair.

He circled the others and seated himself behind his desk. He waved to Deering and the latter closed the office door, remaining inside.

"Now, what is this about Sir Walter Maples, Commissioner?"

"If I may, sir —"

The duke gestured Easton to a seat, Harrel to another.

"Plum here found him," Harrel volunteered. "Soon as he fetched me I could see poor Walt was as dead as a doornail. Look on his face as if he'd seen a ghost. More like he is one, now, eh? Blood spattered all over the walls, coverlet soaked, what a mess, what a mess."

"Thank you, Harrel," the Duke nodded. He kept to himself his opinion of the man, that Harrel was an unspeakable wretch, little better than cockney trash. But he was one of the colony's wealthiest and most influential citizens, a force in the legislative council. One put up with what one must.

The duke asked the houseman, "What have you to say for yourself, Plum?"

The negro closed his eyes as if gathering his thoughts. He held his fisherman's cap in both hands. He shifted his weight from foot to foot. How like Deering, the duke thought.

"Well?"

"Sah, Sah Walter ask me last night. Your Highness and her ladyship takes your partings and leaves Tradewinds for Government House and he ask me, can I take him out this morning. Early, 'fo' sunrise."

"Yes. And did he say what the destination was to be?"

"Chub Cay, sah."

"Chub Cay?" The Duke appeared startled.

"Yes, sah. I reckon, we could pick up a nice easterly this time of year, make it to Chub by midmorning, easy."

The duke lifted a briar pipe from the rack on his desk. He held it in one hand and tapped its bowl in the palm of the other. "Did Sir Walter say what he wanted to do at Chub?"

Plum shook his head from side to side. "No, sah, he did not. He is my employer, sah, and he is entitled. He was my employer, I should say."

"Quite. Well, go on, Plum."

"I woke up and went to Sir Walter's room. I knocked on his do' –"

"What time was this?"

"I don' know the hour, sah. I just know, when I went to bed, I tol' my mind to wake me up good an' early cos' Sir Walter want to get an early start. But he didn't answer my knock, so I went in, Sir Walter's door wasn't locked, and that was when I found him. Sah."

The duke returned the pipe to its place in the rack. He slipped a cigarette case from an inside pocket of his jacket, extracted a cigarette and lit it from a heavy lighter before Deering could spring across the room and hold a flame for him.

He blew a plume of smoke into the air. "Mr Harrel, what can you add to this?"

"Not much, Your Highness. I was sleeping like a log."

"Where is the room in which you were staying?"

"Cross the hall. Down the way from poor old Walt's."

"Do you stay often at The Tradewinds?"

"After last night I didn't want to drive home. Hard to get petrol these days, eh?"

"Indeed. Well, continue."

"So Walt, he said he was a bit low on petrol himself so he couldn't drive me home, eh, so put me up in his guest room."

"This was solely for the purpose of saving petrol?"

"Well, I'll level with you, Governor."

"Please."

"I was kind of, well, two or three sheets to the wind. Had a couple of drinks before the meal and a few glasses of wine and a snifter afterwards, Your Highness. So I thought it wasn't such a grand idea to drive, you see."

"I do indeed. Commendable of you not to risk it. Commendable of Sir Walter to put you up. Were you part of this plan to visit Chub Cay?"

"Not as I can remember."

"Did you and Sir Walter stay up talking last night?"

"Not as I can remember."

The Duke turned sharply toward Plum once again. "You're sure that Sir Walter made no mention of his purpose in visiting Chub Cay? Think hard, Plum."

The negro scratched his head. "I think he might 'o said something, sah."

"Well, and what was that something?" The duke made an effort to contain his impatience.

"Something about countin' on it, sah."

"Counting on it?"

"Somethin' like that, sah."

"It couldn't have been something about the count, could it? Count Grenner?"

Plum looked as if he was going to explode from the strain of concentrating. He held his breath until his eyes bulged, then exhaled explosively. "Sir Walter, he might could have said, 'Count When.' I thought he said, 'Count When.' Like when you pourin' a drink fo' yo' frien' and you say, 'Say when,' he might could have said, 'Count When.' "

"Thank you, Plum." The duke closed his eyes and pondered. He realized now that it might have been better had he questioned Plum in private. Count Max Grenner was to be his partner and front man in the development of Chub Cay. The duke, Walter Maples, and Count Grenner.

It all had to do with the economy of the colony. The Bahamas had been a sleepy backwater for many years, until the Americans had put in their law prohibiting the manufacture and sale of alcoholic beverages. Then, ah, then the Bahamas had boomed! Whiskey was imported from Britain, schnapps from Germany, wine from Italy. Freighters docked in the Bahamas, their cargo off-loaded onto small, fast craft and smuggled into the States via Florida.

It was saddening to realize that a single slip of the tongue, an exercise of candour when discretion should have dictated a wiser course, could bring one down. There was that American who had parleyed capital raised running rum into a fortune in film production and risen to the ambassadorship at the Court of St James, only to be laid low by a single foolish remark regarding the inefficacy of democracy.

The fact that he was right did nothing to alter the circumstances.

The duke addressed the houseman once more. "I want you to take me where you were to take Sir Walter."

Plum said, "You want to go to Chub Cay, sah?"

"That is correct."

Plum tilted his head, obviously deep in thought. "I s'pose I c'd take you, sah. My boat, she's all outfitted. I was plannin' to take Sir Walter this mo'nin', I c'n take you instead, sah."

"Very well, then." The duke stood up. Commissioner Easton leaped to emulate him, Christopher Harrel lazily following suit. "Easton, Harrel, you will hold yourselves in readiness should I need to question you further. Deering, you may return to your duties. Plum, you shall await me on the verandah of Government House."

"Yes, sah!"

The others stood, heads slightly inclined, as the duke strode from the room.

He climbed the broad staircase leading to the family quarters and tapped once more on the duchess's door. Her familiar voice called out, "Come!"

He found her within, reclining on a *chaise longue*, garbed in a Mainbocher dressing gown of pale blue silken faille. She wore matching blue mules, each topped by a fluffy cotton pouffe. A star sapphire pendant rested against her throat and a cuff of matching stones circled one wrist.

"My darling," he said.

"Yes, David, what is it?" He observed that her breakfast tray had been removed and the bed straightened.

"I don't suppose, my dear, that you would care for a brief sail today?"

"A sail? You just told me that Walter Maples was dead. And you're going sailing?"

"I am investigating his death, my dear. It appears that he came to a dreadful, bloody end, but he had planned an expedition this morning to Chub Cay and I thought to follow his planned route, don't you see."

"I see plenty, David. I see you trying to play Sherlock Holmes. Don't we have our own little Inspector Lestrade on this dreadful island? Can't you leave the investigation to the official police?"

The duke frowned. "You forget, my darling, that as governor-general I am the colony's chief law-enforcement officer."

"Yes, and you're the commander of its military force, but I don't see you drilling recruits on the parade ground."

The duke blinked. She was in one of her moods. Well, who could blame her? Being awakened to the news of the murder of one's closest friend – well, one of one's closest friends, anyway – would surely put any sensitive person into a state. He drew a breath; waited until he was certain that she was not going to speak further, and resumed.

"Walter was my friend as well as yours, my dear. Not to mention a prospective business associate. This war is not going to last forever, you know. We have to think of the future."

"You know what our future should have been," she grumbled bitterly. "We should be at Belvedere if not Buckingham Palace this very moment instead of that stammering weakling and his simpering little wify. If you weren't such a fool –"

"Stop it!" He felt the pressure within his head and knew that his face had turned a bright red. Rarely did he stand up to the duchess, but there was a single topic on which he would not brook her criticism. "He is my dear brother!"

"And see how he treated you once you had made him Caesar," came the hissed reply.

"My family is sacred. That is the end of it."

He spun on his heel and left the room.

He found Plum awaiting him downstairs, standing respectfully near the tall cut-glass doors. The duchess of course was right. It was such a tragically far cry from Buckingham Palace and Belvedere and the life of pomp and privilege they had known before the abdication, to this hot and isolated post. If only he could go back and change things – but he could not.

"Pardon, Governor sah, but yo' shoes –"

The duke managed a rueful grin, the first of the day. Of course. This would be no Mediterranean cruise such as he and the duchess had shared on the palatial *Nahlin*, nor a Caribbean jaunt like those hosted by Max Grenner aboard *Stella Australis*. What could poor Plum own but a little sailing dinghy?

"Have you suitable footwear for sailing, Plum?"

"Sah, I sails barefoot."

"Then I shall do the same," the duke rejoined, grinning broadly. They strode side-by-side between the white pillars of Government

House, past the duchess's precious Buick sedan and down sleepy Blue Hill Road toward Prince George's Wharf.

Plum's craft was as the duke had expected. The duke removed his shoes, socks and garters and left them on the quay. He waited while Plum climbed into the dinghy. Plum helped him into the boat, cast off the painter, then used a pair of heavy oars to propel the dinghy away from the quay.

Plum raised a much-patched sail, swung the dinghy to port, caught a late-morning breeze and guided the craft through the narrow channel separating Nassau from Hog Island.

A few scrawny goats wandered the hilly island, cropping sparse vegetation. As the dinghy rounded Hog Island and swung to the north, toward Chub Cay, the duke permitted himself a fantasy. A U-boat would rise from the sparkling turquoise sea. Its captain would emerge from the conning tower, take the duke onboard and return with him to a subdued Britain where he would resume his temporarily abandoned throne.

He would offer his brother and his consort better treatment than the stammerer had offered him and his wife. That much generosity he could afford. Wrongs would be righted, mistakes would be corrected, injustices would be undone. The rightful king would reign once again!

"They be Chub!"

The duke abandoned his reverie with reluctance, but there indeed was the Cay where he and his partners had planned to build their resort once the war had ended. When the Americans repealed their prohibition of alcohol they had crushed the booming economy of the Bahamas, but there was another prohibition in the United States, against gambling. It was carried on legally in one of the arid western states, he recalled, and was winked at in the city of Miami.

But a full-scale luxurious casino in the style of Monte Carlo, located in the salubrious surroundings of the Bahamas, would be his bonanza. His and the duchess's, of course, assuming that she did not abandon him for a fresher and more energetic companion, as she had previously abandoned one husband for a second and that husband for himself. She'd already picked out her fourth mate, the duke suspected, but that liaison had been scotched, there was no longer any danger from those quarters!

"This where Sah Walter was wantin' to go this mo'nin', sah."

Plum was standing at the tiller, a line in one hand running to the little dinghy's boom. "You want me to put in, sah?"

The duke shook his head. "No, Plum, there will be no need for that. Could you circle the Cay, I'd like to survey it today, then return to port."

As the man moved to obey, the duke questioned him. "You say Sir Walter had bled copiously when you found him, Plum."

"Sah?"

The duke blinked. "You say there was blood spattered all over the room."

"Yes, sah."

"I didn't think a bullet to the brain would cause such bleeding."

"Bullet, sah?"

"Yes. Was Sir Walter not killed by a gunshot?"

The black man shrugged. "That man's throat be slashed and his belly sliced open. Whoevah done in Sir Walter was one mean person. I didn't see no bullet hole, sah."

After a moment the duke asked, "Do you sleep at The Tradewinds, Plum?"

"No, sah." Plum shook his head. "I go home every night to sleep, I come back to The Tradewinds every mo'nin'."

"So you would not have heard a gunshot. And Chris Harrel was drunk."

Beating back through Nassau Harbour, the duke half expected to see Max Grenner's *Stella Australis* moving majestically toward the open sea, but she was nowhere to be seen, nor was she tied up at Grenner's usual dockage. Come to think of it, the grand yacht had not been at her place when the duke left Prince George's Wharf hours earlier with the negro Plum.

Once again shod, the duke returned to Government House and telephoned the harbour master. He learned that *Stella Australis* had sailed at daybreak. Only the Count and Countess Grenner were on board, aside from the crew, of course. No, sir, the harbour master did not know their destination, although he thought it might be either the count's villa at Tampico or his mansion at Veracruz.

The duke slammed the telephone down. Damn Grenner! He and Maples had been the main financiers of the planned casino at Chub Cay. The duke's allowance from the Crown was a precarious pittance, hardly enough to cover the duchess's clothing budget. And his brother, he knew, was plagued with constant health problems. Should he die the sceptre would pass to his elder daughter, and who knew how she would treat himself and the duchess? They had been close when he was prince of Wales but cracks had appeared in the family structure during his brief reign and since the abdication he had not seen either of his nieces, nor received as much as a greeting card from them on his birthday.

He had to make a go of the casino! Now that Maples was dead, Max Grenner's role was more important than ever. It was vital. The dead Walter Maples had come from humble enough roots: a rough diamond prospector he had found a mother lode in South Africa and made his fortune. That would pass now to the detestable Lady Margarethe, maybe even fall into the hands of the son-in-law, the vile Delacroix. There was no counting on that money any longer.

Grenner's fortune was even more unsavoury. He maintained his residency in neutral Sweden, built guns and sold munitions to both sides, cash and carry, no questions asked. The Crown was after him, the PM had personally sought his extradition, but the duke exercised his official prerogatives and gave Grenner free run of the Bahamas.

But what if Grenner had heard of Maples's death early this morning? What if word had spread even before notification reached Government House? Grenner held the exchequer for the planned casino, including the portion put up by the duke. The amount was modest enough by the standards of the likes of Walter Maples or Max Grenner. The duke's chief contribution to the scheme was the prestige of his name, the glamour that he and the duchess would provide to the eventual establishment, that would draw wealthy gamblers from the entire western hemisphere if not from Europe. But he had insisted on putting up a share of the capital that represented a huge investment by his standards. Had Grenner decamped for Mexico with all the money?

The duke raced up the broad staircase to his wife's boudoir. She was not there.

He found her shortly in the garden, sunning with her terriers. She had changed her costume to a day-frock of cornflower blue linen. A broad-brimmed hat protected her delicate skin from the rays of the sun, and she wore a pair of oversized spectacles of smoked-glass in harlequin frames of jewel-decorated tortoise shell. She was seated beneath an oversized parasol, a cold glass beaded with condensation at her elbow, a novel opened in her lap. She looked up as the duke literally ran to her.

"What is it, David? You're as pale as a ghost!"

"Where were you last night?" the Duke demanded.

Behind her dark glasses, did he detect a blink? In her always-confident voice, did he hear a hesitation? "Why, I was with you at dinner, of course. Colonel Deering drove us there in the Buick."

"Afterwards, afterwards."

"Why, we returned here, David. What's the matter with you?"

"You did not go out again? You did not return to The Tradewinds and – and see Walter Maples?"

"David, don't make an ass of yourself. What are you implying?"

"I am implying that you took the Buick. Late at night. Quite late at night. You took a knife from the pantry here at Government House and drove yourself back to The Tradewinds and entered the house. Only Chris Harrel was present, other than Walter Maples, and Harrel was immobilized with liquor. You made your way to the master bedroom. You found Maples dead to the world and with the knife you slashed his throat and belly."

"David," the duchess laughed nervously, "why would I do such a horrible thing?"

"Because Maples was your lover and he was losing interest in you. You follow the same pattern, my dear, but this time you couldn't simply divorce me and move on. You couldn't continue to satisfy Maples. I know you, I know you now, at last. Perhaps you hoped for a reconciliation but when you couldn't even waken him you flew into a rage and used your knife on him."

She removed her sun glasses, folded them and placed them in the gutter of the open book in her lap. She glared at him coldly. "He would not even stir," she said.

"That was because there was a bullet in his brain already." The duke started to walk away, then halted and turned back to face his wife. He stood beside her, aware that to her eyes he was a menacing black silhouette against the blazing Caribbean sun.

"Max Grenner and the countess are gone. Sailed away with Walter's money," he paused dramatically, "and ours."

She gasped and started to rise.

He placed his hand on her shoulder, pressing her back into her seat. "It seems that we are fated to remain together for the rest of our lives, my dear. We deserve each other."

Author's Note

Edward Albert Christian George Andrew Patrick David Windsor's reign as Edward VIII was brief (20 January to 10 December 1936). His romance with the American Mrs Bessie Wallis Warfield Spencer Simpson, his abdication for the sake of "the woman I love" and their subsequent marriage led to long years of gilded exile and luxurious vagabondage. Their lives have been seen variously as the poignant and bittersweet romance of starcrossed lovers, or as low bathos bordering on tragic farce.

Created Duke of Windsor, the ex-king served as governor-general of the Bahamas from 1940 to 1945. It is speculated that this relatively obscure post was mindfully chosen to keep him from doing mischief, for his unsavory political sympathies and friendships were well known and regarded as highly dangerous. He had been close friends with Joachim von Ribbentrop, German ambassador to the Court of St James and later foreign minister in the Nazi government. Further, chilling photographs survive of the duke and duchess hobnobbing cordially with Adolf Hitler and lesser Nazis, and reviewing Wehrmacht troops.

The murder of Sir Walter Maples as described in "News from New Providence" is based on the actual murder of Sir Harry Oakes in 1943. Other characters in my story are fictionalized for good reason, but none are cut from whole cloth. Thus, while there was no Count Grenner, there was Axel Wenner-Gren, a controversial arms merchant who did flee the Bahamas for Mexico. There was no Marcus Plum, but George Thompson, a black Bahamian citizen, did play a role of quiet heroism in the real events of 1943. And while there was no Antoine Delacroix, there was a real Alfred de Marigny, son-in-law of the real Sir Harry Oakes. De Marigny was in fact arrested for Oakes's murder, tried and acquitted.

Many volumes have been written by and about the Duke and Duchess of Windsor, including, not surprisingly, self-serving auto-biographies. Other less flattering volumes, several of which I utilized in preparing "News from New Providence," include Gone with the Windsors, *by Iles Brody,* The Life and Death of Sir Harry Oakes, *by*

Geoffrey Bocca, Who Killed Sir Harry Oakes?, *by James Leasor, and Alfred de Marigny's own account of the case,* A Conspiracy of Crowns. *More general information is derived from* Debrett's Kings and Queens of Britain, *by David Williamson.*

All of the above notwithstanding, let me state most emphatically that "News from New Providence" is a work of fiction. Readers interested in the truth of the Oakes case should consult sources such as those cited in this note.

Richard A. Lupoff

Princess Anastasia ❧

WOMAN IN A WHEELCHAIR

Morgan Llywelyn

One of the great mysteries of the twentieth century is what became of Princess Anastasia, the daughter of Nicholas II, last Tsar of the Russias. Was she killed when the Tsar and his family were assassinated in 1918 or did she survive? That's what our final story sets out to solve.

Summers in New York City are a special form of penance. For a woman who spends much of her time in a wheelchair they can be hell. Though I am able to get up and walk about a little, for the most part I just sit and sweat. Not "glow," not even "perspire". My life is reduced to fundamentals. I sweat.

I am never entirely free of pain.

From behind the desk where I sit I can read, in reverse, the name painted on the frosted glass door to our office. Peters & Ehrenfeld, Private Investigations. I'm Martha Peters, my partner is Max Ehrenfeld. We sound like a vaudeville act, a comedy routine called Max and Martha. There are few laughs in this business, however. And I am not as inclined to laughter as I used to be.

The calendar on the desk read 23 August, 1949. In the aftermath of the second World War our firm began specializing in finding D.P.s – displaced persons. Not always alive, of course.

Max is the legs of the partnership, I am the brains. Like a giant spider at the hub of a spiderweb I crouch here and send him out along the strands.

Between us we know Europe very well. Max is a Polish Jew whose uncle once owned a factory in Poland. Ten years ago the uncle sent Max to America on business for him shortly before the Nazi invasion. That was when I met Max and discovered we had a great deal in common.

The Germans destroyed the Polish army in five weeks. Then they scourged the west with genocide. Max never saw any of his family again. He dreams that one day he will find them quite by accident as he pursues some other investigation. Go around a corner and there they are.

He won't, of course. Life is not like that. But I understand his dream.

On this sweltering afternoon I was waiting for him to return from his latest trip and hoping it was successful. Every small triumph matters to him; to us.

When the thin-faced, aristocratic man in the black suit entered our office, I observed that he was sweating too. Yet his jacket was buttoned, his tie knotted, and he even wore pearl-grey gloves. Removing one, he extended his hand to me. His nails were perfectly manicured. "My name is Matthew Ogilvie," he said in clipped tones.

I kept my own hands folded on the desk and just looked at him. I have been told I have a piercing gaze. After a moment he handed me a card. The card bore no personal name, only The Bank of England embossed in copperplate. I examined it noncommittally and handed it back to him. I am not easy to impress. "What can we do for you, Mr Ogilvie?"

He half-lifted one eyebrow. "Do I detect the trace of an accent? German, perhaps?"

I mistrusted him at once for opening a conversation with such a personal remark. "Here in the Village are people of every nationality," I replied in a voice as frosted as the glass in the door, "and I tend to acquire the accents of those around me. The way I speak is not your concern. I repeat, what can we do for you?"

He smiled nervously. My aloofness put him off balance. "Forgive me. You are Mrs Peters?"

I replied with a curt nod.

"You are not quite what I expected."

"I'm sure. Do I understand that you represent the Bank of England, Mr Ogilvie?"

"Let us just say that my principals prefer to remain anonymous for the moment. But they are most anxious to confirm the whereabouts of a certain individual."

Taking a pencil from the ceramic mug on the desk, I held it poised above a lined yellow notepad. "The name?"

His eyelids tightened almost imperceptibly. "Grand Duchess Anastasia Nicholaevna."

For once I could not conceal surprise. "The daughter of the murdered Russian tsar? Are you serious?"

"I assure you I am."

I put down the pencil. "Then I fear you have made a mistake in coming to us, Mr Ogilvie. There are only two of us in this firm. It is common knowledge that Anastasia died with the rest of her family over thirty years ago, but even if somehow she had survived, finding her after so many years would be quite beyond our . . ."

"I disagree. Your agency is exactly right for our purpose. As I'm sure you know, the bodies of the tsar and his family were never found. We have reason to believe the youngest grand duchess may still be alive. As you can appreciate, this is a matter of considerable delicacy. Your firm is small enough to avoid attracting undesirable attention from the press.

"We have made inquiries about you," Ogilvie went on. "You possess a remarkable intuition for locating missing people, even those long presumed dead. Your partner speaks half a dozen languages and has contacts throughout Europe with access to records no one else can get."

I responded with another minute nod, giving away nothing. Then I eased forward in my chair and fixed my eyes on his.

"I am listening," I said.

"Matthew Ogilive knows quite a bit about us," I told Max the next evening. We were in the apartment I maintain adjacent to the office. He had just returned from Toronto that afternoon. As I had suspected, the elderly amnesiac in a Toronto hospital was the long-lost father of one of our clients. Max had come to give me his report before he went home. He lives in Brooklyn somewhere. I never visit his house because his wife is stupid.

As usual, Max was drinking black tea. I prefer stronger drink. I finished my second and cast a meaningful glance toward the bottle on the sideboard.

Max got up to refill my glass. "Not everything, surely."

I smiled. "Who knows all there is to know about anyone?"

"What's Ogilvie's interest in Anastasia?"

When I had drained the glass I replied, "Before the Russian Revolution the imperial family had a lot of money deposited with the Bank of England. On the day the Bolsheviks seized power the British government froze all Russian assets held in English banks. With accrued interest it is now a staggering amount. Ever since the tsar and his family were murdered in 1918, their surviving Romanov relatives have pressed to have the funds released to them. But the Bank of England won't even acknowledge they have the money.

"As the only surviving member of the imperial family, a living Anastasia would be the legitimate heir. She could force them to open their records. The bankers expect the matter to wind up in the courts eventually but they want to postpone it as long as possible. Meanwhile the money continues to make money."

"So Ogilvie wants to be certain Anastasia's dead."

"He was too discreet to put it that way. But yes."

"What did you tell him, Martha?"

Taking a small bottle of eau de cologne from the table beside my chair, I rubbed some on my hands. Scent is one of my few luxuries. "I'm surprised you even ask. I told him we would take the case, of course. The fee will be substantial no matter what the outcome. So pour your partner another drink to celebrate – and fill my glass to the rim this time."

I have great sympathy for the victims of war, any war. My own parents died during what was once called the War To End All Wars. I can understand the anguish of survivors of the Second World War who found themselves wandering through a devastated land with no idea where their people were, or if they were still alive.

After Max had gone home I sat in my chair for a long time, staring out the window at the surprisingly European streets of Greenwich Village. The Village is an unusual location for a firm such as ours.

But we have clients who would be uncomfortable in a modern office building.

Just around the corner is Jack Delaney's, a pub with sporting prints on the walls and saddles for seats at the bar. Max goes there for classic Irish stew, thick with mutton and glistening with fat. Occasionally he brings me some for my lunch, although I really prefer a mug of hot clam juice from the Sea Shell, with a lump of butter melting on top. I haven't much appetite. My needs are very simple.

Which is a pity, really, in a city that can cater to any taste. But on this evening I was not thinking of contemporary New York. Instead I was concentrating on a world long since vanished; a world of grace and manners and certainty, cushioning wealth and extended family. Edwardian England, Imperial Russia.

As one of the Romanovs, Russia's ruling dynasty, Anastasia had been born into such a world. It was shattered in one night of horror. Sometime after midnight on 16 July 1918, Nicholas II, Tsar of All the Russias, together with his wife Alexandra, their four daughters – the grand duchesses Olga, Tatiana, Marie and Anastasia – and fourteen-year-old Alexei, the tsarevich, were taken to a cellar room in a house in Ekaterinburg, Siberia, to face an execution squad.

If anyone had offered the tsar and his family sanctuary outside Russia when the revolution began in 1917 they would have been safe. But even though the tsarina was a granddaughter of Queen Victoria, her royal relatives had not lifted a finger to protect them from onrushing fate.

I sat staring into the gathering twilight, trying to recall what I had read of their tragedy. Once it had made newspaper headlines around the world.

When a rescue party of tsarist supporters finally reached Ekaterinburg they had searched the house. The bloodstained cellar resembled an abattoir but no bodies were found. Then in the months that followed the truth slowly bubbled to the surface like gas in a cesspit. The secret was to big too keep. Unlike dead bodies, it could not be hidden.

The tsar and his family had been slain in cold blood, cut to bits in a hail of gunfire. Those who did not die fast enough were attacked with rifle butts and bayonets. So were their personal physician and servants, and even little Jimmy, their spaniel.

The sheer ferocity of the deed was appalling.

The outside world shuddered over the story for a brief time. Then the Russian Revolution was eclipsed by the euphoria accompanying the end of the First World War, and the murder of Nicholas II faded from public consciousness.

After a time, perhaps inevitably, the rumours began: the tsarina and the children had been spared and had gone into hiding; others were killed in their place and the bodies burned to avoid identification; an infatuated soldier had spirited one of the girls away from the carnage in the cellar; the young tsarevich had been seen in London, heavily disguised.

For thirty years the rumours had continued.

Max and I spent the next couple of days poring over stacks of newspaper clippings and magazine articles, some yellow with age. From these we planned to shape the framework for our investigation. They told a bizarre tale. Over the years a number of missing "royal heirs" had appeared, each eager for recognition.

"It's like splinters of the True Cross," Max said with a chuckle. "If every one of these was a child of Nicholas II, I'm not surprised he had no time to run the country properly."

I made an impatient gesture. "The majority of them are out-and-out impostors, easily discredited. Some aren't even the right age. Remember that Olga, the eldest daughter, was twenty-two in 1918. Anastasia was only seventeen."

Max was studying photographic portraits of the four sisters. "They were beautiful girls," he commented admiringly. "A guard might have fallen for any one of them and tried to rescue her. Judging by this, Anastasia was the least lovely of the lot. Puppy fat, a sharp nose, thin lips. Marie, though; there was a charmer. She's rumoured to have escaped to Romania. There's also a belly dancer from Constantinople who claimed to be Tatiana, and a woman in Italy who insisted she was Olga."

"Forget about them, Max. Those are just fanciful stories. It's Anastasia who worries Ogilive. He spoke to me at some length of a woman called Anna Anderson who has convinced quite a few people that she really is the tsar's youngest daughter. We are to put together a full dossier on her as soon as possible. Anything that might prove or disprove her claim."

Max ran his thumbs under his braces and scratched his chest, a gesture as habitual with him as mine of clawing my fingers through my hair. "Where do you want to start?"

I handed him a newspaper clipping. "Begin with this. It says here that in February of 1920 a young woman attempted suicide by jumping into the Landwehr Canal in Berlin. She was rescued and taken to a hospital to recover. There was no identification on her nor would she identify herself. She seemed disoriented and confused. They called her Fräulein Unbekannt – 'Miss Unknown' – and put her in an asylum because there was nothing else to do with her.

"After months of refusing to speak, she began to talk rather incoherently to her nurses. They were surprised to discover that she spoke Russian as well as German. In the asylum there happened to be a magazine containing pictures of the Russian imperial family. When a nurse commented on the mystery woman's resemblance to the Grand Duchess Anastasia, Miss Unknown began saying she was Anastasia."

Max extracted another clipping from the pile. "A Russian baron from the Baltic took Fräulein Unbekannt out of the asylum in 1922 and made her a guest in his Berlin apartment. Numerous people visited her there, eager to see if she really was one of the tsar's daughters or an impostor.

"While staying with the baron the mystery woman began calling herself Mrs. Tschaikovsky. She explained this with a wild story of having been rescued from Ekaterinburg by a soldier. She knew him as a Pole called Alexander Tschaikovsky, who noticed that she was still alive as the bodies were being taken from the cellar. Tschaikovsky smuggled her out of Siberia in a peasant cart and took her to Bucharest in Romania, some 2,000 miles away. Along the journey he raped her. She subsequently gave birth to a son who was placed in an orphanage.

"When she found life as a soldier's woman unbearable, she decided to go to Berlin and appeal for help to her mother's sister, Princess Irene of Prussia. With no money and no passport, she set out to walk across Europe . . ." Max was shaking his head in disbelief ". . . crossing borders at night to avoid detection. Then when she finally reached Berlin she could not find Princess Irene, so she threw herself into the canal in despair!"

He turned toward me. "How could a young woman who had been

gravely wounded and then recently given birth to a child walk across
Europe? The journey alone would have destroyed her!"

"It is a fantastic tale," I agreed. "But so fantastic it just might be
true. Would anyone make up a story like that and expect to be
believed?"

Together we worked through the clippings, painstakingly con-
structing a profile from them.

After the time she spent with the Russian baron, the so-called
"Anastasia" had a chequered history. Various people took up her
cause and offered her sanctuary. She moved from place to place,
never staying very long with anyone. Both her physical and mental
health were unstable. Added to that she had a difficult personality,
alienating those who tried to help her with imperious demands.
Dowager Empress Marie, Anastasia's grandmother, who surely
could have resolved the question of her identity, flatly refused to see
her.

Marie's daughter Grand Duchess Olga met her, however, and
believed the woman was Anastasia – until other family members
talked her out of it. Some people who had known Anastasia
personally before 1918 saw the claimant and commented on how
different she looked. But they were astonished by the wealth of
intimate details she related. Only the real Anastasia could know such
things. It was argued that her changed physical appearance was
simply the result of all she had been through.

Controversy raged. The members of the Romanov dynasty
vacillated, then began to close ranks against her.

Anastasia's cousin, Princess Xenia, had married a wealthy
American and moved to his estate on Long Island. She invited
"Mrs Tschaikovsky" to come to America and stay with her. Over a
period of six months' observation Xenia became convinced that her
guest really was Anastasia. Then the two quarrelled and the mystery
woman moved on – and on, and on. Because some of the attention
she attracted was very unpleasant, she took the name of Anna
Anderson to avoid the press.

Max read aloud, "In 1927 it was claimed that the alleged
Anastasia was actually a runaway Polish factory worker called
Franziska Shanzkowska. Wounds on her body were identified as
wounds Shanzkowska had received in a factory accident. A woman
who ran the Berlin rooming house where Shanzkowska had lived

testified that she gave her the clothes she was wearing when she was pulled from the canal."

I took the newspaper article from him, squinting to read the small print. The evidence included statements from people who had known Shanzkowska back in Poland. They denounced her for trying to perpetuate a fraud. It was in keeping with her character, they said: self-deluding, discontent, always putting on airs.

Yet no one could explain how a Polish peasant knew so much about the real Anastasia. Anna Anderson's partisans refused to believe the Shanzkowska theory. One wrote to Anastasia's aunt, "It is easier to understand a crime permitted by a gang of crazed and drunken savages than the calm, systematic, endless persecution of one of your own family."

"This is really quite tragic," I commented. "The poor creature has spent her life trying to prove her identity, always dependent on the charity of others. How miserable and confused she must be by now!

"Max, you're going to Europe to pick up a trail almost thirty years old. Start where she first appeared, in Berlin. Investigate the case as if it's never been investigated before. Then locate Anna Anderson herself. I want to know exactly where she is and how she is – and what you think of the authenticity of her story."

"That's going to cost a lot," he said dubiously.

"Our client has promised to pay all expenses." I allowed myself a small smile. "It's an excellent opportunity, is it not?"

While Max was away I kept busy with my own investigations. What we had was a mystery in which we knew who the killers were, but the victim might not have been murdered. To complicate matters, it was in the interests of almost everyone involved to obscure the truth.

There is nothing unusual about political assassinations during a revolution, but even the monolithic government of the Union of Soviet Socialist Republics would prefer not to be connected publicly with the brutal slaughter of helpless children in a cellar.

As for the surviving Romanov relations, the possibility of a living Anastasia had become an embarrassment to them.

I wrote to Max, "If the claimant Anna Anderson were proved to be the grand duchess, then her relatives would undergo the censure of the world for their treatment of her over the years. She is indisputably eccentric, perhaps even raving mad, but that does not justify their behaviour."

Max, who wanted more than anything else in the world to find his own family, would never be able to understand the Romanov attitude. He wrote back: "I would love to be able to prove that Anna Anderson really is Anastasia, if only to see her established in luxury while the rest of her family crawls at her feet, begging for crumbs!"

Max is so emotional.

Building the case was not easy. We must find our way through a tangled forest, with plenty of opportunity to go off at a tangent. To serve as a road map I drew up a large chart and pinned it on our office wall. The result resembled two crooked roads; one for Anna Anderson dating from the day she was pulled from the canal, the other for Franziska Shanzkowska up to the moment their two lives intersected.

I also managed to obtain copies of documents attributed to Anastasia's uncle, the Grand Duke Ernest Louis of Hesse. These I studied very carefully. The Grand Duke had gone to considerable trouble – and expense – to prove that Anderson and Shanzkowska were one and the same. Yet still there were grave doubts. She simply knew too much. No wonder Ogilvie's employers were concerned.

Meanwhile Ogilvie grew increasingly unhappy with the expense accounts I was submitting. I kept upping the figures, waiting to see if his studied British reserve would crack. On a rainy afternoon in late October he arrived at the office just as I was pouring myself the first drink of the day. When I handed him the latest invoice he glanced at the figures and exclaimed, "Radi Bog!"

"I beg your pardon?"

Ogilvie's tailored topcoat smelled of damp wool. "Merely a pet expression, some nonsense from my childhood," he told me. "Are you certain this much expenditure is necessary?"

"It is costly to conduct any investigation in eastern Europe these days, but without going to Poland and Romania we could not have the whole picture. You must understand that information is not easy to obtain. The Communists demand more bribes than capitalists. It will be over soon, though," I assured him, "and we will be able to give you the information you want. Here, you look chilled. May I offer you a drink?" I gestured toward the decanter on my desk.

I waited politely while he lifted the glass to his lips, took a delicate sniff, then drained the glass in one long swallow.

"You like that?" I inquired.

"Very much indeed, thank you. Now, what about our business? *Is* Anna Anderson Anastasia, or not?"

"You will have the information you want," I repeated.

Next day I went out into the city in my wheelchair, negotiating with difficulty the many obstacles put in the way of the handicapped. It was necessary that I talk with the little community of Russian émigrés who lived in New York. Most of them were willing enough to speak to me. They saw only the wheelchair, and felt sorry for me.

Max did not return until almost Christmas. If I had a heart left to ache it would have ached for him. He looked defeated. The dark pouches under his eyes were more pronounced than ever.

"Was there no trace of your parents anywhere?" I asked gently.

He shook his head. He was getting very bald. "None. But thank you for the opportunity to search."

"What of your uncle, that kind, generous man?"

"Even his factory has been razed to the ground. It's like the earth opened up and swallowed him."

"As it did Anastasia?"

With a sigh, he hoisted a battered leather satchel on my desk. "Everything you asked me for is in here, Martha. An up-to-date dossier on the woman who claims to be Anastasia. No one knows more about her than this, I assure you."

He sank wearily into an armchair and watched as I removed a sheaf of handwritten pages and flipped through the report, rapidly scanning. It told a sad story. In 1932 Anna Anderson had returned to Germany from America to spend six months in a psychiatric hospital, courtesy of an American friend. After that she had begun wandering again, reiterating her claim to anyone who would listen.

Doors were – figuratively – slammed in her face. A dozen of the Romanovs signed a document officially denouncing her as an impostor.

By a miracle she had survived the Second World War, though she was in Hanover during the bombing. After the war Prince Frederick of Saxe-Altenburg used his own limited funds to settle her in a tumbledown former army barracks on the edge of the Black Forest. There Max had met and talked with her and taken several rolls of photographs.

I examined the black-and-white snapshots with curiosity. They showed a tiny troll dressed in unfashionable clothing, standing in a garden choked with overgrown shrubbery and briars. Her jaw was asymmetrical, as if it had been battered with rifle butts and healed crooked. I shook my head, smiling at myself. How easy it was to let the imagination run away with one!

"You talked with her, Max?"

"I interviewed her for hours over a period of several days. At first she refused to see me. But then she became all warmth and charm. Like an impish child, she was. Her eyes danced with mischief and I found her captivating – until I tried to question her about the murders in Siberia. Then she got crazy. Crying, waving her hands. 'I will not speak of that dirt!' she kept shouting."

"So. Did you find her convincing?"

Before he could answer the telephone rang. After I hung up I said to Max, "As soon as I told him you had returned, Mr Ogilvie insisted on coming right over. Take down that chart on the wall, will you? He might as well have it along with the rest of the material. He must not think we're holding anything back."

I pushed my chair back from the desk and wheeled over to the wall safe. Max started to help me but I waved him aside. Opening the safe, from the very back I removed several worn notebooks. These I added to the dossier on the desk.

Ogilvie arrived within minutes. I did not offer him a drink. Instead I introduced him to Max, then tapped the pile of material on the desk with one forefinger. "You will find we have been very thorough. Everything you want is in here, Mr Bienenstamm," I said.

Ogilvie went positively ashen. "What did you call me?"

"Your real name: Arnold Bienenstamm. You come from a White Russian family that has been loyal to the Romanovs for generations. You are no more than an agent of theirs, a tool. You were foolish to present yourself to me as an Englishman, Mr Bienenstamm. Your accent was excellent and your mannerisms sufficient to deceive most Americans. The illusion was almost perfect. But I am not an American, and the art of illusion has been a lifelong interest of mine.

"I suspected you almost at once, but you really gave yourself away when you exclaimed 'For God's sake!' in Russian. To be certain, I then offered you a glass of slivovitz which you drank off in one swallow. Only a Russian would do that. Plum brandy that strong would leave an English banker gasping for air. You see, my dear Bienenstamm, you have not mastered the art of impersonation as well as you thought. One must be scrupulous about the smallest details and never have an unguarded moment."

Max was staring at me. "Isn't this man from the Bank of England?"

The other interrupted, "I never said I was. I told Mrs Peters that my principals wished to remain anonymous."

I kept my eyes fixed on his face. "You wanted us to believe you had a huge and reputable banking firm behind you, instead of a conspiracy of second-rate Russian nobles who were desperate to keep the tsar's money from going to its rightful heir.

"I have talked with people who know you," I went on relentlessly, "and who know those behind you. Many of the Russian émigrés here think, as I do, that the remaining Romanovs have behaved disgracefully in this matter. The people I spoke with would not say so for the record, of course, but they were willing to confide in a poor old crippled woman over endless glasses of tea."

"When I look into your eyes I find it hard to think of you as a poor old crippled woman," said Bienenstamm.

"The spirit behind these eyes is not crippled, Mr Bienenstamm."

"Then why pretend?"

"I am not pretending. My spine and legs are permanently damaged, I shall never walk like a normal person. But I am not so helpless as I appear. That is an illusion I find useful."

"Even if it keeps you confined in a wheelchair?"

"We are all prisoners of our illusions, Mr Bienenstamm. Each person lives in the world as he imagines it to be. My world is not yours. In your world people are willing to kill one another, even for something as meaningless as money."

"Money can hardly be described as meaningless, Mrs Peters." His eyes strayed from my face to the pile of papers on the desk.

"The tsar possessed a great fortune," I said. "Did it save him, his wife, his children? No. All it meant was that the hidden jewels sewn into the corsets of the girls turned the bullets for a while, so in the end they were bludgeoned to death by their frantic executioners. Their wealth only brought additional pain.

"Now for the sake of money you want us to identify the only survivor of that horror so her loving relatives can quietly extinguish her too." I pressed my hands against the arms of my wheelchair and half-lifted myself out of the seat. "But fortunately she is beyond their reach!"

The anger in my voice was unmistakable. Bienenstamm met my eyes again, then took an involuntary step backward.

"The Grand Duke of Hesse went to a lot of trouble to prove that Anna Anderson was really Franziska Shanzkowska," I went on. "He hired witnesses to perjure themselves and paid them from his own pocket. The cost to him was negligible compared to the possibility of getting his hands on a share of the imperial fortune.

"But Duke Ernest wasted his money just as you have wasted yours," I told Bienenstamm with satisfaction. Turning to Max, I said, "Now, Max. I want the truth as you know it. You have spent months investigating this case. You have interviewed Anna Anderson at length. Tell our client: is she who she claims to be?"

Max looked puzzled. "Are you sure, Martha?"

"Tell him. *The absolute truth about Anna Anderson.*"

"Very well," Max said dubiously. "In spite of all the evidence in her favour, Mr ... Bienestamm, Anna Anderson is not Grand Duchess Anastasia. She is a remarkable actress, yes; someone who absorbed information about the imperial family like a sponge and fed it back most convincingly. The Grand Duke of Hesse paid witnesses who were really only confessing to the truth – Anna Anderson is a Polish impostor. There was no reason to fear her. She would never have been able to prove her claim."

"It's all here," I said, drawing Bienenstamm's attention to the dossier once more, "including notebooks crammed with details she memorized all those years ago. They are the ultimate proof of her deception, though by now she probably believes the lie herself. Remember what I said about each person living in the world as they imagine it to be?

"Understandably your employers want their interest in this matter kept quiet, so I suggest they simply put these documents away somewhere. Should it ever become necessary they can produce them in court."

Bienenstamm said, "But if the Anderson woman is a fraud, what about the real Anastasia?"

"Anna Anderson was the nearest any person will ever come to being the grand duchess. No other with as strong a case has come forward in thirty years and it is far too late for one to turn up now," I replied confidently. "Rest assured that Anastasia Nicholaevna is dead, Mr Bienenstamm. She cannot be resurrected. She died with her family in Ekaterinburg."

The agent hired by the dead girl's greedy relatives began gathering up the material we had given him, hefting it in his gloved hands as if its weight would testify to its veracity. He disgusted me. "Get out of here," I told him. "You have what you came for, just go and leave us alone."

After he had gone I drained the bottle of slivovitz. I did not even feel it. Max was watching me with a worried expression. "I hope you haven't done something very foolish after all these years, Martha."

"There were grave issues at stake. A terrible crime was perpetrated on the tsar's family in 1918. I should not like to be responsible for another. Those who hired Bienenstamm are quite capable of hiring others like him, only worse. If they became convinced Anna Anderson was Anastasia, they would have her killed. Now she is safe."

"But what about the real Anastasia?"

"I told Bienenstamm the truth. That girl no longer exists, she's been dead for thirty years, since that night in the cellar."

"You told him more than that. You said the assassins' bullets were deflected by jewels sewn into the girls' corsets."

I sank back in my chair, suddenly feeling very weary and older than my forty-eight years. "Did I say that?"

"You warned him about having an unguarded moment, then had one yourself. You went to such trouble to create the perfect illusion – finding a substitute Anastasia and coaching her – then with that one little slip you might have given it all away. Fortunately Bienenstamm wasn't paying much attention to what you were saying. He was too anxious to get his hands on the dossier."

"I did not find the substitute, Max. That I owe to your uncle, as I owe him my life. 'Jews understand about trouble,' he once said to me. 'We will help when no one else will.' I still remember the sound of his voice. So warm, so kind . . ."

I drifted away for a moment. Max's sympathetic hand on my arm brought me back and I found myself retelling the story he already knew. "If your uncle had not noticed me lying exhausted in a ditch beside the road to Krakow I would have died, Max. Instead he took me home with him, brought doctors to me, listened to my story and offered to help me get out of Europe altogether.

"Franziska Shanzkowska worked in his factory, you know. 'She is always play-acting,' he said to me. 'Why don't we give her a great role to play?' So we did it between us, your uncle and I. He arranged to send her to Berlin with a cover story when she was ready, and I taught her everything she would need to know . . . to become me. She was good, very good. So eager to learn. She truly thought it would bring her a happy life."

Remembering, I was racked by guilt. But at least she was safe now. Her deception had kept me safe for three decades. As long as the world thought Anna Anderson could be the grand duchess, no one looked elsewhere. Especially at a woman in a wheelchair.

"Poor Anna," I murmured to Max. "Little do they know that now she really *is* all that remains of Anastasia."

THE CONTRIBUTORS

John T. Aquino, "The Mysterious Death of the Shadow Man". John Aquino (b. 1949) is an American author with a special interest in the Elizabethan period, especially its relationship with the demise of the world of faery. Another of his stories featuring the investigator Henry Bagnet, "The Name-Catcher's Tale", will be found in *Shakespearean Detectives*.

Cherith Baldry, "The Friar's Tale". Cherith Baldry (b. 1947), a former teacher and librarian, is best known for her children's books, particularly the *Saga of the Six Worlds*. She has also written children's books under the alias Jenny Dale.

Paul Barnett, "Two Dead Men". Paul Barnett (b. 1949) is a Scottish writer and editor who has written most of his fifty or so books under the name John Grant. His fantasy novels include *Albion*, *The World* and, under his own name, the more recent space opera series starting with *Strider's Galaxy*. Among his non-fiction books are *The Encyclopedia of Walt Disney's Animated Characters* and *The Encyclopedia of Fantasy* (edited with John Clute).

Stephen Baxter, "The Modern Cyrano". Stephen Baxter (b. 1957) is one of Britain's leading writers of science fiction. His related novels include *Timelike Infinity, Flux, Ring* and the collection *Vacuum Diagrams*. One of his most popular books was *The Time Ships*, a sequel to H.G. Wells's *The Time Machine*.

Jean Davidson, "A Stone of Destiny". Jean Davidson is the pseudonym of literary agent Dorothy Lumley under which name she has published six romance novels, an historical gothic and a crime novel, *Guilt by Association*. One of her distant ancestors was a Comyn so she may well be descended from the victim of her story.

Martin Edwards, "Natural Causes". Martin Edwards (b. 1955) is a practising solicitor and has used his experience as the background for his series of novels about Liverpool solicitor and amateur detective Harry Devlin. The series began with *All the Lonely People* in 1992 and there's been a novel a year ever since. Edwards has also edited the crime anthology *Northern Blood* and others in a regionally related series.

Robert Franks, "A Secret Murder". Robert Franks (b. 1946) is a Canadian by birth but has been a teacher of art in the Los Angeles school district since 1972. He has published a number of articles on such diverse subjects as H.G. Well's Time Machine, Doc Savage, Diaghilev and Lawrence of Arabia. This is his first published story.

Margaret Frazer, "Neither Pity, Love nor Fear". The Margaret Frazer alias originally hid the identity of two writers, Gail Frazer and Mary Monica Pulver, who between them produced the popular series of Dame Frevisse novels, which began with *The Novice's Tale* in 1992. Gail is now continuing the Dame Frevisse series on her own, but keeping the pseudonym. Both halves of Margaret Frazer are, however, present in this anthology.

Susanna Gregory, "The *White Ship* Murders". Susanna Gregory (b. 1958) is the author of the historical mystery novels about Matthew Bartholomew, a teacher of medicine at Michaelhouse, part of the fledgling University of Cambridge, in the mid-fourteenth century. The series began with *A Plague on Both Your Houses* in 1996. She previously worked in a coroner's office, which gave her a special insight into criminal behaviour.

Claire Griffen, "Borgia by Blood". Claire Griffen has previously appeared in *Classical Whodunnits*, *The Mammoth Book of New Sherlock Holmes Adventures*, *Shakespearean Detectives* and the magazine *Boggle*. She is Australian, and spent several years as an actress and dramatist before turning to writing fantasy and mystery stories.

Edward D. Hoch, "The Day the Dogs Died". Edward Hoch (b. 1930) is a prolific American short-story writer with over 700 to his credit. He has created many fascinating detectives, including Captain Leopold, Dr Sam Hawthorne, Nick Velvet, Ben Snow and Simon Ark. His stories appear regularly in *Ellery Queen's Mystery Magazine* and *Alfred Hitchcock's Mystery Magazine* but only a small percentage has made it into individual story collections. Well worth tracking down is his Simon Ark series, *The Judges of Hades*, *City of Brass* and *The Quests of Simon Ark*, the Nick Velvet books *The Spy and the Thief* and *The*

Thefts of Nick Velvet, and the Sam Hawthorne stories, a few of which have been collected as *Diagnosis: Impossible*.

Liz Holliday, "Provenance". Liz Holliday (b. 1958) is an author, journalist and fiction editor of the science-fiction magazine *Odyssey*. She has written three novelisations of the television series *Cracker* and one for *Bugs*, whilst under pseudonyms she's also written novelisations of *Soldier Soldier*, *Thief Takers* and *Bramwell*.

Tom Holt, "Accidental Death". Tom Holt (b. 1961) is best known for his popular comic fantasy novels, which began with *Expecting Someone Taller* in 1987 and include *Who's Afraid of Beowulf?*, *Ye Gods!*, and *Faust Among Equals*. A lesser-known fact is that Holt is an expert on ancient Greece and Rome and has written two novels set in classical Greece, *Goatsong* and *The Walled Orchard*.

Andrew Lane, "The Gaze of the Falcon". Andy Lane is 35 and a full-time civil servant. In his spare time he has written four original *Doctor Who* novels, one *Bugs* novelization, two *Babylon 5* episode guides and several short stories, as well as co-writing a book on James Bond. He is married and lives in London.

Morgan Llywelyn, "Woman in a Wheelchair". Morgan Llywelyn (b. 1937) is perhaps best known for her novels of Celtic history and fantasy, especially *Lion of Ireland*, *The Horse Goddess*, *Bard* and *Druids*. She has written several straight historical novels including *The Wind from Hastings*, *Grania: She-King of the Irish Seas* and *1916*. It was her work on the last-named book that sparked her interest in the last Russian Tsar and the fate of Anastasia.

Richard A. Lupoff, "News from New Providence". Richard A. Lupoff (b. 1935) is a writer whose work is so diverse that he defies categorization. Most of it is probably best defined as science fantasy rather than science fiction, including *One Million Centuries*, *Into the Aether*, *Sword of the Demon*, *Lisa Kane*, and *Lovecraft's Book*. He has since moved into the mystery field starting with *The Comic Book Killer*, the first of his series featuring insurance investigator Hobart Lindsey. Comic books are a special enthusiasm of Lupoff's and one on which he wrote extensively in *All in Color for a Dime*, and which also feature in the psychological thriller *The Triune Man* (1976).

Edward Marston, "Perfect Shadows". Edward Marston is the best-known pseudonym of author and playwright Keith Miles. A former lecturer in Modern History, Miles has written over forty original plays for radio, television and the theatre, plus some 600 episodes of radio and television drama series. He has written over twenty-five novels. Of most interest in the historical mystery field are his two series. The first features Nicholas Bracewell and his company of Elizabethan actors which began with *The Queen's Head* in 1988; the second features Ralph Delchard and Gervase Bret who resolve crimes as they travel the country helping compile *The Domesday Book* in 1086 – this series began with *The Wolves of Savernake* in 1993.

Amy Myers, "Happy the Man . . ." Amy Myers is best known for her books featuring the Victorian/Edwardian master-chef with the remarkable deductive powers, Auguste Didier who first appeared in *Murder in Pug's Parlour* in 1987. She was previously an editor for the publisher William Kimber for whom she compiled the *After Midnight Stories* series of anthologies. She has also written a series of novels under the name Harriet Hudson, including *The Wooing of Katie May*, *The Sun in Glory* and *Look for Me By Moonlight*.

M.G. Owen, "The Snows of Saint Stephen". Owen is the pseudonym of a teacher of English as a foreign language who has travelled widely in three continents and taught in four countries. He has published several stories in magazines.

Mary Monica Pulver, "To Whom the Victory?". Mary Pulver (b. 1943) was, until recently, one half of the Margaret Frazer writing team, and co-author of the Dame Frevisse series of historical mystery novels. Under her own name she has produced a series about mid-west cop Sergeant Peter Brichter, starting with *Murder at the War* in 1987. Under the alias Monica Ferris she has started a new series, starting with *Crewel World*, featuring the spinster sleuth Betsy Devonshire.

Tina and **Tony Rath**, "Who Killed Fair Rosamund?". Tina and Tony are a husband-and-wife writing team who have produced several stories both together and individually. Tony is currently working on an historical novel set during the Napoleonic Wars – history being one of his specialities; Tina is working on her PhD thesis on "The Vampire in Popular Fiction", vampires being one of her specialities. Tony tends to provide the ideas and historical detail and Tina develops the plot and characters.

Mary Reed and **Eric Mayer**, "Even Kings Die". Mary Reed and Eric Mayer are another husband-and-wife writing team whose short stories include a series about John the Eunuch who investigates crimes in the early days of the Byzantine Empire, and a series about Inspector Dorj of the Mongolian Police. The first John the Eunuch novel, *One for Sorrow*, appeared in 1999.

Peter Tremayne, "Night's Black Agents". Peter Tremayne (b. 1943) is the pseudonym of Celtic scholar and historian Peter Berresford Ellis who, under his own name, has written many books tracing the history and myth of the Celts, including *The Celtic Empire*, *Celt and Saxon*, *Celt and Greek* and *Celt and Roman*. In the fiction field he established an reputation for his Dracula series collected in the omnibus *Dracula Lives!*, and the Lan-Kern series based on Cornish mythology, which began with *The Fires of Lan-Kern*. He is perhaps now best known for his series of historical mysteries featuring the seventh-century Irish Advocate, Sister Fidelma, which began with *Absolution by Murder*.

Renée Vink, "A Frail Young Life". Renée Vink (b. 1954) is a Dutch author and translator who also sets questions for a television quiz series in Holland. Her books have hitherto only been published in Holland. They include a volume of fantastic stories set in medieval Scandinavia, *De Runen van de Dwergenkonig (The Dwarf King's Runes)* plus a series of historical mysteries about Floris V, Count of Holland, which began in 1995 with *Floris V en de Schotse Troon (Floris V and the Scottish Throne)*.

Derek Wilson, "The Curse of the Unborn Dead". Derek Wilson has written over thirty books of history, biography and fiction, including the acclaimed family biographies, *Rothschild: A Story of Wealth and Power* and *The Astors 1763–1922: Landscape with Millionaires*. He also also written two fascinating books on the circumnavigation of the globe, *The World Encompassed – Drake's Voyage 1577–1580* and *The Circumnavigators*. In the world of mystery fiction he has created the character of Tim Lacy, international art connoisseur and investigator whose cases have been chronicled in *The Triarchs, The Dresden Text* and *The Hellfire Papers*.